# A VERY FAMILIAR KILLER

I woke drenched in gasoline. Vapor filled the room so thickly you could almost carve it with a knife. The sheets were dripping. My pillow had become a wet sponge. The landing light shone through my bedroom door to reveal a figure.

The fumes made me cough. "What are you doing?"

When the figure stepped into the light its face became clearly visible. The simple fact was: I saw myself standing there. Or, rather, I saw the man who'd stolen my face. He raised a hand that held a cigarette lighter. His thumb rested on the wheel that would ignite the flame that would turn my bedroom into a furnace, in turn that would cremate me where I lay in the gas-soaked bed.

The monster with my face smiled. "There can only be one of us, can't there?"

# SIMON CLARK

# THIS RAGE OF ECHOES

LEISURE BOOKS  NEW YORK CITY

*For Janet*

A LEISURE BOOK®

November 2007

Published by

Dorchester Publishing Co., Inc.
200 Madison Avenue
New York, NY 10016

ISBN 10: 0-8439-5494-9
ISBN 13: 978-0-8439-5494-4

Printed in the United States of America.

10 9 8 7 6 5 4 3 2 1

Visit us on the web at www.dorchesterpub.com.

# THIS RAGE
# OF ECHOES

# CHAPTER ONE

*When he becomes you, then who are you?*

Say again, what's the question? Okay, listen to this: It's in us. We make it happen. Somehow.

Does that make sense? Not that I'd believe for one minute that you'd understand from the start what was happening to us. After all, the mechanics of it are a mystery to us as much as anyone else. But I can't stress this enough: it is important you do understand, because if the kind of trouble I'm facing now comes your way, then what I write here might help you not only make sense of it, but fight it. And stay alive.

I guess this isn't clear, what I'm telling you. But I'm going to try as hard as I can to make it understandable. Damn, this feels like I'm sitting on my stupid butt and lecturing you. As if I'm just about to say, "Take out your textbook, turn to page thirty-one, and compare and contrast the merits of killing with a knife or a shotgun. . . ."

And that's a bunch of balls—big, hairy balls with fucking bells on. No. Your life—and whether you keep it or not, or whether you spill your hot, steamy blood all over the damn floor—just might depend on what you read in the next five pages. So I'm going to dive right in and describe one occasion when they tried to take us by surprise; then I'm going to tell you how we killed them; then I aim to describe what they are. And why they are dangerous. Not just dangerous to me but to you, too. After all, deep down, you know they're out there, don't you?

So, picture this. We're living in a house that isn't ours. The owners are on vacation—it says so on the calendar in the hallway, so no mystery there how I uncovered that fact. I'm baking frozen pizza. Here in the kitchen with me are four people in their twenties. Two men, two women. Casually dressed. I'm the guy in the black T-shirt and jeans. There's that hot-oven smell, a mixture of hot oil, meat juices, herbs—the ghost of a thousand roasts. This conversation might not have taken place word for word: it's an edited mix of conversations we've had before. Oh, and by the way, this is where I change tense from present to past. It reads better like that. Parts of this are story; parts are a bit like the commentaries you get on DVD. That's where I try to explain "this happened because . . ." Okay? And, yeah, this seems like a dollop of muddle because life's like that—a muddle of events, of intimacy, fear, anticipation, blood, bacon wraps eaten too fast because you're late for the bus, answering e-mails, washing clothes, bedtimes, broken nails, the dog whizzing on the rug—all that stuff you deal with. You try to weave it into a pattern that you hope not only makes sense but is meaningful as you go along. So, even if this isn't as clear as the glass in your living room window, one thing is rock-solid certain: this is the start.

As I fed pizza into the smoky mouth of the oven, Ulric said, "Why couldn't they have been vampires? These days who's frightened of vampires? You throw garlic at them, then nail them down dead with a stake." Ulric's Norwegian, a Viking warrior of a man with blond hair and the kind of face that seldom hosts a smile. Even when he speaks in a friendly way there's never a grin; his ice-blue eyes are always hard, but then, they need to be.

Ruth, on the other hand, smiles a lot. I even saw her smile when she threw an Echoman's head down a well with, "If you can get out of that we'll call you Houdini." At the moment she was rattling bottles of beer out of the refrigerator. Smiling. Of course she was smiling; she always smiles: her eyes twinkled, her face was framed with short black hair, and at that moment she joined in with: "Or why couldn't it have been werewolves? They only appear when the moon is full."

"Then we could zap them with silver bullets," Ulric added.

"Exactly."

Dianna matched her classical name. Tall, slim, long blond hair, athletic body. Do all Diannas in the world look like that? Blond goddesses one and all. She set out plates on the kitchen table. "After guzzling out of paper bags for the last three weeks we'll be civilized for once and eat off proper plates."

Ulric was stone-faced as he watched her. "Or why couldn't it have been zombies?"

Paddy leaned against the door frame to the hall, keeping guard. "Because vampires don't exist. Neither do werewolves, gorgons, demons, or leprechauns."

"You're Irish," I told him. "You have leprechauns in your blood."

"My grandmother was Irish. I know squat about Ireland

apart from one thing: the Irish are sick of tourists with their leprechaun jokes." Paddy is a big man with plenty of muscle and bushy dark hair that gives him a grizzly-bear look. Above his eyes are a pair of black eyebrows that are as bristly as those caterpillars that you sometimes find creeping into your house in early spring. Paddy enjoys comfort and food. It doesn't have to be good food, but he likes plenty of it. Right at that moment he eyed me peeling a plastic membrane off another pizza.

"How many of those things are there?" he asked.

"Eight."

"Might as well cook them all," he said. "We don't know when we'll get to taste another."

"Paddy?" Ruth raised an eyebrow. "You do realize that's two pizzas each?"

"There's five of us," Ulric said.

"No," Ruth insisted. "I hate pizza. It's all I can do to bear the smell."

"That's the garlic," Paddy told us. "Ruth is a vampire."

Ulric didn't smile. "There's no such thing as vampires. Remember?"

"No, but there's something else that's following us. So that's why I'm standing here at the door." Paddy nodded as he recalled the mayhem. "The danger's still out there."

I warned you earlier that this conversation didn't happen exactly like this. I've cut words; I've added a phrase or two. Paddy didn't actually utter "the danger's still out there," but it sort of captures the essence of similar conversations while we've been on the run.

And we have pizza. This would be the first real sit-down hot meal in ages. For the last couple of weeks I craved pizza. I drifted away to sleep in the back of the truck thinking about pizza. I imagined how the world's best pizza would smell. In truth, I'm not even a pizza addict, but, my God, I developed a craving for it. Perhaps it's because I couldn't have it. At home when I opened my freezer door those dough wheels all covered in cheese, pepperoni, onions, bacon, chicken, spicy beef, teriyaki turkey would come tumbling out. I'd curse those pizzas because I wanted chicken fillets at the back, or frozen peas. But like the devil himself had willed it, I'd be engulfed with pizzas every time I flipped open the door. And just two floors beneath my apartment was a pizza restaurant. I breathed pizza vapor from noon until past midnight. Pizza-delivery folk would tramp the apartment corridor with arms full of steaming, aromatic pizza. It was only when I was cut off from a world seemingly engulfed with those Frisbee-shaped circles of bread topped with bubbling cheese, tomato sauce, and toppings galore that I craved pizza. Now I had pizza. After the fifteen minutes' required baking time I would sit at the table with my gang and stuff my gullet with it until I felt like bursting.

Ulric watched me slide another pizza into the oven. "You might find this ironic, but the pizza we eat isn't like the native Italian dish. It doesn't look or taste the same. The product we eat has stolen the identity of the genuine item. It's not really pizza. We only think it is pizza because we've grown up with a product that pretends to be the real thing." Yeah, Ulric really does intone things like that.

Paddy shook his head. "If that's supposed to spoil my enjoyment of eating them, then you're mistaken."

"Ah, but did you enjoy the irony of the situation? The entire world is becoming counterfeit." Yup, he can get blood out a stone the way he riffs on a subject that fascinates him.

Ruth glanced through the window as the sun dipped

behind the mountains. "More important, did you know that there's someone's in the tree?"

"Echoman?" Paddy picked up the shotgun from where it reclined against the wall.

Ruth nodded. "There's just the one, as far as I can tell."

Ulric gazed through the window. "The garden's full of trees. There might be more of them."

"No worries," Paddy said. "I'll take care of them."

"We'll give you a hand." Dianna drew a handgun from a leather satchel she carried everywhere. "Mason, make sure the pizzas don't burn."

*They still think of me as the newcomer,* I told myself. *They'd been together six months when I joined them three weeks ago. I'm still the outsider. They don't see me as part of the team.* I slid the pizza out. Its three-cheese topping had started to blister.

"You've got ten minutes until this one's done."

"This should only take five." Ulric turned to Ruth. "Bring a carving knife. I want to see what's under this one's skin."

They talked in whispers as they headed for the back door of the house. They'd circle around the building, then take the Echoman in the tree by surprise. I'd seen this happen—or something very much like it—a dozen times by now. So I concentrated on baking pizza. If anything, it irked me that they still treated me as a stranger who just happened to tag along with them rather than an integral part of the gang. I positioned myself so I could see through the window without being noticed by the Echoman in the tree. Not that I could see much of him—or her—either. A branch flicked as he climbed about twenty feet off of the ground. A few chestnut leaves spiraled lazily down where the intruder had dislodged some greenery.

*What if it's just some kid? And they're just climbing a tree for fun? In thirty seconds Paddy and the rest are going to hit that tree with a lot of hot metal. But who else could it be? This place is at least two miles from the nearest house. It has to be an Echoman.*

"Stupid Echoman," I murmured as I found a pizza cutter. "Don't you shit-wits ever learn?"

The roasting cheese, spicy meats, and herbs smelled wonderful. People talk about "making your mouth water." It had never happened to me before, but mine was suddenly awash. I was just aching to sink my teeth into a slice of savory heaven.

At that moment I caught sight of a dark shape moving on the periphery of my eye. Quick, no noise, more shadow than solid figure. It vanished by the time I turned to get a better look. Whatever it was had passed by the open doorway, along the hall in the direction of the stairs. Okay, so I was armed with nothing more formidable than a pizza cutter, a little steel wheel at the end of a rubber-coated handle. Nevertheless I needed to check what was there.

Gunfire rattled the windowpanes. Outside, Ulric, Ruth, Dianna, and Paddy exploded the tree. The blast of shotgun, handguns, and rifle made the branches billow. Cascades of leaves fell, a green rain that covered the lawn. From the smell of the pizza it must have been almost done. This was time to move quickly, before the crust burned. Did I tell you I have an addiction to pizza these days? Any will do. Any but tuna, that is. I can't stomach tuna. Tuna smells like dead people.

I stepped into the hall as I hunted the invader. Immediately I saw it—him?—sitting on the third stair from the bottom. A gaunt figure with dark red skin. Its eyelids were closed. There was no hair on its head. The scalp was a mess of cracks with holes that revealed a bare skull of dull brown bone.

Even though his eyes were closed as he sat there on the stairs, I knew he watched me. One leg was straight so it lay flat against the risers. The other was crooked so the knee was raised toward his bandaged chest. One hand rested on his lap so it resembled a spider lying on its back, only one with red skin; the fingers were partly curled inward. Despite the body being a ruin the fingernails were perfect ovals the color of pearls. The man didn't move.

"I haven't seen you since I was sixteen years old," I told him. It surprised me that my voice was so matter-of-fact. "What brings you back?"

I didn't wait for a reply. The pizza would burn if I didn't get it out of the oven now. As I recrossed the kitchen to the stove I saw that Paddy and the others had killed the Echoman. His legs must have caught in a branch of the tree. He dangled headfirst with his arms straight down. He was my age, my build. Ruth had already started to cut away his face with the carving knife.

Once I had the pizza safely out of the oven. I checked the hallway again. The figure had gone. Okay, I realize I could have described him better, but why use a bunch of words when I can say: you've all seen an Egyptian mummy on TV, haven't you? Well, that's what had sat on the stairs. Listen, when I was a kid that same ancient Egyptian mummy turned up nearly every night, this three-thousand-year-old priest, officially known as Natsaf-Ty, keeper of the sacred crocodiles. He'd gone all crusty as a pizza base on the outside—all hollow on the inside. Having an ancient dead man chat to you on a regular basis tends to kill the fear. If any other monsters come your way they aren't so hard on the nerves. So, you see, I have a lot to thank Natsaf-Ty for.

I told you from the start that these events were perplexing to all of us. But it's a case of dealing with them. If we didn't the consequences would be lethal. So, please bear with me. After this I'll explain the mystery of the talking mummy and something about what the Echomen are.

A tap sounded on the window. I looked out to see Ruth standing there. She held the Echoman's chopped-off head by the hair. She'd carved away the face to reveal the muscle structure beneath. Blood hung down in sticky red strings from the neck. Its open eyes stared back at me.

Brightly, she sang out, "Hey, Mason! This one's you!"

# CHAPTER TWO

*I want to go home.* The decision came as I sliced the pizza. What made me change my mind wasn't seeing the Echoman with my face hidden beneath his own. No, not at all—it was the return of the mummy. Natsaf-Ty was his name, and three thousand years ago he was the keeper of the sacred crocodiles in Alexandria. *Uh-oh, what's next?* you'll be asking yourself. *Now that we've had a mummy that walks (even if we haven't heard it talk yet), will angels fly through the window to steal the pizza? Or maybe a dinosaur lurks in the basement? Is beautiful Dianna going to hear a noise from outside and say in a carefree way as she nibbles pepper-*

*oni, "I'll just go see what it is. Don't worry. I won't be
long"? She goes outside, never to return, because there's
a great, dirty beast lurking outside.*

No. These are the facts. When I was eight and my sister
was six months old, my mother couldn't stomach living
with her in-laws while my father worked on an oil platform in the Arctic. As opposed to a marital breakup,
where Mom walks out on Dad, she left my grandfather
and grandmother. Shortly after what I suppose was a
traumatic time for all of us (I say "suppose" because
back then I didn't have the maturity to think of it in those
terms), that's when I visited a museum with my class-
mates. In the overseas history section was a near-naked
mummy by the name of Natsaf-Ty. He lay in his coffin
with his eyes closed and his tongue slightly protruding
from his lips. He was dry, crusty, all hollowed-out inside.
The other kids, me included, made funny comments,
squealed in mock fear, pressed our faces to the glass
case to try to see his three-thousand-year-old willy. After
that we went to play in the museum gardens. A couple of
days later Natsaf-Ty appeared at the house. For some reason after that first visit I'd wake just after midnight when
everyone else was asleep and invariably I'd find the
Egyptian mummy, Natsaf-Ty, keeper of the sacred crocodiles, sitting on a step near the bottom of the stairs. You
can only ignore an ancient corpse–turned–museum exhibit for so long, so eventually we started to chat. Oh,
how we talked. World events, television, school, birthday
presents, family—you name it. Of course, the glib answer to why a mummy came visiting is because of the
family breakup. Psychologists will identify Natsaf-Ty as
an externalized memory of my absent grandfather,
whom I liked a lot. And whom I no longer saw.

In the kitchen that evening we ate pizza. It tasted as

wonderful as it smelled. Ulric tutted when a blob of tomato sauce fell onto his lap. That spill annoyed him even though the blood streaks created a kind of tiger pattern on his jeans. Ruth smiled when he mentioned how much he was looking forward to sleeping in a real bed. *For now, things are looking up.*

I finished my pizza before I broke the news. "I'm going home," I told them.

Ulric responded tartly. "That's not a good idea."

Ruth smiled. "I'm afraid he's right."

"What's so wrong with staying with your buddies here?" Paddy drained a beer in one go. "We're not so bloody awful, are we?"

Dianna laid her hand on my forearm. "You're getting to know our funny little ways by now, aren't you?"

"I know Ulric is a walking compendium of revolting habits." Paddy wedged a whole quarter of a pizza into his mouth. "Buff ee ziz orrr . . ." Or words to that effect. Ulric scowled at him.

"You have us now." Ruth's smile was compassion itself. "But the reality is that you must forget your old life."

"Whatever you decide"—Ulric sounded prim—"there isn't a shred of a possibility of you going home. It's not an option."

"C'mon." Paddy ripped off a bottle cap with his teeth. "Have another beer with me. Tonight I'll have a party . . . and you're all invited." His booming laughter rattled the dishes. "The drinks are on me."

Dianna moved from resting her hand on my bare forearm to gently rubbing her palm against my skin. "Stay with us, Mason. You're liked more than you think."

I smiled and told them of course I'd stay. I wouldn't dream of leaving.

But I'd made up my mind. *I'm going home.*

\* \* \*

I lay awake in bed. The time had long since crawled past midnight. Now the clock downstairs chimed a somber one in the morning. Outside, a breeze rustled the trees. My bedroom belonged to a child. A cartoon wallpaper depicted robots chasing after comic-looking cars; shelves were crowded with more robots in the form of electronic toys. One startled me with the words, "Good night, Thomas. Nighty-night. Sweet dreams. And if you should die before you wake . . ."

Great sense of humor the parents had, whoever they were. They programmed child Thomas's android to remind him that death is inevitable. The Romans had a similar saying: *memento mori*, remember you must die.

In the next room Paddy made love to Ruth. Their voices came through clearly enough. Even though I couldn't make out any words (not that I tried, you understand) the meaning was clear enough. *I love you, you're beautiful, that's wonderful, don't stop, faster, faster, that's it, that's amazing.* Like I need to tell you what lovemaking sounds like? I clamped the pillow over my head but I could still hear. Worse, I pictured Ruth naked as Paddy caressed her full breasts. I tried to think about other stuff: the mummy, the Echoman with my face, even the pizza feast, but images barreled through my skull of Ruth's smile, her gleaming teeth, her flushed cheeks, her sparkling eyes as Paddy wiggled on top of her. Worse, I felt that body-tingle. Hearing other people make love is a turn-on. I didn't want it to be, but how do you block a million years of evolution?

I needed everyone to fall asleep. Then I could go. As simple as that. Okay, I had lied. No way would I return home, I assured them. But the moment my gang of heroes fell asleep I'd slip away into the night with my toes pointing homeward. Not the apartment I'd lived in for the last six months, but back to the house where I grew up.

Maybe it was the moans of the pair reaching ecstasy that triggered the robot's sensor. The electronic voice whispered a seductive: "Good night . . . sweet dreams . . . if you should die before you wake . . ." Fucking robot. I wanted to smash its android brain. I hated the parents of the child whose bed I slept in. You don't do that kind of crap to your kid.

"Oh . . . oh . . . oh! More!" Ruth enjoyed the orgasm of the year. A huge, convulsing cum that not only rattled the bedsprings but must have vibrated the atoms of the house. Even the corpse of the Echoman lying under the bushes outside must have been twitching merrily to that kind of earthshaking boning. It sent a rush of blood to my groin. I thought of past girlfriends. I tried not to, but you know how it goes.

The robot responded with: "If you should die before you wake . . . if you should die, do not lie screaming in your grave. Lie still; wait for worms to eat your brain."

*Crap!* I jumped off the bed, knocked my knee against a chair in the dark, cursed some more, snatched the robot off the shelf, then returned to the bed, where I fumbled in the dark to open up the battery pack so I could kill it.

"If you should die, rot in peace." *I see the work of a big brother or sister here*, I told myself as I fiddled the battery from the back of the 'bot. "Nobody will remember your name." They'd programmed the toy to give their brother a midnight scare. "Graves are lonely places . . . deep, dark . . . filled with pain. . . ." As I sat on the bed with the robot on my lap the bedroom door ghosted open. A dark figure materialized to peer at me yanking out the toy's innards.

"Mason? What on earth are you doing?"

I recognized Dianna's silhouette. "It's one of the toy robots. . . ."

"Is it bothering you?"

Lucky she couldn't see how embarrassed I was by the question, or how foolish I felt. "Something's activating it. It's keeping me awake."

"Oh? Do you want me take it out of the bedroom?"

"I've got it." I held up the battery. "It'll stay quiet now."

She moved through the gloom to sit beside me on the bed. Although it was too dark to make out much, I could see her legs were bare, and did I tell you she had such long, long legs? I saw the gleam of skin as those legs ran up to disappear under the T-shirt she was wearing. I noticed her legs as I heard sex coming from the next bedroom. The grunts of rapture were faster now. *They're hungry . . . there's pent-up lust there*. Despite myself I pictured a tangle of naked limbs. And now here was Dianna. I saw the glint of her eyes in the darkness; there was no mistaking her perfume either. From her glances at the partition wall I knew full well she heard lovemaking, too.

I shoved the robot back on its shelf. "That's the toy silenced, but there's no stopping those two."

Dianna gave a breathy chuckle. "Ruth and Paddy have been an item for a while now." Then she said quickly, "I don't know what the effect of hearing people making love has on you, but . . ." Her eyes fixed on me. "It makes me so wet."

"Dianna?"

"Can I get into bed with you?"

*Hell*. What a question. Dianna was beautiful. A willowy goddess of a woman with long blond hair.

She reached out to grip my forearm. "Mason. I really

want to." Heat flowed from her skin into mine. "You're nice." Hot, driving sex in the next room? Dianna's hand on my arm? A divine presence? Yes, my heart pounded. "Mason. Do you mind if I get in?"

"Dianna?" That was Ulric's voice. A door creaked down the passageway.

She clicked her tongue in frustration and slipped out of the bedroom, leaving me alone with the sounds from next door. *Damn, what now?*

# CHAPTER THREE

They slept—I went. Paddy lay in bed with Ruth, Ulric with Dianna. There wasn't time to ponder Dianna's bedroom encounter. As quietly as I could I left the house before the sun rose. Even though it was spring, the air was cold as winter. My breath showed as white gusts as I walked down that lane flanked by fields to a main road. There I hitched a ride on a truck heading into England's northern lands. At that time of the morning there wasn't much in the way of traffic, so the trucker could push his wagon hard. If we could maintain this speed I should be seeing my mother and sister in three hours.

It seems to me that men who drive trucks usually have a shrine to Elvis either in their cabs or in their hearts. The driver I'd hitched a ride with boasted sideburns and slicked-down black hair with a suggestion of an Elvis Presley fringe. This one was about forty-five, putting him fifteen years my senior. Sure enough, here was an Elvis doll in a black leather comeback-tour costume that danced on a spring on the dashboard. As the guy drove, I was sure the look-alike hummed snatches of "Are You Lonesome Tonight?" Truckers are solitary animals, but it's often the case that you get an opposite character trait. Elvis was trucker turned star. Most truck drivers I've met enjoy the solitude of the open road, but they yearn to be showmen, too. They dress for their rolling stage. Often something with a Wild West twist— cowboy boots maybe, or eye-catching shirt; the vehicle is their billboard: they announce their name either painted above the radiator grille or on the door or on a plastic sunshade strip blazed across the windshield. When they drive alone I'm sure they hold the wheel and engage the gearshift and apply brakes in the same understated way your grandma tootles her car to the supermarket, but let the trucker gain a passenger and they drive to impress, with great, sweeping turns of the wheel and big, exaggerated movements of their hands as they turn up the King, blasting out "Viva Las Vegas." With that rousing anthem, they slam home the gears while sounding the horn with enough aplomb to make the dead cover their ears.

My trucker drove—no, not just drove, but DROVE in capital letters. He made it look like the work of heroes, as if the very way he hurtled that three-ton machine along the highway saved the free world. All this in a cab that smelled of fried bacon overlaid with spearmint gum, and he when he saw himself in the mirror he knew he was magnificent.

"Where you headed?" he asked as he nodded to the rhythms of Elvis.

"Home."

"Wife?"

"No, mother and sister. I've been working away."

He glanced to see if my hands were ingrained with honest grime. "Salesman?"

"No, I make TV programs."

"Any I might have heard of?"

"I don't think so."

"Try me."

"It's sliver-casting."

"No, I've not heard that one."

I glanced across as he worked the wheel with so much energy. His hands were clean, too. Even though parts of his truck were crusted in dirt and slippery with grease, he apparently never touched them. On the back of each of two smooth, hairless hands he had a dragon tattooed.

"Sliver-casting," I explained. "It's program making targeted at a small but specific audience. Mainly it goes out on the Internet."

"Ah . . ." He understood. "Porn."

It was easier to smile and nod. In truth I make programs about real estate developments, vehicle road tests, niche hobbies, and product profiles. Rather, that should be I *made* programs. All that had changed, of course, in the last three weeks.

"So you're not married, then?" he asked.

"Used to be."

The driver sounded his horn. I didn't see any other vehicles near enough to be any trouble; maybe for him the horn blast kept the road clear of demons.

"I joined the same club." He grimaced as if he'd tasted something he didn't like. "Bitch doesn't let me see the kids anymore."

The driver next to me was silhouetted against the stars through his window. I pictured him spending solitary nights sailing this battleship of the road, while listening to sad songs ghosting from the Elvis discs.

We made small talk for a bit; then the hypnotic drumming of tires on blacktop lulled us into silence. Later, sunrise over the hills held our gaze. I'd never claim to be a fan of Elvis Presley, but his slower, moodier songs have a way of unlocking something inside of me. Memories started to surface. Until yesterday I'd almost forgotten my old buddy the mummy, Natsaf-Ty. I've already mentioned that when I was a child I saw the mummy in a museum. He had a scanty covering of bandages, mainly around the waist. His torso and head had been exposed to reveal a wise old face with closed eyes and the strange effect of the tip of his tongue protruding through his lips. After that chance meeting I found that Natsaf-Ty came to visit me most nights. If I slipped out of bed up after midnight I'd find him sitting on the stairs, invariably the third one from the bottom with his back resting against the wall. Even though his eyelids were closed I knew he'd be looking up at me in that solemn way of his. He didn't move much, and then only very slowly. When I was eight I thought of him as having a liking for stillness. Now I describe it as being serene. He had this aura of tranquillity as he sat there and talked to me, almost a shadow in shadow. And I've been through the possibility—or probability—that it was my imagination that evoked him there. After my mother took me away from my grandparents I missed them and invented the macabre substitute. Natsaf-Ty was always interested in what I'd done that day at school. In his wise old way he offered advice if I was being bullied or was worried about those things that seem so important when you're eight. You know: How tall will I be when I'm grown-up? Will I always get Christmas presents or is there a cutoff age? How long will my hamster live? How does it feel to be dead (after all, that dusty guy must be an expert at it; he'd been dead three thousand years)? This relationship with the mummy went on until I hit twelve. In retrospect I guess things changed with puberty. Oh, don't get me wrong. He didn't vanish in a puff of purple smoke one night. Ty remained there, guardian of the nighttime stairs, until I was in my mid-teens. It's one of those strange things. Even when I was fourteen I'd still glimpse him there sitting on the stairs, with his hands resting on his lap, only I'd long since stopped talking to him by then. Like he was a chair or a picture on the wall, I'd half notice him, but it no longer occurred to me to say hello, never mind regale him with stories of how my day had been. Natsaf-Ty was slowly fading from my life. I was changing. I careered on the hormonal roller-coaster ride of being adolescent. I listened to music with friends. Getting courage to ask girls for a date seemed to be an ongoing process, not to mention an insoluble problem. Life happens, and I was enjoying it happening too much to find time to sit and talk to some antique Egyptian. But he's the loyal kind. He returned every night to occupy the third stair from the bottom, his step, the one that he found so comfortable for his three-thousand-year-old bones.

The week after my sixteenth birthday I heard that my best friend had been with a girl I'd planned to ask on a date (after days of building myself up to it I'd finally mustered enough courage). The truth hit me as hard as an avalanche. Some kid at school I hardly knew said to me in the cafeteria, "Hey, did you hear about Tony Allen? There was a party over at my place on Sunday and we heard shouting coming from the back lawn. We

all went out to find your pal Tony screwing Susan Shepherd on the grass. They were slamming away like a runaway train."

*It's okay*, I'd told myself that evening when I went
around to Tony's. *He's my best friend. I'm all right about
it. So I won't get to date Susan Shepherd, but it's not as if
she's my girlfriend, is it?* I'd never asked her out. The
most I'd ever done was talk to her now and again, with
all that ancillary stuff of lots of watching with aching
longing from a tantalizing distance.

Tony invited me into the kitchen. His parents were
out. The radio played a love song. In a civilized way I
chatted about us going to see a band at an end-of-term
ball. He never mentioned Susan. It was only when he
turned his back to me to pour boiling water into the
cups that the rage came down. How could he have sex
with Susan Shepherd so casually? He'd teased me when
I confessed I'd mustered the courage to ask her out. At
that moment, in my imagination, I had to endure the
mind-searing picture of Tony saying to her at the party,
"Fancy coming outside for a quick poke?"

"Sure, why not?" she'd reply.

Why was it all so easy for Tony to charm the girls, yet
all so tongue-tying for me? Fury hit me so hard I
couldn't speak. I shoved Tony against the kitchen
counter. Boiling water slopped out of the kettle and
onto his hand that held a cup.

"Hey!" It came as a yell as much as a word.

"You think you're so fucking clever!" I screamed at
him with all my sixteen-year-old angst. "You know I fancied Susan!"

"Shit, Mason. Look at my hand!"

I shoved him again. "Don't you lay a finger on her
again."

It was teenage madness. The hormonal tidal wave that knocks years of friendship out of your head in one jealousy-driven whoosh. Tony then knocked me off my feet with a single punch.

As I came to he was mopping spilled water from the counter. "Look at the mess. My mother will go mad when she sees this."

Roaring out death threats I blasted to my feet and swung another punch at him. He sidestepped it; my fist smacked into a steel rack that held fish slicers, ladles, and a sieve. Ten minutes later I made it back home with a huge gash in the back of my hand that didn't just bleed; it erupted red stuff. I was a blood explosion. That crimson discharge could have been an expression of my anger.

That night, at half past midnight, I crept to the stairs as my sister and mother slept. A shadow sat on the third riser from the bottom. I looked down at Natsaf-Ty. He raised his ancient mummy face, a wise face I knew as well as the back of my wounded hand. His eyes were closed. The tip of his tongue protruded from his lips. The tawny skin of his hairless head seemed to be an assembly of atoms that exuded a subtle glow rather than an actual physical presence. Even with his eyes closed he appeared to watch me as I sat down on the step halfway up the stairs. I sat all hunched and miserable there before managing to get out the words that had stuck in my gullet.

"I don't know why . . . I tried to kill my best friend today." My shoulders began to shake. "I feel sick at the thought of it. I knew I shouldn't have, but I couldn't stop myself from wanting to hurt him." My hands were shaking too as I bunched them into fists. The cut beneath the bandage pulled as if the sliced skin were being dragged open again. "I didn't even manage to hit him. I punched a rack on the wall and did this to myself." I held out my right hand for Natsaf-Ty to "see." "I'm an idiot. I deserve smashing my hand up."

Gently he pulled back the bandage to examine the wound, tilting his head to one side as he studied the damage there. The sight of the scab sickened me as much as that stupid outburst of anger at Tony. I felt betrayed by the emotion that had made me act so bizarrely.

The mummy sighed.

"You're right," I muttered. "I deserve it. It'd serve me right if I got gangrene." In the gloom I stared at the wound. The cut formed a Y shape of vivid red lines. The tips of the V shape at the top of the Y ran from my knuckles to converge at the center of the back of my hand, while the horizontal column extended as far as my wrist.

My eyes were burning. "I'm sorry I ignored you for so long. Remember how I used to come down here and we'd sit on the stairs and talk every night?"

He gazed at me with the closed eyes. His face was expressionless.

"Why won't you speak to me now?" I asked, feeling as miserable as anyone could. "I know you must be offended because I ignored you, but I need you to speak to me now."

He looked down at the Y-shaped wound in the flesh. He stared at it so intently I found my gaze drawn to it, too. A crimson Y that resembled a forking road on the skin. One road led to the left, one to the right. In life and love, which road would you choose?

Tires drummed the road. Daylight spread across the surrounding fields. The truck had turned off the main highway onto a narrow lane. Not that I'd noticed. I'd been so wrapped up in the past. I found I was still looking down at the back of my right hand as I rested the palm on my knee. The Y scar was still there, as plain as if I'd used a bloodred pen to draw it there. Apart from that scar my hands were unmarked, not like the trucker's, with the dragons tattooed on the back of each one. I glanced across as he drove to the sounds of Elvis's angelic voice singing, "Glory, glory hallelujah." I saw the dragons had vanished from the trucker's hands. Instead there was a red scar on the back of his right hand in the shape of a Y.

# CHAPTER FOUR

"I've got to go," I told the trucker.

"A piss?"

I nodded.

"The lane's too narrow to stop right here." He applied more weight on the gas pedal with his cowboy boot. The engine roared. Bushes at either side of the truck blurred green; low-hanging branches clumped against the roof. His hands shoved and tugged at the big wheel. Just half an hour ago there were tattooed dragons there; I'd swear it. Now they'd gone. On the back of his right hand was that Y-shaped scar, and such a vivid, blazing red I couldn't have missed it the first time around.

When I'd first climbed into the truck after hitching a ride I put the guy's age—this Elvis look-alike—at forty-five. Now in the light of day he struck me as being closer to thirty-five. Somehow the sideburns didn't seem so noticeable now. The fifties bouffant had been replaced by a fringe that looked a lot like mine. His hair wasn't dyed black after all; it was naturally dark. Like mine. Meanwhile, the trucker blinked as he drove, as if he'd been dazzled. He rubbed his eyes, then noticed the backs of his hands. He frowned as if trying to fish something from his head that he'd forgotten.

"I really need to go," I told him.

"There's no stopping here." He pulled on the horn cord. The thing cried out like a monster in pain. "You're going to have to wait."

"Don't think I can." I grimaced. "I was drinking a lot last night. Brewer's revenge." I tried to make light of it, but all I wanted at that moment was for him to stop so I could jump from the truck and run. Because I knew for sure that the trucker was going Echo on me. He was starting to sound like I sound. I had the same mannerism of pushing the side of my mouth with my thumb when I got tense. He was doing it. I was doing it. That hand with the flaming red Y on the back of it. It was a stigmata on both our hands.

"You like Elvis?" I tried to be conversational.

He shrugged. "He's not terrible, I guess."

"I really need to go now."

"Can't stop here. We'll get rear-ended."

"You've got a lot of Elvis CDs?"

"I just haven't gotten around to changing them."

"It's embarrassing." I smiled, trying to make light of it. "But if I don't go in the next five seconds you're going to get wet upholstery."

He flashed a grin at me. Didn't he have blue eyes five minutes ago?

Then we both said the same thing at once: "Brewer's

revenge." Our thumbs pushed at the side of our mouths despite the smiles.

"Really," I said. "It's hurting."

"God should've used more cloth when he cut our bladders," he said. *That's the kind of thing I say after too much grog*, I told myself. "What's your favorite kind of grog then?" he asked.

Grog? Only I used the word *grog* in those mental conversations with myself. *Grog* and *ale*.

"People say German beer's the best in the world, but I prefer—"

"Belgian." He sounded the horn. "Me too. Belgian has flavor. German beer's got the purity but doesn't have the depth of taste."

The trucker had gone Echo on me; there was no doubting that. Where did the name Echo come from? The gang back at the house always used it for those people who began to spontaneously convert into copies of us. At first I thought of them as shampires. A variant of *vampire*, of course. Shampire—the *sham* part meaning inferior copy; the *pire* bit suggesting that as vampires rob their unwilling victims of their blood, so the shampire stole our identity. The bottom line is: I am me. But at that moment the Elvis-ish trucker was becoming me also.

Biological copies happen all the time in nature. After all, aren't identical twins genetic copies of each other? Okay, that happens in the womb. But if you didn't know for a fact that identical twins exist (because you've seen them with your own eyes, haven't you?), would you believe that such a thing was possible? And at that moment this stranger was becoming my twin. Only it wasn't occurring in a womb but in this cab that smelled of spearmint, with a leather-clad effigy of the King dancing to the rhythm of the speeding truck. And all the time tree branches hammered like the fists of crazy people trying to batter their way in.

*I need to urinate*, I told myself. *I really need to go. There's that pain in the pit of my stomach. That insistent pain, the pent-up sensation of pressure that needs release. Urgent, annoying, intrusive: this is what it feels like when you're bursting for a whiz.* Okay, I didn't really want to go to the bathroom, but this guy beside me had turned into an Echoman—an echo of me. His hands were like mine (complete with scar); his hair resembled the hair I saw in the mirror every morning. Just like me he preferred Belgian beer to German (though if I'd discussed the merits of Germanic and Flemish brew with him last night he'd have stared blankly at me). He pushed the side of his mouth with his thumb when perplexed. So, sure as Elvis is the King, he must be feeling the same as me.

*Need to go . . . need to go . . . need to go . . .* I pushed the words through my head with memories of being seated on a bus or standing in a supermarket queue with that bursting need to reach a lavatory.

"It's starting to hurt now," I said. "Can you pull over?"

"All this talking of 'going' has made me need to piss, too," he said matter-of-factly. "I'll stop as soon as there's a place." He chuckled. "Brewer's revenge." Even though he laughed as he pushed the side of his mouth with his thumb, thoughts troubled him. Although he was clearly becoming an Echoman, he hadn't realized it yet. He grunted. "You know driving a truck beats driving a car? You're so high above the road. It's like looking out from the top of a house. It gives you a sense of security."

Echomen favor height. Often they launch their attacks from trees. I could see that this one was for the first time marveling at how high the truck driver is above other traffic. Truckers are the titans of the road. They look only their own kind in the eye. Everyone else they gaze down on from their Olympian altitudes.

I grimaced. "Please. You don't know how bad this feels right now. It'll only take a minute."

The man smiled. "Here'll do fine."

Air brakes hissed as he pulled over onto gravel beside the road.

"I won't be long," I told him, but I had only one thought. That was, *Run!*

After bringing the machine to a stop he turned to me with a knowing smile. "You know, I think we've got a lot in common, you and I."

I opened the door. "I'll just be a minute."

"You're not thinking of running away from me, are you?"

"No. I really need this ride."

Before I had chance to climb out he leaned sideways and cupped his hand behind the back of my neck.

And did I tell you that Echomen don't want those whom they duplicate to live? Before he could put both hands around my neck I yanked the plastic Elvis from the dashboard and slammed it into his face. Its metal dance spring scratched his cheek. After letting fly with a blistering curse, he swung a blow at me. Instead of pulling away, which would have given him ample room to swing his right hook, I lunged at him. With my heel pressed against the dashboard I could use the strength in my legs to keep pushing him hard against his door with my shoulder. The lock of the driver's door popped and out he tumbled into the road. His head struck the blacktop first, with his legs trailing behind out the cab.

The six-foot drop knocked the sense out of him for a few seconds. And somehow in the struggle the hand brake had been knocked out of the locked position. As he lay there in the road, his face twisted in pain, gasping for air, the truck slowly moved forward. I was vertically above him, looking right down into his eyes as the huge tires crunched road grit. The wheels kept on turning as the wheels at the back of the tractor unit smoothly crept over his hips to crush the man beneath the waist. As he howled his hands shot up to the underside of the three-ton vehicle. For an entire sequence of moments he pushed upward as if he truly believed he could lift the metal monster and stop it from squeezing the life out of him.

I know nothing about trucks. Nevertheless, I managed to drag the hand brake back into the locked position to stop the wheels from mashing his stomach and chest. That done, I leaped out of the cab. The lane here was quiet—apart from the man's howls, that is. The trucker turned Echoman must have planned it like this. He intended to find a quiet place to stop, then kill me as the transformation took place—from *he* to *me*.

The rest of my gang killed Echomen like you or I would use a piece of tissue to crush a bothersome fly against a window. I'd never killed an Echoman before. I hadn't yet. This had been an accident. The guy fell under the wheels of his wagon. Besides, he wasn't dead yet. A lot of liquid, some of it scarlet in color, ran out from between his legs where the five-foot tires had crunched his body to paste, but he was still noisily alive. And he was begging me to save him. His eyes locked onto mine; one of his arms reached out to me, as if he were a child who'd fallen into a hole and cried to his father to simply lift him out. The man had three tons resting on him. What could I do to save him? Then . . . why should I save him? He'd kill me the first chance he got.

I glanced around. The sun was above the horizon. Flanking the lane were trees. Nobody would have seen the accident yet. There was a knife in my bag. The gang always cut away the Echoman's face to see which one of us he resembled. This was hardly a tricky problem here. The same scar that adorned the back of my hand now blazed a brilliant red from the back of his. A short while ago he looked every day of his forty-five years. Now, even though he vented blood from his mouth, he didn't appear over thirty. He no longer resembled Elvis Presley. And although he wasn't *me* yet, he was on the road to *me*, figuratively speaking. Literally speaking, he lay on the road and howled with a lusty strength, even though his hips and pelvis must now resemble cake crumbs. I reached into the cab to get my bag. This wouldn't be easy—it would be bloody and messy; I'd have to cut his throat to shut him up—but I should maintain the practices observed by my gang. The man had turned Echo, so he had to die. That was rule number one. Two, we observed the results of the process and made a written record; therefore, when he stopped squirming I had to cut away the face to reveal the new features forming beneath the old skin.

When I got close he grabbed my ankle. I kicked his hand away. He lay flat on his back with the tire depressing the pit of his belly, and he screamed so loud my ears hurt. Quickly I pulled out the knife, then crouched down on the road just above his thrashing skull. At the second attempt I got my hand under his chin, then pulled it back to force his throat to rise, a mound of speckled skin that revealed razor burn (just the same as mine) and forty-eight hours of stubble.

"No . . . please. Don't do this. Get help. For God's sake, please get help." He spoke remarkably clearly for someone with three tons of steel riding his nuts.

I leaned forward so I could rest the blade's cutting edge just below his Adam's apple. When you sliced someone's throat open, did you saw the blade like cutting bread for a sandwich? Or would it be better to exert a firm downward pressure, as if halving a block of cheese? The man stopped screaming. With his bloodied teeth gritted together he stared at me with huge eyes that were full of pleading and sheer, out-and-out terror.

Then came one of those moments that people speak about, only you don't really know what it's like until it happens to you. A sense of someone staring at me made my skin itch all over. The road was still deserted. Apart from my own respiration, and that of the Echoman, all I could hear was the morning breeze stirring the leaves. There wasn't even any birdsong. I checked out the trees behind me. And wouldn't you just know it? There he was again. Natsaf-Ty, keeper of the sacred crocodiles, stood watching me from the forest. I was in sunlight, he in deep shadow, so it was difficult to make him out clearly. The shadows appeared to mutate there. Even so, I sensed him watching me through those closed eyelids. His head was slightly to one side, as if somehow he listened to my thoughts. I let go of the guy's head as I stood up; his skull clunked on the blacktop. Quickly I scooped up my bag from the road and slipped the knife inside. I couldn't kill the man if Natsaf-Ty was watching. Okay, even if the mummy was a product of my imagination, it brought back all those memories of late-night conversations on the stairs. Though the individual beneath the wheel was an Echoman, I couldn't slit his throat in front of Natsaf-Ty. It would be like using the F-word in church.

Instead I ran across the road toward the shadow figure. Something was happening inside my own head if an Egyptian mummy kept popping up. If I asked Natsaf-Ty why he was there—regardless of whether he was extruded from my imagination or not—then maybe some deep-seated psychological conundrum would be answered, and dried-out old Natsaf-Ty would return to whatever knot of neurons inside my noodle from whence he came. The moment I entered the cluster of trees I saw he'd vanished again.

Nevertheless, I tried. "Natsaf-Ty. I saw you. What do you want? Are you trying to tell me something? I know you saw what I was going to do to that man on the road. But we're all in danger now. Only it's a danger that nobody can understand or believe is a real threat unless they experience it for themselves." A bird fluttered in the branches overhead. Leaves spiraled down. "I don't want to kill, but for people like me we don't have a choice. We're trying to find a way to prove to the rest of the world that something bad is happening. Even we can't explain it. It's like an invasion, but we don't think it's coming from outside. It might have been inside of us all along. Listen. Won't you come back so I can talk to you?"

In the shadows were more shadows and gloomy tree trunks. It was like nighttime in there. I took another dozen steps into the forest. Then I heard the sound of a vehicle braking hard on the road. Doors slammed. Running feet, shouting voices. So the trucker had been found. And Natsaf-Ty warned me just in time that somebody was coming.

Softly, I whispered into the shadows, "Thanks for the heads-up, old buddy. If you hadn't been here they'd have caught me red-handed."

The road wasn't the place to be right now. Instead I headed deeper into the forest, well away from the police when they arrived ten minutes later with the ambulance.

There's something else about Echomen I haven't explained. Sure they begin to resemble us; they adopt our mannerisms; they feel what we feel. That's why I used the trick of remembering the discomfort of a full bladder to encourage the trucker to make that bathroom stop. But it's a two-way street. Whatever magic or telepathy that drives it is a mystery to me, yet as I weaved through those trees I felt what the truck driver felt. A dull pain roved through the pit of my stomach like a creature chewed on my bowel. If I closed my eyes for too long I saw what he saw, from his point of view as he lay on the road, looking up at the men and women from the emergency services who tried to help him. Snatches of conversation ghosted through my head.

*"Don't worry," says a man in uniform, "we'll soon have you out of there."*

*A woman smiles down in that caring way of a professional who has seen it all before. "What's your name, sir? Can you tell me your name?" Then another surge of pain that doubles me over—the real me. "Quickly! We're losing him!" My/his eyes look down at his/my stomach as blood erupts from a torn artery.*

Then the phantom words, images, and feelings stopped, and I knew he was dead.

# CHAPTER FIVE

Question: Is an empty wallet heavier than a full one? Stupid question, right? The answer's obvious: the wallet that is bereft of banknotes is the *heaviest*. At least, it seems like that. You're aware of the cashless wallet riding for free in your pocket, doing no work, and enjoying a pointless existence.

After leaving the dead Echoman to be shoveled from the pavement by the police, I walked through the forest until I saw a town in a valley. There I found a railway station and bought a railway ticket, leaving just enough money for coffee and a doughnut for breakfast on the platform as I waited for the train home. I guess whoever made the doughnut knew he was going to be fired, because he must have emptied a whole drum of cinnamon into the mix. The first bite of the doughnut set my mouth on fire. In a hurry to spit out the revolting mouthful of doughnut, I set the coffee down on a seat. The paper cup fell sideways. A moment later I was left with an inedible snack and my breakfast beverage forming a steaming pool on the concrete. *Great. Just great.*

The train was due in ten minutes. Just time to get to an ATM for some more cash. Life on the road, sleeping in a van, being tracked by Echomen does mad things to your head. I'd lost track of how much money I had, so for whole moments I stared at the screen blinking INSUFFICIENT FUNDS. *I have sufficient funds*, I told myself. I had the machine print me a statement of my last dozen transactions. There you have it . . . I'd left my old life in the city in a rush. So I'd not canceled the bank debits. The bulk of the cash had gone on a month's rent for rooms I no longer lived in—and would never see again.

I could have eaten a bag of coffee beans right then, never mind drinking a cup. A night without sleep and the battle with the Echoman trucker had left me with a craving for caffeine. But without so much as a coin in my pocket all I could do was return to the bench on the platform, stare at my puddle of spilled coffee, and wait for the train.

The train arrived in my hometown of Tanshelf at midday. If a supreme Being does control the weather, then that Being had decided that despite all the lousy stuff that had happened to me in the last three weeks, I still looked too perky for my own good, so the heavens opened wide to dump their deluge on me. Without money for a taxi or bus back home, or even enough for a coffee in the station café, I had to stand in the overhang of the town hall as rain blasted the streets like liquid gunfire. Tanshelf is a market town. If you ever doubted that this was a place farmers brought their harvests and livestock to trade, the street names and tavern names would beat that pernicious doubt right out of you. Where I stood beneath the canopy I could look through the falling water at streets that radiated from the town square—Beastfair, Horsefair, Oatsfair, Cattlefair, Oxfair, Goosefair, Swinesfair (*fair* being the old English word for *market*). Then the taverns that comprise a fair-sized chunk of the town's businesses; they allude to a market heritage, too—Beastfair Vaults, the Drovers, the Ancient Shepherd, the Lamb, the White Swan (known locally as the Mucky Duck), the Wheatsheaf, and so on.

The weather played jokes on me. Rain suddenly eased. Blue sky appeared over the Corn Exchange, so I set off on what would be a half-hour walk to my mother's house. Only I'd gone a mere twenty paces when the rain blasted along the street again, driving shoppers inside and me into something called the Buttercross. This is an archaic structure in the town square where merchants would make their deals. It comprises eight stone pillars that hold aloft a tiled roof. The open archways don't keep the wind out, but it keeps the rain off. I ducked inside. In its center was a wooden bench that was maybe twenty feet long. The only other person in there was the town vagrant. He'd occupied the place for the last thirty years, so I recognized him from childhood when I'd cross the market square to catch my bus home. I can't remember his real name, but everyone called him Old Snotter.

Now here was Old Snotter lying on the opposite end of the bench from where I now sat waiting for the rain to abate. Old Snotter hadn't changed. He had a huge ginger beard that hid most of his face. Ginger eyebrows bushed over his eyes. More ginger hair stuck out from under a ball cap. The impression you got was of a big, gingery orangutan. You couldn't really tell what clothes he wore because he made a kind of overalls out of black plastic sacks. He tied one each around his legs; then he tore holes in another for his arms and head and pulled it over his torso as if it were a glossy black fetish T-shirt. You never talked to Old Snotter. He never talked to you. Old Snotter lived in his own alcoholic world a billion miles from planet Earth.

So I waited for it to stop raining. As I waited it sank into me that I was back in Tanshelf for the first time in half a year. All those months ago I crossed this very square to the station, no doubt Old Snotter had been snoozing here on the bench; then I boarded the train that carried me to the capital city, where I had well-paid work making TV for the Internet. For six months I labored hard all day, crafting films that won praise and (more important for my boss) premium rates for the piggyback commercials. I lived a permanent state of *now*. When I wasn't shooting with my camera I was at parties with friends, the kind of parties that never seemed to have a beginning or an end. Sometimes I left a party in the morning, worked all day, then returned to the same party at night that was still blazing along. Then three weeks ago, the world I believed was relatively sane, stable, and set to continue in its rock-solid orbit went *pffft!*

*So here I am back in Tanshelf*, I told myself. If it's not overly poetic, this is a place paved not merely in Yorkshire stone but with memories. Over there by the bus stop is where I won my first real kiss from a girl. Outside the Mucky Duck, that's where I threw up so violently after my first boozy night that my watch strap broke, and I carried my vomit-smeared watch home in my pocket. I found it glued to the pocket lining in the morning. As I sat there on the bench near Old Snotter, with the rain hissing against the roads, I marveled at how Tanshelf looked so familiar, yet so strange, even though it had been only six months. There was an iron sculpture of a tree where Tony Allen climbed to impress a girl and all his money fell out of his pockets. The coins went rolling everywhere; a bunch of ten-year-olds pounced on them before vanishing into the back alleyways.

The church clock chimed one. I'd been sitting there for an hour. Old Snotter still snoozed on the bench. The muscles in my rump were aching from being perched on those antique bench timbers that had accommodated rear ends for the last hundred years or more. Through swirling rain one of the natives of Tanshelf would come hurrying across the square to briefly appear before vanishing again. On one occasion I was sure the old mummy, Natsaf-Ty, loomed through the mist of raindrops. I fancied I glimpsed the arid red face (magically protected from the wet), the closed eyes, the tongue protruding slightly from the lips, the slow-motion movements of the withered arms and legs. Only the dark figure veered off to disappear into the storm before I had it in clear view.

"Natsaf-Ty?" It was a halfhearted call on my part. I knew he'd already gone.

The bench quivered as Old Snotter turned over on it as if he rolled over in bed. His suit of black plastic sacks made scrunching sounds as he wriggled to make himself comfortable again on the concrete-hard wood. Ginger beard tufts stuck up in spikes; they'd been stiffened by who knew what. My backside ached like fury from sitting there for an hour. Old Snotter must have anesthetized himself good. A green bottle with a couple of inches of liquor waited within his reach on the stone slabs.

As water cascaded down I watched cars crash through flash floods in Beastfair, Swinefair, Goosefair, and the rest. What buildings I could see through the swirling murk had their own cache of memories I could evoke. The bookstore where I had a Saturday job when I was in college. In my mind's eye I could see myself walking through the doors to check out the latest releases before taking my bag of sandwiches upstairs to put them in the fridge until lunch. Next to that was the bank that was held up at gunpoint five years ago. Now it was a coffeehouse.

The memories still ran through my head when the church clock chimed twice. Two o'clock. The pain in

my backside from the bench lit bonfires inside of me. I
stood up and thought I saw Natsaf-Ty's dusty flesh looking at me from the entrance to the bookstore. When I
took a closer look I saw it was a woman in a brown
jacket waiting for a break in the rainstorm. As for me, I'd
been sheltering under the Buttercross canopy for the
best part of two hours. It's times like that, when you've
nothing to occupy your mind, when it falls prey to all
those anxieties you hide away. Now the lack of money
began to bother me.

*I should have canceled the payments for the rent and
utilities. Now they've cleared out my account. I've no job
anymore. There's a couple of hundred in an old account,
but I need to give a month's notice to get hold of that.
Maybe I should have listened to Ulric and the others and
not come home after all. But what kind of life is that?
Sleeping in the back of a van, or breaking into an empty
house to steal time in someone else's bed and eat their
food until we have to move on? If I go to the police, what
then? How can I convince them that Echomen not only
exist, but are a threat?*

I stared into a puddle that featured never-ending expanding rings as drips fell into it from the roof. *But think
it through, Mason. You tell the police, then what? They
don't call in SWAT; they call in the psychiatric-duty doctor. Then they make some inquiries after I tell them what
happened. First of all that leads the cops to the truck
driver who fell under the wheels of his rig when he attacked me. My prints will be on the door handles; my
DNA will saturate the spearmint gum in the trash bag
hanging from the hook in the cabin. Hell, come to that
my DNA will be under the dead guy's fingernails. There's
a scratch he made when he grabbed the back of my
neck. Would the Y-shaped scar on the back of the*

*trucker's hand be enough to prove that some bizarre spontaneous cloning was taking place?* I laughed. There was precious little fun in the laughter, because I knew that rather than being celebrated as a monster-killer, I'd be shot full of sedative and sat before the TV in a psychiatric ward at Tanshelf General Hospital.

The church clock struck the quarter hour. The doom-laden chime died on the rain-soaked town. Fried-food smells drifted from cafés. When had I eaten last? Pizza? It had to be the pizza last night. We ate two pizzas each. That seemed such a long time ago. Ruth had shown me the Echoman's head that wore my face. It seemed unreal now. Had the last three weeks really happened? Or did I fall asleep on the train home, then dream it all?

A pair of bikes flashed across the square ridden by girls who rang their bells for the sheer joy of it.

"Rain." I muttered the word as if I had to say it to believe it. Then, at last, the clouds turned from gray to white. The buildings were glossy, as if they'd been given an instant coat of varnish. The rain made the roads glisten, too. But at last the storm had passed. Now for the walk home. Until that moment I hadn't thought of how I'd explain my sudden reappearance to my mother. I stepped over the big puddle that hosted the spectacle of ever-expanding rings of water. I'd easily cleared the inch-deep puddle when all of sudden I was toppling backward again. A second later I slammed down into it with a splash. The instant I realized someone had attacked me was the same instant that the sky was blacked out as a heavy shape pressed down on my face as I lay there. When I tried to shout out I felt a smooth plastic sheet with my tongue. The smell of old perspiration mixed with stale booze raced up my nostrils to provoke my stomach into a retching spasm. Only I couldn't breathe. Old Snotter's homemade plastic suit had sealed off my airways. The weight of the hobo felt like tons rather than pounds. The force of falling—that and rapping my skull on the flagstones—fucked up any chance of figuring out what had happened exactly, other than that Old Snotter had dragged me off balance and now appeared to be trying to suffocate me with his great slab of a chest. Beating his back with my free arm was useless. My other arm was pinned beneath my own body. Kicking my legs was easy to do, but fruitless. A lot of fireworks started spitting sparks inside my head. My heart ached, it beat so hard. For a moment I was sitting on the stairs at home again. I was ten years old and asking wise old Natsaf-Ty, who sat on his habitual third step, "How old do you think I'll be when I die?"

I tried to bite his chest flesh through the sack, but all I managed to do was taste salt and dirt on the plastic membrane that he'd wrapped himself in. I wasn't up to asking myself why he'd attacked me, thinking only that I'd come all this way to die at the age of twenty-eight, in Tanshelf's town square on a wet Monday in April. Old Snotter's body movements became more convulsive. Then I saw light. Old Snotter was rising away from me. All of a sudden the air rushed back into my lungs. My coughing sounded more like barking as I sat up in the puddle. Three guys were dragging Old Snotter off of me. They were shouting to one another to hold on to him. A moment later, however, he twisted out of their grip. After that there was a glossy black blur as he raced away into the back alleyways.

"Did you see the old devil run?" One my rescuers had nothing less than admiration in his voice. "He's at death's door, but he moves like a greyhound."

One of the others pulled me to my feet. "What did

you do to Old Snotter? That must be the first time he's turned vicious on anyone."

I wiped puddle water from my face. "I've never seen him talk to anyone, never mind want to wrestle." Old Snotter's taste clung to my tongue. That had to be the least pleasant thing I'd ever had in my mouth. "Thanks, by the way."

"You're local, then? You know him?"

"I used to see him every time I came into town." I wished I had something to rinse my mouth with. "Old Snotter . . . all he ever did was sit or lie on the bench. That and drink himself to sleep."

The three men were dressed in blue mechanics' coveralls. They were bemused by the man's sudden violence.

"What did you do? Try to steal his bottle?"

I shook my head. "I never touched him."

"He's certainly taken a dislike to you."

"Dislike? He tried to kill me." As I got recovered my senses I realized what had happened. He'd been too close to me. He'd turned Echo, too. This was getting bad. They never changed so quickly before.

"He wasn't trying to kill you." One of the mechanics picked up my wallet from the ground. "Old Snotter was after your money."

The other mechanic disagreed. "He's never stolen before. To my knowledge, anyway."

"Believe me," I told them, "he wanted to kill me."

They exchanged glances, not sure what to do next.

"We should report it to the police," said one.

"No," I disagreed quickly—no doubt too quickly, because they were surprised by my reaction. "No. I must have woken him in the middle of a bad dream."

They laughed, secretly relieved that they wouldn't get involved with giving witness statements.

"Yeah, it'll be something like that," said one of the men.

"He probably saw you as a pink elephant," added another.

The third still had doubts. "It was Old Snotter, wasn't it? He moved fast for someone as decrepit as he is."

"Sure it was."

"But Snotter's got that dirty great ginger beard. Didn't the guy who attacked you have short dark hair?"

"It had to be Old Snotter," another of the mechanics said. "Smelled like him. And he was wearing his plastic suit."

"Whoever it was, he's gone," I added. "And thanks again. I appreciate it." I held out my hand and shook each of theirs in turn. Suddenly I felt uneasy to be in the company of others. If this process was speeding up, was I the cause? Was I infecting people? Of course, I was the architect of another problem. I'd decided to go home. Wouldn't the same happen to them?

# CHAPTER SIX

These thoughts: *Am I doing the right thing? Of course I'm* not *doing the right thing! I'm going home to my mother and my sister. This "event"—whatever it is that's happening to me—is going nuclear; it's just exploding into something else. If I get too close to another person—and that includes sitting ten feet from a total stranger—then* strange *things start happening. They start turning into me. They become my physiological echo.*

But the simple action of going home ripped any doubts out of my head and kicked them out of the arena. I was home. My mother and sister were so thrilled to see me they looked as if they could burst. Add to that I was so exhausted I could hardly keep on my feet. And did I mention hungry? The emptiness in my stomach was a painful void.

"Mason, why didn't you phone to let us know you were coming home?"

I muttered that I'd been given a couple of days' leave from work at short notice and wanted to surprise them. "They're refitting the studio." The reason was vague yet faintly plausible. "Wires all over the place."

"I've stripped your bed; all the sheets are back in the loft."

Eve, my twenty-year-old sister, was as delighted as my mother to see me. Suddenly the practical one, she shrugged away problems. "My spare bedding's in the cupboard. Mason can use that."

"Pillows?"

"He can use my new one."

"And there's his clothes."

"New toothbrush . . . clean towels in the blanket box."

Eve and my mother live together in the house. I could see they'd forged such a tight-knit team they anticipated what the other would say and had formed a vocal shorthand, which they understood but left me flagging. Even so, I knew they had everything I needed to make me comfortable.

My mother checked her watch. "If I go by four I can get to the butcher in time for him to cut me some nice sirloin."

"Whoa," I broke in. "Don't go rushing around after me. I'll be fine. A frozen pizza will—"

"Not on your life." She grinned with such happiness it made her face light up. "We'll have steak and potatoes, then cheesecake. You'll want a beer with that, won't you?"

"It's not necessary, really. I didn't come home to put you to all this trouble."

"It's no trouble. I'll go now. Do I need a coat? No, I'll risk it."

Eve saw I was more than a little tatty around the edges. "You look as if you've walked all the way here from London."

"Only from town."

My mother must have seen the stubble along with the dark rings under my eyes, but she was wise enough not to start a reunion with questions that could be construed as criticism. "Right. I've got my keys . . . purse. Eve, can you make your brother a coffee and a sandwich to keep him going until dinner? There's chocolate cake, too; I'm sure he won't turn that down."

"Unless London's turned him funny." Eve pitched it as a joke, but she kept doing this double take of me that suggested I'd changed after living away from home.

That's my mother, Delph, and sister, Eve. My mother could pass for mid-thirties. She has short blond hair that's so unfashionably curly that it drives Eve to distraction (with plenty of "Mother, you're not going out with me looking like that"). Personality-wise, Mom's lighthearted, good at making jokes, very good at comic impersonations of people—not anybody you've ever heard of; she mimics some of our odder neighbors, family members, people she's seen in the supermarket. She's so good at it that she's had us choking with laughter. As mother and father rolled into one, with her being a single parent, she can unblock drains, change car tires, and cook amazing meals (but hates fiddly baking—"I haven't time to do fancy," she'd tell us). Perhaps her nicest trait is to be so likable that she can make a neighbor's day just by chatting to them over a fence. Eve, at twenty, is at college as a mature student. She'd left school for office work, then realized qualifications do help career advancement. Though she'd deny it she'd begun to resemble our mother a heck of a lot—not the blond, frizzy hair, though. Even from the age of twelve Eve took the trouble to straighten her long, dark hair. Once I even caught her using the clothes iron to flatten it against the table. Eve seemed even taller and slimmer than the last time I'd seen her. When she stood beside our mother I could see she beat her regarding height.

After walking through the door into the house followed by a tumultuous greeting with plenty of kisses, I was all of a sudden left in my own company. Mom darted out to her little green car for the drive to the supermarket. Eve said she'd make me a sandwich, then added pointedly, "You'll be wanting a bath, won't you? Towels are in the usual place."

Did I really stink that much? Then when had I showered last? Add to that some of Old Snotter's aroma that must have transferred to me when he attacked me just a couple of hours ago and I'd be attracting flies as readily as something hairy lying dead in a ditch.

I ran a bath as deep as I could get it without it overflowing the sides. The prospect of lying immersed in hot water tempted me more than words could say. A lot of my toiletries were still lurking in the back of the cabinet. There were also the usual clutch of disposable razors so I could scrape away the stubble as I wallowed up to my jaw in the tub. Bathrooms are other worlds. You do what comes naturally there without being self-conscious. I don't know if it's the same for everybody else, but my bathroom thoughts run along different tracks. As I steeped my flesh in the tub I gazed at my distorted reflection in the bath faucet chrome. It made my face look like a naked thumb with eyes resembling dots on a page. Everyone's face in the world is different. Of course they are. Even twins aren't exactly identical. There are minor differences in face shape, or the habit of raising an eyebrow. The way the bath chrome took my reflection, then distorted it to look so bloody peculiar, like a thumb with black hair at the end, made me wonder how a stranger could end up wearing my face. Trying to imagine what infinity is really like leaves you with that sick feeling, as if you're about to topple from a cliff, so it made me nauseous when I tried to understand what process turned people into me. As I dragged the razor down the side of my face to cut away the stubble I realized that I'd blocked questions about what the Echomen really were and why they were changing into duplicates of me. I'd even distanced myself from reality when Ulric, Ruth, Dianna, and Paddy had killed them, and I'd seen them kill so many in the last three weeks.

It's a way of protecting my sanity, I guess. Even in the early days I'd mentally censored my reaction to the slayings. Just how many slayings? I closed my eyes: a blur of exploding heads, hands clutching at bullet holes in chests, groins, backs, necks, faces, throats, breasts, arms, hands—faces were the worst. A face shot deflated the head like it was a ball shrinking to half its normal size. I shaved harder. The water swirled around me, that familiar smell of soap. The warm fluid enclosed me in a liquid grasp.

But I wanted to remember a single incident, not mixed images of falling bodies with the shit blasted out of them by that gang of four strangers. The very same strangers who came out of nowhere, picked me up out of the street, and then carried me away on this insane carousel ride of mayhem. My hand shook as I chiseled at my face with the blade, while my mind whirled madly, trying to catch a tail of all those running memories.

Then this:

On the third day with the gang, I'd gone to buy sandwiches from a gas station on a road that ran through open countryside. Ulric had parked at the back of the building, well away from other cars. A guy in his twenties followed me back to the van. He wore a red ball cap that carried the logo of a canoe passing through a hoop.

"Can you give me a lift?" he asked.

"You don't know where we're going," Paddy replied.

"That doesn't matter." The man had a bright smile. "I'm one of the restless sort. I just keep moving around."

He was clean shaven; the jeans and sweater he wore were in good shape; so were his sneakers. In one hand he carried a plastic bag with what must have been groceries, and I remembered he was chewing a large wad of gum—bright green gum that moved around the inside of his mouth like it had a life of its own, as if the guy in the red cap had taken a liking to chewing on bright green caterpillars.

"Sure you can come along," Paddy told him. "That is, if you don't mind riding in the back with all our stuff."

"No worries." The hitcher's smile was a sunny day in its own right. "I'm just happy to be moving. One thing that irritates me is sticking in any one place too long."

"You must have gypsy blood," Ruth told him.

"Something like that."

"I'll open up the back." Paddy swung open the doors. "Try to make yourself comfortable."

"Thanks."

As he climbed into the back Paddy and Ulric jumped him. They used their body weight to hold him down. At the same time Dianna emptied the plastic carrier bag of its groceries; then she and Ruth slipped the bag over his head. They held it there with the open end sealed with their hands around his neck. When he exhaled the bag ballooned. When he inhaled it sucked tight around his head. The plastic film molded itself so closely around his skin you could see all his features: even the way his bulging eyes formed raised mounds like a pair of little domes. I watched without emotion over his demise. If anything, I was disappointed that the carton of chocolate pudding Dianna had tipped from the bag with the other groceries had burst open. I watched the chocolate sauce leaking out and thought how good it looked.

When I started to walk away from the four who suffocated the hitcher in the back of the van, Ulric snapped, "Mason? Where are you going?"

"I want one of those puddings," I told him.

Paddy grinned at me as the guy's struggles morphed into predeath fits. "You can get me one as well."

"Anyone else want chocolate pudding?" I asked.

Ruth shook her head. "But you can see if they've got any gum like he had." She pressed down on the dying man's face with the palm of her hand to make sure no air reached his nostrils.

"That bright green stuff?" I asked in surprise. It looked disgusting.

"Yeah, I'm ready for a change."

"Okay."

I strolled across the parking lot to the gas station store.

Behind me they'd have started cutting the guy's face off, just to check which one of us he was turning into.

The bathwater had turned a funny color. I'd been miles away—and more than two weeks in the past. I hadn't noticed that I'd sawed away not only facial hair with the razor but a lump of skin too. Blood dripped from my chin into the tub. I realized I still had feelings after all when I rubbed the cut with the sponge: it hurt like hell.

# CHAPTER SEVEN

That evening was like the old family evenings.

"What did you do to your face, Mason?" Eve stood behind where I sat in the chair and without any shyness grabbed my head and pushed it sideways.

"Cut myself shaving; mind my beer." A dollop of ale plopped out of the glass to roll down my shirtfront.

"Cut yourself shaving?" My sister never did display any reticence when it came to seizing hold of my head or a limb if she wanted to examine it more closely. "You look as if you've been trying to chop your own head off. And look at this zit on the side of your neck. If it bursts it'll blow the windows out."

"Eve, you're twenty. You should be more ladylike." Mom used her scolding voice as she sat in her favorite armchair, but she was smiling; she enjoyed having the old sibling banter back in the house again. "He hasn't come two hundred miles to have his face debated."

Eve laughed. "It's a face only a mother could love."

She gripped my nose to give it a playful shake. "Don't visit the elephants at the zoo—they might not let you out again."

After being on edge for so long my body hurt as muscles relaxed. I found I couldn't stop smiling, too. "Mother. She says my nose is too big."

"Oh, don't start telling tales on each other again."

"It's Eve." I grinned. "She's wicked to me."

"You deserve it. All brothers deserve it." She sat on the chair arm to playfully put me in a headlock. Maybe she still felt uncomfortable hugging her big brother in an affectionate way; a bit of play-wrestling smuggled that hug in anyway. "What are your plans?"

"Oh, nothing much."

Mom poured herself a glass of white wine. "Say no if you haven't time, but the branches of the apple tree are hanging over Jack's fence."

"I'll cut them back in the morning," I told her, then managed a drink of beer between Eve playfully crushing my head. "Ouch. Watch the brains, dear."

"What brains? You once greased your bike's gears with olive oil. Garlic-flavored olive oil at that. Whenever you rode it you smelled like a deli."

"Never mind, it kept the shampires away."

"Idiot." Another vigorous head squeeze. "What's a shampire?"

"Same as a vampire, only they steal your looks, not your blood."

"Listen to him, Mother. Away six months, then comes back full of psychobabble."

She tickled my neck, which nearly left me choking with laughter.

"Are you sure about pruning the tree?" Mom worried

that she was imposing on me. "Eve and I can do it if we use the long-handled clippers."

"No, I'm looking forward to some lumberjacking." I swigged the beer. "I need to burn some calories anyway. These days half of my time is spent in the editing suite juggling film clips."

"And the other half in a bar, judging by those bags under your eyes."

"Eve, I told you not to tease your brother. He doesn't have bags under his eyes. He's just tired."

"Speaking of tired . . ." The clock on the bookshelf told me it was ten p.m. "I'm going to have an early night."

Both Eve and Mom had enjoyed themselves so much that they pressed me to stay up for another beer. I was dog-tired. Of course, I'd lied to them about work. There'd be no job for me there at Sliver-cast Imaging, as I'd not turned up at the office for the past three weeks. Neither had I even hinted at recent events. How could I explain my troubles to my family?

"You can't go to bed just yet." Eve leaned against me as she sat on the chair arm to keep me in the seat. "We haven't interrogated you about girlfriends."

"Eve." Mom's gentle warning.

"Mason, I'll get you a beer."

"I'm whacked."

"Aw, c'mon, just one more. You haven't told us about all those celebrity parties yet."

"Okay, then." My smile was an exhausted one, but felt genuine enough. "Just one."

It was so much like old times, the three of us joking and laughing in the living room. Once more this whole business with the Echomen—and the killings—moved into the background, where it seemed like a dream.

\* \* \*

"What's that you said? No, you didn't ask the question, did you? It was me thinking it." I looked downstairs at Natsaf-Ty sitting on the third step from the bottom. In the postmidnight darkness he was motionless, his eyes closed, the wise old face expressionless. Then he raised his chin until I had a sense of him gazing at me.

I'd woken at one in the morning with the rank taste of stale beer sticking to my tongue, so I went to the bathroom for a slug of mouthwash. The mint was so powerful it felt as if I'd taken a mouthful of electric shocks. When I crossed the landing in the direction of my bedroom I'd noticed the dusty scent of aromatic resins that signaled the return of an old friend. I can't describe the appearance of Natsaf-Ty as being a shock or even a surprise. I'd seen him at the house yesterday when Paddy and the others shot the Echoman in the tree. I'd glimpsed Natsaf-Ty several times since. If this ancient Egyptian mummy with the scalp full of cracks that revealed dry bone was an imaginary friend from childhood, then he was back again.

The herb scents and resins that the embalmers used to stuff the torso when they emptied out the internal organs were distinct in the night air. Sights of that dried husk of a body, the reddish skin, the crisscrossed bandages across his chest: they were real enough at that moment. So as I'd done night after night as a child, I settled down on the top step. Natsaf-Ty rested on the third step from the bottom, one leg raised, so the bulbous knee bone almost touched his chest, while he sat twisted to one side so he could rest his back to the wall. And as usual the other thigh supported one hand, revealing perfectly preserved fingernails that were the color of pearls. And the face . . . same as always: eyes closed, tongue slightly protruding between lips that would be as crisp as cheese crackers. A sensation that the wise old man gazed at me, as if he wondered about what I was really like, about what I planned to do, and what would motivate me to behave in a certain way. Right now I sensed his expression as being one of accusation. *Why did you do that, Mason? What made you kill the truck driver?*

This made me angry. Even though I risked waking my mother and sister, who slept in their rooms nearby, my voice grew louder as I talked. "What's that you said? No, you didn't ask the question, did you? It was me thinking it." My hands clenched into fists. "I didn't mean to kill the truck driver; he fell out of the cab and the wheels crushed him. But you know something? I would have killed him anyway. And do you know why? Because that man was turning into me."

Natsaf-Ty regarded me through those closed eyelids as I ranted on: "Why was he turning into me? I don't know. But as I sat beside him in the cab his hair changed color to the same as mine. He had tattoos on the backs of his hands, but they vanished, and then there was this scar on his hand." I held up mine to show the Y-shaped lines on my skin. "Right now I'm thinking you don't believe me, but here I am talking to someone who died three thousand years ago, so if I can believe you're here in this house, then you've no right to doubt what I'm telling you."

I was breathing hard; my voice grew louder. "Just as there's no rational explanation for us sitting here like this, then there's no rational explanation—yet—for the fact that something happens to certain people when I get too close. It takes hours, not minutes, but gradually they become me. I know what they're thinking. I start to see through their eyes. Why can't you damn well tell me what's happening? When I was a kid you always had this wisdom—you'd advise me when I had a problem. But you don't fucking speak to me anymore. You just sit and stare at me like it's *me* who's turned into a freak!" I jabbed my finger at the mummy's placid features.

"Three weeks ago I was walking home through a park at night when a guy tried to kill me. The worst part of it was that he looked like me. Not resembled me! Not a bit like me! But *exactly* like me! Same hair, same face, same voice! Everything the fucking same. Right down to this scar on my hand. I froze. I couldn't fight him. I thought I'd gone insane and this was all a hallucination. He would have killed me if it hadn't been for these people who dragged him off me. Paddy, Ruth, Dianna, and Ulric, the same people at the house a couple of nights ago. You see, they've been under attack for months. They're hunted by versions of themselves. Their physical echoes. What else could I do? I joined them. I asked them what was causing this. They don't discuss it. They tell me this isn't the time for philosophy; it's the time for survival. They're on the move all the time, sleeping in the van, or breaking into an empty house for a bit of extra comfort."

Natsaf-Ty just sat there. He didn't move; he could have been a red statue. Only there was this sense of him staring, as if he were saying, *Mason, I accuse you of being a freak. I accuse you of murder. I accuse you—*

"No, you don't fucking accuse me!" I roared these words at the dead Egyptian. "I accuse you! When I was ten you would have explained what was happening. You'd tell me what I could do to help myself, like when those kids were stealing my lunch money. How am I supposed to work this out for myself? Where do these people come from who turn into me? And you know something? They're bloody useless monsters. They're so fucking easy to kill. So why do they bother to attack us? Last week we were in the van and one walked up to the window. Paddy pulled out a shotgun and Ruth said, 'No, don't fire.' 'Why not?' asks Paddy. She replies, 'Because we've only just cleaned the blood off the van from the last one.' Paddy laughs. 'Good point,' he says, then reverses the van twenty feet, leans out through the driver's window, and blows the woman's head clean off. 'Damn.' He's annoyed with himself because he's destroyed the head. 'Now we can't see which one of us she was becoming.' Ruth pats him on the arm. 'Not to worry. Besides, I'm sure that one was becoming me.' " I slammed my fist down on the step I was sitting on.

"Don't you see? Sometimes it would be better if they fought harder. Sometimes when they kill one of these Echo creatures I find I'm asking myself, 'What if they've just killed an innocent member of the public? What if they haven't turned into an Echoman and we made the wrong identification?' "

Natsaf-Ty, keeper of the sacred crocodiles and long-time dead man, tilted his head to one side. Through an egg-size hole in his skull I could see the void where the brains would have been. After death in ancient Egypt the embalmer shoved a metal spike up the corpse's nose to pierce the soft tissues of the nasal passageway so they could then insert a wire hook to yank the brains out. Imagine the brain coming out like a series of big, bloody boogers. How long would it take before the skull was empty? Then they'd use the spike to ram in onions to make the rancid corpse smell a little sweeter. What remained of the human being, Natsaf-Ty, was little more than a pastry crust; picture a slightly overbaked apple pie with the filling teased out. This empty pie of a man was what I'd spent my childhood chatting to. Now he'd returned, but he no longer conversed. There was only that long, accusing stare that condemned who I'd become. *I kill Echoboys and Echogirls, don'tcha know? Echomen are strangers that turn into me.*

Once more anger boiled inside. "You were there in town yesterday, weren't you? You saw Old Snotter change into me. You just stood there and watched him try to kill me. Why didn't you stop him? Yesterday morning I was with the trucker when he was dying under the wheel. You appeared there to warn me that people were coming, and that I'd be caught. So why warn me yesterday that I was in danger, then stand back today as a wino tried to commit murder?"

The impassive face regarded me. At that moment time stuck to the side of the universe. A force glued it there. What came unstuck were the events of the last three weeks. It's not easy to describe. All I can say is that instead of remembering all those battles with the Echomen, those fucking useless monsters, it seemed to me as I sat on the top looking down at Natsaf-Ty that it all happened again.

*Nearly home, the lamps on the path lighting my way through the park. The fist hitting the side of my head; then I turn around to find my attacker is me. There's my face looking into mine. The expression is determined, like someone attempting to climb a wall he knows is too high for him. He knows he'll fail. Yet it's something he's got to do. I could have fought back, but I'm so surprised by seeing this fist-swinging doppelgänger I can't move. Shit, I don't do anything to save myself; he pushes me over, then crouches down so he can punch my head. These people appear from nowhere. The girl I will know as Dianna uses a big glittery blade to open his neck. "No need to cut his face off," she says to me. "This one's you."*

*The days follow. I watch as they shoot Echomen in the
same casual manner you or I would employ to bat a fly
with a rolled-up newspaper. Then it feels I'm back at the
truck trying to get my knife into the guy who looked like
Elvis, then looked like me. He's lying on the floor screaming at me to get help. Now Old Snotter is flinging himself
on me in Tanshelf after the rain.*

Time unpeeled itself from the side of the universe. I
sat on the stairs. Natsaf-Ty tilted his head slightly to one
side as he gazed at me through closed eyelids. My scalp
prickled as I finally understood. "You're trying to warn
me, aren't you?" I clenched my fists. "They're changing.
Transformations are faster. Everything's speeding up.
You're warning me that they're going to do something
different. What are they planning? Are you trying to tell
me that my mother and Eve are going to change?" Unease ran through me like some dark electricity. "Tell me
what I've got to do. Please. How can I stop this thing
from happening to my family?"

A car prowled along the street. Maybe the *boom-boom-
boom* of its sound system woke me. I'd slept so soundly
that for a moment I thought I was back in the van again,
where we'd sleep like dogs curled up on blankets. That
sensation lasted only a moment. When I peeled my eyelids open I saw this was the bedroom of the house I
grew up in. All my old posters had gone; Mom had re-
painted the walls a pale blue (once they'd been a seri-
ously decadent purple; my choice). Birds sang like lives
depended on it. Sunlight blasted through the window. I
fumbled for my watch on the bedside table. Five minutes to ten. I hadn't slept this long in weeks. A neighbor
called her dog in from the garden. The dog didn't seem
in any great hurry. I heard the name, "Billy," voiced with

more irritation every time it was repeated. Then the sound of a shutting door suggested that Billy had eventually complied.

With a luxurious yawn I sat up in bed, half expecting to see Natsaf-Ty there, leaning against a wall like a three-thousand-year-old punk who was bored with immortality. *Last night why didn't you answer my questions?* Even as I asked the question, as if Natsaf-Ty's spirit hovered nearby listening to my thoughts, I knew the answer. I was thinking what you're thinking now: I dreamed that encounter on the stairs. The Egyptian mummy was a product of my nocturnal imagination. That in reality, when I was venting all that angst, I was asleep in bed.

As I sat there a set of knuckles smacked against the door. A moment later Eve's smiling face appeared. "We were beginning to think the sandman had carried you off. Sleep well?"

I grinned back. "Dead to the world, I was."

"Well, if you can reanimate yourself, I'm making bacon sandwiches downstairs."

"Eve, I told you not to go to any trouble."

"I'm enjoying it; it's nice having my brother back home. I've got someone to torment again."

"Thanks."

"Now hurry up or I'll tip this glass of orange juice over you." She set down a full glass on the bedside table. This morning she wore jeans and a white T-shirt. I noticed a bracelet of plaited pink strips on her wrist.

"Eve, you're going to have me feeling guilty; you mustn't spoil me."

"I'll let you owe me."

"Just you wait. I'll make you lunch; then you'll know what suffering really is."

She laughed, then paused in the doorway. "Mason?"

"Hmm?" I sipped the juice; a lovely iciness rushed down my throat.

"When did you start speaking in your sleep?"

"I didn't know I did."

"Last night I heard you talking."

I made light of it. "Probably the hideous shock of seeing my sister's face again."

"Ha-flipping-ha." Then the smile fixed in a way that stopped it from being a happy smile. "Mason, when you were talking it didn't sound as if you were in bed. It seemed to be coming from the landing."

"I'm sorry if I disturbed you." I smiled to put her at ease. "I've been under a lot of pressure at work." So, a little white lie—what else could I say?

"It must be something like that." Then her hand flew to her mouth. "Oh, the bacon! It'll be burned to a crisp!" Eve ran from the room.

# CHAPTER EIGHT

By ten thirty that morning I'd finished breakfast. Mom had already left for work. Eve cleared away the dirty dishes, but I was determined not to lie around while she did all the chores.

"You're making me lazy," I told her. "I'll see to those."

"I don't mind washing the dishes."

I grinned. "You've certainly grown up. I remember my sister being the little rascal who sneaked out to play when it was her turn to clear the table."

"That was when I was ten. I'm twenty, remember?"

"Okay, but I'll make lunch once I've finished pruning the apple tree."

"Ready for another coffee?" She filled the kettle.

"Thanks."

She glanced back at me. "Have you decided how long you're staying?"

"Two or three days." That sounded fairly noncommittal. The trouble was, I had nowhere else to go, no money; the events of the last three weeks had built a brick wall between today and tomorrow for me. As Eve busied herself with rinsing the mugs I ran hot water into the bowl. *All I can do*, I reasoned, *is live day to day in the hope that everything returns to normal by itself. But will it?* Last night Natsaf-Ty appeared to warn that things were about to get a whole lot worse. Okay, okay, I know ancient Egyptian mummies don't materialize at the dead of night as messengers of impending death and destruction. You know as well as I do that the dead—whether domestic or alien—tend not to make social calls. And, yes, Natsaf-Ty has to be a product of my current anxieties, and yet . . .

"Mason!"

"What?"

I glanced back, startled, as Eve shouted, "Your hand! You're scalding it!"

Damn, I was so deep in thought I hadn't even noticed I'd left the hot-water faucet running onto the back of my hand. Its searing jet had been striking the flesh, turning the Y scar a vivid red.

"Mason, are you okay?"

"Fine. Just miles away."

"No, don't dry it. Run cold water on it." She grabbed the affected hand and played the cold faucet onto the reddened skin. "It's something when the little sister has to take care of the big brother. I'll be mashing your food for you next."

"Thanks."

"There . . . just dab your skin with the towel; don't rub." She smiled. "I'll finish the dishes. You make the coffee." She smiled. "But don't go fiddling with the water in the kettle, will you?"

"Listen, you've been to the museum in Tanshelf, haven't you?"

"Of course."

"Then you've seen the Egyptian exhibits?"

"Why the sudden interest in the museum?"

I poured boiling water into the mugs. Eve kept a close eye on me, perhaps thinking I'd suddenly douse my head in the searing liquid. "So you've seen the mummy?"

"Loads of times. When we were kids we'd try to look under that bandage loincloth he wears. Ye gods, we had dirty minds. How's the hand now?"

"Fine." I handed her a coffee. "The mummy's called Natsaf-Ty. He was the keeper of the sacred crocodiles."

"How do you keep a sacred crocodile? You mean he was like an old type of zookeeper?"

"I guess it was more involved than that. He was a priest at the Temple of Aten."

"You've got a retentive memory, Mason. I was eleven when we did the priest's story at school. Heck, I remember we had to produce a comic strip of a day in his life in five hundred B.C. or whenever it was."

Sudden exasperation made me edgy. This was the moment I should be explaining to Eve about the Echomen and these weird visions of Natsaf-Ty. Hell's bells, I had to get it all off my chest. My coffee was so hot it stung my lips. "Blast."

"Mason, are you all right?" Before I could answer there came a knock at the door. "I'll get it." Then she slipped down the hallway to open the door to our caller. A second later she called back, "Mason, it's Tony Allen."

Tony Allen, you'll remember, is my friend from school. In a fit of jealousy once after the Susan Shepherd incident I tried to punch him. That was the fight that left me with the Y-shaped scar on the back of my hand. I hadn't seen Tony in a couple of years. His career in computers took him away from Tanshelf for weeks at a time, so we gradually lost touch as our lives followed separate paths. When Eve showed him into the kitchen I was already refilling the kettle to make him coffee. He'd gained a few pounds. His hair was short and crinkly these days instead of the bizarre dandelion frizz he used to sport in college. Gone were the torn denims, too, in favor of casual office wear—a short-sleeved shirt in pale blue with dark gray pants. Whereas he once had had rounded features, the years had made his face leaner, so the thing you noticed first about him was his jaw. It gave structure to his face: this could have been a marine on a mission. Tony was—of sorts.

With a broad smile I held out my hand to shake his. "Tony, it's great to see you. How's the family?"

He didn't shake my hand. Instead he launched a verbal attack. "What the hell are you playing at?"

"What?" I glanced at Eve in case she knew what he was talking about. She merely flinched at the boom of his voice.

"You know damn well what!" he roared. "Not twenty minutes ago you tried to push me off the platform in front of a train."

"Tony—"

"You nearly killed me. If it wasn't for people on the platform I'd be dead now."

"Tony, it wasn't me."

"Of course it was you. We were standing face-to-face when you did it. I asked you in a completely civil way how you were, and you launched yourself at me."

"Listen, Tony, it wasn't me." I kept my calm. "You're mistaken."

"Don't treat me like I'm crazy, Mason. You might be— I'm not!"

"Tony, why on earth would—"

"You know why. You're still hung up on what happened. Remember this?" He pointed at the scar on my hand. "You need help, Mason. And if you come near me or my family I'm going to the police. Got that?"

"Tony—"

"Back off, Mason. I'll break your face if you take a step closer to me."

Eve snapped out of the shock. "Tony, my brother wouldn't hurt you. You were best friends."

"Right, *were* best friends. And as for not hurting me, you should have been at Tanshelf Station twenty minutes ago. He tried his hardest to throw me in front of a train. God help you, Mason. God help you!" Tony's massive jaw worked as he tried to stop himself from punching me.

Eve stared at me, then turned to Tony. The look in her eyes suggested she'd looked into a pit and seen monsters thrashing there.

"Tony, you're mistaken. I—" Big mistake—I took a step toward him. He launched himself at me with his fist bunched. Eve sprang between us. The force of Tony's forward movement bounced Eve's slender form into the kitchen table, but she recovered her balance fast enough to put herself between Tony and me before he started slugging.

"Tony." Eve gestured with both hands to calm him. "Tony. It can't have been Mason."

"Can't it? You don't know what he's really like."

"Listen, he was here with me all morning. Twenty minutes ago he sat at that table eating breakfast."

Tony set his face hard. "It's loyal of you, Eve, to defend your brother, but he's not worth it."

"Damn it, Tony! He was with me all the time. He couldn't have attacked you."

Tony shrugged as the anger started to drain from him. "Of course it was him. I've known your brother since we were kids."

"I don't know what happened to you at the station just now," she said, "but it can't have been Mason. He simply wasn't there."

Tony glared. "Mason, have the guts to own up. You were there on the platform, weren't you?"

"What did I do?"

The question surprised him; nevertheless, he answered: "I stood at the edge of the platform as my train came toward the station. Someone touched my arm. When I turned around you were standing there, but really close . . . strangely close. We were face-to-face for a second; then you pushed me off the platform onto the line. Luckily I managed to land on my feet. There were people waiting for the train who dragged me back." His nostrils flared at the memory. "But only just in time. Three seconds later I'd have been under its wheels."

"Where did I go?"

"You ran for it. Lucky you did or I'd have beaten the crap out of you." His tone suggested that he'd decided beating me was a good idea after all.

"And you're sure it was me?"

"Of course I'm sure. Now, are you going to admit to attacking me?"

"When I was sixteen I took a swing at you in your parents' kitchen . . . and missed. That's the only time I was tempted to hurt you."

He stared at me.

"No, Tony," I told him in all seriousness. "I wasn't at Tanshelf Station. I haven't left the house today."

The man's sense of purpose when he strode into the kitchen had been a force to be reckoned with; now he suddenly became doubtful, his shoulders dropped, the air of menace evaporated. "But I'm sure it was you, Mason. We were face-to-face." He put the palm of his hand a foot from his nose. "This close."

I threw him a question that startled him as much as a slap. "When I got close to you this morning, did I smell?"

"Smell?" He rolled his eyes. "You stank to high heaven. You reeked like a monkey."

"And now?"

"You want me to smell you?" He gave an uneasy laugh. Even my sister raised an eyebrow.

"If I smelled as bad as you say, you'd have a noseful right now."

He blinked. "And you've managed to shave, too."

"All in twenty minutes after trying to murder you at Tanshelf Station."

Tony appeared to deflate. With a sigh he leaned against the kitchen counter. "It . . ." He shook his head. "It really looked like you, Mason. Same height, same shape face, same eyes, same . . ." He gave a defeated shrug.

Eve spoke gently: "It must have been someone who resembled Mason."

"Resembled?" He clicked his tongue. "My friend, you have a doppelgänger out there. And he's dangerous."

Over coffee we talked; the more we did so, the more it drifted into small talk, until we chatted about the music we listened to as kids.

"Mason, do you remember the time we told everyone at school that we were going to see a band in Langthwaite?" He chuckled. "Listen to this, Eve—the band was part of a short-lived—very short-lived—new wave called sex metal, so it was strictly adults only, and we were just fourteen. When we were turned away at the door we made a pact to pretend we'd seen the band so we could impress everyone at school. The next day we described their filthy stage act right down to the last movement; everyone wanted to hear what we'd seen. The only problem was, the concert had been canceled, so when people found out, our credibility went down the toilet."

I smiled. "At least we enjoyed being the coolest kids in the school for five hours."

"Bother." Tony glanced at his watch. "If I don't move now I'm going to get fired."

Eve said, "Someone tried to kill you this morning. Tell your boss you're having the day off."

"For my boss, being murdered is a reason to take time off; attempted murder doesn't count in his eyes." He grinned. "Sorry about the ruckus, folks." The grin faded as he remembered. "It's just so weird. I could have sworn it was you, Mason. I even shouted out your name as you"—Tony shrugged—"*he* pushed me off the platform."

"Can I call a taxi?"

"Thanks, but I'd parked my car at the station, so I just

picked it up after the . . . you know what." He gave a grim smile. "Turned out to be an interesting morning, huh?"

"Too interesting, if you ask me," Eve said with feeling.

"Bye, Eve." He kissed her on the cheek. "Good luck with the exams."

After the farewells I walked him to the car.

"You don't think it was me at the station, then?" I asked as he opened the car door.

"You? No, impossible. As I said, you stank like a monkey, had stubble all over your face, a right mess."

"What was he wearing?"

"He looked as if he'd dressed himself at random out of a charity sack. Baggy old jeans, plaid shirt with the sleeves flapping. Cruddy shoes with the soles hanging off."

"The kind of shoes Old Snotter would wear?"

"Exactly what Old Snotter would wear."

"Did you notice him today?"

"What? Old Snotter? Probably not. I didn't go into the square."

There was a pause before I asked, "Do you think it could have been him that attacked you?"

"Old Snotter?" He laughed. "The municipal derelict? He's as much a fixture as the railway station. He wouldn't hurt a fly. Besides, it looked nothing like him." He frowned. "Whoever attacked me certainly stank like him, though. Why do you ask?"

"It doesn't matter. Nice car."

"Yeah, they give me a car for the job, then pay me a pittance so they can balance their books." For a moment Tony took in the scenery as if this row of peaceful houses interested him. "You know, Mason," he began, "I really believed it was you who shoved me in front of the train."

"You think I could do such a thing?"

He gave me an odd little smile. "Mason Konrad. The nicest guy in school. The kind of guy who gives up his seat for the elderly on buses . . . never says mean things about people behind their backs. Mason Konrad: people praise him for being pleasant and considerate, with never a cross word."

My laugh was forced. "Stop it, Tony. I'm no saint."

"No, you aren't a saint, Mason." He glanced around to make sure he wasn't overheard. "Because I've seen another side to you, haven't I? One that made me believe that you could throw me onto a railway track, where I'd be cut to pieces."

"If you're talking about what happened that New Year's Eve, it was a long time ago."

"It was. Yet I still remember it like yesterday, don't you?"

I said nothing.

He'd gone too far to stop now. "A drunk shoved you out of the way. The Mason Konrad I'd grown to know would have shrugged it off. Not that night, though. You punched him so hard I threw up when I saw the state of his face."

"It's ancient history, Tony."

"Two days later my dad read aloud from the newspaper that the guy had been so badly beaten he was still unconscious in the hospital. My dad reading that over breakfast comes back to me so clearly, I can still remember how the scrambled eggs tasted. I haven't eaten them since that day."

"Tony—"

"You nearly killed that drunk, Mason. Only you and I knew who did it. And we've kept quiet about it for twelve years, but you know something? Keeping a secret is corrosive. There's not a week goes by when I don't think about the guy with half his face hanging off."

I stayed silent. But it was a taut silence. The same edgy quiet you get before an earthquake lays waste to a city.

Tony gripped the top of the car door as if he needed something firm to hang on to. "And you ask me if I thought you could push me in front of a train? What do you think?"

A moment later he drove away down the street. There are some things you force yourself to forget, aren't there? Then there are other facts that you keep to yourself. The drunk who pushed me, then tried to put a knife in Tony's back. Tony never saw the knife. He only saw me knock the man down. I shook my head as I returned to the house.

# CHAPTER NINE

Summer days. The sun works its magic on mood. If it had rained for those three days since I returned home, or we were gripped by churning fogs that could have seeped from some old Dracula film, then I'd have brooded over what had happened to me in recent weeks. Call it repression. Call it selective amnesia. But I didn't dwell on all those slayings I'd witnessed—not even the man who'd been crushed beneath the wheels of his own truck.

They were three busy, sunlit days. I tackled that tree to my mother's and my neighbor's satisfaction. Jack gave me a bottle of his homemade parsnip wine that gifted me with the best night's sleep in ages. I painted the kitchen, dejunked the garage, fixed a cabinet door, did a pretty nice valet job on Mom's car, then turned my hand to alfresco barbecue meals. If only life could remain like that.

On the night of the third day—that fateful night—Eve

and I skimmed a purple Frisbee to each other on the back lawn. The air was still. A red sunset painted the horizon. Mom sipped a glass of chilled white wine on the patio as she glanced at her magazine. A time of family togetherness when we were happy, content to be living in the warm, tranquil moments of now and not thinking about anything in particular.

"I'll varnish the lawn furniture tomorrow." I caught the Frisbee. "The weather looks set to stay fine."

"You're supposed to be having a break." Mom sipped her wine. "You're my son; you don't have to earn your keep."

Eve laughed as the spinning disk nearly flew over the fence. Deftly she plucked it out of the air. "I'll give you a hand, Mason. My first class tomorrow is in the afternoon."

"Don't let me keep you from your studies. . . . By the way, good throw; it nearly took my head off." I grinned as I made a pretense of fixing my head back on my shoulders.

"It would have been a big improvement. Sheesh, I can't believe how warm it's getting. Anyone for ice cream?"

"I'm fine with this, thank you." Mom waggled her glass to show it was still half-full; then she added, "Don't use the chocolate fudge; that's left over from Christmas. There's a new tub of cherry at the back of the freezer."

"Okay."

Of all the memories of my family I have, those moments are the ones I replay most.

I woke drenched in gasoline. Vapor filled the room so thickly you could almost carve it with a knife. The sheets were dripping. My pillow had become a wet sponge. The landing light shone through my bedroom door to reveal a figure.

The fumes made me cough. I was convinced the figure was the Egyptian mummy that had visited me in my childhood. "What are you doing?"

When the figure stepped into the light its face became clearly visible. The simple fact was, I saw myself standing there. Or, rather, the man who'd stolen my face. He raised a hand that held a cigarette lighter. His thumb rested on the wheel that would ignite the flame that would turn my bedroom into a furnace; in turn that would cremate me where I lay in the gas-soaked bed.

The monster with my face smiled. "There can only be one of us, can't there?" He straightened his arm as a prelude to setting fire to the bed.

*"Get out!"* A second figure seemed to explode through the doorway. It collided with the Echoman; the cigarette lighter flew from his hand. Mercifully the lighter wasn't lit.

That second figure was Mom. For a split second I stared as she wrestled the Echoman back so forcefully he lost his balance to crash back against the closet.

"Mom!" I yelled as I sprang from the bed. "Get away from him. Call the police!"

"No," she shouted as she struggled to hold on to the writhing version of me (a version she couldn't have recognized yet in the gloom). "We're going to get this thug out of the house first! He's poured gasoline all over the stairs. If he gets the lighter . . ." She didn't say any more; she didn't *need* to say any more. That mental image was blistering in its own right. *If this thing gets a flame to the fuel the entire house will explode—it'll take us with it.* Our plan came as an instinctual thing: Just get the man out of the house. Then call the police.

At that moment I heard Eve shouting as we dragged the guy out onto the landing. She was in her pajamas; my mother was in a nightdress. This was no way to fight a war with the intruder, but we had no choice. Gasoline fumes filled the stairwell. The intensity of the stench sickened me. All it needed was a spark . . . a tiny little spark. . . .

Spluttering, choking, coughing, eyes streaming, we wrestled with the Echoman.

Eve was saying, "Oh, my God, oh, my God . . ." I knew she'd seen the man's face. She realized he was identical to me. All that separated us from indivisibility was that I wore shorts and a T-shirt; the monster wore jeans that were too big for him and a plaid shirt with sleeves open at the cuffs so they flapped like a bird's wings.

Eve cried, "Mason, there's someone on the stairs!"

For some reason I can't explain I expected to see Natsaf-Ty sitting there with his wise old face turned up to watch the battle raging on the landing. Only running up the stairs came a middle-aged guy with short silver hair. A stranger, for sure, yet I knew *what* he was. In his fist he carried a wrench. And, yes, I knew what he'd do with that. He applied it to the back of my head with enough violence to prove he didn't care whether I lived or died. The landing walls flew away from me into darkness. Whether I hit the floor hard or gently I can't say.

# CHAPTER TEN

*My eyes are open. I know they're open. I've touched my eyeball with the tip of my finger to make sure. It's there: moist . . . spherical . . . an organ that can alternate between an internal or external existence—okay, I've established that. So if my eyes are open why can't I see a damn thing?* If I've thought those words once I've thought them a hundred times as I lay there. When I woke after being knocked unconscious in the house I found myself on a flat, tiled surface. Kitchen floor? Bathroom floor? A morgue? The morgue thought sends strange notions through my head. *If all the dead came back to life would they fill the morgues with the living? Then would they bury all of us who are still alive in the cemeteries? Listen, you must never, ever trust a dead man; they become such slippery characters. . . .* At that moment I was too dizzy to sit up straight, my thoughts too muddled.

But then, a lot of things made no sense to a brain that felt inflamed and swollen inside my aching head (my fingers had already explored the cut in my scalp where the wrench had smacked it). I heard running water. A skittering sound came close my ear with a smell of animal; when the skittering came closer I reached out to feel a small body covered in fur. It darted away from me. Then a thudding, something like a gigantic heartbeat. After that footsteps—only they made a clanking sound, as if someone walked on a steel grid. These footsteps moved above me, backward, forward, halt, forward again. They weren't rushed. Just a measured pace, as if someone went about their business on a metal grid above my head. Then came a scream. The sound shocked me into sitting upright. Eve? It sounded like Eve. Instantly the scream stopped. Silence. A long silence, the kind your ears fill with the gush of your own blood pumping through arteries. Next: those clanking footsteps again, someone walking without hurrying across their metal grid. Now what? Shout hello? But the danger there is if it attracts unwanted attention. It might be safer to stay silent.

*Get moving*, I told myself. *Find a light switch*. Even
though my head echoed with the pain of being
whacked by a wrench I reached out. For a moment
there was only air around my fingers; then I found the
flat, vertical plane of a wall. This felt like concrete. A
moment later my fingers traced a line of mortar, so a
wall of concrete blocks above a tiled floor. No window
frames, no cable tacked to the wall that I could follow
to the switch. With no other option I used the wall to
guide me through the darkness. Still I couldn't see a
thing—not a glimmer, not a pinpoint of light. Darkness
clogged my eyes; I stared hard into that essence of dis-
tilled night. This was darkness and silence fused into a
world of nothingness. I'd moved perhaps fifteen paces,
with my fingertips fumbling along the wall, when my
foot stopped sliding across the tiles because it struck an
object. I bent down to feel what it was. Cold tiles.
Grooves in between. I moved my hand a few more
inches in that total darkness.

Then my fingers touched a soft object. Bare skin,
splayed digits. Another hand. Undeniably another hand.

"Mom . . . Eve?" Wherever I was, they had to be here,
too. The Echomen must have brought us. "Mom? Is that
you?" Relying on instinct, I reached out to where the
head must be if this figure in the dark was sitting on the
floor. My fingers made contact with a face; it was easy
to find the shape of the nose, a cheek, then a jaw covered with stubble. My gasp of surprise seemed to act as
the trigger. The man grabbed at me from the darkness.
Even though I couldn't see him I sensed the bulk of the
guy as he grabbed hold of me to tug me down to the
floor.

"It's okay; it's cool," I panted. "I won't hurt you." My

hands went up in a way to show I didn't mean any threat, but could he see them? Of course he couldn't, so he threw punches at me. Though I didn't see them I heard his grunt as he struck out; his fists buzzed by my ear. Then he hooked his hand around the back of my head. When he dug his fingers against my head wound it stung so much that I quit being gentle Mason Konrad.

"Hey, hey. Stop that." I managed to ward off his swinging arms. "I'm not here to hurt you. Hey, what did I tell you? Stop trying to hit me." The punch slammed into my ear. "Damn it, I'm like you. They put me here. Now, stop . . ." He grabbed my head, then tried to bash it against the concrete wall. I heard him grunting with exertion, but he said nothing. The smell of his perspiration was acrid; if anything it reminded me of animal cages at the zoo.

"Enough!" When he didn't quit I reached up to find a mess of straggly hair. Though I couldn't see it, I knew I had a good grip, so I dragged his head back by his locks. Grunts of pain exploded from his lips. "Stop it! Stop fighting me!" I don't know. Maybe he was deaf, or he couldn't speak English. Instead of the pain from having his hair yanked persuading him that fighting in total darkness wasn't a good thing, he came back at me throwing punches. Okay, I couldn't see them, could I? I felt them. So I punched back, landing a few in his face. The blows broke up his grunts to create a stuttering effect. Then I had an idea. As quickly as I could I got the wall to my back; when I judged he was coming back with a flurry of punches I slid downward. Just in time. A succession of thuds came from just above my head as the stranger boxed with the wall. This time he cried out in pain as he planted what must have been a terrific punch into solid concrete. Now I was crouching in front of him with my head level with his unseen waist—and not far from his equally unseen groin. But it didn't take night vision to judge where his balls were. I threw a vicious uppercut between his legs. With a howl he went down. This time I didn't waste time. In a moment I'd gotten the bastard on his back; then, with my legs straddling him, I felt where his face was with my left hand; then I let him have the full force of my rage with my right fist. I held the head down by the hair as I delivered ten full-blooded punches into the center of his face. When I was too breathless to punch I used the flat of my left hand to bear down on his throat. Of course, it was too dark to see what effect it had on him. But after a minute of using my body weight to compress his windpipe I climbed off the guy as I panted, "Leave it now . . . no more fighting. . . ."

The choking sounds he made were the loudest noise there. In fact, they echoed back like they were amplified. Exhaustion wrung me out. All I could do was lean against the wall. My guts shook; the pain in my hand from punching hurt more than the pain in my skull.

A moment later a light shone down from above. It plunged vertically through the darkness like a column of fire. It not only dazzled; it seemed to drive hot wire into my eyeballs. Confusing images leaped at me. Gray concrete walls. White tiled floor; a black strip running across it. The floor sloped. In the center of the column of light the guy I'd fought lay flat on his back. Both arms were out by his sides; one leg was raised so the knee pointed up at the ceiling. There wasn't much to make of his face because it was such a fucking awful mess of blood. Shit, it looked as if pieces of raw steak protruded from his right cheek. His straggly blond hair radiated from his head like a fan of spikes. Most noticeable was the way his mouth was open wide—so wide you could have popped a whole apple in there. And he was making this croaking sound as he struggled to breathe. Then the light went abruptly out.

One image stayed, though. I'd seen the back of his hand. There, as clear as day, had been a scar. A Y-shaped scar. Just same as mine. Here in the darkness, I'd just fought an Echoman.

Minutes later, a shuffling sound. Someone crawled over the tiled floor. I saw in my mind's eye that the stranger was coming to attack me again. Even though his face was a bloody, crapped-up mess, he had just one thought: to kill me. I readied myself. Even when the noise vanished to be replaced by silence, I tensed myself. At any second the attacker would launch himself at me from the darkness. This time I couldn't afford to stop short of killing the man. Either it would be me or Echoboy. Mercy was weakness.

Instead of hearing movement I felt the figure bump against me. Again, I'd seen nothing. The first I knew was physical contact. I grabbed for where I guessed the neck would be; what I must do was get hold of the throat, then strangle the monster.

A surprised gasp followed by, "Please . . ."

That had been a female voice. This wasn't the time for being timid. By instinct alone I felt for her arm. Instead of a limb I found I was touching her upper body. What my fingers found left nothing to the imagination: a pair of naked breasts, then a smooth torso that was bare as far as the outward curve of the hip. Below that I didn't go. Five minutes ago a stranger tried to murder me. Right at this moment I had a naked woman in my hands.

# CHAPTER ELEVEN

The woman's body had a warmth that made me reluctant to withdraw my hand. Even though she was naked there in the darkness, she didn't attempt to flinch away from my touch or make any protest—or make any comment whatsoever.

Taking a step back and putting my hands by my sides, I asked, "What's your name?"

"Name?" Instead of anxiety or fear she appeared calm—strangely calm.

"I'm Mason Konrad," I told her. "Have they harmed you?"

"Why should they?"

"Your clothes . . . did they take them?"

"They made me uncomfortable. I threw them away."

So! This was no ordinary girl. I took another step backward in the darkness. That absence of light got under my skin now. I mean, if a naked girl spoke so oddly, what did she look like? Her breasts felt normal, as did her waist. But why did she speak that way? As if detached from the reality of being, in some black hole God knew where.

"Mason?" Her voice came as whisper through the darkness.

"Yes?"

"Where are you?"

"Don't worry; I'm close to you."

"Good."

"Are you frightened?"

"Frightened?"

"Do you know where you are?"

"I'm with you." There was a shimmering quality to her voice. "Will you hold out your hand so I can find you?"

My hands were staying firmly by my sides until I knew what I was dealing with here. I tried my questions again. "What's your name?"

No reply.

"Where are you from?"

Silence.

"Did they bring you here?"

No answer. *This is getting bloody crazy*, I told myself. *She's turning out to be a figment of my imagination just like old Natsaf-Ty, keeper of the flaming crocodiles. Deep breath, Mason. Try again.* "You must remember your name?"

"I'm sorry; I'm making you angry."

"I'm not angry." *Slap her; make her talk.* Okay, that was one of those devil-speaking-in-your-ear moments. My nerves still jangled from the attack by the Echoman. Hell, part of me suggested strangling her before she could do anything freakish. Or was it my balls telling me to do something freakish to her? I remembered the way my veins tingled when I touched her naked breasts.

"Why have you stopped talking to me?" The huskiness of her voice brought back the tingle.

"I haven't, but you're not so generous with your answers, are you?"

"I'm sorry—"

"You've already apologized once."

"Sorry—"

"Three times." Was I being snappish because there was a danger I'd speak in a way that would soon become overfriendly?

"It's difficult to explain," she murmured. "I want to tell you my name is Madeline—"

"Why don't you then? I won't bite."

"I'm sure it is Madeline, but for some reason it's not important anymore. I'm standing here in the dark. In one way I know I should be scared, but it just doesn't trouble me. I'm okay about it. Does that seem strange to you?"

"You're probably disoriented. Madeline?"

"Yes." A breathy *yes*, as if she relaxed.

"Did you see who brought you here?"

"No."

"They didn't hurt you in any way?"

"I'm fine."

"You must feel cold."

"Do I feel cold to you?" An invitation to touch her. Was that innocence on her part? Or guile?

For now I kept my distance. "I'm wearing a T-shirt," I told her. "I'll hand it to you."

This quickened her voice. "You're giving me your clothes?"

"The T-shirt, anyway. Are you okay with that?"

"Yes, I'd love to wear your T-shirt." For the first time there was some heat in her tone. Before I could even re-move the garment, however, a light shone down from above. Of course, once I'd shielded my eyes against the dazzling blast it was only natural to squint up against the glare and see who the hell was there. But all my eyes were rewarded with was that searing shot of light. Still shielding my eyes, I turned my attention to the woman, Madeline.

She was naked as she stood there beneath the brutal light. Her eyes were part closed against its brilliance. Here was a woman around my age, twenty-eight. Neither plump nor skinny, her body was athletic without being chunky. Her naked limbs revealed subtle bulges of muscle; her breasts were dark-tipped; her hips had a pleasing breadth to them; and there's no denying I felt a tingle of desire. Madeline had the tautness of a long-distance runner. That formation of firm muscle extended to her face. Rather than soft, her features were sharply defined—high cheekbones, a strong nose and jaw, a pair of sharp, dark eyes beneath black eyebrows. Her short, dark hair emphasized the strength of her face. And she stood naked and unashamed and magnificent. For a moment the power of her attraction held my attention so that I noticed nothing else. Thrills of arousal titillated my nerve endings. Then, at last, I forced myself to pay attention to my surroundings. Unlikely that there would be an easy exit; however, I needed to form a picture of my prison, because surely that was what had happened. The Echomen had jailed me.

*So this is my cell: visualize it. A long, narrow room formed by two concrete walls around seven feet high; they're hastily built; mortar squeezes from joints; the blocks are uneven; at the base are careless gaps; this has been built in a hurry. The floor is tiled; these have been here years. They've had decades to mellow, so white tiles are speckled with tawny flecks. Every five feet a row of black tiles six inches wide run from left to right. My cell is thirty feet long. It ends in a white-tiled wall at each end. Not far from me is a brown blanket next to a plastic bowl. In the bowl are bottles of water and cellophane-wrapped cookies. They don't want me to starve. File that; it's important. They're keeping me alive for a little while longer. But what of my cellmate?*

Madeline was faintly familiar. If she came from Tanshelf we might have attended the same school. She was the right age for us to have been there together. Then again, I might have simply passed her in the street from time to time. Heaven knew, she was beautiful enough to have made an impression on me.

"You are cold," I told her.

She looked down at her breasts. "Gooseflesh. You noticed this?" Which could be Madeline-speak for "Sheesh, you were staring at my boobs."

"Here." I handed her the T-shirt. Eagerly she slipped it on, taking clear pleasure from my body heat still warming the cotton. I followed up with: "Don't I know you?"

"I'm not sure. Do you?"

"You're from Tanshelf?"

"Hmm." She folded her arms in such a way that she could stroke the fabric that had been next to my skin. I took the *hmm* to be an affirmative rather than an expression of sybaritic pleasure at being clad in what I'd been wearing just a moment ago.

"You look familiar," I told her. "Very familiar." A creeping unease worked its way up my backbone. "Have you seen me before?"

"I don't think so." She smiled.

"Never heard the name Mason Konrad?"

"Mason Konrad?" She liked repeating the name. "Mason Konrad."

"Madeline, are you putting me on?"

"I don't know what you mean."

"Have you seen this scar before?" As I showed her the gouge marks I called upward into that retina-drenching light, "Hey! Is she one of yours?"

No reply from above, although I heard my voice echo as if it had gone booming up into some high-roofed cavern.

Hugging herself, she beamed at me with so much sex

in the smile it reached out and teased my balls. "Mason, you're nice."

"Am I?" It took effort to keep my voice cold. "Am I really?"

"You smell nice, too." In a way that was both pretty and winning she lifted the collar of my T-shirt so she could give it a mischievous little sniff from the inside. Without trying, I pictured her beautiful body beneath the flimsy fabric. I stared at her short dark hair. My hand immediately went to my own hair—my own short, dark hair, and possibilities began to whirl inside my head.

"So you've never seen this scar?" I flashed her the Y again.

"Nope."

"Nope?" I mimicked her carefree *nope* as I snatched hold of her left wrist and looked at the back of her hand. My grip was brutal. Madeline smiled as if I'd only brushed the skin with the lightest of touches. I knew what I expected to see there. What would be etched deeply into the skin. I'd seen the Y-shaped scar duplicated on the back of the trucker's hand, and on the hand of the man who attacked me here in my cell just minutes ago.

"What have you found?" she asked with such a lovely giggle that my heart lurched in my chest.

I took a deep breath before delivering the answer. "Nothing." Both hands were unblemished; okay, a freckle or two, certainly no scar. "Madeline? Can you remember anything else about yourself? Where you live? Have you—" The killing of the light stopped my voice dead. Once more we were in total darkness, me holding her wrist. The skin made mine tingle. She rested her hand against my chest in such a gentle way that a delicious shiver ran through me. I released her wrist then put my arm protectively around her shoulders. She allowed herself to sink against me. Why I hadn't done this before I don't know, but I lifted my free arm above my head to feel for the top of the concrete wall.

Now that the darkness was back it would be a good time to climb over the barrier and vanish from the Echomen's lair—because lair it undoubtedly was. Lair and jail. Maybe death chamber? The bastards wanted to kill me—remember the truck driver? Remember Old Snotter? The once harmless drunk who tried to suffocate me? And where was Eve? Where was Mom? The darkness stabbed me through and through with edgy thoughts. Had they hurt my mother and sister? The moment I reached up, though, expecting to find the top of the wall with thin air above it, disappointment dropped like a stone inside of me. Although I couldn't see it now, or against the glare of light earlier, I realized that a metal grid formed a roof to my cell. So that was where the clanging footsteps came from. Echomen walking on the "roof." The metal grid rested (bolted probably) on top of the concrete walls to form the lid that kept me in.

Then these three things happened:

One: from the darkness above a cascade of gasoline doused us.

Two: a narrow beam of light shone directly downward through the grid roof. It illuminated a man of around fifty with a wild mane of silver hair. He stood twenty paces from me, probably entering the cell through a hatch when we were plunged into darkness. With the light came a second cascade of gasoline that drenched him from his bushy head to the brown boots he wore. The boots were the same color as the leather belt he wore with a wolf's-head buckle in gold-colored metal. It didn't match the rest of his clothes, that belt. Was he given it as a present and felt obliged to wear it? Was it a souvenir from his youth? The wolf's head might have had huge meaning for him in his teens. Now when he buckled the belt around his waist it might reconnect him with happier times from the past.

Third: exactly halfway between the silver-haired stranger and me, a small object dropped from above to clatter onto the tiles. The illumination revealed the object to be a cigarette lighter.

Soaked with gasoline? The appearance of the gas-drenched man and the lighter? The significance wasn't lost on me. The newcomer started to run at the same moment I did. Only after five paces I fell to my knees.

# CHAPTER TWELVE

In that cell the sole source of light was the narrow beam that shone directly downward behind the man who now ran toward the cigarette lighter on the floor. Even so, enough light bounced from the wall and white tiles to make the wolf's-head belt buckle flash, while the man's eyes blazed at me as if they were balls of blue fire. Madeline didn't appear freaked by the approach of the gas-soaked man. She merely stood back, then watched with a serene expression.

Already the fumes made me gag; they filled my chest like I'd been abusing solvent; a giddy vertigo tried to topple me. Even so, by the time the stranger reached the cigarette lighter I deliberately dropped to my knees. The cold spirit raged on my lips where the gasoline had run into my mouth, stinging the flesh. Thoughts spat through my head: *Gas-soaked man grabs lighter; he'll rush at me. No doubting what his plans are. He'll put the flame on me. The gas will turn me into a human blowtorch.*

I knew I couldn't hope to use the lighter on him. The moment I ignited it, the vapor would ignite, then we'd both ignite. As far as I knew, there was no place to get rid of it, even if I reached it first. We'd end up wrestling all over the fucking floor for possession. So here I was on my knees. The guy armed himself with the cigarette lighter. He ran toward me, fumbling at the little silver wheel on the thing. Scrape . . . scrape . . . scrape . . . as he rotated igniter against flint.

I'd thrown myself to my knees where the blanket and bowl had been left. My leg bashed the bowl across the floor to scatter cookies and water bottles. Then I had the blanket in my hand. Straightaway I rubbed at my face, hair, shoulders, and bare chest, trying to soak up that drenching of fuel. No way could I dry myself properly; it was like I'd bathed in gasoline; it dripped from me; it sprayed from my hands when I shook them. I left gasoline footprints on the tiles. But I got the blanket good and moist with premium-octane fuel. The silver-haired man bore down on me, eyes blazing, mouth becoming a leer, a human shark coming in for the kill. *Scrape, scrape, scrape*—his thumb worked the igniter wheel to produce the spark. Gasoline soaked him, too; more so than me because he wore more clothes, the fibers holding it there, a volatile mixture that's not just flammable; it's explosive. If you've seen a burning car explode you know what I mean. When lunatics drink fuel and light a cigarette their lungs blow out through their chests in sheets of flame. That stuff is liquid dynamite.

Five paces from me, Gas Man was slowing so he could concentrate on getting his fuel-slippery thumb a purchase on the silver wheel. *Scrape, scrape . . . I'm ready.* The moment he grunted with fascination as the blade of yellow popped from the end of the lighter was the moment I threw the blanket over the guy. It would have been no trouble to him to swat it aside but he used the hand that held the cigarette lighter. The fuel-drenched blanket caught fire. His arm burst into flame. That arm became a living fuse that carried the blue fire up to his shoulder, where it exploded the vapor streaming from his hair. One second later he erupted. He was a whirling, screaming meteor, running blindly into the concrete wall. The impact left pieces of burning man on the block work. That howling, mortal fireball attempted to run at me, but his eyes must have been seared by now; he couldn't see a thing and tripped over the water bottles. Past the point of no return, he lay writhing in agony as the gasoline-soaked clothes blazed with all the fury of a furnace. Gone.

"He can't hurt us now!" I shouted this back to Madeline, who stood watching. All the time she showed no horror. A little smile turned up the corner of her lips. The golden fire lit up her eyes.

I was still stinking with fuel, still dangerously volatile in more ways than one. So I kept my distance from the burning Echoman. No doubt about it, he had to be one of those creatures. Although he didn't resemble me. Or anyone I knew.

The second his movements slowed as the blood began to boil inside his heart I heard a roaring. What I took to be negligent construction work that had left three-inch gaps between some of the concrete blocks where the wall rested on the floor became obvious. It became obvious where we were, too. This was a swimming pool. A disused one that had been partitioned by concrete walls. Sure enough, water gushed through gaps in the block work. This was no trickle. It was a full-blooded torrent of freshwater. It swirled around the burning corpse to kill the flame. Soon it was up to my knees. I made use of the water, too. I was dressed only in shorts, so I'd dry fast with or without bath towels.

Despite the biting cold of the water I plunged myself into it to flush the gasoline from my skin. It was no fun wearing a coat of high-octane to start with. I didn't want the Echomen repeating the trick with the cigarette lighter. Even though the water didn't get any deeper than my knees, I managed to completely immerse myself. Madeline did the same. Even as I climbed to my feet the water began to run back out again. Shallower, shallower, shallower. In moments it did nothing more than slick the tiles at the bottom of our customized swimming pool. My attacker was nothing more than a charred mess now. The force of the draining water had carried the body against the wall. Now it lay beached on the otherwise clean expanse of white tile.

This was a good moment to tell my jailers what I thought. "You made it so fucking easy! Call that an attempt on my life? I killed him like I'm going to kill all of you!"

Madeline looked at the grid above her head, too. Her face had a pleasant, relaxed expression, as if she did nothing more than gaze up at an attractive harvest moon.

When the lights went out I moved fast. Guiding myself by touch alone, I found the burned corpse. With luck, the Echomen didn't use any kind of nightscope to see us in the dark. Sure as eggs are eggs, they'd remove the body in the dark, just as they did with the other guy who attacked me. *First I want to see what's in your pockets.* The guy's clothes were crispy, to say the least. Artificial fabrics had fused with his skin. Again by fingertip searching I located his pockets. You never knew—there might be a knife or a gun. I figured that he would have carried some additional armament, but . . . *Damn it.* Nothing. Not even a handkerchief. Clanging footsteps sounded overhead. *The Echomen are coming to collect their fallen hero.* Some fucking hero. They'd made an incompetent attempt to murder me. Patting the burned corpse, I searched for anything that would help me survive down in this cell. The body smelled like roast pork. The face had become a hard crust with a nose that felt like a lump of baked pastry. A loud clang came from above my head, a hatchway opening?

*Damn.* Frustration made me want to curse. Yet this might be the only chance I got to salvage something of use. My hand closed over the man's belt. I remember it was a sturdy strap of leather. It should have survived the fire, to a certain degree anyway. Fumbling for a moment in the darkness I finally discovered that wolf's-head buckle. Heat still lingered there despite the soaking in cold water. Even though the hot metal stung my fingers I opened the buckle. More sounds from above; they were coming for their comrade. If I didn't move quickly they'd find me there, too. *Come on, come on* . . . I prepared to pull the belt through the pants' loops. No need: the fire had burned them to ash. The belt slid easily from that dead meat's waist.

*Quickly: before the lights come back on.* As tightly as

I could get it I rolled the belt up, then found one of those gaps in the concrete blocks by touch in the blackest of black. It took some shoving, but at last I inserted the rolled belt into the gap where it couldn't be seen. With luck—plenty, plenty of luck—the belt with its wolf's-head buckle would be waiting for me when I needed it.

# CHAPTER THIRTEEN

The Bible describes a plague of darkness as a "darkness to be felt." In the disused swimming pool it was that kind of darkness. Five minutes ago I'd been instrumental in burning the stranger to death. I'd taken his wolf's-head belt away from him, then hidden it by wedging it into the gap between the concrete blocks that made up the walls, which in turn formed the long, narrow cell. In this darkness I was dripping wet.

Madeline, the otherworldly woman with the beautiful athletic figure, embraced me, whether in an amorous way or to help keep the chill from my near-naked body, I don't know. By then I wished I'd checked the dead guy's wrist for a watch. Down in this abyss of blackness I had no way of telling the time. Too late now. From the scraping sounds the burned corpse was being hauled away. To attempt an escape would be crazy, even though the cell must be open. It was too dark to see where the exit would be; nor could I see how many Echomen were there. Being living is better than being dead. So for the time being I'd keep it like that.

Minutes later the sliding sounds had vanished. With

the darkness came silence. Madeline said nothing. For the time being she was content to keep her body pressed hard against mine. After a while I put my arm around her. She was so smooth to the touch; her breath warmed my chest. Another moment later she put her head on my shoulder. The softness of her hair released such a wave of pleasure inside of me. *Getting sexy . . .* That feeling I didn't put into words; it suggested itself the way my skin tingled. Despite being locked in this weird cell, *despite* the attack by two strangers, my blood lit up with erotic sparks. Sex vibes weren't titillating just *my* flesh either. Madeline pressed closer. One arm embraced me. Her lips were the softest purveyor of kisses. A kind of hunger drove her as she kissed my bare shoulder, then moved to my face. Mouth on mouth, her kisses were passionate. That passion I returned with a heat of my own. I wore shorts, nothing else; all she had was my T-shirt. Her nakedness beneath that could have been a surreal generator that pumped out waves of sheer erotica. Listen, people make love in the strangest places. In cemeteries they call it drinking wine in the graveyard at midnight as naked bodies writhe on tombs full of bones. In aircraft it's called the mile-high club; in public lavatories it's cottaging. Sex in other public places is dogging. What do you call full-blooded bodily penetration in a prison cell after you've burned a guy to death? Write your own answer here . . . make it a powerfully descriptive one. Make it resonate with the act of fucking under the watchful eyes of hidden jailers.

*There we are, standing on wet tiles as we hold each other. Here are the firm contours of that athletic body of hers. I kiss her on the mouth while heat surges through my body. Her supple back arches as her hips push against mine. My hand slides under the hem of the T-shirt to stroke her bare stomach before traveling upward to cup a breast, the hard nipple pressing deliciously into my palm. Her murmurs encourage me to go further; she loves this. She wants more. . . . A sigh of pleasure in my ear as I move my hand downward over her stomach. I glide over her navel, heading south, deep south, way down south. . . .*

*Bang!* The lights came on. Three narrow beams of tungsten brilliance that blasted downward through the steel grille above our heads. Through the dazzling glare Madeline's smile shone at me. She didn't care that she was in this swimming pool–turned-jail. She was happy to be with me; that was all that mattered.

With the light I expected a third stranger to arrive. Taking a step back, I tried to look up through the grille just a foot above my head. I even reached up to slip my fingers through the mesh.

Then I raged at them: "Bastards! Do you think it's funny? Are you getting a kick out of this? Why didn't you leave the lights off? You could have waited until the change was complete. Then you could have laughed yourselves to fucking death!"

I lunged at Madeline. "You knew this would happen, didn't you!" I didn't shout this at the woman. (She still smiled; she wanted loving; place and circumstance were unimportant to her; she wanted it there and then; yeah, I'm telling it so raw and so coarse because that was the state of *me* right then.) No, it wasn't beautiful, mysterious Madeline I yelled at: it was the invisible jailers. Because her mystery had just evaporated. I held up her hand. "You waited long enough, then you switched on the lights and showed me this!"

*There, that's why the mystery's gone. Madeline stands*

*smiling. I'm brandishing her hand. There's a scar, a Y-shaped scar on the flesh. That's right, I was kissing me. Or something* becoming *me.*

"Great joke, guys! You are so fucking brilliant!"

A smiling Madeline, still expecting sex, touched my face. I pushed her against the wall. With one hand I gripped her hair; the other I pressed to her throat.

"She's your crash-test dummy, isn't she?" I roar the words into the void. "You stuck her in here so she'd be close to me. You wanted to see if she'd turn into me, just like the others. Okay, your experiment worked. Now I'll complete it for you. You sit there and watch me kill her. How do you want me to do it? Quick or slow? I can beat her head against the wall. Or I can take my time . . . just leisurely strangle her nice and slow. Eyes pop out, tongue protrudes, lots of gurgling, twitching." My heart pumped hard in my chest as I psyched myself up. "She might be one of your kind, but you'll not be worried about losing her, will you? And what about me? Why should I worry? If this creature is becoming me I can't be guilty of hurting another individual, can I? No, because in reality I'll be hurting me. And when I kill her with my bare hands I'll really be killing myself."

For the first time I saw real fear in her eyes as I held her against the concrete wall. And now those eyes were the same color brown as mine. The dark arch of the eyebrows was the same as I saw in the mirror.

"If you follow me I'll kill you. Understand?" I tightened my grip on her hair. "I said, do you understand?"

A frightened nod. With that I let go of her so quickly she could have been burning-hot metal. Thirty feet was as far as I could go in that narrow cell. She stood against the wall, the image of the abandoned waif, shivering in a T-shirt that barely reached the tops of her naked thighs. When the cell was plunged into darkness again, I told myself: *Big mistake, Mason. She's turned Echo. You should have killed her while you could.*

When I woke I found myself sitting against the wall. A figure stood ten paces away. I knew it was completely dark, yet I still saw it. For a moment I thought Madeline had crept toward me. Whether it be an Echoman or an Echogirl, they turn evil; that much I know. As well as adopting my appearance she'd soon be driven to kill me. So in a snap of movement I was on my feet. There, looming from the darkness, a tall, thin figure. Despite the absence of electric light I made out the familiar shape of a hairless head. The more I stared, the clearer the image became; the atoms of the thing itself seemed to glow.

"I hadn't expected to see you here," I murmured. He was back. Natsaf-Ty, my childhood imaginary companion, and for the last fifty years premier exhibit of Tanshelf Museum. For a second I gazed at the near-naked figure with just parts of his body still covered. Whatever archeologist unwrapped the mummy when it underwent scientific examination had retained the bandages around the loins to no doubt spare the more sensitive museum visitors. Natsaf-Ty stood in the center of my long, narrow cell just as I remembered him: a gaunt Egyptian mummy with dark red skin. Cracks formed a crazed pattern on his scalp. As of old he cut an impassive, even serene figure. He didn't move. There was a spirit of the eternal about that utterly still form. The glow that emanated from the mummified Egyptian grew a little brighter so I could make out the face: its eyelids were closed; the tip of the tongue protruded through lips as arid as the desert that once entombed him.

When I spoke the words seemed flippant, but that

was to mask my anger at being a prisoner. "Natsaf-Ty? Thank you for dropping in to see me. I hope you're here to show me the way out?" No reply, no movement, nothing; not a whisper nor sigh nor inclination of the head to hint that he'd heard me. Natsaf-Ty merely "gazed" at me through those closed eyelids. "I preferred it when you were chattier . . . of course, that's when I was child. Imaginary friends just aren't the same when you grow up. . . ." I paused. "Come on, Natsaf-Ty. Speak to me. Just like you used to do when I was ten years old." I clenched my fists. "Hey, hey! What do you make of my companion, huh?" I could just make out a hunched mound that was the sleeping Madeline at the other end of the narrow cell. "You can see for yourself what's happening. Three weeks ago I started meeting people who were turning into me. Me and my friends call them Echoes. That was a code word that could be used in public; although by turns we refer to them as Echomen or Echofolk. Now here's a woman who's turning into an Echogirl. More to the point, she's becoming me. What do you suggest, Natsaf-Ty? You were always the one with wisdom. You advised me what to do when I was bullied at school, or when I wanted to find my father wherever he sneaked off to. Back when I was ten you were so patient when you explained the reasons why my grandparents never used to come and see me. But you're dumb now. You never speak! Come on!"

I advanced on the motionless figure. Tongue protruding slightly, eyes closed, yet looking at me—always damn well looking at me in the same way, as if he read my mind. What a mind I owned! What a screwed-up mind!

"But you know something? That's my mind; it's the only one I've got, yet somehow nature or the devil or bloody dick-eyed Martians have found a way of duplicating me—and maybe even my screwy mind. So, welcome to my home, Natsaf-Ty, keeper of the bloody sacred crocodiles. Why don't you shake me by the hand, because I'm the photocopied man. They say no man is an island; well, I'm a whole archipelago. I've been pirated. There are other Mason Konrads out there. So what do you suggest I do? I mean, are you here to help me? Or are you here to watch me die? Because sure as dogs crap in the park, that's what's going to happen."

I advanced on the figure with the ruined body of dried, cracked skin that had been turned red by the embalmers' salts—a medley of reds, coruscating from rust red to faded tangerine. Never before had I touched—or attempted to touch—this three-thousand-year-old mummy. At that moment, however, I not only wanted to touch; I wanted to punch, kick, mutilate. "I'm sick of you appearing from nowhere just to stare at me. Why do it? Aren't you comfy in your coffin anymore? Go haunt some other fool. If you've not come all this way to help me, then what's the point? What's the fucking point!"

*Yeah, smart move, Mason. When you can't do anything to escape from here, why not get angry and beat up your imaginary friend? What's more, you're shouting but you haven't woken Madeline. Doesn't that suggest something, Mason? You must be dreaming. . . .*

Whether I was dreaming or not, the notion of venting my fury on what must have been a product of my imagination came down like a crushing weight on me. I turned my back to the wall, then slid down until I was sitting on the tiled floor. When I spoke my voice cracked with emotion. "So why do you come here?" I was closer to the mummy now, so I had to tilt my head back to look up at the serene face with the closed eyes. "Come on, old friend, we've known each other for a long time. You can tell me, can't you?" From this angle I also looked up through that steel grid of a roof. Beyond the three-thousand-year-old face, I could just discern the ceiling beams of the swimming pool. Perhaps a little illumination crept in from somewhere, because there were the lights (unlit, of course) dangling at the end of their cables. There was another object hanging there, too. For whole moments I stared at it. Then, with a surge of heat blazing through my veins, I climbed to my feet.

Natsaf-Ty was close enough to touch now. Close enough to punch—not that I wanted to punch. At that moment I wanted to hug his ancient, crusty flesh. "I know why you came now." My voice rose. "Even though you couldn't tell me you could show me!" I laughed— were there flecks of hysteria in the sound? "You wanted to show me a sign. And a sign you have shown me!" I laughed louder. "Behold the sign!" Standing on my toes, with my head tilted back so I could see through the crisscrossed bars, I gazed at the sign Natsaf-Ty had revealed to me. The words were painted on a board six feet by four feet, suspended just beneath the roof lights. I read that sign aloud: " 'No Pushing. No Splashing. No Ducking.' " My eyes watered from the force of staring through the gloom. "And someone changed the D in Ducking to an F. My God, how they did that I'll never know." I shook my head with amazement. "I'm at Tanshelf High School. I came here for years. Long, long years. This is the old swimming pool. Every time we saw that sign it made us laugh—oh, boy, we had dirty minds back then." I read the sign again that some trickster had doctored. " 'No Pushing. No Splashing. No Fucking.' "

Did this help me? Did knowing that I was held prisoner in my old school have the potential to save me? I didn't know. But knowing where I was being held set the blood racing in my veins. If knowledge was power then I'd just become that bit more powerful. I was no longer a beast in a cage.

*So . . . old Natsaf-Ty had a valuable reason for being here after all. I'm in a place I know; this must give me an advantage.*

"Thank you . . ." I thanked the air of my prison. Natsaf-Ty had gone, whether back to his glass case in the Tanshelf Museum, or whether his image had retreated into some quirky fold of my brain I couldn't begin to say. That's the territory psychiatrists and occultists battle over for possession.

*I know where I am . . . I know this place.* That knowledge comforted me. Proverbially, I was standing on solid ground again.

Bang. Lights on. Dazzled. I could see nothing. Screams. More screams mixed with, "No! Don't!" I shielded my eyes to see what happened at the far end of my cell. Madeline had woken up. She moved from side to side as if trying to bounce herself from the concrete walls. When I shielded my eyes from the glare, that was when I saw what they were doing to her.

# CHAPTER FOURTEEN

*Simple: they're trying to kill her.*

Was it an ego thing? If Madeline was slowly undergoing a transformation into me, did I feel as if I had possessory title over her? Whatever went through my mind at that moment, I found myself racing along that narrow corridor of a cell.

"Leave her!" I shouted at her tormentors. "If you want to stick someone try sticking me!" Because I'd seen what they were doing to her. At least two people must have stood on the steel roof above her. Through the gaps in the bars they were spearing her with broom handles—broom handles that had been sharpened to a lethal point. She screamed when one of the spears drove through her T-shirt into the upper part of her chest. When she used both hands to grip the pole I saw the Y-shaped scar—the same Y-shaped scar that graces the back of my right hand: it's a raw conjunction of lines that are still bloodred after all these years. A lasting memorial of the night I was driven by jealousy to swing a punch at my best friend. The punch missed and I ripped open the back of my hand. That was then—this is now: the men, or women, above her were invisible against the downward glare of lights. All I could make out were moving silhouettes that jabbed the wooden poles down into Madeline's body. A bloody patch formed around a rip in her T-shirt at the shoulder. Her red lips pressed together as the pain nearly overwhelmed her.

"Leave her alone! She's one of yours!" My rage thundered. I gripped one pole, tried to twist it from the unseen hands above, but it slipped through my fingers. A second later they jabbed it through another section of cage roof to stab at Madeline. Tears rolled down her cheeks from those oh-so-familiar eyes.

I roared at them, "Stop it! You're hurting her!"

She sobbed brokenheartedly now. When she tried to protect her face from a sharp point it cruelly dug into the palm of her hand. Instead of pulling I yanked the pole backward; the pressure of the steel bar against the shaft snapped it. A few fibers of wood held the pole together, and it was quickly withdrawn. A pity. I'd have loved to have one as a weapon. Another pair of poles appeared to try to stake the woman, who seemed so fragile now as she hunched her shoulders and cowered before the makeshift spears.

There wasn't a great deal I could do to fight back, as the attackers stood on the grille above us. Instead I grabbed hold of Madeline. Hugging her tightly to me, I used my body as a shield. The salvo of jabs I expected didn't materialize. Instead it went suddenly silent. For a long time I held Madeline close, her head tucked in against my chest, my head projecting over hers to protect it.

"I know you hate me," she whispered at last. "I don't want to be like this. I don't know what's happening to me."

It wouldn't be long before the lights went out—our captors were predictable. Gently I told her I should check the wounds inflicted by the spears. Without hesitation she gripped the hem of the T-shirt and slipped it up over her body, then over her head. If I'd expected any involuntary change of gender, what I saw there in the harsh lights proved me wrong. I saw smooth female skin, breasts, and adult womanhood just where the supreme deity or Mother Nature intended. Without a murmur she allowed me to lightly touch the puncture wounds in her shoulder and upper chest. A little blood smeared the otherwise flawless skin, but the injuries weren't at all serious. Her eyes locked onto mine as I examined her.

"They'll be sore," I told her. "But they've only just broken the skin."

"They don't want to hurt you yet," she said.

"I wouldn't gamble on it staying that way." I helped her with the T-shirt.

"You called me a crash-test dummy." Her dark eyes were unnerving. "They're going to keep hurting me, aren't they?"

"Madeline." I stepped back from her but kept my hand on her arm. "For the time being, I'll protect you."

"For the time being?"

"It's hard to explain; you're changing. Soon you'll want to hurt me."

"Mason." She was hurt by my suggestion. "I'd never hurt you."

"You might think that now. . . ." I shrugged.

She held my gaze for a second, then: "When you were asleep I saw someone standing right where you are now."

"Go on." For some reason a shiver ran down my spine.

"It was too dark to see him properly. There was something strange about him. I don't know how he entered the cell, and he kept very still."

"Did he say anything?"

She shook her head. "I couldn't make out any features; it was just a figure . . . or a suggestion of a figure. Very indistinct, but it made me feel strange when I saw him. Like I was losing my balance." Recalling the visitor appeared to trouble her, so after shaking her head again as if to dispel the disturbing memory she took hold of my hand so she could compare it with hers. The Y-shaped scars matched perfectly. "We both have the same scar. I've never had a scar there before. Inside me I feel unreal. It's a way I've never felt before. What I can see of my body is changing, too."

"That doesn't strike you as freakish?"

"I know that it should, but it doesn't." She released my hand as if reluctant to do so. "Mason? You think the change is going to go deeper than my features changing, don't you?"

"If you're talking about gender . . ." Once again I shrugged. "The things I've seen in the last three weeks have been so strange I wouldn't be at all surprised if I have to start calling you mister in the next few hours."

"I won't change my sex. It doesn't work like that."

"How do you know?"

"When we're conceived we are neither male nor female. It's only when the embryo has been in the womb for a number of weeks that the sex of the child is triggered. I was born female, Mason. There's no reason I'll change spontaneously."

"So you'll be my identical twin. Only a female identical twin." I grimaced. "If human biology has gone so topsy-turvy then anything's possible." I'd barely gotten *possible* through my lips when a crash sounded from above. We both looked up. At any moment we expected to find the sharpened broom handles jabbing down into our faces. As always the glare of the lights was too intense to see much other than flitting silhouettes. Only then came another crash. On the other side of the bars appeared a face. I didn't recognize the man. His blue eyes were like fire as they blazed down at me from a distance of a foot. I drew Madeline toward me to protect her as best I could if they attacked. Only it wasn't us they attacked.

They must have held the stranger facedown on the bars of the cage that formed our ceiling. There they beat him. Whether it was with sticks or whether it was kicks I don't know. For ten minutes they gave him their undivided attention. His eyes were wide-open all the time, staring down in shock at us, as if he were indignant beyond belief that they were doing this to him. The blows were loud; his face jolted to the rhythm of the beating. Soon he howled loud enough to shake Natsaf-Ty's old bones in the Tanshelf Museum. The noise could have been akin to that made by a buffalo tangled in razor wire, an impossibly loud bellowing with hardly an intake of breath. Blood released by the man's wounds dripped through the bars onto the white-tiled floor. I had ample time during the attack to speculate. The stranger was an Echoman; that's what I figured, anyway. By now I began to suspect that I saw a certain look in their eye that gave them away. As the man made the bovine bellowing I found myself gazing dispassionately at the face as it became a visual expression of the agony he felt as his bones snapped.

Why do Echomen destroy their own? Could it be they don't understand that a human body can survive only so much physical injury? Did that indicate that whatever created the Echomen wasn't familiar with human beings? Were they punishing the man for a misdemeanor? Had he avoided some chore? Was this an experiment to test the human body to destruction? If so, why conduct the experiment so me and my doppelgänger roommate could witness it? Did they beat one of their own to demonstrate what they could inflict on me when they decided it was my time to suffer? Or—and this suggested their ignorance of human psychology—did they mutilate the man in front of me to encourage me to do the same to Madeline? You've watched a TV cooking program and become ravenous when they set the sizzling steak on the plate, haven't you? So, did the Echo mind believe that this was a way to stimulate my appetite for violence?

*Think again, you idiot monsters.*

After they delivered a hundred or so whacks with great gusto, the man stopped howling. Blood dripped from his mouth; he had difficulty focusing his eyes. After a moment or two the flitting silhouettes above us dragged him away. The lights went out.

We slept. Once I opened my eyes to see Natsaf-Ty "looking" down at me through those closed eyelids. I recalled the old fairy tale where a man had such powerful sight that he could look through the world. To see normally he must bandage his eyes. Natsaf-Ty had a stare that could peer into every hidden corner of your mind. At this moment I couldn't remember if I ever pulled the legs off a spider when I was child. No doubt Natsaf-Ty could peruse my memories to confirm whether or not I did mutilate arachnids.

When the light returned it shone at a different angle. This time the light beams were horizontal, not vertical. They didn't illuminate us in our cell; they revealed a figure standing on the steel grid roof. Posing there, as if for a formal photograph, was a boy of around eleven years of age.

"Dear God," I breathed.

"Do you recognize him?" Madeline asked.

I nodded. "Me. Or rather, me as a child."

"Then don't watch what they do to him."

The boy stood above us on the bars in such a position that I could clearly see the face with the dark brown eyes and the dark arches of the eyebrows that were distinctively mine even back then. The boy didn't move. The building was silent.

Only after several minutes had elapsed did the boy move back into darkness. His place was taken by a man of at least fifty. He had white hair, but his eyebrows were strikingly black arches above his brown eyes.

"What's this?" Bitterness crept into my voice. "The seven ages of man?"

"They're showing versions of you at different ages. You as a boy, you as a middle-aged man."

I growled, "They're mistaken if they think this is going to break me."

The middle-aged man standing on the cage bars held out his hand.

"Same scar." My voice was matter-of-fact. "You're going to have to do better than that," I told my invisible captors. Then I sat down with my back to the wall and paid no attention to what happened above my head.

# CHAPTER FIFTEEN

The lamps stayed lit.

"Come on; work with me, Madeline. Why are they doing this to us?"

"To provoke us to react."

"That's it? Don't you get the feeling they're testing us?"

"They're setting challenges."

Our voices shimmered in the swimming pool that had been converted into our prison. After watching the guy being beaten to a pile of crimson crap we started talking, whispers at first; whispers became a buzz. Now we talked loudly, not caring if the Echomen were making notes. This was a brainstorming session that had set us on fire. We were upbeat, enthusiastic. *Here we are: Madeline is naked apart from the T-shirt. Her bare legs move endlessly as she paces barefoot on the tile. That pacing bug has me, too. We walk, we pitch ideas, bounce phrases, get the conversation simmering merrily. Our eyes are bright; thoughts blaze inside our heads.*

"So what do we know about the Echomen? One?" I held up a finger.

Madeline answered in a flash. "They are outwardly normal people who turn into replicas of others. Two?"

"The change is physical and mental. Our minds begin to overlap. Three?"

"Initially they are friendly. Then they become hostile."

"Right. The copy desires to kill the original. Four?"

"We know the change begins within minutes of the stranger being infected."

I paused. "So the process is a result of a virus?"

"A virus, or something like a virus. Five?"

"Why?"

"Why is this happening?"

"In the natural world there's a reason for everything." She rested her thumb against her bottom lip. "Invasion?"

"From where?"

"From another planet?" She shrugged. "Another dimension?"

"Okay, it's only speculation, but go with the idea."

Madeline continued to pace. "All right. Imagine this: in the past societies have suffered, sometimes even collapsed, when a more technologically sophisticated people comes along."

I rested my thumb on my bottom lip. "The superior society might not be hostile, they aren't invading the less advanced people, but they might as well have slaughtered them anyway."

"Absolutely, the end result is the same. The less advanced of the two societies feels inferior. They lose their drive to achieve goals. Rather than follow their traditional route in life they either become a shadow of their former selves as their settlements decline into squalor, or—"

"Or they are absorbed by the dominant society and become exactly like them, adopting their belief systems, culture, currency—"

"They'll even dress the same." She ran her fingers through her hair as the ideas came faster. "So, what scenario do you have?"

"Echomen are a weapon."

"Sent by?"

"An alien civilization."

"How?"

"They seeded the earth with spores or a virus millions of years ago, so they'd lie dormant until they were needed?"

"Why are they needed now?"

"Human beings are becoming technologically advanced. We can travel to other planets."

"But not the stars?"

"Not yet." The heat of certainty flooded my veins. "Not in spaceships, but our TV and radio signals have been washing through the galaxy for a hundred years."

"So, if there are life-forms out there they know we're here. And that we might pose a threat to them?"

"Exactly." I slammed my hand against the overhead bars of the cage. They rang like a huge bell. "Okay, these alien creatures might be peace-loving, stay-at-home kind of guys, but they know what we know, which is . . . ?"

"When two cultures meet the strongest destroys the weakest."

"It may not be through war or any kind of hostility, but that's the outcome. Regardless of how benevolent the most powerful civilization is, it results in the death of the inferior society."

"So they send the Echomen."

"Exactly." Triumph at finding the answer blazed inside of me. "But they haven't sent them in the conventional sense of dispatching an invading army. No, the aliens can't risk coming to Earth in person, so they leave the Echo virus here."

"How does that keep the alien home planet safe?" she asked.

"Because the little green men with their bug eyes—we can picture them like that if it helps—because they know from our TV broadcasts that eventually we'll build spaceships and find their planet. Then either human beings or ETs will be wiped out. It doesn't matter if we go in peace and they receive us in peace; the dominant society will cause the inferior one to atrophy and eventually die out. So the ETs plant their time-bomb virus on any planet that develops life. Therefore, the Echomen's purpose is—"

"To cause chaos."

"That's right." A smile spread across my face. "It's not necessary for the aliens to conquer us. The Echo virus has a simple agenda. Infect us. Replicate humans. Cause chaos. Create disruption. Spread disharmony."

She clapped her hands together at the revelation. "So we'll be so busy trying to clean up the mess the Echomen make that we won't have the time or the resources to even contemplate traveling beyond the solar system. Wait . . ." She gripped my arm. "Mason? This theory explains so many things. . . ."

I grinned. "Our Echo theory? As titles go it needs work. . . ."

"But aren't you thinking what I'm thinking? Terrorists, hijackings, drug trafficking, credit card fraud, computer viruses—they are engines for chaos. All of them! Mason, this has been happening for years. What if good people have been replaced by evil copies?"

I scratched my head but I was still smiling. "You mean Hitler really was a peaceful art lover who was replaced by a duplicate of himself, one hell-bent on destroying civilization?"

"Didn't Hitler very nearly succeed?"

"I agree." The smile died on my face at the same time as an immense coldness crept inside of me. "I agree with you. You agree with me." Madeline beamed at me like this was the happiest moment of her life. "Madeline, you used a phrase a few seconds ago: 'aren't you thinking what I'm thinking?' Bingo." I took a step closer. "Hit me."

"What?"

"Hit me."

"Why?"

"Surely you know?"

She shook her head.

"I told you to hit me." I added a fake smile to my face. "It's part of our Echo theory. It'll prove that what we talked about is true."

Madeline appeared puzzled, but this time she nodded.

"Okay." I presented my face to her. "Make it a good one. I really, really want to feel it."

The slap stung, all right. She was no weakling. As I

flinched at the pain of the blow Madeline cried out at that same moment. In a second she covered her cheek with her hand; her eyes were watering; the pain brought a trembling spasm that shook her entire body.

My hand rested against my burning cheek. "It's like looking into a mirror, isn't it? No . . . it's more than that. We agreed so eagerly with each other because when it comes down to it, we weren't talking to each other. We're two heads with a single mind."

The hand she pressed against her sore face bore the Y-shaped scar. She'd slapped me, yet she'd felt the sting, too. Fear returned to her eyes.

"You're an Echo." I jabbed my finger at her. "And I've been stupid enough to let my guard down." I strode away to the far end of the cell.

When the voice started I thought I imagined it. This was a time of evil miracles. When normality was wrung inside out and made to do weird things. Echoboys, Echogirls. The stranger who became me. Or was it vice versa? They hadn't switched off the lights, yet at that moment there was a darkness there in our swimming-pool prison. Shadows wormed their way from the walls. The light from above cast net-shaped patterns on my skin. The tiled floor had become a crisscross pattern of light and dark. The darkness was winning. I realized that now. Those fucking inept monsters, the things we'd laughingly called Echomen (well, there was an element of desperation in that laughter)—whatever—the Echomen had proved easy to identify, then almost embarrassingly easy to kill. So easy, in fact, that I sometimes wondered whether Paddy's gang were murdering innocent men and women.

All that had changed. The Echomen had captured me. They imprisoned me here with their own version of the crash-test dummy, Madeline. *Other than being female, she's an identical version of me. We think alike; we look alike. Picture the beautiful children we could spawn.* That thought made me laugh out loud—such cold, dark laughter. As dark as those shadows that flowed into the swimming pool. Shadows like that could drown a man. And now I heard a voice whispering my name. The shadows brought paranoia. The Echomen were winning. My mind was cracking. The Echo theory? The one about intelligent life from another planet being so insecure that they created chaos on neighboring worlds? Sweet Moses on a motorcycle! That had seemed so cogent, so accurate. It explained terrorist atrocities. You could even apply it to the cybersaboteurs who disseminated viruses on the Internet. Echomen were on a quest to cause chaos. To disrupt society. To interfere with technological progress. And maybe, in the name of a borrowed faith, to load into the backs of ice-cream trucks black-market nuclear bombs, then drive them into the heart of your hometown and . . .

*. . . and why haven't I concentrated my efforts on escaping this place? Here I am in a makeshift prison cell built in the swimming pool of my old high school. If I haven't tried to escape, does that mean that there's an Echoman inside my head? Not Madeline. Another one— another version of me—close by . . . feeding me ideas . . . suppressing thoughts of getting away . . . suggesting that I walk down to where Madeline leans against the wall in that T-shirt that barely touches the tops of her thighs. And what? Have sex? Even now I'm picturing kissing her face and her breasts. There's a fiery heat inside of me. I'm imagining the sense of release it could give me if I could pump that excess heat into her cool belly. Isn't that what she craves anyway?*

"Mason . . . Mason . . ."

Whispers rode the back of shadow. With the phantom whisperer I expected to see Natsaf-Ty. Maybe this time he'd bring those sacred crocodiles he was entrusted with way back in ancient Egypt? The mental image of the mummy with a line of high-stepping crocs wasn't exactly amusing; even so, my head swam as if I'd taken a hefty swallow of brandy. "Get out of my head," I muttered. "I know you're trying to dig your way in there. You want my memories, don't you? You're not content with looking like me; you want me body and mind." My mutters were directed at the unseen copy of me that I suspected lurked nearby.

"Mason, listen. It's me. . . ."

"Go away," I told the invisible whisperer. Thirty paces away, at the other end of the narrow cell, Madeline stared. She wondered if I was talking to her. By now she feared me again. She had every right, because here I crouched in my shorts, muttering to myself.

"Mason." The whisper strove to reach through my paranoia. "It's me."

"Mom?" I shook my head. "No, they're screwing with you, Mason. This is a trick."

"Mason. Down here."

The angle of the single lamp made the section of floor where it met the wall nothing less than a ravine of shadow. Nevertheless, the voice brought me to my knees.

"Mom, is that you?" My God, a lame question, but I had to ask it or go mad.

"I'm in the next cell," came the familiar voice. "Eve's in the one next to me."

"How long have you been in there?"

"Just a few minutes. We're in the old high school.

They kept us locked up in the basement. I don't know why they moved us."

"They haven't hurt you? Or Eve?"

"We're okay. They haven't touched you?"

"No, I'm fine." So, a white lie of sorts.

"Are you alone?"

"They locked me in with a girl. Madeline. I don't know who she is apart from her name." Another white lie. *So, go right ahead and explain to someone how a stranger becomes you. "There's this clone virus, you see. Soon they begin to acquire your characteristics, then . . . See? It's better to show than tell."*

"Mason, let me see your face. Please—I thought they'd killed you when they attacked you at the house. Let me see that it's really you and you're okay."

"I am. Believe me."

Her voice caught on the emotion. "Listen, Mason. If you get right down to the floor there are gaps in the bricks. Can you see?"

I shuffled on my hands and knees like some mutant bottom-feeder, the side of my face sliding along the tiles as I looked through each gap in the blocks. Then I saw a glint of an eye through one of the spaces.

"Mom, I can see you."

"I see you, too." Her voice grew a little louder as she called, "Eve? Your brother's here. He's safe."

"I'll get us out, Mom," I promised. "Whatever it takes, I'm going to make sure we go home soon."

A sound came as a metallic roar of thunder. I guessed someone had just stamped with all their might on the cage roof directly above me. Raising myself to my knees, I looked up. A figure stood on the bars. All I could see were the soles of their shoes. Then the feet moved, the flat of a palm now pressed against the bars. Whoever was up there above my head had crouched down in order to study me. I glanced at Madeline. Tense with fear, she stood hugging herself. My eyes lifted to stare into the darkness above the metal grille.

A calm voice drifted down. "Mason Konrad. This is a good time to introduce myself." With a click came a glow. It was directed into the face of whoever gazed at me. Can I say, hand on heart, this came as a shock? No, I cannot. This is inevitable. Sooner or later I'd experience this encounter. The man up there wore the same face as I did. We were identical in every feature.

# CHAPTER SIXTEEN

When the light went out it effectively vanished the man—that man with my face. My features, my hair, my smile that says, *Prove to me that I can trust you.* The lamp at the other side of the building still shone; it cast a spiderweb pattern of shadows on my bare chest. The sound of running water started, a gushing roar that reverberated from the walls. They'd turned on the water before to snuff out the flames on the burning Echoman. This time I knew what they planned to do.

"Mason?" My mother's voice reached me over the roar. "What's that sound?"

"Water. They're going to fill the pool."

"I heard someone speaking to you. A man's voice . . . who was it?"

"Nobody you know." Silver oozed through gaps at the

bottom of the wall. "It's going to be cold, Mom. Tell Eve to keep out of the water for as long as she can. That goes for you, too."

"They're going to drown us?"

"I doubt it. They're aiming to push us to the breaking point." Water sluiced across the tiled floor. Thirty paces away Madeline looked down as it washed over her bare feet, in that light, liquid silver.

"Mason, it's coming through the gaps in the wall."

"I know. Listen, don't worry. I'm going to get us out of here."

*Easy to speak the words . . . just how, pray?*

I ran across to Madeline. She flinched back, probably expecting me to strike her. "Did you see who was up there a moment ago? Have you seen him before?"

She shook her head.

I pushed on as the blasting roar echoed around the swimming pool. "Did you see how they brought us in here? Listen to me—is there a doorway or a hatch?"

"I don't know." The cold water had reached her calves by now.

"Right, I'll force them to show me." I called out. "Nat-saf-Ty. I need your help! It's time to pay me a visit. Come on; I want you here. You've got to help. Show me what you can do. You were keeper of the sacred crocodiles—that meant something important back then, didn't it?" What was Natsaf-Ty? He was an exhibit in a museum; okay, I knew that. Psychologists would explain that he was a projection of my subconscious when I went through troubled times as a child. But if the Echoman that wore my face had somehow been feeding my mind with ideas, then this should be a two-way street. I'd feed his mind with images of my old imaginary friend. Where the shadows were deepest I pictured Natsaf-Ty standing there. A red figure with crisscrossed bandages across his chest and loin. Skeleton-thin arms. A gash in his side where embalmers removed his internal organs. A hairless head with a cracked scalp, complete with an egg-sized hole that revealed the void where the brain had been. Now, the final details. The lightly closed eyes, the noble, serene face. Then the quirky feature that made museum visitors laugh out loud: the tip of a dry tongue slightly protruding from the lips. Sometimes it came across as an expression of him concentrating on solving a problem. Other times it said, *Go on and look at me; I don't care. I'm immortal; are you?*

When I'd pictured Natsaf-Ty against that wall masked by shadows I closed my eyes so I could put all my energy into visualizing him. A gaunt figure that glowed dull red with shuttered eyes that somehow had the power to scan the mysterious hidden places of the universe and the human heart alike.

Presently I heard feet approach over the sound of rushing water. *You want to see for yourself, don't you? My look-alike thinks he can see a third figure. One that glows with a red light. You're puzzled, aren't you? And because you've been reaching into my head you've seen a memory of this figure. You believe it must be real.* I sank to my knees as I kept the image of wise old Natsaf-Ty there. How my doppelgänger must wonder what powers I possessed to conjure a stranger into the cell— one that might prove to be dangerous to the Echofolk.

*Damn, that's cold water.* It swirled around my waist as I crouched there. What the man on the cage bars above me couldn't see was that I reached into the gap where I'd hidden the belt, the one with the wolf's-head buckle that I took from the attacker after he'd fried in his own body fat. The copy of me knelt down on the cage roof to stare at the luminous figure of Natsaf-Ty. The sight of the mummy fascinated him, even though it existed only in my imagination. In some nebulous, tele-pathic way the Echoman picked up what was in my mind's eye.

What he didn't see was me lunging upward with the leather belt wrapped around my fist, the metal pin that normally went through the belt hole now protruding wickedly between my first and second fingers. A foot above me the man had his face pressed against the bars; his eyes (that were identical to my eyes) gazed at Natsaf-Ty.

*Bang!* I punched the metal grille directly beneath his face. The steel buckle pin that wasn't much thinner than a nail you'd bash into timber went straight through. It punctured the skin of his left cheek; there it embedded itself in the roots of his teeth that were set in his upper jaw. The howl of agony made the water's roar a gentle whisper in comparison. In effect, I'd nailed the buckle to his upper jaw. Even though he tried to pull away from me, the stout pin held him down by the face; the force of the blow must have folded the point over to form a barb. I held on to the leather belt; it was singed, cracked, burned bits came off in my hand, but it held. Like a hooked fish he twisted his head from side to side to loosen the pin from where it nailed his face. Blood squirted. He was yelling now. Madeline ran to help me. She was an Echogirl. She should have helped the guy who thrashed his limbs on the cage roof, but maybe she hadn't finalized her allegiances yet, because she reached through the bars to hang on to his hand. And what a hand. A hand like mine, complete with a scar in the shape of a bright red Y. Just like mine. Just like Madeline's.

Mason Two screamed as if he were being murdered. And, by God, I'd have murdered him if I had the chance. Help came in the form of the guy we'd seen beaten to crud, but he was still somewhere between life and death. His broken arms swung as if they were joke limbs made from foam rubber.

"You should know better than to mutilate your own people," I yelled up into the bloody face that was connected to the wolf's-head buckle by a pin that must have decided that when it came to its finest moment of existence it would never break. Although from the way the Mason Two's cheek became extruded into a pyramid I realized it was starting to withdraw. Whatever happened now I couldn't let him escape. There he was, his face held down against the cage by the single steel buckle pin. In a second it would rip free from where I'd embedded it. As soon as it did he'd scramble away. And because the bars of the cage roof were between me and my flesh-and-bone photocopy there'd be nothing I could do.

"Hold on to his hand!" I shouted at Madeline. "We've got to force them to show us how they access the cell!"

The guy whom they'd beaten, just so they could prove to us that vicious assaults were something they accomplished without difficulty, collapsed onto the bars above us. There he lay groaning. A useless piece of man meat. Mason Konrad Two still howled. Yet any second now he'd be free. Then he'd vanish. What then? Nurse his wounded face as he enjoyed the spectacle of us drowning in the pool?

The pin started to slide. Blood jetted from the wound. It created pain in the Echoman's face that could only be guessed at. Howls broke through his lips; the force of it sprayed saliva onto us. His eyes crimped shut tight.

"Suffer, you bastard! Go on, suffer!" Then I called to Madeline, "Put your other hand through the bars. Get your fingers over his wrist. No! Don't try to hold on to it. Plait your fingers together! Form a cradle; then use your body weight to hold him."

She plaited her fingers over his wrist as his forearm lay flat against the bars above us. Good God, I wish I had a knife to jab into his belly. At last the pin slid out, ripping the flesh of his cheek as it exited. Instantly a sudden stinging flared up in my left cheek. *That's the Echomen's magic trick*, I told myself. *I'm starting to feel my duplicate's pain.* Nowhere near as intense, but it made my eyes water. Speaking of which—cold water swirled around our waists now. The pipes that fed the swimming pool must be raging at full power. As they vented, as Mason Konrad Two roared with agony. As I threaded the free end of the leather belt through the cage bars, the Echoman who'd had his ribs pounded into something that must have resembled mashed potato struggled to help his comrade. Although his arms were broken he fumbled with metal fastenings on top of the bars that formed the roof over our head. These must be catches or bolts, which meant sections of the roof could be raised. *That's the way out.*

Pain troubled this Echoman, too, because he made an extended "eeeee" sound as he struggled to unfasten the hatch.

"It's come out!" Madeline yelled. "He's free!"

"No, he isn't!" I'd looped the stout leather strap over Mason Two's forearm that lay flat against the bars above me. Even though the pin had popped from his cheek, allowing him to raise his head (his bloody head, at that), I held his forearm down on what formed *his* floor and *our* roof. The strength in my arms wouldn't be enough, so as I gripped half the belt in one hand and half in the other, I swung my feet up until I rested them on the roof bars. There I hung, doing a fair imitation of a sloth as it hangs by its front and back claws from a branch. My body weight accomplished what I couldn't have hoped to achieve by muscle power alone. The belt formed an effective restraint around one forearm. Mason Two bellowed louder. His accomplice caroled that "eeee" note as he fiddled with the catches. Below me water gushed into the cell. No doubt both my mother and Eve heard the screams of pain from their cells and they were crying out to me to find out what was happening, but the level of noise was so formidable I couldn't hear them.

How long that scenario would have lasted without us being interrupted I don't know. However, a pair of figures raced across the metal grille; their feet clanged as they pounded toward us. They knew exactly what they had to do. One got hold of the Echoman by the hair; with no hesitation he threw the broken man aside as if he were a piece of trash. Both newcomers flicked back the catches, raised the steel grid, then reached down to deliver a blow to my head that turned the noisy building silent as death.

# CHAPTER SEVENTEEN

Wet . . . Thunder . . . Screams . . . Lots of wet . . . choking wet. That was what I woke to. And what a strange waking . . . Let me tell you, they don't get any weirder. When I opened my eyes I was no more than five inches from the steel grid that formed the cell roof. A face loomed from the shadows above. It was the man with the same face as mine. This was the Echoman who was a duplicate of me. Every detail of his features was identical, apart from the wound in the middle of his cheek made by the belt buckle pin. The rip in the skin was big enough to admit the end of a pencil. A shiny plug of congealing blood formed a stopper to prevent any more bleeding. Immediately around the wound was a ring of bloodless white skin; encircling that, a fearsome blue bruise resembled a rain cloud. I'd hurt him. Dear God, I'd hurt him. All these thoughts floated through me in a dreamy way. We seemed to stare at our mirror images for a long time. He didn't blink; the brown eyes were cold. As well as physical appearance he'd robbed me of my mannerisms. The one he employed now was the way I had of pushing my thumb against the corner of my mouth when I was tense.

"You shouldn't have done that," he told me (my voice, my teeth down to the slight gap in the middle of the upper two). "I'm not like the rest. What you've done has forced me to be inhumane. Even though there was no option other than keeping you locked up, I made sure you were safe from harm. Because of this"—he touched the wound—"we know that you'll stop at nothing until you've escaped. Now we're forced to destroy you."

The cold hit me. The roaring sound, the screams pierced the fuzz in my head left by the knockout blow. A bare arm encircled my throat; a solid body pressed against my back. *Someone's behind me.* I began to struggle.

Madeline's voice sliced through the cacophony. "Mason, don't fight. It's okay . . . I've got you."

That must have been the moment I came to my senses. Madeline supported me in the flood of water. We were so near the roof bars of our prison because we floated above the bottom of the pool. Madeline had one arm around my throat as she battled to save me from drowning; her other hand gripped one of the bars as she kept our heads clear of the icy liquid gushing in through the pool's feeder pipes.

"They're going to flood the place," she shouted. "Once the water reaches the roof bars we won't be able to breathe."

"Mom!" I yelled. "Mom! Eve!"

I thought I heard their voices call my name. The din had become thunder. All the time the swirling inrush of water tugged our bodies.

"Where did he go?" The figure on the bars above our heads had vanished.

"They've got problems with the other cells. They hadn't figured on the weight of water. The walls are collapsing."

"Mom! Are you there?" If this botched structure in the swimming pool had started to give way then Mom and Eve might have escaped. "Madeline, can you find the locks on the hatch? It's right above us."

Even though my hands consisted of numb bunches of fingers that were nearly useless after being immersed for so long, I gripped a cage bar with one hand while I reached through to feel with the other. Madeline helped me.

"I didn't see how they fastened them," she shouted.

"They must just twist off, something like a butterfly nut."

"Locking screws?"

"Too time-consuming for them."

"Here!" Despite the exhaustion clouding her face her eyes suddenly blazed in triumph.

I found one. "It's a butterfly nut. Turn it—"

"Counterclockwise."

I nodded. There we were, both holding on with a right hand, the one that bore the same Y-shaped scar. It reminded me to be on my guard. Madeline had saved my life. She was also one of the Echo creatures, a female replica of me. Just how much could I trust her?

I covered my sudden doubt by talking. "They were in too much of a rush after slugging me to do these properly. They're only finger-tight. Maybe before they had someone keep watch in case we discovered how they secured the hatch."

"Pray they're too busy now to keep checking on us."

A muffled thump. "Must be one of their bloody useless walls falling down."

"Got the last one. Push!"

Together we pushed upward with so much force it drove our own heads back underwater. I came up gasping. Madeline had vanished apart from a pair of forearms that thrust out of the water to heave the grille. Again my attention was drawn back to the red scar that carved those lines on her sopping hand. This would be a good moment to prevent the woman's escape—permanently. Yet, even though she was without doubt one of the Echofolk, she still hadn't turned against me. Here we were, working together. Allies. I knew I couldn't kill her yet. Maybe that would prove to be a fatal mistake, but how easy would it be for you to murder another human being?

The air gap between the surface of the pool and the bars had narrowed to about three inches. We'd have to exit soon or drown. I reached down underwater to pull Madeline's head up so she could grab a lungful of air.

"It's not hinged," I shouted. "As soon as we lift it above the frame, push it sideways."

The hatch matched the gridwork, difficult to differentiate from the rest of the cage roof, but fairly light. Working together—no, more than together; this was pure harmony. Whatever force of nature, or supernature, transformed Madeline into a female copy of me nudged us into thinking alike. In ten seconds we'd pushed the hatch aside. Easily she hauled herself out, that marathon runner's body of hers making light of the work. Then I pulled myself up onto the roof.

*Bang!* It hit me what the Echomen had done. In the disused swimming pool of my old school they'd built concrete walls that ran across it widthways. On top of that they'd added what must have been steel sections of fence, only they'd laid these flat across the tops of the walls. Despite the botch-quality workmanship, this must have taken some forward planning, not to say hard labor. Imagine a swimming pool drained of water; in your mind's eye add a dozen concrete walls topped with steel grids to create cells some five feet wide by thirty feet in length; they run from one side of the pool to the other, bizarre corridors to nowhere.

Now that they'd filled the pool with water only the wall tops and grille roof were visible. At the far end of the pool where it was the deepest some walls had given way under the weight of the water. I figured there were other captives here that had escaped as the tumbling walls brought that section of cage down. Now there was nobody on the cage roof but Madeline and myself . . . oh, the Echoman that had his bones broken as a lesson to us all sat on the grille twenty paces from us.

He was of no use to his comrades and no threat to us. He sat hunched, slowly shaking his head while grunting with pain. All this I absorbed in a snap.

"Mom? Eve?" What was important now was that I found them. I ran across the steel grid to peer down into the cell next to mine. A pair of hands gripped the bars, keeping a head above water.

"Mom?"

There she was. I crouched down to touch her fingers. Her eyes instantly locked on mine.

"Mason. Thank God."

"Don't worry. I'll get you out."

"No!"

I crouched over the hatch. There were six wing nuts holding it down. Two inches beneath the bars swirled the water's surface; my mother's face could have been a two-dimensional mask floating there.

"Mason! Listen to me," she shouted. "I'll be fine. Get Eve out first."

"The water's nearly up to the bars." I tried to unscrew the butterfly nuts. They didn't move. "Damn. They've used a wrench to tighten them."

"Mason . . . Mason." Her voice grew calm as she reached through the bars to hold my hand. "Listen to what I'm going to tell you. Don't worry about me. I'm fine. Focus on getting Eve out of the cell. She's very cold. I can hold on. Eve's losing her grip on the bars. So, you see, Mason, you have to save her first." All this she said with such calm and such dignity that it stopped my struggling with the fastenings. "Mason, there'll be ample time for me. Now go save your sister."

The wing nuts were screwed as tight on Eve's cell. What shocked me most, however, was that only Eve's forehead and nose appeared above the water. Her fingers had turned bloodless as she gripped the bar to lift herself as high she could—only it wasn't high enough, was it? Water ran up into her nostrils. Her face shook as spasms struck her.

"Damn. That's why they weren't worried about us escaping. They used a wrench to make these so tight you can't loosen them with your fingers!"

Madeline got to her knees so she could reach through the bars to take hold of Eve's head. Supporting it like that relieved my sister of some of the strain of keeping her face pressed hard against the bars to snatch those last few breaths before the water rose to lethal levels.

"Blast!" My sopping fingers slipped off the wing nut. "It's no good. I need a tool to shift them."

Madeline's brown eyes met mine. She knew that Eve was dying. "Try the hatch cover. Use it as a hammer."

I raced back to the roof of what had been our cell. By this time my feet splashed as the water rose above the bars toward the lip of the pool itself. The broken man shuffled on his knees toward me. He stared at me with a dogged determination; he knew what I was doing, and in his smashed-up kind of way he planned to stop me. Like empty sleeves his shattered arms swung uselessly. It would have been so tempting to punch him in that swollen face of his. . . . I thrust the thought out of my mind. Eve and Mom came first.

As I ran back to Eve's cell I shot a glance at Mom to reassure me. Her hands still clasped the roof bars. A second later I used the hatch to beat the wing nuts. The hatch was a little larger than the kind of tray you'd eat your supper from. There wasn't much weight, so I had to take a swing at the fastenings. Sometimes I missed and struck the cage bars. At that moment I tried not to notice Eve's face vanishing beneath the water's surface. After I'd struck the wing nuts a couple of times Madeline leaned sideways. Still supporting Eve's head with one hand she began work on the first wing nut.

"It's moving," she shouted. "Keep hitting the others."

This went faster. The blows loosened the wing nuts. By the time I'd done the last one Madeline had unscrewed four of them. Then together we spun off the last two. As I wrenched the hatch off the cage Madeline caught hold of Eve. She drew my sister out onto the cage roof, where she lay coughing water; her lips had nearly turned black; her eyes were screwed up with pain.

"I'll look after her." Madeline pointed. "Get your mother out."

*Splash, splash, splash.* I was running through water.

Running through water?

Beneath the level of my ankles I saw the crisscross pattern of the grill. Beneath that my mother lay on her back. The water was icily clear. My mother drifted there, her hair fanned out, her eyes open, staring up at me . . . only they weren't staring . . . not really staring. In fact, they were not seeing anything.

The broken Echoman became the vessel into which I poured a tiny fraction of my rage. Yet at that moment there wasn't a space big enough in the entire cosmos to accommodate my anger. He reared up on his knees as I approached him. The flip-flop action of his shattered arms had no effect as he tried to punch me. One push put him on the cage facedown. I had no shoes, of course; kicking him would only have shattered my own bones in my feet. With the blood roaring in my veins I stamped his head down against the bars five or six times until he showed no interest in moving his fucking useless limbs. The water reached above my ankles as I pressed my heel down on the back of his head, grinding his face against the submerged grille. It only took a couple of minutes for the guy's lungs to fill with water. Nevertheless, I kept holding it there. Just to be sure.

Madeline's voice sounded in my ear. "Mason, leave him. We've got to go before they come back."

# CHAPTER EIGHTEEN

So, you're faced with this problem. You need to move three people a distance of four miles from a derelict school to a suburban house. Add to that that one of the three wears nothing but shorts; the second is naked apart from a skimpy T-shirt; the third is clothed in pajamas, but has narrowly escaped drowning, and is suffering from shock. Add just a little more shit to the mix: all three are exhausted, cold, hungry, still soaking wet. While you're at it, toss in another pinch of misery (when you're vulnerable life's good at piling on woes, isn't it?): the mother of two of the group died just twenty minutes ago. Oh, and there are individuals somewhere in the former school that are driven by an alien instinct to kill the three at the earliest possible opportunity.

That was what we faced. It should have made the journey home sheer torture. But that four-mile walk home? I don't remember it. We could have glided there by magic carpet, for all the discomfort I remember. All that comes back to me now is seeing the sun rise as a flattened red ball over Tanshelf. I hadn't experienced a dawn like it before; the sun resembled a huge, bloodshot eye. Were we spotted by members of the public as we trudged along? I can't say. Did a worker returning home from a night shift, or a youth delivering newspapers challenge us? If they did I've no recollection. We walked but we could have been brain-dead. No smells registered. Madeline and I were barefoot; later I realized my feet bled from the four-mile stroll sans footwear. I didn't notice so much as a prickle at the time.

Looking back, I figure I followed my old route home from school. This was always faster than even catching the school bus that dropped off at every street corner and took detours to Upper Tanshelf before reaching our neighborhood. So I must have taken Eve and Madeline, dripping like wet bath sponges, along the farm track across the cornfields to where it ran by the end of the road where we lived.

The house hadn't changed. After what had just happened to us did I honestly expect it to have died of grief or something? I don't know. It just seemed to me that those redbrick walls should have a different appearance. Instead they were resoundingly indifferent. At times like this logic is a slippery thing . . . too slippery for a traumatized mind to cling to for long. So, I failed to perceive the illogic of expecting the house to be suffering in tandem with its residents.

Nobody spoke as we walked along the side of the house. By now it must have been around six a.m. Soon clock-radio alarms would be alerting neighbors to heave their bones out of bed. Still on autopilot I climbed onto the garage roof, then in through a window with a broken catch, a route I'd followed many times before in childhood. Eve and Madeline shivered by the back door as they waited for me to let them in. On the way I collected dry bath towels. Considering we'd been ab-

ducted by force from the house, the Echomen had left
our home remarkably tidy. Even the gasoline smell had
gone. On reaching the back door I unlocked it, handed
out the towels, then stood back to allow the pair in.

Eve entered first. Her eyes could have been the windows of an empty house. A staring blankness. She
paused.

"The woman can't come in," Eve intoned. "I know
what she is. I won't have her in our house."

The escape from the flooding prison cell, then la-
boring to rescue Eve before the exhausting walk home
had left Madeline with a beaten look. Matted hair
stuck in spikes; a bruise darkened her cheek, no doubt
acquired in the struggle to climb through the ceiling
bars.

"You can't come in," I told her.

Her large dark brown eyes held mine as a weary mind
calculated her options. "I've nowhere to go." Her voice
was hoarse. "I don't even know who I am anymore."

I turned to Eve. She shook her head. "Please, Mason."

The loss of our mother had broken my sister's heart.
No way would I make her feel more wretched by inviting
Madeline into our family home. "Don't worry, Eve. Go
change into some dry clothes. I'll deal with Madeline."

*"Madeline?"* The way Eve phrased the name had the
same resonance of someone saying, *Edible?* when
served up a rotting pig's head with an assurance that it
was lovely grub.

When Eve retreated upstairs I began to close the
door in Madeline's face. She stared with pleading eyes,
yet she never actually said anything. With the door just
inches from shutting her out I leaned into the gap.

In a whisper I told her, "The side door of the garage

will be open. You'll find the car unlocked. Make yourself comfortable in there. I'll bring you some clothes later. Here." She already had one towel but I handed her a second one. "Wrap yourself in both; you look cold."

You could debate the niceties of hospitality any other time but this one. Madeline was a monster—no, worse than a monster: she was a version of me. I remembered how I'd drowned the Echoman a couple of hours ago. If I was capable of killing in cold blood, what whims and fancies might be lurking inside of her?

# CHAPTER NINETEEN

A day wrapped in fog. That was what it seemed like now. We'd been in the Echomen's jail for nearly forty-eight hours. Eve and I had made it home. Exhaustion smashed our will to keep going. We slept in the bedrooms we'd occupied since children. In the garage Madeline must have slept, too, because the few times I looked out the window there was no sign of movement. At one point in the day I got up to eat something from the refrigerator—I can't remember what—and I noticed that Eve had taken down all the photographs of Mom.

When I returned to bed Eve stood at her bedroom door. Her eyes were hollow things, more like raw wounds than the pretty features that attracted the boys.

In a broken voice she said, "Mason, I know I should be asking you what happened to us . . . but my brain feels dead now. . . . I can't think about anything . . . nothing that makes sense anyway. . . ."

"You should try to sleep. You'll feel better."

"Better? I can't believe I'll feel better ever again. Mason?" There was a pause as she held me with a wounded look. "We're not going to the police about this, are we?"

"Not yet."

Eve had every right to ask me my reasons, or simply to call the cops. Instead she stepped back into her bedroom. I waited on the landing, just in case she did change her mind and started asking questions. After all, there were plenty: Why were we kidnapped? Who were these Echomen? Why did they do that to us? *How come Madeline looks an awful lot like you, brother, dear?*

After I heard Eve climbing into bed, then it falling silent in her room, I decided to return to my own. Sleep is supposed to be the great healer of emotional wounds—I don't know how true that is, but sleep is an ideal escape from reality. You see, this was eating into me: if I'd moved that bit faster I could have saved my mother. All I needed was an extra sixty seconds after releasing Eve. Memory replayed scenes of what *could* have been: *Unscrew the wing nuts that hold the hatch on my mother's cell; she's pressing her face up to the bars to keep above the water flooding in; then (and I see this more than anything) flip back the hatch with a shout of: "That was a close one, Mom! Don't worry; I'll help you out." And out she comes, dripping wet, panting, but alive as you and me.*

I realized I'd sat down on the top step of the stairs. Grief, anger, frustration, remorse—they boiled inside to make me sick to the bone. I gripped my knees so hard my fingernails turned white. In the shadows at the bottom of the staircase a figure sat on the third step. With his back to the wall, his face was tilted up at me. Eyes lightly closed, tip of the tongue protruding through dead lips—just the same as usual, right down to the cracks in his scalp, reddish skin, bandages that were as much dust as cotton threads. *Unmoving, unspeaking, the serene god of stillness . . . Natsaf-Ty, keeper of the sacred crocodiles, he's looking at me. He knows the secret me. Why, all those years ago, wasn't he there in the shadows to witness what really happened that evil New Year's Eve? That I knocked out the drunk to prevent him from stabbing my best friend in the back? Natsaf-Ty sees me replaying that scenario of saving my mother if I'd only moved faster. He also sees the secret I've been working so hard to keep from myself—*

I snarled. "Don't you dare accuse me of that—don't you fucking dare." My fingers curled into fists that ached to punch out. "Madeline means nothing to me. I'm not obsessed with that woman—I never will be!"

The figure on the stair didn't move—not a single wise old bone in that crust stirred.

I sighed. "Mom always used to say . . ."

Grief comes in a wave. You see it approach; you know it's coming; only you can't dodge it or reduce its power over you. The wave hits, overwhelms . . . you, too, have experienced grief. There's no need for me to elaborate.

A day wrapped in fog. Sleeping, waking, eating cold cuts, nausea: the food rebounds. As the day passed in a blur I alternated naps poisoned by nightmare with checking that Eve was still safe. In the afternoon gales brought rain that lashed the house with the force of a whip. Drafts made human-sounding groans in the chimney. Ice-cold air filled rooms as if they became a doppelgänger of the swimming-pool prison that had filled with icy water. While Eve slept I delivered clothes along with food to Madeline out in the garage. Cool logic dictated that I take either Mom's or Eve's clothes to the woman. But I saw only too vividly how Eve would freak at the sight of Madeline—the she-monster that wore my face—wearing either her clothes or our mother's. So the garments I presented to the woman huddled in the backseat of Mom's car had to be mine. Even though Madeline's a hundred percent female, with no trace of becoming a hermaphrodite, the woman closely matched my height.

"Put these on." I dropped the clothes through the vehicle's open window. "There's a hairbrush in the glove compartment." Rain clattered against the garage roof as if drawing the world's attention to these strange events taking place. *Come look at this*, the rain-on-roof code seemed to say. *The woman looks like him; soon she'll be slipping into his clothes. Where do these freaks go from here?*

"Thank you." Madeline's shyness mingled with gratitude. She not only studied the garments but squeezed the fabric between her sublimely feminine fingers. This was no beauty pageant finery; I'd dug out a white T-shirt, a hooded sweatshirt, black jeans, sneakers—all pretty much unisex anyway. Did I bring underwear? Think about it: supplying my own underwear would have made Sigmund Freud sit up in his grave and commence some furious note scribbling.

In the confines of the rear car seat she shrugged off the towels, then the T-shirt she'd worn in the cell. When I turned away to avoid watching the rear-of-car strip show, I glimpsed a figure skim by the garage window.

An Echoman? It had to be. It made sense for them to follow us home from their homemade jail, then finish the job. Taking just enough time to grab a wrench from a shelf I raced out of the garage. Thoughts of Mom lying drowned in the swimming pool, hair fanned out, eyes staring, boiled up inside of me. If I could get my hands on one of the bastards . . . The heavy steel wrench felt good in my hand at that moment.

Like a rhino I went charging through the bushes. Its head would burst like a watermelon when I swung this lump of metal at it. Nobody in the bushes, so I charged back to the front of the house. Rain stabbed my eyes. Gales screamed through the chimney. A figure lunged from a doorway. A shout. My hand raised aloft the wrench as if it were a sword of divine retribution.

"Mason, it's me!"

Madeline stood there. Her eyes were bright with fear as she anticipated falling victim to my bloodlust.

I lowered the wrench. "Have you seen anyone?"

She shook her head. "Mason, what are you going to do with me?"

"Do with you?"

"Have you thought what will happen to me in the future?"

"It's nigh on impossible to figure out a plan for the next three hours, never mind your entire future. Besides, whatever's happened to you doesn't make me your owner. Why don't you just go home?"

"Even if I could remember where I lived, what would my family say if I turned up like this?"

I stared at her face—or, rather, a close copy of my face, albeit a feminized one. "Don't you remember your family?"

"When I try all I can see are the faces of your mother and sister." She looked away. "Sorry."

Madeline was so emotionally wounded that part of me wanted to give her a hug, but my own emotions were too scrambled to get involved with anything approaching physical contact with the woman.

I took a deep breath. "There doesn't seem to be anyone around. It might have just been a kid sneaking by the garage for a dare." I shrugged; even to me that explanation wasn't convincing. "But it's likely those people who abducted us will want to finish what they started."

"If it's not safe, will you let me come into the house?"

"My sister's ripped up about what happened." I shook my head. "It's not a good idea."

"All right."

I know, I know, she should have protested. I mean, if your life is in danger you need to be in the company of people you know. Here I was, telling her she was in danger; then I denied her the protection of being in a house with the doors locked. Relative protection, that is. If Echomen appeared around the corner with guns, what could we do to save our necks then? So instead of demanding to come with me she returned to the garage, her demeanor achingly submissive.

Lamely I added, "The main doors are locked. You can bolt this door from inside." Then this statement that, if it were a horse, was so thunderously lame the poor bloody beast would have been shot dead: "Stay in the back of the car with the blanket over you . . . you'll be safe there." *Yeah, why not glue together a jacket made out of Kleenex and tell her it's bulletproof?* That would make her just as safe as hiding in the back of the car if the Echomen returned. With the rain still hitting my head as if it had taken a dislike to me, I returned to the house. Eve stood in the hallway.

"I saw the pair of you," she accused. "If you know what she is, why are you so obsessed with her?"

"Do you want me to turn her out into the street?"

"Mason, she's not a real human being; she can't be. She won't have feelings."

*Madeline saved my life. She saved yours. Damn it, that's the truth. I'll tell Eve these facts now.* "Madeline is—"

"My God. You should see the expression on your face! You *are* obsessed with her. . . . Mason, you make me sick!"

"Eve . . . Eve! Let me explain. . . ." But she fled, howling with sheer rage.

For the rest of the day I saw nothing of Madeline, nor of Eve, who remained in her room, door locked, ears blocked, the way siblings can to (a) sever communication with the other sibling, and (b) sever that communication in such a way as to generate frustration at not being able to argue further or even apologize. After that, there were other false alarms. More than once I woke in the sure certainty that I heard feet climbing the stairs. When I checked they were deserted; even my old imaginary friend Natsaf-Ty appeared to shun me for abandoning Madeline to the uncertain safety of the garage. And when your imaginary friend gives you the cold shoulder, that's when you know you're in trouble. Twice the telephone rang. "Hello?" No answering hello.

The Echomen stayed away. Our enemy didn't attempt to slaughter us in our beds, or burn down the house, or even hurl stones with threats tied to them. No. When the Echomen returned it was in a way none of us could have predicted.

# CHAPTER TWENTY

The next morning I woke to find I'd slept ten hours. After a shower to blast away any tenacious jail odor I dressed, then went downstairs to the kitchen.

My mother sang out a bright, "Good morning. Sleep well?" She wore a summer dress with orange flowers on a green background. At that moment she busied herself in the sunlit kitchen as she whisked eggs in a bowl. "You were going to cut back the apple tree for me, weren't you?"

People will tell you that you always see a loved one at least once after they die. The truth is, for a second I didn't believe I saw a ghost. For that glittering, surreal instant I believed the last seventy-two hours hadn't happened. That I was strolling into the kitchen like any other morning to find my mother making breakfast with a spring in her step. Just like times gone by, when we'd chat about our plans for the day, about what chores needed to be done—would I be meeting friends later? That sort of thing. And for a whole moment I clung to the illusion as hard as I could. Then:

"Get out."

"Mason, will you pass me the pan? The one with the wooden handle."

"I said get out." My voice came as a low growl, something close to the sound a dog makes before it attacks.

"And would you like bacon with the scrambled eggs?" Her voice had a lightness to it—not a care in the world.

"You're not my mother."

"Mason, the pan."

"I told you to get out."

"Okay, if you don't want to pass the pan I'll use the copper one, but it's always difficult to clean." She tipped the whisked eggs into another pan, then set it onto the gas ring. "Will you keep stirring while I get the bacon? That copper's a nightmare if anything sticks. . . . Oh, good morning, Eve. Sleep well?"

Ten expressions in one millisecond. At least, that was what seemed to pass across my sister's face: happiness, confusion, disappointment, alarm—the works.

"Mason." Eve froze in the doorway. "It's one of those things. It's followed us here."

"Eve, stay back."

"I don't know what game you two are playing." The thing that wore the smiling face of my mother put the bacon on the table. "But I haven't time for it this morning. After breakfast I have to drive Mrs. Robinson to the hairdressers'. Ever since she had that fall last month she's not been able to use her own car. Now, will you stop staring at me as if I'm wearing a fish on my head and make yourselves useful? Eve, fetch the coffee, will you? Mason, keep stirring the eggs or they'll burn."

The door that led outside from the kitchen was open. From it came a shape that moved so quickly it was a blur. A second later it lunged at the creature that had stolen my mother's identity. Another second and I recognized the figure as Madeline. Deftly she slid a transparent plastic bag over the clone's face, then gathered it tight around her neck. The expression on the face inside the bag changed from a happy-go-lucky smile to one of fury. Her eyes narrowed as she tried to grab Madeline by the throat.

"Help me!" Madeline yelled.

Eve acted first. She caught hold of the creature's flailing arms. This freed up Madeline to reach out, grab the flex from the kettle, and wrap it around the neck of the thing that posed as my mother. The woman tried to scream, but the sound came out as a gurgle. The pressure on her trachea, however, wasn't great enough to stop her breathing. The bag inflated as she exhaled, then shrank tight to the face like shrink-wrapped meat when she inhaled. A patch of fog appeared around the mouth where moisture from her breath condensed. The eyes changed from being gentle Mom eyes to slits that blazed hatred.

"Mason!" Eve shouted.

"Help us get her onto the table." Madeline used the electric flex as part reins, part hangman's noose to both pull and choke. "Hurry, Mason! She's breaking free!"

I went to help, then froze. What I had to do was obvious—only that woman really did look like my mother. *Exactly like her.*

"Mason!" Eve yelled again. "Help us!"

The plastic bag continued to inflate-deflate. When it sucked tight to her face as she breathed in it created a polyethylene fright mask that had precious little in the way of humanity about it. When it inflated it formed a misty halo around a face and head that were exactly the same as my mother's. What if it wasn't my mother that died in the pool . . . what if it was one of those Echo creatures? Now we were choking the life from the woman who gave birth to me. That puddle of air in the bag would be poisonous now. Her chest heaved as she breathed a gallon of toxic gas.

Still she struggled, though. She'd grabbed Eve by the throat. When Madeline had the chance she balled her fist, then whopped it into the creature's gut with enough force to make her grunt. The pain was also intense enough to stop her from fighting for a moment, giving the pair time to drag her across the table so she lay on her back with her legs dangling at one side and the two women holding her by the arms at the other. The kitchen table had become a sacrificial altar. The bag still inflated-deflated. Bad air rushed in and out of her lungs.

Eve turned to me, her hair flying out, eyes fiery. "Mason. Get a knife!"

I stared in disbelief.

"Use it on her before she breaks free."

My eyes went to the knife hanging on the magnetic strip; the ten-inch blade glittered. It sang its own bloody possibilities to me. *Grab the knife. Plunge the point into the woman's belly. Twist it around; rock the handle downward so it forces the blade up toward the heart.*

"No!" I pushed both Eve and Madeline away, then dragged the plastic bag from the woman's head. Instantly she scrambled to her feet.

"Mason, you should have killed her while you had the chance."

"What if we made a mistake? What if she's our mother?"

The woman who wore Mom's face managed a smile as her chest heaved for air. "I can be your mother. Listen to me . . . they'll cut a deal. As long as you don't interfere with them I'll stay with you as long as you want."

Eve lunged for the knife on the wall. I caught her before she could slash the monster's face with it.

Strangely, the creature appeared uncaring about her safety. She smiled as she rubbed her bruised throat. "Like I said, children, if you want me to be your mother, then I'll be Mom for as long as you need me." She took a step back. "I'll come back later. Just to make sure you make the right decision."

With that she stepped through the back door. By the time I ventured out there the woman was nowhere in sight.

"Mason, get that thing out of the house."

"Madeline needed to—"

"I don't care! Get rid of her!" Eve went to her room.

"Sorry about that," I told Madeline. "Eve's . . ." The words didn't come easily. "Brokenhearted. Our mother was still young . . . full of life."

"If you want me to go, I will." Madeline watched my face, no doubt searching for clues as to what I was thinking . . . but then, sometimes we shared stray thoughts. As she'd waited out in the car inside the garage I had lain in bed and felt what she felt—the terror of knowing her identity had been supplanted by another; the fear of being alone in the garage when an Echoman might have been approaching with the intention of killing her. Then I'd picked up her craving for human company, yet with that had come self-disgust, because she knew Eve and I saw her as some kind of monster.

Lost in my own thoughts I hadn't answered, so she gently repeated the invitation. "Mason. I can go. All you need do is ask."

"No. You've nowhere to go. I'm not going to abandon you."

She smiled. "I'll keep out of Eve's way."

"For the time being that might be a good idea." I found myself smiling back. "Seeing that Eve has gone back to her room, I'll cook you something." I got busy, partly to suppress the headful of questions I had buzzing around in there. "I do a great steak smothered in melted blue cheese. Do you want to give it a go?"

"If you like it then I will."

"So we share the same tastes as well as the same features." I touched my nose. "I'm sorry you ended up with this beak, by the way."

"I've been admiring it in the mirror. I had time to kill in the car."

"Yeah, that can't have been much fun."

"I didn't mind. Sometimes I saw you looking out of your bedroom window."

My face grew warm. "It's hard not to be concerned. After all, if those people came back . . ."

As we talked I took packs of steak from the refrigerator. Madeline pulled the big old pan from the back of a cupboard—it was the one I always used for steak. Neither of us mentioned the obvious question: if she'd never been to this house before, how did she know it was there? Because the answer was obvious: Madeline was dipping into my memory. So what was the extent of her knowledge about me? How long before she could read my mind like you read words on a sign?

*Die, Madeline! Die!* It was a crude experiment in mental projection, and I kept a close watch on her face. But when I shouted the words inside my head she didn't give the tiniest indication that she'd picked up on them. Now, that was a relief. I didn't want her knowing every little thing that slipped through my mind. It was one thing to share the same face, another thing entirely to share the same thoughts.

She smiled. "You crumble the blue cheese, rather than grating it."

"You must have read my mind." I made a joke of it. "Yep, if you crumble the cheese into a bowl, then—"

"Sprinkle it on the steak once it's cooked and pop it under the broiler until—"

"—bubbling." I nodded. "Whatever it is that's happened to us, at least it means we don't always have to explain recipes to each other."

"Or how we feel?"

That question of hers might have required more explanation; however, I noticed the plastic bag on the floor. It had a smear of pink lipstick on the inside. Taking a deep breath I picked it up. "Sometimes it seems recent events are a dream. Then this." I crumpled the bag in my fist. "Hard evidence."

"So the Echo people made a copy of your mother, like they made a copy of me out of you?"

"You're not a copy like the others. You're different. Can you wash the tomatoes, please?"

Wash tomatoes? Open the potato salad? Cut some bread? Pour orange juice? I know, it made me angry. But I've this tendency to evade the painful parts of reality by doing normal, humdrum things. If I'd begun this conversation with Eve she would have demanded answers. Madeline didn't want to know how I was really feeling about Mom right now. Don't you know it? Madeline's a chip off the old block. She's me to a T. So without any social awkwardness we lapsed into small talk. *This butter's a lovely color, Mason. Would you prefer coffee or orange juice? Look, there isn't a cloud in the sky. You've an eyelash on your cheek; here, let me get it for you.* See? Small talk. Avoiding confrontation with reality. A Mason Konrad trait. Now a Madeline trait.

We ate lunch early, so call it brunch. Madeline loved her steak covered with melted blue cheese and made a lot of expressive "ooohs" and "mmms." The kitchen was no longer as silent as the proverbial tomb. The radio played upbeat music; we chatted in a lively way. When I cut a tomato it squirted into my eye, which had us laughing as I wiped away the juice.

That was how Eve found us, both laughing, Madeline leaning forward across the table to dab away a tomato seed stuck to my eyebrow. Seeing my sister standing there with reddened eyelids, her face puffy from weeping, hit me like a slab of cold concrete. Madeline immediately stopped laughing, then lowered her head in a submissive way that reminded me of a housemaid who knew her place.

I started attempting to excuse the scene. "We were both hungry, so we decided to have an early lunch. Sorry if we woke you." My fork went down on the plate harder than I intended. Madeline flinched. "Damn it, Eve. We can't stop living. What happened to our mother is terrible; that doesn't mean we've got to crawl into our beds and stay there."

"You're right, Mason. It's essential to eat." Eve spoke in a way that was more restrained than I could have believed possible under the circumstances. "It's also essential to take action. So I've reached a decision."

"Go on."

"You said that we couldn't go to the police until we had evidence?"

"That's right."

Eve nodded at Madeline. "Then take her to the police. They'll take one look at her; then they'll know we're telling the truth."

"Do you know what the authorities would do to Madeline?" Cold and heat flushed through me simultaneously. "They'd experiment on her like a lab rat."

"I figured you wouldn't be parted from her. So now I'm proved right."

"Eve, it's not like that. I don't—"

"Don't explain. It's not necessary." She surged on: "So the decision I did come to, one that I expect you to agree with, is that we go back to the school and find hard evidence that the police will accept."

"You know the danger of going to the police?"

"Yes, and it's not that they'll think we're insane. They'll find the cells built into the pool, and maybe even our mother."

Madeline tilted her head to one side. "Why, then?"

Eve replied with a lick of fire in her voice, "Because we're in danger from your kind. Once we go to the police they'll force us to stay here." She turned to me. "Madeline's not the only one thinking like you, Mason. If we have to remain in this house while the police investigate then we're easy targets." She took a deep breath. "And don't look at me as if I'm going to break into pieces. Mom's dead. I'll grieve for her when this is over. Now, whether you come with me or not, I'm going to search the school."

# CHAPTER TWENTY-ONE

Tanshelf High sprawled over three acres between cornfields and an expressway that thundered with traffic. I'd been schooled there, and so had Eve. For years parents complained that the school was too remote from Tanshelf; finally they'd gotten their way. A new one had been built closer to town. Although the old site had been zoned for redevelopment, the business community considered its out-of-the-way location as instant death to any commercial opportunity. They kept their cash in the bank. Tanshelf High kept to itself as it quietly rotted into the ground.

We arrived midafternoon. The sun shone warmly enough, but the place made the blood run cold. In that scattering of blocks that housed the gym, cafeteria, classrooms, labs, and staff room was the swimming-pool block. Once it had meant a welcome break from class, plus the opportunity to duck friends and ogle girls in their swimsuits. Now it brought more recent memories charging back. The long, narrow cell in the pool. The hours of darkness. The fear. The image of my mother floating dead in the water.

As I drove the car through the school's busted gates I glanced at Eve beside me. Far stronger than I'd given her credit for, she gazed at the school buildings, determined to get in there and find the evidence she needed. In the backseat Madeline's eyes took in the derelict buildings with their boarded windows. Her face held no expression, so I couldn't tell if she was afraid or simply curious about what we might find. On occasions I'd picked up on her emotions; however, nothing reached me at that moment.

"If they've got any sense," I said as I stopped by the main building, "they'll have gotten out when we escaped."

"Don't expect them to do the logical thing." Madeline sounded matter-of-fact. "They don't think like us."

Eve spoke bluntly: "They don't think like Mason and me. You're one of them, remember?"

Madeline didn't answer back. Again there was that sense that she knew her place in the pecking order. Her demeanor was submissive in the presence of Eve.

Eve drove the point. "Not only one of them—I don't trust you either."

"Eve, she's on our side."

"Why? Because she told you so—or because she looks like you, so she can't be evil?" Eve opened the door. "By the way, a car kept driving by our house today. I didn't recognize the people. Maybe your special friend here telephoned the Echomen when we were asleep."

"Eve—"

"Watch your back, Mason." Eve climbed out of the car. "Madeline might be only biding her time."

Despite the air of decay about the place the authorities had made the classrooms blocks secure from intruders. They might be worthless structures that were covered with peeling paint and rampant ivy growth, and containing nothing more precious than air once breathed by three thousand hormone-fueled teenagers, but the windows were covered with mesh screens, while doors were not only locked but padlocked.

"I was unconscious when they brought me here," I said as we walked along an overgrown path. "Did anyone see how they took us into the swimming-pool building?"

Madeline simply gave a little shake of her head. If you ask me her mind had been wiped during the transformation. All she seemed to recall from her old life was her name.

Eve shivered. "They covered my head with a blanket. I didn't see a thing. All I knew was that there were lots of them."

"Lots?" That made me pause. "I only ever saw around half a dozen."

"Trust me, Mason. There are dozens of the monsters."

We moved on through grounds that were nearly jungle. I recognized a brick sculpture of an athlete built by the art class. Once it stood in the middle of a neatly mowed lawn near the gym. Now only the top of a red-brick hand stretched above the bushes, having long since drowned in a tidal wave of greenery. By the time we reached the swimming-pool block I could have vomited. The pale concrete walls seemed to ooze dread. You hear of people suffering from panic attacks—at that moment I began to know its reality. My breathing went shallow; my heart raced; a taste like moldy bread filled my mouth. We pushed through the long grass that touched our hips. Here a way had been trampled where the Echomen had approached the side door. I took a deep breath; this was something I had to do. The Echomen didn't worry me; it was the thought of finding my mother still floating in the pool. By now the long period of immersion would be making a mess of her face.

"I'll go first," I told them as I surged toward the door. "Damn. They've sealed it." For a moment we stared at the massive nails that they'd driven into the timbers in such a way as to hold the door shut. "We'll need tools to get it open."

Madeline scanned the stark walls. "There's no other way in?"

"There are no windows at ground level, and the main door's padlocked."

"I'm not going yet." Eve's expression was determined. "I'm going to stay here until I've found enough evidence to have the police swarming all over the place."

"I'll help you, Eve," Madeline said.

Eve grunted. "Don't bother. I never asked for any help from you."

"We'll check the classroom blocks." As much as anything, that was intended to steer Eve away from a confrontation with Madeline. (Hell's bells, Eve wanted to kick Madeline in the head—I didn't doubt it for a moment.)

Once more we waded through the green lake of grass. Brambles snagged our ankles; thorns pricked through our clothes. That minor physical discomfort was one of the *more* pleasant aspects of this wilderness. Though the sun might be shining, it wouldn't prevent any of the Echofolk who'd spotted three intruders from dashing out of their lair to beat us to pulp in broad daylight. I mean, who'd hear our death screams in a place as remote as this? Eve moved in a resolute manner. She was here to get the job done. Madeline expressed her loyalty to me by sticking close. From time to time she pushed back her hair where it fell across her face. I noticed the Y-shaped scar that was identical to mine.

When I glanced through a grove of trees I saw Natsaf-Ty. He did that thing of appearing to gaze at me through his closed eyelids. Yellow butterflies flitted around his dried husk of a body. One loose end of a bandage swung in the light breeze.

"Mason?" That was Eve's curt whisper. "What have you seen?"

"Uh, nothing." I glanced at both Eve and Madeline to see if they'd noticed the ancient Egyptian mummy standing in the shadows. They hadn't. Or they weren't letting on that they'd noticed anything strange. Well . . . when your childhood imaginary friend returns, what does that say about your state of mind? A good sign? Or a symptom of impending madness?

If anything, it seemed to me that our meager force of three had risen to four. With a renewed sense of purpose I homed in on a classroom block. More peeling paint, cracked boards, torn roof felt—this was the place where I studied history.

"There's no point in going through the doors; they're padlocked." I tugged at the steel mesh that had been used to secure the windows, the same mesh that had been used to form the "roof" of our makeshift prison cells. Eve and Madeline began to test the mesh too, searching for a loose corner. In between tugging the mesh I tried to peer through the windows. Not only were the panes crusted with grime, but it was dark in there. For all I knew there could have been an Echoman staring out at me.

"The nails are moving on this one," Madeline said.

Eve pulled a carving knife from her boot. She noticed my reaction to the knife. "I wasn't going to come here without a weapon. Dear heaven, I wish I'd gotten a machine gun. Out of the way, Madeline."

Eve attacked the nails like she'd wanted to attack those Echomen who'd murdered our mother.

"Let me," I said.

"You think I can't manage?" She ripped out the first nail. "Grab the screen. Let me know when it starts to give."

In less than three minutes the screen had come free. A minute after that I climbed into my old classroom. It wouldn't be hard to imagine seeing my old friends there as fourteen-year-olds when we listened to Mr. Grasse (or Seedy, as we called him. Grass seed? Okay, high school wit was never sophisticated). The place was dry; it retained that distinctive school smell. You have only to walk into a classroom after years of not stepping foot inside of one, and that smell brings with it an entire cargo of memories—of friends, bullies, practical jokes, nice teachers, mean ones, the pangs of forgetting homework or the thrill of dashing out the door at the sound of the last bell. Those recollections rushed at me as I stood in the gloomy void. Although the furniture had gone there were still posters on the walls: Roman emperors, an Inca time line, a picture of the Wright Brothers' plane, complete with the hand-drawn addition of a fart jetting from Orville's bottom. Remember high school wit?

"Is it clear?" Eve whispered.

"Looks deserted." I helped the pair through the window.

Eve looked around. "My old classroom for history." She gave a grunt. "See that blue tack in the wall above the window? I remember Todd firing that from a rubber band." Then in an instant she switched off the nostalgia. Nothing would deflect my sister. "Listen. We'll go through the building room by room."

"We could split up," Madeline suggested.

"No way," I told them. "We stick together."

Classrooms on the ground floor were duplicates of one another: posters on the walls, rooms empty of furniture but bursting with memories. We ascended to the next floor by stairs I'd charged up and down maybe a thousand times before.

Eve rushed ahead.

"Slow down," I hissed. "We don't know if there's anyone in here."

I was proved right. There were people. Lots of them.

# CHAPTER TWENTY-TWO

The next floor: blinds had been drawn in the classrooms. Despite the sunshine outside, in here it was a gloomy light that had a dirty look to it. Dirty light? How could you have dirty light? Yet that was how it appeared. The glow coming through the window blinds had a soiled aspect. What illuminated the classroom upstairs was a grubby yellow. I didn't want to be touched by light like that, as if it would contaminate my skin if it laid its beams on me.

Eve whispered in alarm as she peered into the room, "It's not empty." The blade glinted as her fist tightened around the knife handle.

"Keep back," I hissed.

But Eve surged into the room as if on a suicide mission.

"Eve." I rushed after her, ready to fight for our lives. Madeline followed me, her hand protectively pressed against my back.

"Don't worry." Eve sighed. "They're dead."

Piled here were what appeared to be giant versions of the frozen turkeys you can buy in supermarkets. The iced poultry forms something like a hard, rounded boulder, shrink-wrapped in tough plastic. This was similar. As many as two dozen human corpses had been piled against the classroom wall, partly obscuring posters of Aztec pyramids. The bodies had been folded up like fetuses. Then they'd been vac-packed. Each body formed a lumpy shape with the limbs scrunched in tight to the torso and the head forced sideways so it lay pressed against the shoulder.

"They've shrink-wrapped their own dead?" Eve was mystified. "Whatever for?"

I crouched to examine an old man in a bag. "They don't know what happens to a human body."

"They need to observe the process of decay," Madeline added. "The Echomen are learning about you."

Eve's eyes roved from both myself to Madeline; the way we answered like a pair of twins reading each other's minds made her uneasy. "Or maybe they just don't like the stink of death."

Madeline reached out to lightly press one of the hard vacuum packs. "Mason and I talked about it. We concluded that Echomen are the product of an alien species. They act like a time bomb to disrupt human progress."

"To prevent us from developing interstellar space travel, which would threaten the security of aliens in neighboring planetary systems."

Eve watched as Madeline pressed her finger against the plastic. A green slime oozed out of the eyes of a shrink-wrapped woman to form a layer between the inner plastic and her dead skin. The liquid made squishing sounds.

Without taking her gaze from the cadaver's face Eve grunted. "Aliens? Remote-control security systems? You two have got it all worked out."

Madeline pushed the plastic membrane harder; the pressure caused one of the woman's eyes to bulge from the head, like a new-laid egg popping out of a chicken's rear. I even heard a muffled *flupp*. The dead were rotting at a furious rate.

When Madeline pressed the shrink-wrapped cheek, causing a black tongue to swim through the lips with all the slippery speed of an eel from its underwater hole, Eve barked, "Stop that!"

Eve shoved Madeline. Okay, so she meant to move my deviant twin away from the vac-packed dead, but Madeline blundered against them, causing one from the top to fall onto the classroom floor. The impact made the bag burst open in a flood of juice produced by putrefaction during the warm spring days. Once the compressive force of the plastic membrane had been released so violently, the arms, legs, and head of a dead youth unfurled themselves.

"My God, it's alive." Eve got ready to fight.

The wave of bad-meat stench punched me in the nose. I reeled back like it really had been a physical blow. Meanwhile, the corpse straightened its arms so quickly the hands splashed into that growing pool of crap that leaked from its internal organs and out through every hole in its body—God-given or other-wise. With the pressure of the chest released, it appeared to suck in air with a tremendous gurgle that had the intensity of a whole bathtub of water being dragged down the plughole. Its eyes pressed out against the eye-lids to deform them into two brown domes; then the eyeballs themselves squirted out just as the woman's had done a moment ago, once more with a loud *flupp*. Clearly gas had built up considerable force inside the corpse; the release of the vacuum pack allowed it to exit, spluttering, sighing, burping, from wherever it had been contained.

The stink hit Eve and Madeline, too. They rocked backward as if hit by a hurricane, their faces screwed tight with nausea.

I gulped. "It's dead . . . get out of here. . . ."

We bundled ourselves chaotically from the room,

with me slamming the door shut behind me so prematurely the bottom of it knocked my heel. That stench hurt a whole lot worse, though. It felt as if I'd poured acid down my throat.

Eve coughed; the flavor of the dead even coated itself on her tongue. Then she pushed Madeline in the chest. That symbiosis again—I felt the bruising shove, too, as Madeline gasped with shock.

Eve pointed the knife at Madeline. "You did that on purpose. You knew the bag would burst open!"

"I lost my balance when you pushed me." Madeline pressed her hand to her breastbone where Eve's shove had hurt her.

"Why touch the damn things, then?"

"To help you. I thought they might have given us clues."

"Clues? You bust one open so the stink would stop us from looking any closer."

"I'm sorry." Madeline dropped her gaze in that submissive way.

"You will be sorry."

"Eve," I panted, "this stench is going to kill us if we stick around much longer."

I hoped she'd take the hint to return to the fresh air; instead, my sister marched upstairs to the top floor of the classroom block. If anything, however, the next floor was worse—much worse.

# CHAPTER TWENTY-THREE

For the moment, leaving the god-awful stink was the only matter of importance as we raced up the staircase to the top floor. It didn't smell like the level we'd just left; it didn't exude the familiar school smell either. This place smelled wrong for different reasons. Aromas of the farmyard rolled into us as we cleared the top step, the kind of stink that makes you think of beasts sleeping in none-too-fresh hay. Although Eve hadn't voiced her doubts that the Echomen were the work of a nonhuman race, she'd clearly thought it from her reaction to our statements in the mortuary of shrink-wrapped corpses. What I witnessed now was, for me, evidence that we were dealing with beings that had no morals, scruples, conscience; hell, they hadn't a shred of an idea what pain was. Because the classrooms were full of pain. They housed agony. This was the epitome of torture.

On the top floor of the block a central hallway ran from one end to the other. Leading off from that hallway at regular intervals were classrooms: six of them. The same classrooms where I sat and learned about the history of humanity. Humanity existed here no longer. As for mercy . . .

We moved slowly along the stinking hallway to look in through the glass panes in the doors. In classrooms, bathed in a dirty, yellow light that oozed through closed blinds like pus oozes through a bandage, were figures, around a dozen per classroom.

"Who are they?" Madeline asked.

"Your people, probably." Eve's voice became a whisper.

"Now do you see?" I grimaced. "This is proof. Who-ever did this to them can't be human."

We moved on. At the end of the block lay another stairwell that would take us back to ground level, and that beautiful open window that led to wonderful fresh air, far from this reek of dying men and women.

Eve paused. Through the window in the classroom door she regarded those figures that were nine-tenths dead. Had this been part of a test? Inflict injury. Make a note of their ability to perform tasks with half a face missing or a foot hacked off. Then select another speci-men. Shoot a woman in the guts; time how long it takes her to die.

"My God," Eve breathed. "I wondered why they were so evenly spaced across the classroom; they've been nailed down."

In that rancid light I saw the figures; they either lay on the timber floor or they squatted there. If they lay, they cushioned a head with an arm. If they sat, they raised their knees so they could prop their elbows there, then cradle their heads in their palms. I didn't see any faces. It was as if the weight of those faces ex-erted such a pull that they couldn't lift them from the floor or from their palms. What physically held the fig-ures there were nails, big, gray six-inch nails, as far as I could tell. To keep them positioned tidily in the room they'd been put in two rows of six. Then the Echomen had nailed them to the wooden floor, either through a foot or a hand or both. Nail heads protruded from the tops of feet and backs of hands like metallic tumors. Apart from flies buzzing around to grow fat on the dead specimens there was barely a sound. From somewhere

I heard dripping—big, fat drops splashing onto a hard surface. I didn't investigate further.

"So these are copies of people?" Eve's eyes were large in the gloom.

"They are," I agreed. "But don't ask me where the originals are. They might be dead."

The spectacle of the nailed men and women that remained frozen in the same position hypnotized Eve.

"Hey." I spoke gently. "Eve. We've got all the evidence we need. It's time to go to the police."

She swallowed. "But that means leaving them here. Look at that woman. They've nailed her to the floor by her face."

The metal spike had passed through her right cheek and exited the left to be imbedded in the floor timber. It looked as if she rested on her side with her head to the wood as if eavesdropping on the floor below—but down there the shrink-wrapped dead were silent as the grave (apart from the odd postmortem gurgle, of course). Shadow hid the creature's face: dead or alive? You just couldn't tell.

"Mason's right," Madeline said. "It's time we got away from here."

As I put my arm around Eve to coax her in the direction of the nearest staircase, I glanced along the hallway. Natsaf-Ty stood there. The motionless Egyptian mummy had that watchful appearance, even though his eyes were closed. Although in the gloom, and maybe twenty paces from me, I made out the cracks in the scalp, plus his serene features molded by red skin, which was as arid as the desert that had held him for three millennia. The tip of the tongue protruded between the lips.

What a time for it to happen. What a bloody, unbelievably awkward time. The head tilted slightly to one side. *He's studying me,* I thought. *He's judging me.* That was when I began to understand the purpose of Natsaf-Ty's visits. There was more to this old keeper of the sacred crocodiles than I thought. If repressed aspects of yourself—your inner self, you understand—can manifest themselves in your doodles on newspapers, or in your choice of car, or clothes, or love partner, then that was the bloody awkward, yes, inconvenient moment that Natsaf-Ty's relevance in my life became clear. The old mummy—bandaged loins, withered arms, and all—had seemed like an imaginary companion from childhood. Yet he was more than that. My dusty friend was a projection of those parts of me that I repressed. I'd lived with my grandparents until my mother took me away from them, never to see them again. I, as a child, didn't think, *Oh, that hurts. I don't like what's happening to me.* Back then I couldn't understand this alien emotion. The way you flush something unpleasant down the toilet bowl, so I flushed this unpleasant reaction into the hidden sewer of my mind. Presto! Hey! That mixed-around feeling flushed the pain I felt for myself; it flushed my empathy for others feeling pain.

The shock of losing most of my family—a family I loved—trashed my ability to understand why I grieved, too. Natsaf-Ty was here to guide me through the obstacles of figuring out the way I felt, and to encourage me to say to myself, *Yes, I was hurt and unhappy when we left my grandparents. I loved them. They did nothing wrong to us. So why did we cut them out of our lives?* People like Freud have elegant academic modes for expressing the projection of repressed emotion. What did an ten-year-old know about that? So when I saw the mummy Natsaf-Ty, keeper of the sacred crocs, in his museum case, a little corner of my brain that kept itself busy trying to repair the emotional damage very wisely conjured Natsaf-Ty to me. A mummy who was, in fact, a father figure. He'd sit on his third step from the bottom, I at the top, and we'd talk in those postmidnight hours. His wisdom guided me. His loyalty sustained me. His gentle humor cracked me up—in a lovely way. Say what you like about that gray lump between your ears; it works the best miracles you've ever seen.

All that passed through my mind—housed by that selfsame gray lump—as I encouraged Eve to walk with me to the stairs.

"We've done it," I told her. "Once the police come here we don't even have to explain what's happening; they can see for themselves."

"All this will be over, and we'll be safe." Madeline smiled.

In the classroom a male figure stirred himself. A bottle of water stood against the wall beneath a poster of a temple ruin. His suffering had robbed him of his strength. The struggle to reach the bottle weakened him so much his chin dropped until his face hung downward. The image of broken humanity near death, all he could manage was to reach out that long arm toward the water bottle. Yet he could not close his fingers around it.

I glanced along the hallway. Natsaf-Ty stood there, an immobile red statue clothed in the mysteries of the eternal. *Imaginary friend, you reminded me of the pain I felt. Now that I know that pain, I can understand the pain of that man dying of thirst in the classroom.* That bottle of water—a liquid that could quench the fires in the man's throat—I imagined its cooling wash of sweetness as if I drank deeply of it myself.

"Just a second," I told Eve. Then I opened the door to the classroom. It wouldn't delay us much if I handed the dying man some water.

The instant I stepped into the room all those moribund figures appeared to come alive at once. Although they were nailed to the floor they moved in a single muscular jerk. Those who could turned their faces to me. They should have been strangers. What I saw were half-destroyed copies of my face. Not only that; I saw copies of Eve and my mother, too.

I'd expected to see pathetic expressions and eyes that could barely open. When their eyelids snapped back they revealed a fiery glare. These creatures were angry. What was more, they were angry at me. The woman whose face had been nailed to the floor was nearest. Her hand flew out to grab me by the ankle.

Madeline dragged me out through the door. "Come on; they're waking up!"

We raced for the nearest staircase. This wasn't the one we'd used to ascend to the top floor. But it would be the quickest to the exit. As I ran I looked into the rooms. Duplicates of Eve and me—tortured, broken, maimed duplicates—moved as if a violent life force had entered them. One by one they heaved at the nails that fixed their limbs to the floor.

"It's okay," Eve shouted. "They're nailed down. They can't get us."

"Don't bank on it." Madeline jerked her head toward a doorway. "Look!"

You've seen someone draw a thorn from a finger. Once it comes out it slips smoothly, yet with the relief comes the pain of the spike exiting the flesh. This had something of that resonance. The Echomen that were still alive had begun to exert their strength against the nails holding them down. They had this righteous anger on their faces, as if Eve, Madeline, and I had committed a cruel act upon them. They glared at us as we ran for the stairwell. At the same time they slowly yet surely pulled the nails from the floor timbers—even though the nails were still punched through their own hands or feet.

We reached the stairs and had clattered down at least eight before we saw that more of their shrink-wrapped dead had been piled across the turn in the stairwell—whether it was intended as a barrier or simply a place to store them, I didn't know. With the stairwell blocked, however, we had to go back.

"Use the other stairs!" I shouted, not that I needed to state the obvious. Eve and Madeline had already retraced their steps.

But as we ran back along the hallway, bloody figures staggered from the classrooms.

"Don't stop!" I yelled. "Don't stop for anything!"

# CHAPTER TWENTY-FOUR

In this gloom, figures were a riot of gray faces, shadowy limbs, grasping hands. As the three of us surged along the hallway to the other staircase they shouted at us. In their angry, hurt voices they called, "Eve . . . Mason . . . Mason . . ." Those voices came out of faces that were duplicates of our own—albeit ruined versions. A chaotic whirl of lips that were smeared with blood, bruised cheeks, ripped eyelids. When they raised their hands to grab us, some were still skewered by the six-inch nails that had tethered them to the classroom floor. A face slammed toward me. Even though I tried not to recognize whether it was a copy of me, I saw the blaze of rage in its eyes.

"Mason," the Echoman hissed.

I punched out hard, knocking it down. Madeline fought her way through. Eve used the knife; my God, was she good with it? The sharp edge slit open more than one face, I can tell you. When a mass of hands erupted from the shadows to catch hold of Eve I ripped them from her, breaking the monsters' fingers in the process (and noticing the Y-shaped scars—that old wound I wore as trademark on my own hand). We pushed on by those classrooms that were filled not only with the stench of captive versions of us but that sick yellow glow that had been as feeble as these creatures until our presence roused them into this frenzy of anger.

"Mason!"

"Eve!"

The insistent calling grew louder. Were they trying to kill us? Were they trying to make us stay? Was this an alien expression of affection? For the life of me I didn't know. All I craved was *out*. To get away from these classrooms that had turned into hell on earth. Images of fresh air, open spaces, blue skies nearly drove me crazy. I yelled at these smashed clones with nailed limbs and tortured bodies to get the fuck away from us. If they blocked our escape route I smashed a way through with my fists. I punched heads; I stomped over bodies that were too broken to walk. Eve and Madeline followed. When Echomen held them back I grabbed my sister or Madeline, then bodily dragged them along with me (after grabbing an Echoboy or an Echogirl by the hair, then smashing their face against a wall that might carry a poster of Stalin or Castro).

"Out of our way!" I plowed through them. A geriatric version of me with yellow eyes, white hair, and no teeth lunged forward, his Y-shaped scar visible on his hand as he tried to gouge my face. I shoved him so hard he collapsed under more Echomen streaming out of a classroom.

Eve slipped to the floor.

"I've got you." I lifted her to her feet. Eve's face looked into mine; hers possessed a frame of ratty hair with a rash of oozing zits that turned her right eyelid into a mash of strawberry reds. She was smiling. My fist exploded her face.

"Mason, get down the stairs," the real Eve shouted as she pushed by the replica of herself that I'd just punched.

Madeline, finding her way blocked by the bloody copy that still smiled as she swayed there, gripped hold of the creature's air, then dragged her forward so she toppled over the steel banister. The thing that resembled a ruined version of Eve tumbled through the air to strike the concrete steps twenty feet below with the sound of raw steak being slapped onto a plate.

Even in the heat of that classroom war zone, Eve's glance at Madeline was a telling one. *You wish that had been the real me, don't you? You bitch . . .*

The blue sky glowed every bit as beautifully as I expected. The air was fresher. The grass greener. We gasped with relief as we stood in the lush field and sucked sweet air into our lungs. Inside the classroom block it had been a nightmare of stink, chaotic motion, a kind of inferno of anger and violence. Outside the classroom was peace.

I shoved the screen shut to stop the Echomen from climbing out after us. Madeline snapped a sturdy branch from a tree; then together we rammed it beneath a firmly fixed section of security mesh in such a way that it held shut its loose neighbor.

"It won't hold them for long," Madeline panted.

"It'll be enough." I pulled Eve by the hand. "C'mon! Back to the car."

We raced through the long grass. All around us were more shuttered classroom blocks. What atrocities did those walls conceal? Skulls peeled of skin, nailed genitals, faces dipped in molten metal—imagination fed images into my brain that I didn't want to see. After the gloom of being indoors we shielded our eyes against the dazzling sun as we ran back to where we'd left the car by the main school building.

"Anyone hurt?" I asked as we sped through the deserted complex.

Madeline shook her head.

Too busy making plans to answer, Eve panted, "We've got them. Drive into Tanshelf . . . we'll tell the police. They'll be all over this place inside the hour!"

When we reached the car as it sat there in the sunlight amid an ocean of bushes, we saw that it was occupied. Eve drew the knife; the sun splashed against its blade in silent explosions of silver.

In the front of the car sat two men. One was easy to identify: me. Or at least a version of me. The other was a middle-aged man with white hair. In the back sat a version of our mother.

"Same one that came this morning." Eve grunted. "See the bruising on the face? I did that." My sister sounded so matter-of-fact it was chilling. I did a double take just in case I'd hauled one of the clones out of the classroom block by mistake. No, that was Eve, all right. The real Eve. Anger burned in her eyes at the sight of that second-rate copy of our mother. The copy of me in the driver's seat smiled out through the open window.

"Nice car," he said. "Had it long?" The mutilated cheek told me that this version of me was one and the same that I'd injured with the belt buckle just before escaping the cell. The wound hadn't even begun to heal. In fact, it looked worse. It had become an open mouth of a wound with a gray ring of dead flesh around it, then encircling that a halo of bruising. From the injury oozed a greenish mucus.

Instead of answering his question about the car, I greeted him with, "Looks like gangrene. I'll be a happy man if it is."

"Mason, you mustn't get into a conversation with him," Madeline warned.

"Don't worry; I won't."

The man in the car who wore my face, although one with a wound the size of an egg yolk, pushed his thumb against the side of his mouth—my habit when tense or thinking—and displayed the same Y-shaped scar on his hand. "Any right-thinking person hates it when a volcano erupts and people get killed, but can you stop it from happening? No, you can't. All you can do is deal with the aftermath the best you can."

I growled, "Get out of the car."

He ignored me. "Imagine that what's happening here is a volcano erupting. Five hundred years ago not a man on earth would have been able to explain what a volcano is or what geological forces are involved in its spewing out lava, or chucking out all that ash and poison gas." A trickle of mucus rolled out of the puncture wound on his cheek to creep down his jaw. "You can't explain what's happening to me any more than the fifteenth-century king in his castle could render a scientific explanation of how volcanoes erupt. You, Mason Konrad, don't know the mechanics of how I turned into you. Or how people have been transformed into your mother and sister. Don't look at me like that, Mason. I know you've seen my zoo in your old classrooms." The clone of me smiled back at the clone of the woman who bore me. "We're dealing with the aftermath of a biological eruption. Dormant genes have just gone *kerrump*, and we're working hard to clean up the mess in order to continue with life the best we can. I mean, the last thing I want—or you want—is for anyone to get hurt here."

Eve stepped forward with the knife. "You killed our mother, you bastard."

"Now that you've raised that . . ." The man glanced back over his shoulder. "Over to you, Mom."

The woman who resembled my mother leaned sideways so she could rest her elbow on the car door. "The offer still stands. Leave us alone and I'll come back home with you. I'll be your mother. Things will be just like they were before. No one will ever know what happened."

"Get out of the car!" Eve yelled. "I'm going to cut that face off! You don't deserve to wear it!"

"Big brother," the man said, "exert some sibling authority here. We don't want anyone to suffer."

"That didn't stop you from making us suffer in your jail." Anger flared inside of me. That face . . . I wanted to stick my finger in the wound in his cheek, then rip it open. Even as the mental image flared, my cheek began to itch in the same place as the wound on his face.

Eve advanced on the car, the knife at the ready. "I didn't tell you this, Mason, because things were bad enough, but they tortured Mom."

"I didn't touch her."

"Not physical torture. This *thing* sitting in our car told Mom that he'd cut me to pieces in front of her if she didn't tell him what he wanted to know."

"Look, let's not be unpleasant with one another." The man spoke reasonably, as if smoothing over a spat between old friends. "All I wanted to know was how you did it."

The woman with his mom's face wheedled, "We can be a family again. I'll be your mom."

"Not interested," Eve said.

The man with the hole in his cheek held my gaze. "Did you hear what I said, Mason Konrad? How did you smuggle him into the cell?"

I glanced at Madeline. If she had any idea what I was thinking, she knew I'd attack him. The second man, the one with white hair, merely watched impassively.

Mason Konrad, second edition, my face, my habits, my scar, continued his line of questioning: "In the cell you had a visitor. A figure. I'm certain the pair of you know each other. But what is it? How can a human being move through solid walls to reach you?"

"What's he talking about?" Eve shook her head, puzzled. "What figure?"

"Don't worry about him, Eve." Suddenly I experienced a sense of exultation. "That visitor is an old friend of ours. He's going to destroy these monsters." I pointed at the man in the car. "Including you."

The man with my face smiled. However, uncertainty made it appear forced. So he didn't know who Natsaf-Ty was, or that he was nothing more than a childhood imaginary friend that had taken to visiting me again. That clone of me in the car's driving seat had managed to copy my flesh; what was more, he could pick up some of my emotions. But one thing he could not do was understand that the mental projection—or hallucination, call it what you will—lacked actual substance. Natsaf-Ty was as real as a tree to him. *Yeah, pick the bones out of that, you filthy creature. Burst a blood vessel trying to figure it out.*

My heart pounded as I leaned forward to look the man in the eye. And just for a second I was sitting in the car, looking out at the original of me, and being screwed up inside because I couldn't unravel the mystery of Natsaf-Ty, keeper of the sacred frigging crocodile.

I whispered, "You've seen him, too, haven't you? And you're scared of him."

That Echo of me raised his fist. Clenched there was a knife with a narrow blade fully eight inches long. *So this is it*, I told myself. *We're going to fight it out on the grounds of my old school.*

I hissed at the pair beside me, "I'll grab him. You take care of the bitch in the backseat."

Only it was the Mason Konrad look-alike who caught us by surprise. He turned, then jabbed the point of the knife blade into the underside of the chin of the stranger who sat beside him. With a God-almighty shove he drove the blade up into the man's head. It must have passed through the floor of his mouth, his tongue, then the roof of his mouth and into the sinus cavities.

Maybe the stranger knew all along that this would happen to him, that his destiny was to sit in the passenger seat to wait for the knife to be rammed up inside his skull. In any event, he didn't show much surprise. After blood squirted from the wound, as if his jaw had decided to piss blood, he began to convulse.

"We're going to the police," Eve told the copy of me and the copy of Mom as they climbed out of the car.

"Why don't you do that?" the man answered.

Just for a moment the woman lingered there, as if reluctant to leave. The expression suggested she was going to ask to come with us, but she had a hurt look in her eyes, as if she knew we'd reject her offer a third time.

The man vanished into the green wall of bushes. The creature that pretended to be Mom knew she must go, too, and slipped away into the vegetation. By the time I dragged the knifed man out of the car, several events were taking place at once.

"What are you going to do with him?" Eve asked as I let the stranger sink back onto the lawn.

"Nothing," I replied. "He's just gone and died on me." I ripped up a handful of grass to scrub the big splotch of crimson from the leg of my jeans where the guy's bloody head struck as I tugged him from the seat.

Madeline announced another event that I had been too busy to notice. "The school's on fire."

Eve listened. "Sirens. Do you hear them?"

I clicked my tongue in annoyance. "Those things made plans before we even got here."

A loud bang came from the direction of the swimming-pool block; dark smoke rose in a column.

"They're burning the evidence. The history classrooms are alight, too."

Eve stared at flames bursting through the screened windows. Screams rose in a sustained wail. "We should let them out."

"You've got to be joking. They wouldn't thank us for saving them; they'd kill us the first chance they got."

"But they are proof of what happened to us, Mason. We need them alive."

The sirens grew louder. I grabbed another handful of grass. Bloodstains are stubborn. They don't want to vanish. They want to yell their scarlet truth to the world. *Look! Caught red-handed!*

I shook my head. "We're getting out of here before the police come."

"What? You're crazy. We can show them what happened."

"What they'll see, Eve, are burning buildings and me covered with bloodstains; there's a pool of blood on the car's passenger seat, and there's our friend here, dead in the grass. What are the police going to deduce from that?"

"We can't just run away, Mason."

"Eve, Madeline, get in the car. No, in the back, or you'll end up covered in that stuff."

"Mason?"

"Eve, don't you understand? Okay, so those monsters have won the battle this time. We've got to stay free to win the war."

# CHAPTER TWENTY-FIVE

The car had become a telltale heart, like in the story by Edgar Allan Poe where a murderer is convinced he hears the heart of his victim beating beneath the floorboards with all the force of a drummer pounding at a bass drum. In the tale only the murderer can hear the heartbeat. To him it's a thunderous sound. It's more than a sound, in fact; it shakes the entire universe. So the car—Mom's little green runaround that took her to work and the supermarket—became a latter-day telltale heart. Drive a car with a quart of blood sloshed over the passenger seat; then you'll know what I mean.

As I drove away from my old high school that had flames pouring out of the buildings, including the old swimming pool that had been our jail, police cars and firefighters were surging up the road. Once more my knowledge of Tanshelf's hidden back lanes meant we could avoid meeting the emergency services head-on. Even so, the experience of driving with blood congealing on the passenger seat while Madeline and Eve sat in the back lacked any appeal whatsoever. As I drove my eyes flicked from the road ahead to the brown-red pool on the upholstery that normally accommodated a human bottom. A dozen ravenous flies dove in to feast.

When I sped into the suburbs the blood of the murdered Echoman, the one that my clone had stabbed in the underside of the jaw, appeared to grow bigger. The congealing lumps stood proud of the cloth; indeed, to my eyes they seemed to swell. How long before they became gore mounds that rose above the level of the passenger door to be in plain view of every passerby? Imagination, I know: it's the telltale-heart thing.

"Slow down," Eve told me. "We don't want to draw attention to ourselves."

I drove faster. "The moment anyone sees that blood they're going to be calling the police."

"It looks strange," Madeline said. "There's two of us in the back and you driving, Mason. I should have sat in the front passenger seat. I don't mind the blood."

Eve grunted. "I bet you don't."

In the rearview I saw that Eve had slid along the seat to be as far from Madeline as possible.

"As soon as I can I'll dump the car. First I've got to get us home." The temptation to floor it made the muscles in my foot twitch as it rested on the gas pedal, but that wild, excessive speed really would turn the entire vehicle into a telltale heart: the machine might as well sprout severed arteries and spurt blood all over the road. Instead, I kept the mph down. Minutes later a surge of relief gushed through me as I pulled into the driveway.

"I'll get the garage door." Eve opened the car door before I'd even stopped.

In less than twenty seconds I'd driven the car inside the garage. At least that telltale heart on wheels was out of sight, but it didn't magically make the blood vanish. If the police connected us somehow with the fire at the school, not to mention the corpse on its grounds, they'd find the blood-drenched car in a snap. Suddenly being home didn't seem like a good idea. But where could we go?

For now, my sister tolerated Madeline's presence in the house. Just—only just.

"Mason, I'll allow her to come indoors, but she mustn't come upstairs. Okay?"

"Okay." I nodded. Madeline said nothing, her expression neutral.

"And she's not allowed to touch any of my things. Right, I'm going to shower and change my clothes. The stink of those monsters is still on me." With that Eve went upstairs.

When the bathroom door had closed, Madeline said in a matter-of-fact voice, "Eve hates me, doesn't she?"

"Events have overwhelmed her. All this is going to take some digesting. For God's sake, I'm still trying to understand why there are people out there who are becoming identical copies of us." I sat down at the kitchen table. "What do you make of my doppelgänger? At least I ruined his pretty face." The laugh that escaped my mouth came like a savage bark rather than an expression of amusement.

"You should name him." Madeline filled the kettle.

"I should what?"

"Give him a name."

"He's a monster; why should I do that?"

Madeline regarded me with all seriousness. "If you're going to fight them, you must know your enemy, so you must give him a name. It's a way of taking possession of something if you give it a name."

"But what name? Kevin? Tony? Tone the clone?"

"Nothing flippant. You mustn't underestimate him." She thought for a moment. "Call him Konrad."

"Konrad? That's my surname."

"I know." Madeline spooned instant coffee into a mug. "It's not a name you're going to forget in a hurry, is it?" She glanced out the window. "A van just slowed down as it passed the house."

"It didn't take the Echomen long to come and finish what they started." I locked the door. "Where's the van now?"

"It's not stopped. Do you think it's them?"

"I don't see why not. They're probably checking whether we really are stupid enough to return to the house." I pushed the tip of my thumb into the side of my mouth as I tried to think of a plan. "With luck, this is just reconnaissance."

"Do you think they'll attack? Konrad seemed frightened of the figure in the cell."

"Ah . . ." I smiled. "Konrad, my secret twin. Yeah, he did seem unnerved, didn't he?"

"But who is it, Mason?"

"He's . . ." For a moment I was ready to rattle out anecdotes about old Natsaf-Ty, my childhood imaginary friend, keeper of the sacred crocodiles, but this was Madeline I was speaking to. I was forgetting her nature: she was of the Echo tribe. Could I really trust her, just because she appeared to be on my side? Instead of elaborating I simply gave a knowing wink before adding, "The man who walked through the cell walls is our secret weapon."

As Madeline finished making the coffee I peered around the edge of the window in case the mystery van had returned. It hadn't—instead a young boy stood out on the front lawn, looking directly at me.

Madeline reacted with alarm as I moved. "Mason? Where are you going?"

"They've just pulled another stunt. But I'm not letting them get away with it."

By the time I'd opened the door, the shower of blossoms from the cherry tree was the only evidence he'd been on the lawn. At least it suggested which direction he'd fled. And the boy? Did I think for a moment that he might have been a kid from the neighborhood who'd run onto our lawn for a dare? *No*, I told myself as I pursued him through the bushes, *he's me. Or at least he's me at age ten. The Echomen sent him to screw with my mind. I'm convinced of that.*

The kid—the ten-year-old clone of me—raced through the border of bushes that grew alongside the boundary fence, so now I caught only glimpses of his arm or shoulder as he ducked his way through the branches. Those same branches whipped back into my face; one slapped me right across the eyes, so I blundered along with all the grace of a charging hippo.

"Come back." I growled the order. "Come back. I want to talk to you."

*But do I want to talk*, I asked myself, *or do I want to beat you to a bloody mess? The kid's gone Echo. He might be luring me into an ambush. More of his kind might be lurking in the bushes.* Mental graphics of me falling in agony with a knife blade in my guts exploded into my mind. Right ahead, a high fence where the apple trees grew. The kid would be trapped.

"Stop! I only want to talk!" *Liar, liar, pants on fire.* If I grabbed him this would be evidence to show the police that nature had gone freakish.

Ahead of me, leaves fell where the kid charged through the vegetation. I dragged my knuckles across my eyes to scrape away the water that blurred them. Scuffling sounds, a scrape of foot on wood . . . *Damn, the kid's climbing over the fence.* I slammed through the low branches of the apple tree to find the ten-year-old copy of me rolling over the boards; his legs, body, and head disappeared onto the far side of the fence into the next garden. Only he'd screwed up somehow. One arm was stuck on my side of the fence. I lunged at it.

"Got you!"

I grabbed the wrist. The bones seemed as thin as pencils beneath the flesh of the forearm. Blinking like crazy I managed to focus my eyes. This was what held him: I stared in surprise at a camera that dangled by a strap against the boards of the fence. The strap itself had wedged into a gap where the wood had split. For some reason the kid didn't want to leave without his camera; to continue running all he needed to do was let go of the strap; yet he wasn't letting go. Although he said nothing I could hear him panting with exertion on the other side of the fence. All I could see of him was the elbow, the forearm, and the hand that hung on to the camera strap. By this time the camera swung furiously as I tried to haul the kid back over the fence. And there, right in front of my face, was his hand with that same telltale scar. Just like mine, the scar was a bright red emblem in the shape of a Y.

"Don't struggle," I told the kid, whose face I still could not see. "I don't want to hurt you."

*No? Not even a little bit of hurt? Mason, you know you could twist the boy's thin arm and feel the bones break under the skin. Remember what his kind did to your mother?*

"No," I whispered to myself, "I'm catching you whole. You're coming with me to the cops."

The camera still did the pendulum dance at the end of the strap as I gently yet firmly held the arm while getting ready to reach over the fence so I could capture the boy without hurting him. Only plans don't always go the way you intend.

All of a sudden my right hand that held the boy's wrist jerked upward with such force that it yanked my shoulder muscles. On the other side of the fence the child cried out in pain.

"Stop it, you bastards! You're hurting him."

Clearly someone had grabbed hold of the kid, then hauled him ferociously away.

Originally the boy had no intention of leaving his camera behind—that much was obvious—but this time what choice did he have in the matter? When I pulled myself up to look over the fence he—and whoever had gotten him—had vanished into the trees that clustered at the other side. For a moment I listened, but the only sound was someone mowing their lawn a couple of houses away.

I scooped up the camera from where it had fallen

onto the earth. It was one of the old kind that used photographic film rather than digital technology. Everything about it was manual—you turned a wheel on top to advance the film; the focus could be adjusted by twisting the lens clockwise or counterclockwise; a tiny window revealed the exposure counter and told you how many shots were left on the film, and my God, it was amazing! The instrument appeared to tingle in my hands. I know, I know . . . it wasn't the camera itself—that was cheaply made, not worth a dime these days. It was the circumstances of how it came to me, and who owned it. The boy loved this camera.

This much I knew: the kid was a ten-year-old copy of me. He wasn't even human in the conventional sense. But he must have lavished such care on this clunky old mechanism of cogs and shutters. For whole moments I stood there beneath the apple tree, turning it carefully over in my hand as I examined it with all the rapt attention of someone finding a diamond-encrusted Fabergé egg in their yard. The numbers on the lens barrel had been almost worn away through use, as were the black letters of its maker printed on silver metal above the lens barrel (it was either EDOX or EBCX, not that either name meant anything to me anyway). The thick black strap that had accidentally brought the boy to a dead stop still had the plush, velvety feel of newness. The camera itself, as I said, could have been a worn-out antique. Even the plastic shell of the instrument had been broken, yet the boy—it had to be the boy, I decided—had with such loving care glued the broken parts back together again. He'd even replaced one of the lugs that fixed the strap to the camera with a heart-shaped buckle that must have come from costume jewelry. The whole thing was a miraculous reconstruction of a smashed-up old camera.

But despite the affection lavished on its repair, it was absolutely revolting. The camera belonged to a creature with my face as a child, one of a new mutant breed that had tried to kill me and my sister, and had succeeded in murdering my mother. Through the tiny window at the top of the camera I could see a figure 12. So, Echoboy had taken twelve photographs on a roll of twenty-four. What were the images contained within that camera casing? You can bet your sweet life they weren't of cute puppies, or views of his home, or friends sitting grinning on a wall. This was a camera operated by one of the Echofolk. Wouldn't the photographs be of what obsessed those creatures? Might they record their experiments at the school? The nailed-down clones of my sister and me? Had the boy secretly photographed my mother drowning in the pool? He must have been sent here by Konrad. What for? To screw with our minds? Or to photograph us? Why? For future reference? For wanted posters?

I grew angry. The monsters. The fucking murderers . . .

Or did the boy come here with the idea of photographing Natsaf-Ty? Because it was my imaginary childhood friend that had gotten Konrad so scared. He couldn't work out who the dusty red man was. Okay, Natsaf-Ty didn't exist in the real world, or rather, he existed only as an exhibit in the Tanshelf Museum. But Konrad and the other Echomen couldn't figure it out. Konrad had glimpsed the mental image of the mummified body and didn't have the human cognitive process to understand that Natsaf-Ty just wasn't real. I made him up because I was a scared and lonely kid. And it was either invent an imaginary father figure or sit back and watch my mind flare out under the trauma of being separated from my grandparents, whom I loved.

Now I had the kid's precious camera. The photographs it contained would be revolting. Yet the knowledge that the child treasured this camera so much that it had become an object of mystical power to him stopped me from smashing it against the fence. Even though the touch of it repelled me, this relic that the kid loved so much—that he risked his life for—fascinated me. I've said it before, but it seemed to tingle against my fingers. I'd keep it. I wouldn't let go. . . .

"Mason!" Madeline appeared at the edge of the swath of bushes through which I'd charged just moments ago. "Mason, they're here!" Her eyes were bright with fear. As soon as she'd shouted the warning she rushed back into the bushes as if to find a place to hide; a second later she shrieked in pain. I started forward as I heard what appeared to be heavy bodies shoving through the branches.

"Leave her!" I yelled. "If you hurt her I'll kill you."

"Only us."

I stared as my old buddies appeared—Paddy, Ruth, Dianna, and Ulric. Paddy and Dianna pulled Madeline back by the arms. She struggled, but they were used to dealing with Echomen by now.

Dianna sounded exasperated as she said, "Mason, why did you just leave like that without telling anyone?"

"That shook us up, old pal." This was Paddy. "We didn't know what had happened to you."

Ulric scowled. "And didn't you hear us? We told you not to go home. It's dangerous for your family."

Dianna slipped a noose of bright orange string over Madeline's head, then pulled it tight. So tight, in fact, that Madeline began to choke. Madeline tried to use

the hand with the Y-shaped scar to pull it free but Paddy
pinned her arms behind her. Dianne increased the
pressure. Madeline gagged. Her eyes were full of pain
as her body began to shudder.

The four chatted like old friends who'd dropped by
for snacks.

"At least you're in one piece, old buddy." Paddy kept a
tight grip on Madeline's arms and didn't appear to notice her convulsions as she strangled. "We'd have come
back sooner, but we ran into a friend."

Ruth glanced around at the neighboring houses; she
smiled as she said, "You'll be okay to do the job here. As
long as you stick close to the bushes nobody can see
you from the windows."

Ulric repeated in that mechanical way of his, "We
told you not to go home. It's not wise—not wise at all."

"We traded up to a motor home, by the way." Dianna
increased the tension on the orange string that
cinched Madeline's neck. "It's even got satellite TV. How
cool is that?"

Paddy grinned. "Not to mention the refrigerator.
Hmm . . . ice-cold beer all the way."

"Oh, and we came back for another reason. There's
somebody we'd like you to meet. Nearly done, Dianna?"

"Another couple of minutes. She must have a tough
neck."

That broke the spell. With Madeline's lips turning as
purple as two ripe plums I launched myself at them.

"Stop it! You're hurting her!"

"Hurting? We don't plan on hurting her. We're in the
process of killing her."

"Let her go."

I shoved Paddy back, then dragged the cord from Dianna's hands. With the constriction about her neck re-

moved, Madeline could spew out a whole volley of choking noises.

Ulric's eyes narrowed as he watched me gently remove the noose from Madeline's neck. "What's going on, Mason? Why are you stopping us? She's just one of those things."

As I flung the noose to one side I brandished the camera in Ulric's face. "You'd better listen to me carefully. I've got plenty to tell you. Plenty!"

"And we came here thinking we had important things to reveal to you." Dianna nodded. "Okay. We won't hurt your"—she pursed her lips—"your lady friend. So, Mason, you'd better tell us your story; then we'll tell you ours."

# CHAPTER TWENTY-SIX

So, I did the obvious thing. After telling the four I'd be right back, I went to find my sister so I could introduce her to them. After all, Eve was part of this, too. She would need to hear the information they planned to share with me. Madeline had just about recovered from nearly being strangled, although a red mark encircled her neck where the cord had bitten deep.

Ruth tagged along. "I'll come with you."

"I live here. I'll be fine."

"From the little we've seen it doesn't look fine." She still smiled her permasmile, but her eyes were serious.

"What are you going to do if we bump into a bunch of Echomen? Shout rude names at them?"

"Something like that." Her smile broadened as she

collected a sports bag from where she must have dumped it in the undergrowth when they pounced on Madeline. She showed me the submachine gun lying in the bottom of it.

I smiled. "You could do some wicked name-calling with that."

So we turned the corner and we bumped into Sis. She was having a conversation with the creature who was a duplicate of our mother.

"I can be your mom," she was saying. "Just give me time. I can make it up to you. Everything will be like it was before."

I caught Ruth's eye, then glanced at the Echo. The bruising on her neck told me this was one and the same who had appeared this morning to cook us breakfast as if nothing had happened. Ruth gave a nod, then slipped her hand into the bag to grab the gun. I stabbed a glance at her while mouthing, *No*.

The woman stood at the driveway gate. Behind her neighbor kids cycled their bikes in the afternoon sun. To start blasting lead at the creature would lead to innocent children catching a round or two.

Eve didn't seem to have even noticed I stood behind her on the drive. Or Ruth, for that matter. My sister growled, "You're not my mother. I told you the first chance I got I'd kill you."

What the neighbors made of what happened next God alone knew. Eve advanced on the woman. The way her body language screamed violence I knew my sister planned murder. The creature saw it, too. She fled across the road, then cut along a path between two houses.

"Eve," I called, "there're some people I want you to—"

The red mist had come down on Eve—okay, so it

was metaphorical red mist, but it was dense enough to obscure not only everything in the world apart from the object of her hatred; it clouded reason, too.

"Eve. Come back. Eve!"

But my sister took off with the speed of a gazelle after the monster who pretended to be our mother. In a blur of blue denim she sprinted along the path between the two houses in hot pursuit.

"Eve! Eve!"

And that was what our neighbors must have seen if they were taking a peek through their windows. Eve Konrad apparently chased her mother, Delph Konrad, across the street and into the woodland at the back of the houses. Was this some kind of Konrad family lark? they'd have been asking themselves. Or had the mother-daughter relationship collapsed into raging warfare? I started running after them, then paused as I realized that Ruth ran with me.

"No," I called to her. "Go back and tell the others." I eyeballed the sports bag that contained the machine gun. "But I need that."

"Mason, you don't know how to use one of these."

"I'll figure it out."

If she didn't agree I was going to wrench the bag out of her hands, but she threw it at me. "Make sure the safety's off; then point and squirt."

I weaved between little kids on their bikes as I charged after Eve. Even though there was the temptation to pull out the machine gun so I'd have it at the ready to blast the Mom look-alike, I kept it in the bag. The neighbors might turn a blind eye to what seemed like Eve pursuing longtime resident Mrs. Konrad, but they would absolutely alert the cops if they saw the son toting a submachine gun.

One you were through the gap in the houses, that was where the suburb ended. The path led into a dozen acres of oak and chestnut trees. It tended to be quiet there, but I couldn't rule out dog walkers, or even teenagers indulging in a few beers out of sight of their parents.

"Eve!" Now I yelled as she bounded toward the trees. Ahead, Echo-Mom had vanished into the shadows of a monster oak. "Eve! Leave her! Come back here; you don't— *Damn!*" The shadow swallowed her, too, in a gulp. *Damn it, Eve. What a crazy thing to do—what a bloody crazy thing! Echomen are going to pounce on you.* Even though some raw phrases that described Eve were bursting from my lips, I knew I'd never turn back. Premonitions snapped through my skull. If I didn't catch up with my sister in the next twenty seconds I'd never see her again. Worse . . . hell, a lot worse: I *might* see her again, but like the "Mom" she pursued my sister wouldn't be the same one I'd known for two decades. So I bounded forward like I had springs fixed to my soles, jumping over dumped mattresses, abandoned car tires, builders' rubble because they'd been too bloody lazy to take it to certified dumping grounds. Then I plunged into the shadow ocean, too, beneath the spreading branches. Birds screamed in alarm. A rabbit fled in panic from my thudding feet. Deeper into the forest the garbage assumed a raunchier aspect— hanging from branches were used condoms that had gone all pendulous with the weight of their liquid cargoes pooling in the teat; then there were the withered remains of cannabis roaches, and lying on a bed of purple toadstools were the remains of a bong made from a plastic bottle. Beneath the branches the air had become heavy with that musky smell of wild animals.

Shadow crept in with a density that was not only blinding but suffocating. Whereas before, in the open, I'd been able to view almost a mile in front of me, now I could see only five yards. Tree trunks crowded together as if they yearned to squeeze human beings out of their space.

"Eve." My yell morphed into a whisper. "Eve. Can you hear me?"

I followed the only obvious route, a path that curved from side to side, so I couldn't see more than a few paces ahead at any one time. Every ten seconds or so a branch would snag the sports bag, nearly ripping it from my hands. "Eve!" My voice rose. It was getting wild in here. The heat grew oppressive. Humidity put a squeeze on my lungs so it was hard to breathe. And at any minute I expected to turn a corner to find Eve lying on the dirt with her blood splashed all around. As I ran I searched through my memories of this place, when I used to ride my mountain bike along these paths. I knew a disused quarry lay at the center of the wood. There were also old mine workings here. The mouths of the pits had been closed up with flimsy plugs of fern, so everyone in Tanshelf knew that if you weren't careful you could plunge through the greenery into a pit deep enough to crack every bone in your body. Those were the kind of pits that were black as the inside of a tomb; they also stank of something that had once been alive but was now going rank and rotten. If you dropped a stone into a pit it vanished into darkness for a long, long time before you heard the thud of rock hitting soft, rotting stuff, or maybe you'd be rewarded with a splash that made you wonder what it would be like to tumble in there to drown in the darkness.

So, as I ran, I kept an eye on the earth in front, in case

it presented that telltale circular depression of soft greenery that would admit you to a whole universe of pain. Consequently, when I happened on the figure I couldn't stop, and slammed into it.

"Hell, Mason! Can't you watch where you're going?"

"Eve?"

She grunted. "You clumsy idiot. You nearly broke my damn back." Still rubbing her spine where I'd charged into it, she pushed me back a step; then she put her finger to her lips. "Shh."

"What's wrong? Have you found the woman?"

My sister shook her head; her eyes were so serious I felt my stomach turn chill. "Listen." She gripped my forearms as she locked eyes with me in a way that reminded me of my mother when she revealed bad news. "I'll show you them if you promise to keep your head."

I laughed despite the situation. "After what we've been through? Of course I'll keep my head. What is it?"

"Remember? Promise."

"Okay, okay. Promise."

She stood back to allow me to move to the edge of the tree line. I knew where we were. This was the old quarry. A deep gouge in Mother Earth where, as kids, we'd throw old refrigerators over the edge to watch them splash in a white mess of destruction as they hit boulders fifty feet below. So there we stood, brother and sister, at the edge of the limestone cliff. Beneath us, the bottom of the quarry was a flat expanse of grass with a turquoise lake in its center.

And there they were . . . the hellborn masses . . . the evidence that told me that all I'd done in life was futile. That I'd lost the war after all. In the Bible there are demons that announce, "I am legion." I always took it to mean that the demons numbered in the thousands or millions, but they were all exactly the same. A mass of identical demons—indistinguishable from one another, indestructible.

And there "I" was: Down there in the quarry beneath me, Mason Konrad. There "I" was and *I am legion*. For in that God almighty wound in the face of the earth was me—or that should be five hundred versions of me. The legion of Echomen all wore my face. I knew they'd all have the habit of pushing their thumb into the corner of their mouths when they were thoughtful. And if I had a suicide wish I could have found a path that led down into the quarry, then, at my leisure, checked each and every hand—and don't you know it? Each hand would own a Y-shaped scar on the back—a fork of red lines etched into the skin.

Eve whispered, "They did this on purpose. They used the woman to lure us here. Mason? Mason, I warned you . . . keep your head. Don't do anything stupid. *Mason!*"

My sister had seen the expression on my face. My eyes went wide and probably somehow lost-looking, as if I had looked into an abyss and seen Satan himself in all his demonic majesty rising out of hell's fire to claim me. As one the five hundred Echomen in the quarry lifted their heads to look at me. Their collective sight hit me like a punch in the face. I gasped as I rolled backward at the force of it. Faces that were identical to mine smiled. And something of their minds reached into mine. Just for a second I stood at the bottom of the quarry gazing up at *the* Mason Konrad standing on the cliff top.

"Mason, don't!"

Eve may have struggled to stop me. Only I don't remember. All I do recall is ripping the machine gun from the bag, then hauling back the bolt. *Make sure the safety's off; then point and squirt.* Ruth's words came back to me clearly enough. That was when I squeezed the trigger. Thirty-five rounds of nine-millimeter ammo snapped out of the muzzle to rip into those mirror images of me down below. Heads burst in splashes of glorious crimson. Nearly a dozen Echomen dropped down dead or dying. The others kept on smiling. You see, I'd killed maybe two or three percent of that evil legion. That was all—a tiny, tiny percentage. They knew it. *They knew I knew it.* Fuck, they knew they'd already won the battle.

"C'mon! Mason, move it. They're coming up the path," Eve shouted, but I ignored her. All I craved was to kill those bastards in the quarry. With luck I might have nailed Konrad, the one I'd stabbed with the buckle pin. God, the satisfaction of wiping that shit off the face of the earth would be substantial indeed.

Eve dragged at me. "Mason, get back home! Didn't you hear? They're coming to get us!"

The words punched through that fog of rage inside my head. The machine gun no longer had ammo. I'd spent it all in one vicious discharge. Okay, I'd butchered some of the monsters. The thing was, four hundred of their surviving brethren were intent on butchering my sister and me. *And here they come.* They surged toward a slope where trucks had once accessed the workings to collect the stone. In a couple of minutes they'd be fighting over what was left of us.

So, thrusting the firearm back into the sports bag, I called Eve to follow me. We charged into the trees to retrace our way back to the house.

"Mason. Eve. Let me be your mother." The copy of

Mom stood in shadow, her face the epitome of maternal concern. "Just say yes; I can protect you from them."

Now it might be Eve's turn to deliver bloodshed. But despite the killer look she shot the woman, she kept running. Once more we were in the stifling atmosphere under the branches. Birds screamed in alarm. Rabbits fled from us. We could see no more than a few paces ahead in that choked world of trees, bushes, hemlock, brambles.

"Mister, I want my camera back." The boy who'd visited me earlier stood beyond a tuft of ferns. "Please, I want it back. It's mine."

Eve goggled. "Mason, that boy looks like you when you were—"

"I know; it's one of those things. Keep moving."

"Please, mister." The boy's eyes filled with tears. I'd never seen anyone look so wounded. "You don't know what that camera means to me. I spent days fixing it. I'll never be able to get another."

I encouraged Eve to move with a pull on her elbow. "Hurry up. They'll soon be here."

"Please, Eve," the boy said, "will you make him give the camera back? I'll be good."

He stepped forward. The mat of green under his feet sagged like it was rubber. A second later it split wide as he tumbled through into the old mine working.

Eve screamed, "He's fallen!"

"Good!" I yelled back at her. "Because I haven't got any bullets left to kill him."

Eve slowed. "You're not going to leave him down there?"

"He's not even human. Come on."

From the trees behind us came the sound of what

could have been a massive engine. But that that deep, deep thudding sound wasn't the result of pistons. These were the feet of hundreds of Echomen coming our way.

"If we start running now," I told her, "then we've got at least a chance of making it back to the house."

After shooting me a frightened glance, she nodded. Then she started to run like she'd never run before.

# CHAPTER TWENTY-SEVEN

Eve and I met Paddy as we ran through the gap between the houses.

"Paddy, where did you leave the van?"

"Just around the corner. We didn't want to attract attention."

"You've got attention now," Eve shouted.

I nodded. "Five hundred Echomen are going to tear along this path any minute." Then I noticed the way Eve looked at Paddy, then me as she ran. "It's okay, Eve. This is Paddy. He knows about the Echomen. He's killed plenty of them, too."

Paddy had one of the sports bags as well. Even though I couldn't see the weapon I knew there'd be one inside. Instead of going for the gun, however, he tossed me a bunch of keys. "Bring the truck up to your house. I'll get the others."

"Make sure you bring Madeline," I told him.

This earned a strange look from Paddy. "You do know what she is, Mason?"

"We'll talk later. Those bastards are going to be here any second now."

Paddy darted back to our house. Eve followed me to the truck at a breathless run. Even so, she managed to pant out questions. "You knew about these things all along? Why didn't you tell me?"

"Echomen aren't easy to explain."

"Mason? It cost the life of our mother!"

"I didn't know they'd follow me home. I thought I'd shaken them off."

"You should have warned us!"

"Get in the van! They're here!"

Still glaring at me in fury, she scrambled into the passenger seat. "Mason—"

"Not now!"

I started the motor, slammed home the gears. Soon I had the machine roaring up the street to the front of our house. By this time Echomen streamed along the path from the woods into the suburbs. Not only were they an invading army, they all wore the same face. Mine.

"Why aren't they attacking us?" Eve asked. "What are they doing?"

I watched them running into the gardens of other houses in the street.

"Oh, my God," Eve whispered, "they're going after our neighbors." Then her voice rose into a yell. "And it's all your fault, Mason! You brought them here!"

Paddy, Ruth, Dianna, Ulric, and Madeline sped up the driveway, then piled into the back of the van.

Eve turned on them. "Are you fucking cowards or something?"

Ulric fired the order: "Mason, drive."

Eve couldn't believe what she'd heard. "You've got

guns. I saw them. Stop them from attacking our neighbors—kill them!"

In that frigid Nordic way Ulric stated, "There are too many of them. They'll kill us, too."

So I drove. I hated myself. I hated Ulric. But what else I could do? The hundreds of Echomen would over- whelm us in seconds, even with our machine guns. So, yes, I drove. As I drove I saw monsters that wore copies of my face drag innocent people I'd known for years into their houses—what they'd do to them indoors was a question I didn't want answered.

Dianna peered through the windows in the rear doors as I quit the suburbs in a swirl of exhaust fumes. "We used to think Echomen were stupid because they were so easy to kill. Now they're changing. They've upped their game."

Ahead of me a figure stood at the side of the road. When so many people look like you, how do you tell them apart? Most I couldn't. This one was different. Even though he smiled at me I saw the wound in his cheek. The one I'd made when I punched the belt buckle pin through his flesh. It still oozed a sticky, green pus down his jaw, not that it appeared to pain him at all. I slowed down in preparation for crushing the monster with the truck.

In that monotone Ulric said, "Keep driving, Mason. Ignore him."

"That's the one that killed our mother. Shoot the bas- tard or I'll ram this heap of shit right into him."

Paddy gripped my shoulder. "We can't do anything to draw attention to ourselves."

"Jesus Christ, Paddy. Five hundred copies of me have just slaughtered an entire neighborhood. Don't you think I've gotten myself well and truly noticed?"

"It's going to take time for the police to act. We've got to put distance between that back there and us."

"You are cowards," Eve hissed. "If you'd killed some of them they might have backed off." When nobody replied Eve turned on Madeline in the back of the van. "You enjoyed watching innocent men, women, and children being slaughtered, didn't you?" She tried to strike her but Madeline sat too far away. "I said you enjoyed it, didn't you, you fucking bitch?"

"Hey, Eve!" I shouted.

As Eve sat with her face buried in her hands I drove past the monster who wore my face on the front of his skull. As he smiled he gave me a casual salute. And all I could do was drive on.

A moment later Ruth leaned forward. "Mason. I'm sorry. But this situation has gotten bigger and more dangerous."

I grunted. "Tell me about it."

"We aren't beaten yet, though. The world out there, even though they don't know what's happening, is depending on us to save them."

"Our army numbers all of seven. That doesn't amount to much, Ruth."

"Six," Eve snapped. "Madeline doesn't count."

There was a beat; then Ruth added, "That's why it's important we stay in one piece. But there are more of us. We're going to take you to meet someone who has been fighting Echomen for longer than we have. She knows what we have to do."

After that the only talk was Ruth giving me route directions. Pretty soon we were out of Tanshelf, driving north into open countryside toward where they'd hidden the RV.

Paddy certainly could pick his times. He must have been thinking about this until he couldn't take the internal pressure anymore. "Mason," he said in a low voice. "You and Madeline. What's the story?"

# CHAPTER TWENTY-EIGHT

Eve answered for me, not that I wanted her to, not in a million years, because she announced, "Mason and Madeline were locked in the same cell together. They became very close. Isn't that right, Mason?"

I cast a glare back at my sister.

She continued in lighthearted tones, even though she was sinking blades into my back. "They formed a bond. They're inseparable now. Although you've seen what she is, haven't you?"

I growled, "Eve."

Madeline folded her arms across her chest, a posture of defensiveness. Even though she didn't speak her dark eyes flitted from face to face, especially to Eve.

And speaking of sister, dear sister, she went on: "I repeat, you've all seen what she is, haven't you? Madeline is a female version of my brother." She ruffled my hair as though I were five. "See those jeans and the T-shirt the monster's wearing? Mason gave her those. She's probably even wearing his underwear."

"Eve, that's enough!"

Even Ruth was stunned—the same Ruth who took bloodshed in her stride with a smile on her face. "Dear God, Mason, is that true?"

"No! Well, yes . . . it's true about the clothes."

"Hell, Mason. What were you thinking?"

"But it's not true about the underwear."

Paddy whistled. "Commando?"

"Look, there's nothing between us. . . ." I realized this sounded all wrong—worse, they were making their own assumptions about Madeline and me. "If you give me a chance to explain . . ."

"Hey, Mason." Paddy laughed, but he wasn't amused. "Do you want me to explain the meaning of incest?"

"It's not even fucking incest," Eve snapped. "It's narcissism taken to the ultimate. What my brother is doing is loving himself."

"Listen," I began. "It's not—"

Ulric rode over me. "That is evil."

"It's not bloody natural," Paddy added. "If you want to get all romantic with yourself there's good old-fashioned masturbation, you know? That's cool; everyone does it. Schoolteachers, cops, Supreme Court judges, pastors, chefs, presidents, even the dentist who puts his fingers in your mouth—we all choke the monkey now and again."

Dianna eyed Madeline. "We could just push her out through the back doors."

"Hey! Listen to me!" Before anyone could interrupt this time I jerked the steering wheel, causing the van to lurch; my human cargo bounced off the vehicle's walls. "Now, you hear what I've got to say. Yes, I gave Madeline my clothes, because those bastards shoved her into my jail cell naked. I did consider giving her clothes that belonged to my mother or my sister, but Eve would have exploded at that. So I believed I was being considerate of my sister's feelings." My voice softened. "Especially as she's gone through hell recently. Another thing: Madeline isn't like the other Echomen. She doesn't harbor malicious intentions toward us. She also saved Eve's life."

This seemed to settle my passengers down, because they didn't say a word for a while; they were thinking about what I'd said. This seemed a good moment to advance my manifesto. "That's why I don't want any of you ill-treating her. That goes for you, too, Eve. Besides, we've got a golden opportunity here to understand one of these things firsthand. Madeline might be able to teach us something about their nature. Does everyone agree?" Absolute silence—apart from the motor, that is. I gave the wheel a dance, which in turn gave the van a merry jive. Grunts sounded as those men and women hung on to prevent themselves from being bounced against the metalwork. "I asked, does everyone agree?"

"You're asking us to trust Madeline?" Dianna sounded doubtful.

"That's a big request," Paddy said.

"Okay." I held the van steady. "How long until we reach your friend with all the answers?"

"About an hour."

"Good, I'll tell you what happened to me since leaving you last week. Then you decide. Okay?"

Behind me they must have been shooting questioning glances at one another; then one by one they said their okays. I noticed Eve awarding Madeline a hostile stare, but she didn't disagree.

So as we rode the straight highway between fields of corn, the sun burning down, I related those incidents over the last few days that had hit me with all the subtlety of cannon shells. I described the ride with the Elvis-ish trucker who steadily turned into a Mason Konrad look-alike. After that came the peaceful spell at home before being hauled away in the dead of night to a makeshift jail built in the swimming pool. Either by accident or malevolent design the Echomen had constructed their prison at my old high school. Then I took great care to explain how Madeline had been dumped into the cell with me, how she'd gradually changed into a female version of me, but . . . *but* . . . she wasn't hostile to humans, that she was different from the other Echomen, and . . . *and* . . . I did not engage in any perverse jiggery with her.

"She's as much a victim of this as we are," I added, revving the motor to underline the statement. I finished off by describing our return to the school the following day—Eve, Madeline, and me—the discovery of the shrink-wrapped dead, our tortured clones in the classrooms, and how the Echomen appeared to be testing their own kind to destruction, maybe trying to uncover the weakness and strengths of the human form. Oh, and I mentioned something about the telepathic links, but I didn't have enough evidence to elaborate on it. Rather than the transfer of rational thought it seemed more like an empathy of physical feelings with the briefest of flashes of what the Echomen saw.

Then I clammed up. As I did so I glanced into the rearview to check the reaction of my audience. One person who did look at me strangely was Madeline, the one I least expected to regard me quizzically. However, I figured she must have been asking herself: *Okay, Mason has just given them a thorough retelling of all that happened to us. But why didn't he mention the stranger? The one who walks through walls? The apparition who frightened Konrad? Why did Mason neglect to mention it?*

*But there's a reason for everything, Madeline,* I thought. *The same reason I haven't explained the nature of Natsaf-Ty to you.* With Natsaf-Ty still a secret I had the reassurance of an old-time poker player with a derringer secretly tucked inside his boot. I glanced at her again, just in case that rudimentary telepathy of ours had projected those thoughts into her head. However, she wore a blank face right at that moment. If she had detected anything going through my mind she didn't let on.

"Okay," Dianna said, "for the time being I say we trust Madeline."

"For now. Okay." Ulric bordered on the reluctant.

Ruth nodded. "We can suck it up and see for twenty-four hours."

"I'm fine with it if you are," Paddy added, some of his old heartiness returning. "Anybody got anything to eat? I'm starving."

"There's gum."

"Chewing gum is cheat-eating." Paddy rubbed his stomach. "Just scream out loud if you see a drive-through."

Eve stared at him. "At a time like this? You want to eat?"

"Welcome to our magical realm, Miss Konrad." Paddy sounded lighthearted to sweeten a bitter pill. "From now on it's always 'at a time like this.' We grab food when we've the opportunity, because sometimes you miss dinner for days at a time."

Eve pressed her lips together hard but said nothing. A cold fury burned in her eyes.

*She's angry,* I told myself. *At me first. Then Madeline. Then the Echomen last of all. No, scratch that.* Last of all she was angry at Ruth, Dianna, Ulric, and Paddy. Come to that, you could add God, or Mother Nature, or whoever was responsible for human biology. Right at that moment, my sister held an ice-cold fury in her heart for lots of things.

I switched on the radio. Straightaway a news bulletin report blasted from the speakers. "We're receiving reports of a series of attacks taking place in a Tanshelf suburb. Details are sketchy at the moment, but police are looking for a local man who lives on the street where the incident took place. He's described as being in his late twenties, with dark hair and a slim build. Authorities refuse to release his name at this stage, but a neighbor told our reporter that he'd returned home only recently after working away."

Eve groaned. "Oh, my God."

I glanced back, thinking she'd reacted to the radio report. Instead she stared through the windows set in the rear doors of the van.

"Eve, what's wrong?"

"We're being followed."

"Police?"

She shook her head. "It's one of those things—an Echoman."

Paddy frowned. "How can you tell?"

"Bloody obvious, really. It's driving our mother's car."

"The green hatchback?"

I clicked my tongue. "They must've grabbed the car the moment we took off."

Ulric lifted the sports bag onto his lap. "We're not going to outrun the car in this. I'll get rid of them."

I glanced at the bag with the gun muzzle pointing out. "We can't draw attention to ourselves, Ulric. If you let fly with that cannon you'll bring the police down on us in no time."

"Police would be a good thing, wouldn't it?" asked Eve.

"Think about it, sweetheart." Paddy smiled. "The cops know about what happened in your neighborhood. Your brother's the prime suspect, so they're going to keep you locked up until they get answers, but what happens if the cops start turning Echo on you?" He shrugged. "I can even spell what'll happen in six letters: U-R-D-E-A-D."

"You think I'm just a kid, don't you?" Eve's cold anger suddenly turned hot. "To you I'm just Mason Konrad's stupid little sister."

"No, I didn't mean that; it's just—"

She spoke with force now: "Ulric. Don't fire on them. Mason, take the next left."

"It's just a dirt track."

"I said, *next left*."

If you're a guy and you've got a sister—an older one or a younger one; it doesn't matter—and if your sister uses *that* tone of voice on you, believe me, to ignore her is to do so at your peril. I turned left.

"Slowly," Eve hissed. "Pretend you haven't seen him."

"Is it Konrad?"

"Konrad?"

"He's the leader—at least, he seems to be." For the first time in ages Madeline had spoken. "You've seen him. The one with the face wound. Mason did that." She voiced the "Mason did that" so proudly I felt everyone stare at me.

"Madeline suggested I award him my surname, Konrad. Now it gives me something to take back from him." I clenched the steering wheel so tightly my knuckles whitened. "When I catch up with him."

The van bumped along the track. Overgrown bushes scraped their limbs along the flanks of the vehicle.

Eve leaned forward until her head was level with mine. "Not too far. Just around the corner, then stop. He won't see you until the last minute."

Ulric nodded. "Then I'll take care of him."

"No, you won't," Eve told him. "I will."

"You?"

"Give me the gun."

"You know how to use a firearm?"

"Guns are designed to be used by even the stupidest people. Don't you ever watch television?"

"Even so—"

"Besides, I go skeet shooting."

"But not with one of those," Paddy pointed out as Ulric eased the black submachine gun from the bag. "That's a widow-maker."

Eve didn't waver. "You told me that fighting Echomen is going to be my life from now on." She held out her hand for the weapon. "If there's got to be a first time for me killing someone"—she shrugged—"let this be it."

Ulric frowned. "Do you think killing is as easy as in the movies? Bang-bang, drop down and play dead?"

"Instead of patronizing me, give me the gun. Then sit back and watch what I've got planned for him."

# CHAPTER TWENTY-NINE

Dianna said, "Eve's right, Ulric. She's got to do it sometime."

"No," I told them, "she's not ready."

"Like I said, Mason. Watch me." Eve held out her hand for the gun.

"We're here with Eve." Ulric handed her the weapon. "We can help her if she makes a mistake."

"I won't." She grasped the gun.

As I brought the van to a stop after the next bend in the track, Ulric quickly showed Eve how the machine gun worked. Despite my misgivings, my sister was right about one thing: most guns aren't even as complicated as food processors: just point the hardware, then shoot. Your target's gonna get a gutful of hot lead. Of course, it takes expertise to hit distant targets, or ones concealing themselves, or moving fast, but at short range . . .

*Okay, quit babbling*, I told myself. *You're nervous at what your little sister plans to do. Just get this thing over and done with.*

Now the sequence moved fast. Van stopped. Eve outside. Gun in hand. Ready for the car, complete with unsuspecting Echoman driver, to buzz around the corner to present himself at point-blank range.

The rest remained in the van as Ulric and I followed Eve as far to the back of our vehicle; there we paused as Eve ran as far as the blind bend in the track. A moment later she took up a position with her back to the bushes, and just a couple of paces from the dirt road itself. Sure enough, four seconds later Mom's old green car came skidding around the corner. Due to the sharpness of the bend its driver didn't see the truck blocking the way until the last moment. He stomped the brakes; the car's tires skittered over loose stones. In a cloud of dust the car stopped just feet from the back of the van. Then all this happened fast, only when I recall it now the memory glides into a weird, slow-motion fantasia of bloody images. First I remember with a glittering clarity that the Echoman sat at the wheel. Don't you know it, he regarded me in the mildest way, something like seeing an old friend where you didn't expect to find him. His hands held the wheel in a ten-and-two position. The Y-shaped scar was there, carved into the back of his hand, a fucking stigmata that's haunted me since my teenage outburst of rage at my friend. Now some stranger wore it on his flesh—but did he bear the significance of it carved into his conscience? You bet your bloody life he didn't. This was one of those monsters: an Echoman. Whether Konrad sent him to find out where we were going or to kill us was moot, because that was the moment Eve leaned forward, the submachine gun in her two fists. The surreal kicked in. *Just for a split second I'm the Echoman sitting in the car looking out at me; Ulric stands beside the truck. In the shade of a tree to my left is the dusty old gentleman. Natsaf-Ty had arrived to witness what happens next in this normally peaceful country lane. The Egyptian mummy stands there without moving. His closed eyes "gaze" at the scene as it plays out. Even from here I make out the tip of his tongue protruding between his lips.*

Then, with a sound savage enough to scatter birds from the branches, the machine gun in Eve's hands kicked into life.

"Your sister has missed," Ulric announced.

I grimaced. "Oh, no, she hasn't."

The burst of bullets struck the guy's hands as he gripped the steering wheel. That flight of slugs traveling faster than the speed of sound disintegrated the knuckles while his fingers simply burst into red mist. In surprise he lifted his arms to stare at their mutilated extremities. Eve opened the driver's door before grabbing the guy by his shirt collar in order to drag him out.

Even though lifeblood pumped hard from what remained of his hands, he kept himself from falling flat. Instead he shouldered Eve aside, then began loping across the field. That gave me further evidence that Echomen who were copies of me were capable of seeing Natsaf-Ty. The Echoman reacted to the silent red figure by veering away to run parallel with the track.

Ulric has this permafrost personality. He rarely reacts with surprise, but Echoboy's odd change of direction puzzled him. "Why did he run back to the track? What has he seen?"

So, Natsaf-Ty was invisible to Ulric. But then, isn't that the way with imaginary friends? Ulric saw only an open field and a tree; for him there was no three-thousand-year-old mummy in a scanty garb of a few bandages.

Ulric recovered from his surprise enough to intone, "I should have brought my handgun. We'll face added problems if he escapes."

He'd barely gotten the word *escapes* through his lips when Eve fired another short burst. The bullets ripped up a flurry of grass around the Echoman's feet. Instantly he fell flat on his face in the meadow. His feet had suffered the same kind of damage as his hands. Nevertheless, he still tried to use his shattered hands to push himself upright so he could stand on his bloody feet. He managed it, too. Until Eve caught up with him. One-handed, she pushed him back down to the ground.

By the time Ulric and I had reached her she'd begun interrogating him. "You were following us. Who sent you? What had you been ordered to do?"

Behind us, Paddy, Dianna, Ruth, and Madeline

spilled from the van to join the party. Beneath his tree Natsaf-Ty looked on.

Meanwhile Eve persisted. "Listen to me." She aimed the gun in the center of the man's face. "What were your orders? Were you told to follow us? Or to kill us?"

"Sorry, my sweet," Paddy told her. "They never respond to questioning."

Ruth nodded. "Strictly speaking they're not human, remember?"

Madeline's eyes were wide. I guessed what was going through her mind. Here was Eve, my sister, getting extremely annoyed with a man who resembled me so closely he could have been my identical twin. . . . No, worse than that. The bloody figure on the ground could have been *me*. Eve's eyes blazed in her head as she jabbed the copy of me with her toe.

"Was it Konrad who sent you?" All he did was stare with a pair of large brown eyes, as if she gabbed in a foreign language. "I know you understand me. So talk."

No reply. She squirted a couple of rounds into his knee. The pain jerked him four feet in the air. From the force of his scream we knew that had hurt him.

Eve aimed at the other knee. "Konrad sent you, didn't he?"

*"I'm saying nothing!"*

"Ha." Eve gave a cold smile. "You just did."

"I'm not telling you anything."

Despite the wounded guy insisting he wouldn't reveal any details, Ulric was impressed enough to give a whistle. "Congratulations, Eve. This is the first time I've heard one compelled to talk to us."

Dianna shrugged. "Something tells me we're not going to learn anything from him."

"On the contrary," Eve said. "He's going to teach us plenty." Another couple of rounds exploded his right kneecap. Once more the guy howled in pain.

Even Paddy turned pale. "Finish him. He won't say anything worth hearing."

Echoboy had bitten his tongue in his agony; pink blood frothed from the mouth (my mouth—or that was what it seemed like as I thought, *I'm watching my sister torture a man who looks exactly like me: I'm making mental calculations about this, which add up to me being increasingly uneasy*). She fired another bullet into his thigh. That pool of crimson had grown until the man appeared in danger of drowning in it.

Paddy had a note of pleading in his voice. "Eve?"

"Listen." She fired the word like she had fired bullets into Echoboy. "If he says nothing I'm not wasting my time here. We know that these things form a rudimentary telepathic link with whomever they copy. This monster is a clone of my brother."

I raised an eyebrow.

Eve pressed on. "So if you kill them outright, what chance have we got of learning anything about them?" Her eyes swept to my face. "Mason, I've inflicted enough damage; can you pick up anything he's feeling?"

I tried. But all I saw was my facsimile groaning at our feet.

Eve nodded. "Okay. Anything now?" Her next shot smashed an elbow. Blood vented from torn arteries.

"Nothing," I told her as I asked myself, *How far is Eve going to go with this? Is this torture by proxy for my failing to warn her and Mom about the Echomen? Was it for Madeline's benefit? The message being, See what I'm doing to this Echoman? Watch out. You might be next.*

Ruth appeared uneasy, too, for other reasons. "Although we can't be seen from the road here, it's still too open for my liking. It's time we tidied up and moved on."

Eve had only three or four rounds left in the machine gun. At point-blank range she discharged them into the Mason look-alike's stomach.

Ulric disapproved. "The head or heart would have been best."

As the Echoman curled up into a ball he made disgusting grunting sounds.

Eve shrugged. "I don't care if he takes all week to die."

"I'll get my knife," Ruth said.

"No." Eve handed the submachine gun back to Ulric. "This is research. There's still a chance Mason might form a telepathic link with Echoboy here."

"All I'll get from that," I told her with some venom, "is to feel the pain of the man dying."

"He's not human."

"Nevertheless . . ."

Eve took hold of one of the bloody arms. "Help me drag him into the bushes. He's not going anywhere with his legs in that mess. From what you've told me, these brutes are evolving. If, instead of transmitting emotion and feeling telepathically, they start channeling information, that could give us an edge over them. We might know their plans the moment they make them. Make sense?"

Ulric was impressed. "That does make sense." Almost cheerfully he grabbed hold of the Echoman's other arm to help Eve haul the man into the undergrowth.

"Wow," Ruth breathed. "I'd say that Eve has just made a friend." A knowing smile appeared on her face. "Mason? Does your sister like the tall, Nordic type?"

# CHAPTER THIRTY

After we left Echoboy to his melodious groaning beneath the bushes we headed north. This time Paddy drove while I sat in the back.

Every now and again Eve would ask this question of me: "Mason? Do you feel anything yet?"

"Hungry, tired, ready for a shower."

"You know what I mean. The Echoman I shot . . ."

"Do you mean, can I feel his pain?"

"Well, do you?"

"No. Nothing." In truth, a cold throbbing spread from my stomach to my chest. By whatever medium carries telepathic thought I detected the chill sensation of the man's impending death. Eve had mutilated that monster who was identical to me with so much relish that I decided that to admit to sharing his suffering would give her satisfaction; therefore, I kept silent. You're right: sibling conflict can be an ugly thing.

Ulric, on the other hand, continued to marvel at Eve's treatment of the guy. "In the future," he said, "we should consider whether we need to destroy Echomen outright. If possible we should capture a specimen, then conduct our own experiments."

"You mean torture?" Madeline rarely spoke, but her own anxieties were surfacing. "How can torture ever be considered justifiable?"

"Your kind are monsters." Eve regarded Madeline coldly. "So it's impossible to describe us as inhumane.

We'll do whatever's necessary to extract the information we need to survive."

I knew what they were thinking as they stared at the female version of me. "Madeline's not like the rest of them," I insisted. "We might discover that there are more of them that can become our allies."

Eve responded with, "Madeline isn't here for a drive in the country. She has to accept that we'll be watching her. She might increase our knowledge of the enemy."

"You're not torturing her. That's final." I glared at the others in the truck as they stared back at me. "Eve, Madeline saved your life. You owe her."

"Do I really?"

Now the rest appeared uneasy at the animosity surfacing between brother and sister.

Paddy called back over his shoulder as he drove, "You're very much alike, you and Eve, did you know that? Two chips off a block. And you know something else? I'm not easy to frighten, but the pair of you scare the Holy Ghost out of me. No wonder Echomen want to become copies of you. You stop at nothing, so if they become you neither would they." He grimaced. "The pair of you are angels of death."

Look. Everyone's entitled to enjoy themselves. Nobody can survive in a permanent state of anxiety that would make even a psycho's eyes leap out of his head and fly across the room to pop against the wall. So what I did next I did to release the emotional pressure that was building inside of me. You might determine that how I acted was wrong. Or even insane. But I did it. I did it because I had to. You judge whether it was an act of madness or salvation.

# CHAPTER THIRTY-ONE

I met her in a place called the Tavern o'er the Well, where she worked behind the bar. It happened in one of those villages that had been prosperous once, but paint peeled from the houses and nobody seemed to care anymore. When she said to me, "You're not from around here, are you?" I'd replied, "I'm just passing through." Her heartfelt response had been, "Lucky you. I'd do anything to get out of this dump. *Anything.*"

So there you have it. Madness arrives. Right at that very moment I decided to hunt that woman down. Not in a murderous way but out of animal lust.

The events of the last week turned my blood into a boiling mass of anger, frustration, you name it. What the Echomen did to my mother whipped me into a killing frenzy—I wanted nothing more than to slaughter every last one of the monsters. Yet when I saw this woman in the tavern, something worked a transformation on all that rage. Like alchemists labored to turn lead into gold, so all that fury became a craving to nail that woman to the bed. By God, I lusted for orgasms. I craved to feel that pent-up emotion gush out of me. So with murderous rage transmuted into desire I stayed at the bar and chatted to Scarlett. The tavern was so dowdy in an everything-a-shade-of-brown kind of way that Scarlett had transformed herself into the epitome of feminine glamour. All soft, beautiful curves, golden cleavage, shining red hair. At that moment, for me, she appeared like the goddess of love. Even her perfume seemed a breath of paradise.

"I've never asked a man this before," Scarlett murmured over the bar to me, "but would you like to come home with me tonight?"

I maintained eye contact with her, yet it was as if a sixth sense of mine mapped the curves of her body beneath that clinging white top of hers. Nodding, I told her I would.

As she went to serve another customer their beer, I turned to a figure standing in the shadows at the end of the bar. "What are you looking at? Never seen a man and woman planning to have sex before?"

Natsaf-Ty had a real talent for following me. I only hoped he'd keep his crusty old nose out of my business in the hours to come. That business would be an erotic entanglement. I didn't want a three-thousand-year-old Egyptian mummy as a voyeur. Imaginary or not.

When I crossed the courtyard at the back of the Tavern o'er the Well, a man stood watching me from an archway in a wall.

Without pausing, I grunted. "Can't you take the hint and clear off?"

"Just how many have you had, Mason?"

"Paddy?" At first I thought Natsaf-Ty had returned.

"The others were wondering what had happened to you."

"Just enjoying a beer or two with a new friend."

"A beer or two? Aye, and the rest." Paddy stepped into the light. "Come on, old pal; I'll walk you back to the van."

"I'm not sleeping in any stinking crap wagon tonight."

"Mason." He moved as if to take my arm so he could guide me.

"I'm not drunk," I told him.

"No, you're not," he agreed too readily. "But we'll head back to the van. Might not be too safe around here."

"Fuck the Echomen. Fuck the van. Fuck you."

I left him standing there, staring after me. Paddy may have worn an expression of hurt, but that might have been a product of the same imagination that conjured the dusty old gentleman Natsaf-Ty to watch me with that quizzical air. *Fuck that.*

The church clock beat the chimes of midnight. From Scarlett's directions her house was easy to find. The first one in a row beside the village pond. In the dark the stagnant water evoked an image of a big, wet eye staring up at the stars.

Okay, Paddy had been right to figure I'd had a good many beers, but I felt sober as a nun. Maybe I didn't harbor nunlike thoughts, though. Scarlett had managed to leave work early to get ready for my arrival. And I arrived at the red door of her house as lustful as a wolf.

Before I knocked she'd opened the door so I could slip inside. When I began to talk she put her finger to her lips. In the gloom I saw she wore a kimono of dark green silk. It had the same smooth coolness to my touch as her lips when they lightly pressed against mine. But that almost nonsexual kiss abruptly blazed into passionate mouth-on-mouth. Her fingers raked through my hair before she held on to the back of my neck to maintain the kiss until both of us had to break away gasping in the end. By this time my heart was pounding. What seemed like flows of lava jetted into my bloodstream. That heat sped down into my belly.

That heat went nuclear as I saw the way her eyes flashed in the gloom of the hallway—those eyes were so full of joy and laughter and, make no bones about it, an eagerness for sex.

A moment later she climbed the stairs. My heart pounded as I followed with a picture in my mind of a king-size bed up there with cool, clean sheets. Just the thought of the mattress waiting for our arrival fired up the nerve endings in my groin. However, I'd ascended only as far as the third step when she stopped me from going farther. A dizzying swoop of disappointment rushed through me. *She's changed her mind,* I thought. *Scarlett's going to say, "Sorry, this is a mistake. I want you to leave."*

Instead, however, she touched her lips again for silence. Then, in a whisper that was so soft I could barely hear it, she said, "Stay there. We're not going to rush this."

Her perfume, her beauty, with that red hair tumbling down the green silk kimono, her body language . . . listen to this: I was captivated. I found myself sitting on the third step from the bottom so I could gaze up at her in the gloom. Even at that moment a little part of me realized I'd adopted the same pose (and the same riser— third from the bottom) as Natsaf-Ty when he used to visit me at home when I was a child. Now here I was gazing up at the woman as she danced her way to the top of the stairs.

Don't let me hear you utter the word *seamy*. Something inside her knew my spirit was in need of repair. Intuitively she understood how to mend the damage. Her eyes glinted as she shot me provocative glances. In that soft whisper of hers she sang to herself as she danced for me at the top of the stairs. With her back to me she eased the kimono off one shoulder to reveal bare skin, then eased it back up before sliding down the garment to reveal the other naked shoulder. Still with her back to me she opened her kimono. If I'd been in front I'd have seen what she revealed. From the back I saw the garment resemble a pair of vast silken wings. Then, closing it again, she turned sideways before extending a leg forward, the toe pointing, until I saw as far as the stocking top midway up her thigh. The woman knew. She stoked erotic fires inside me until they were incandescent. By postponing the moment of full sexual contact she heightened the anticipation. And I gazed up at her as if she really were the goddess of love.

Then the dance ended. She turned her back on me, then whispered, "Mason. Come and take me."

All the pain, anger, grief—the truckload of emotions that had been boiling inside of me—were channeled into that orgasm. Every muscle in my body pulsated to the rhythm of me driving into Scarlett's body as she lay there under me. Fireworks, explosions, a sense of discharging more than semen, but electricity, a weird but wonderful—oh, so fucking wonderful—electricity. There were torrents of sensations that made me forget entirely about who I was and what I'd experienced. As I lay down beside the beautiful redhead there was one of those moments of bliss that comes after sex, when you feel as if somehow you've melted into the fabric of your surroundings. There are no concerns. There's only the throbbing ecstasy of living in that moment of *now*.

As we lay panting there, she turned to press her naked body against mine.

"Mason?"

"Hmm?"

"In the morning, take me with you." Her cool lips kissed my chest. "Please. Pretty please."

*How can I refuse?* I told myself, still deep in that sexual glow. *Scarlett can come along. And we can do what we've just done over and over again.* I smiled. Not for a moment did I think about repercussions. For that matter, I didn't consider what the others would say to a new passenger. Madeline, of course, would submissively accept Scarlett into our circle. With a cocoon of warm satisfaction all around me I merely smiled as Scarlett moved smoothly until she sat astride me. A moment later she ground her own body against mine. In the darkness her head formed a silhouette with tousled shadows where her hair had been mussed during our passionate meshing. She took a delicious twenty minutes to bring herself to climax. After that her mouth took over. When at last she lay down to sleep beside me I saw her lazily lift her arm to the glow of a streetlight filtering through the window.

As I drifted into sleep she murmured in a way that was equally drowsy, "Look at that mark . . . I must have gotten lipstick on the back of my hand."

I kissed her hand in the dark, the implication of what she'd seen slipping by me unnoticed at that moment. "Hmm. In the morning we'll shower. And I'll wash it away. Give it my personal attention."

Nearly asleep now, she whispered, "I'll like that." She cuddled into me. "You will take me with you in the morning, won't you?"

*Daylight. Scarlett's bedroom full of people . . . urgent murmuring . . . dry mouth . . .* I awoke with those impressions. Yet even as I opened my eyes to people moving around the bed I thought, *You're still sleeping; this is a nightmare.*

A figure lay on the bed beside me. It was wrapped so tightly in a white cotton bedsheet it had the appearance of a pale grub on the mattress.

"It's all right."

"Paddy?"

"Stay there. We've nearly finished."

I blinked against the glare of the sunlight streaming through the window. Paddy, Ruth, Dianne, and Ulric were in the room. Paddy tied a thin red cord around the ankles of whoever was wrapped in the sheet.

Then the occupant of the shroud couldn't be a mystery. "*Scarlett.*"

Ruth soothed me with, "Don't worry, Mason. It's over. Everything's under control."

Dianna perspired because she twisted a loop of cord from the bedside light around the neck of the figure inside the sheet. When the convulsions in the body stopped she released the noose with a sigh. "That did it." Dianna wiped her forehead with her wrist. "You can take it away."

"It?" I grabbed hold of the cotton fabric that parceled the head. "Why are you doing this to Scarlett?"

"Why do you think?" Ulric's coldness made me shiver.

"No." I shook my head. "She was fine." In disbelief I wrenched at the sheet covering her face.

Ruth pushed me away. "Mason, stop it."

"I've got to see."

Paddy gripped my wrist. "For your peace of mind, forever and ever hereafter"—grim-faced, he held my gaze—"you're better off not looking."

But as they hauled the body of Scarlett away, or what had once been Scarlett, I saw a bare arm slip free of the sheet. Nobody said anything; their eyes said it all when I saw what was on the back of that hand before Ulric pushed it out of sight.

I stared at the same Y-shaped scar on the back of my own hand. For a moment I wondered if my teeth would be strong enough to rip away the skin that bore the revolting stigmata.

They carried off the body in silence. I followed, still buttoning my shirt. As they bundled the corpse into the back of the van that stood just outside the front door I glanced back along the hallway. A door opened at the end of the passageway. What I had assumed to be a downstairs lounge revealed a single bed with a radio standing on a table beside it. A figure emerged from the gloomy interior to move down the hallway.

The man stopped five paces from me. Although his hair was mostly silver he still had red strands there, the same color as Scarlett's. His green eyes appeared to gleam in the dim light as he looked right at me.

"Scarlett?" He reached out. "I heard footsteps. Scarlett, is that you?" He took another step forward, a white-tipped cane trembling in his hand. "I'm sorry I got angry with you yesterday. But it frightens me when you tell me you want to leave home. Scarlett?" His blind eyes roved over me, then across to the kitchen. A note of fear crept into his voice. "Scarlett?"

On the stairs Natsaf-Ty appeared to look down his nose at me as I stepped into the sunlight.

When I walked away the blind man called out, "Scarlett? Where are you?"

# CHAPTER THIRTY-TWO

Later, in the van, a brutal mood pushed its hooks into me. "Why did you have to kill her?"

"You saw her hand." Ruth touched the back of mine where the scar wrought its crimson Y.

"So she'd gone Echo on me. You still didn't have to kill her." I buried my scarred hand inside the other.

I rode in the back of the vehicle with Ruth, Dianna, and Ulric. Paddy called back over his shoulder as he drove, "If she'd woken first she would have killed you. Lucky we got there before either of you woke, old pal."

"Old pal? Don't 'old pal' me."

Ruth began, "I'm sorry that we—"

"Don't apologize," Ulric said in his customary monotone. "We saved Mason's life. He's still under the spell of the woman's vagina."

"Listen," I demanded. "When Scarlett turned Echo she was like Madeline, right? A female version of me?"

Nobody answered.

"Well, was she?"

"Here will do," Paddy announced. He turned the van off the main road into a lane that twisted away into a forest. Nobody looked me in the eye as they dragged Scarlett's body, still wrapped in the sheet, out of the back doors, then dumped it into a ditch.

Once more Paddy drove, the other three in the back with me and the passenger seat vacant.

"I must be popular." My voice was grim. "Everybody

wants to ride with me. Is it my new aftershave that's so irresistible?"

Ulric, the epitome of Scandinavian honesty, responded by sniffing the air inside the lumbering truck. "You're not wearing aftershave, Mason. The woman's perfume rubbed off on you when you were having sex."

"You should have let me see the body."

"Bad idea."

"I needed to see the extent of the transformation."

"No."

Ruth touched my hand again in a gesture of sympathy. "There's no point in worrying about it, Mason. Put it out of your mind."

"Speaking of putting things out of mind, what have you done with Madeline and Eve?"

Again nobody replied.

"Eve hasn't hurt Madeline?"

Ulric appraised me. "Would you mind if she had?"

I spoke doggedly. "Madeline's on our side. She saved Eve's life."

They exchanged those glances again, as if they recalled secret conversations they'd had about me. Perhaps Eve had speculated for their benefit. *I don't know what happened between them when they were locked up in that cell together—naked—but they've become very close.* I pictured the knowing expressions, every single one of them visualizing the mating of man and monster: a monster who was a female copy of Mason Konrad. Very kinky, very Freudian. I punched the metal wall of the van so hard it clanged like a cathedral bell.

"Isn't anyone going to tell me anything?"

"Mason—"

I yelled; "You've left Eve alone with Madeline! Do you

know what my sister is likely to do to her? Do you! And where the hell are you taking me?"

"We've already told you about the safe house," Dianna replied calmly. "Eve's gone ahead with Madeline in the RV."

"That's going to make some road trip." My voice became a growl. "Did you debate how long it'd be before Madeline's butchered by my sister?"

"Madeline's safe," Paddy said as he cruised the truck along the highway. "She's important now. We've realized we have to . . ." He stiffened as he realized he'd told me something he should have kept under mental lock and key.

"You've realized you've got do what—*exactly*?" Rage flowed freely through me again. "I've had enough of you people. Since the first day we met you've never treated me like I was part of your group. You never gave me weapons so I could protect myself. If anything, you behaved as if you were an armed guard escorting me to . . ." Understanding detonated inside my head. "That's it, isn't it? I never was one of you, one of the gang, because I'm cargo, aren't I? I'm a package you're delivering to someone else!"

"It's not like that," Ruth said. But their expressions told me different.

"Who are you taking me to? More important, *why*?"

Ruth gripped my arm. "Mason. They won't hurt you."

I tugged away. "Hey, Paddy! Pull over. My ride ends here!"

Ulric exuded permafrost. "Stop the van? Don't you want to see your sister?"

"Or Madeline?" Dianna made sure her question sounded suggestive.

"Fuck you," I retorted.

Paddy slowed the vehicle. "What's it to be, Mason? Jump ship here or find your sister?"

What else could I say? I sat with my back to the steel wall and my face set like stone.

Dianna smiled. "I figure Mason's decided to stay with us for the time being."

Listen. When you're nauseous, you'll happen upon a dead bird seething with maggots. If you're suffering the leviathan of all hangovers, a neighbor will decide to hammer nails into solid timber. When you slip on a ba- nana skin, it's not only in your best clothes; it's in front of the boy or the girl you're trying to impress with your cool poise—not that stupid flop onto your fanny. Yeah, you get the drift of this. If something bad happens it's never just one thing: there's invariably the complemen- tary package of other woes just to add insult to injury, or *another* injury on top of the original injury. So, where I'm going with this line of thought is, as I sat there, ex- periencing nothing less than fury at the death of Scar- lett, and tormented by questions of how close to resembling me she'd become . . . *and* knowing that Paddy and his gang had duped me; that I wasn't a fel- low member but some kind of package to be delivered to a third party, it . . . *it* happened to me again. That rudimentary telepathic link established itself with the Echoman that Eve had shot yesterday. We'd left him to die under the bushes. Now, after all this time, he'd done precisely that. A sense of coldness filled me; then came a slow, wrenching drag, as if the remnants of his life were ripped out of him—something I can describe only as the sensation of thorns that had been embed- ded in flesh being pulled one after another. As I stifled the groan at the aching sense of loss transmitted to me by the dying man, I suddenly thought of Madeline. Just for a moment I saw through her eyes. In front of me/her my kid sister's face hove into view; a second later pain shot through Madeline's stomach. The pain reached across the miles to drive into my belly too. I winced as my knees rose in an involuntary spasm.

*Eve's been left alone with Madeline,* I told myself. *Eve's making the most of the time. These pains . . . she's driving a knife blade into Madeline's belly.*

I masked the torture in my stomach so the others wouldn't notice. Madeline, whether intentionally or not, telepathically transmitted the pains to me.

This went on for ten more minutes; then Paddy announced, "This is it." He pulled over to the side of the road. "Mason, I promised you I'd take you to your sister, and here she is."

With spasms of agony diving through my stomach muscles, I had to lumber unsteadily from the back of the truck. Just in front of it was parked a silver RV with Eve leaning against it.

Eve looked me over. "You're pale," she said. "You've not been eating shrimp again, have you? It gives you a bad stomach."

"Thank you for the touching reunion, Sis. No, I haven't been eating shrimp. I've just been through a whole universe of crap, through."

"Commiserations."

"Where's Madeline?"

"Inside." Eve appeared to be searching for the right word before adding, "Resting."

"What have you done to her?"

I wrenched open the door of the RV. Straightaway I saw Madeline sitting on one of the sofas. Her lips were pressed together in pain while she rested her palm against her belly.

"Damn it, Eve. You didn't have to hurt her."

"Ah . . ." Eve understood. "So it's that telepathic thing. You're feeling what she feels?"

"What did you do to her? Knife her?"

I sat beside Madeline on the sofa. Her dark eyes held mine, the hand with the Y-shaped scar pressed against her stomach as the hurt returned. Behind me, Dianna and Ruth climbed into the vehicle's lounge area.

"You really feel what's hurting her, Mason?" Ruth appeared amused.

"Which means I know you've been torturing her."

"So, Mason." Eve spoke with satisfaction. "You're feeling the pain in Madeline's stomach. And it's something you've never experienced before—not exactly, anyway."

All three were smiling. I scowled.

"What's the matter, Mason?" Eve's smile broadened. "Haven't you heard of period pains before?"

The three women laughed. Even Madeline allowed herself a timid smile. Outside the doorway of the RV, Paddy and Ulric exchanged grins, but noticeably refrained from making any comment on menstruation.

My anger dropped. "You mean you haven't hurt her?"

"It's her period, Mason; she's old enough to take care of herself." My sister enjoyed my unique—for a male—discomfort—a discomfort both psychological and physical. "As for you, I can get you a painkiller if you like."

When the others had stopped laughing, Dianna said, "We need to get moving. After what happened back in Tanshelf the police will be hunting for the pair of you."

"Unfortunately," Ulric added, "considering last night's episode when Mason got drunk and left us for sex, we cannot guarantee he'll be willing to keep a low profile."

Ruth turned to Eve. "We discussed this eventuality last night. Do we have your permission?"

Eve became grave as she nodded.

This caused my hackles to rise again. "Which eventuality, and what permission?"

Madeline leaped to her feet. "No! Don't touch him!"

Eve wrestled Madeline to the couch as the others grabbed hold of me.

Ulric's hand came into view holding a syringe full of pale yellow serum. "Mason. It's for the best." Then he plunged the needle into my face beneath the right eye. It seemed to me in the moments that followed I remained awake. Only the image had frozen in time of Paddy, Ruth, and the others holding me down. However, the colors, one by one, slowly faded to monochrome, until it seemed I stared for hours at the scene in black and white.

# CHAPTER THIRTY-THREE

"Sleep well?"

"I didn't sleep; I was drugged."

"You're healthy? No nausea? Double vision?"

"Two questions: Who the hell are you? And where are we?"

I scanned the room of a country house: bare floor timbers so ancient they were black, a stone fireplace big enough to spit-roast wild boar. Apart from three straight-backed chairs, the most striking furniture was a gigantic plasma TV screen hanging from a white-painted wall. Twenty feet from it a woman sat at a small table that accommodated a laptop. She wore a smart peach suit, giving her the appearance of a business executive; without doubt the most salient feature was that her hair had been plaited until it resembled a glossy black rope. Without a glimmer of gray it hung over the back of the chair until it almost touched the floor timbers. She'd not looked around at me when I asked the questions. Beside me stood Madeline, Eve, and Ulric. From what I could see of the woman's face it possessed a hardness, perhaps like that of an aging cop who'd seen so many murders that the veteran law enforcer could read a mutilated corpse for clues like you can read a page. As she watched the six-by-ten-foot plasma screen about a hundred different images appeared as thumbnails—shots of buildings, trees, open meadows, a walled garden.

"Thank you very much, Ulric. If you haven't eaten you'd best do so soon, before they arrive."

Ulric gave a respectful nod, then turned to fix me with a look that meant business. "Mason. You'd better listen carefully to what Dr. Saffrey has to say. She's going to tell you the truth." Then he glanced at my sister. "Eve?"

"Aren't you staying?" I asked, although I noticed her little glances at Ulric. She always had that look with new boyfriends.

A faint blush colored her cheeks. "I'll go with Ulric. I've already heard what Dr. Saffrey has to say."

I grunted. "I guess I was under for longer than I thought, huh?"

Madeline vented some anger. "They kept you under for twenty-four hours. I told them it wasn't right. They might have killed you."

"I swore an oath to deliver Mason safely." Ulric became prim. "That's what I achieved."

"Bastard." Madeline's eyes flashed.

Dr. Saffrey turned to appraise me. "Mason, you've a formidable ally there, haven't you? She's like a tigress protecting her young." The woman smiled. "I'll talk to Mason, Ulric. Go enjoy your meal with Eve."

My sister and her new flame withdrew from the room in a way that suggested that Dr. Saffrey had authority here.

"Mason. Madeline. Please sit down." She was close enough to pat the seat of the nearest straight-backed chair.

"I'm going to stand." Did I sound defiant or just plain grumpy? Dr. Saffrey didn't bat an eyelid.

"Madeline, I have no prejudice against you. I don't expect you will desert your master, but feel free to sit if you wish."

"I'm not her master," I said.

"No? Don't you see the look of devotion in her eyes, Mason? If you asked Madeline to throw herself in front of a truck she'd do just that. Happily, willingly, joyfully."

"Listen, I don't know who you are—"

"There." She tapped keys on the laptop. The thumbnail images assumed a rippling effect as they showed dozens of different views in the course of a matter of seconds. Somehow this woman, who was hardly in the first flush of youth, appeared to monitor every image at once, alert to any change.

"It will be wasteful of both time and energy if we start our relationship with misapprehensions about one another." Her almond eyes flicked from my face to Madeline's, then back again. "You said you don't know who I am. My name is Dr. Saffrey. I'm a doctor of law, not

medicine, so don't come running to me with any embarrassing itches or stomachaches." She smiled, an attempt to put us at ease. "I won't tell you where you are,
other than that we're tucked away in the wilderness. It
was a military site reserved for the testing of weapons,
none of them radioactive or biological, as far as I
know." Her keen eyes locked on mine. "On the other
hand, I've learned about you, Mason. Eve told me your
personal and family history, and what happened when
you were held captive at the school in Tanshelf. I'm
sorry about your mother, by the way. Ulric has explained how he and his squad—"

"Squad? That sounds military to me."

The doctor continued without a blip. "—managed to
acquire you . . . your subsequent adventures, the second attack in the quarry near your home, and the re-
grettable incident with the woman you slept with. I also
know about Madeline, of course. And I must say she is
astonishingly similar to you in appearance. Which, in
our experience, makes her unique."

"So what is all this?" Anger crackled along my nerves.
"Are you going to tell me you're responsible for creating
the Echomen? After all, you must work for the military,
don't you?"

"The answer to the first question is, I wish we were
responsible for the mechanism that turned Madeline
into a copy of you. Then we could probably stop this
mess from getting any worse. Second question: yes, the
army pays my pension. But to elaborate: if the government knew what we were doing here I'd either be jailed
or . . ." She shrugged. "I'd meet with an unfortunate car
accident."

I frowned. "What exactly are you doing, then?"

"Did you know that every nuclear power plant keeps

a team of retired scientists and technicians on their payroll?"

"How does that explain this?"

"That team consists of men and women who are all over seventy years of age, most over eighty."

"They fix leaks." This came from Madeline.

Dr. Saffrey nodded. "They're so old a big dose of radioactivity won't make much difference to the elderly one way or the other. If the leak of radiation is a bad one they'll willingly serve as a suicide squad to block any holes and mop up any radioactive spills. They do this because they are good people who don't want to expose young men and women to mortal danger; what's more, they know the end of their lives isn't that far off anyway; they don't have many years to lose if they should be contaminated with a lethal dose." Her eyes roved over the plasma screen again, checking those thumbnail images. "Not long now," she announced. "But long enough to share with you what I know. And why I mentioned those silver-haired nuclear technicians who are prepared to sacrifice their lives in order to save others'."

I shrugged. "Okay, you've told us that nuclear power plants employ the elderly. Forgive my lack of amazement, but I don't see the point here."

"And why it's relevant to us," Madeline added.

"An eighty-year-old scientist plugging a radioactive leak accepts the risk of death." Dr. Saffrey turned from the screen to look me in the eye. "I am eighty-four years old. By sitting in this room with you I am accepting the possibility that whatever's inside you might turn me into what Madeline has become. Your female doppelgänger."

"Why single me out? You know as well as I do that

Paddy, Ruth, Ulric, and Eve have been duplicated. This can affect anyone of us."

"True. But you contaminate faster. You produce Echoes of yourself across a broader spectrum of ages. If you are close enough to someone then they often becomes a version of you. Follow?"

"So you're saying this is Mason's fault." Madeline's eyes flashed with anger. "You're accusing him of being some kind of plague carrier?"

The elderly woman shook her head. "This contamination of the human race is widespread. It's not confined to Mason. Yet Mason is unique when we talk about rapidity of transformation, extent of transformation, and the ability to cross boundaries of sex, age, and race."

"You're going to dissect him." Again this came from Madeline. "I won't let you. He's a good man."

"Ah . . ." Dr. Saffrey smiled. "That's where I can agree, only not for the reasons you think. Mason could very well be good for the human race. We just need to investigate his body, and his mind, more deeply." When Madeline took a step toward her, Dr. Saffrey smiled. "That doesn't involve so much as parting a hair from his head. We will observe him and you; that will be valuable enough."

"So," I said, "what are your plans for me?"

"Initially it must be quarantine, I'm afraid."

"Ah, the laboratory cage awaits?"

"It'll be far more congenial than that. Look at the screen." She tapped a key on the laptop. Instantly one of the thumbnail images expanded to fill the TV. "This is the Rose Garden. We need to house you there for a few days. You'll be comfortable. More important for us, you'll be living apart from our staff."

"So I really am such a danger?"

"I'm afraid so, Mason. One of our soldiers who helped carry you in when you were drugged is now, to put it bluntly, a replica of you. So far, we've learned that not everyone you encounter will be transformed into a duplicate of you. Some are immune *so far*. Paddy and his team haven't been affected. Corporal Naylor was unlucky. Before you ask, I have to admit we don't know why some people change into copies of you, Mason, or into copies of those who, for want of a better description, carry the transformation bug. I confess, the rules regarding the transformation are perplexing. Our scientists are as bewildered as anyone else. If anything, it points to the random biology of the Echomen. Until we encountered Madeline here, one thing we've been pretty sure of is this: It's the nature of Echomen that they become hostile to the rest of humanity."

With the words rolling smoothly from the woman's tongue I watched the screen. There, a garden full of roses lay inside walls that stood a full fifteen feet high. In one corner appeared to be an old cottage beneath a red-tiled roof. If anything what caught my eye were two figures. Strolling hand in hand, Eve and Ulric followed a path between a lake of pink flowers. The idyllic scene lay at odds with the machine guns they carried over their shoulders. They paused to kiss.

Dr. Saffrey smiled. "If only what the wise say is true: love conquers all. Then young people like that will destroy evil." Her face hardened. "But it will take more than love. We must hate, too. Hate what the Echo creatures are doing to ruin the human race. Mason, make no mistake: we are fighting for the survival of our species." She'd no sooner uttered that when a red block began to flash in the center of the screen. Eve and Ulric reacted to a sound by running toward a door in the garden wall. "Ah," Dr. Saffrey murmured. "There goes the alarm. We have contact."

# CHAPTER THIRTY-FOUR

The six-by-ten-foot screen rippled. An image of Eve and Ulric running through the Rose Garden toward the door in the hall changed to dozens of thumbnails. Most of these revealed shots of open countryside: fields, meadows, trees, bushes. I glimpsed one thumbnail showing a front-of-face shot of Natsaf-Ty. The ancient mummy "gazed" at me through closed eyelids. As ever, the tip of a tongue that was dry as a raisin protruded between the lips. The picture of the red face ruined with cracks and holes couldn't exist anywhere else but my mind, of course. Dr. Saffrey didn't see it as she studied the screen; maybe Madeline caught some suggestion of it as her mind lightly brushed against mine in that telepathic way gifted by whatever mechanism generated the doppelgänger transformation. The way Natsaf-Ty regarded me with his head tilted to one side had a quizzical air. Once more I found myself asking; *Why are you haunting me? What do you expect from me? Is there something I should be doing?* Thumbnails melted to be replaced by a single six-by-ten image of a strip of grassland that ran between two areas of forest. A low sun illuminated this green highway.

Dr. Saffrey murmured, "Here they come. Right on cue."

Figures cast long shadows as they walked toward the camera.

"Echomen?" I asked.

"Indeed they are."

"How far away are they from here?"

"No more than a quarter of a mile."

"You're not concerned?"

She gave a grim smile. "Everything is as it should be. Just you wait and see."

Madeline examined the screen. "What are they carrying?"

"We'll find out soon enough."

The figures were in a long shot; both the angle of the camera set at about knee height and the setting sun created the impression of tall, spindly men and women with overlong legs and torsos that were topped by small skulls. These were shadowed so I couldn't see the faces. I counted thirty of them. Each one carried a bundle over their heads. Because these, too, were in silhouette I couldn't make out what they were. They were perhaps the size of sports bags, of no particular shape, nor apparently heavy.

"Weapons?" I asked.

"You'll see," Dr. Saffrey replied coldly.

Madeline said, "You were expecting them to come here."

"Expecting? More than that, we lured them here. The more Echomen we remove from society the safer the world becomes."

The huge screen hanging from the wall showed the slow advance of the men and women who'd become those Echo creatures. They'd just been like you and me once. Now? Well, they could be *you* or *me*. They were duplicates of ordinary individuals, only now their minds had been reprogrammed to hate the human race.

Ulric appeared in the doorway. "Dr. Saffrey?"

"Go ahead, Ulric; there's no need to acquire any for testing this time."

He withdrew. The woman pressed a key on the laptop. Small thumbnail images formed a frame around the main central one. I saw a concrete wall. Behind it a dozen or more soldiers stood with machine guns and rifles resting on top of the concrete blocks. More thumbnails revealed close-ups. Ruth, Dianna, Paddy, and Eve were amongst the troops. They were armed with automatic rifles.

"You lured the Echomen here," I said. "How?"

"The Internet reaches everywhere. We have our intelligence team creating blogs, message boards, short films, you name it, all of which purport to be from individuals who know abut the Echomen. We create a fictional community of people on the Web who are sharing information about the creatures. There are also references to a safe house for ordinary men and women who are fleeing from them to come to this location." She sighed. "Echomen believe they are cleverer than us. They think they've discovered vulnerable people they can destroy."

"But you lure them into a trap?"

"See for yourself."

As the elongated figures approached the camera, growing larger on-screen, the armed figures behind the wall, one of whom must be my sister, fired their weapons. The doomed Echomen didn't scream; there was no running; nobody panicked. When the figures approached the perimeter wall where the soldiers had positioned themselves, they simply sank to the ground as bullets struck them. I watched as a single heavy-caliber tracer moved in apparent slow motion through the evening air. Like a sluggish shooting star it closed in on a man dressed in a leather coat. When it struck him in the face his head turned into a spray of dark droplets. Headless, he took another step before toppling. The bundle he carried struck the earth in front of him. Coolly professional, the soldiers chose a target, fired, destroyed their target, picked another target, and so on.

The Echomen didn't charge the wall; neither did they run away as their numbers were depleted by the searing blast of gunfire. They simply walked forward. Maybe in some strange way they'd already decided this would be their destiny. I recalled the Echomen that had been nailed to the floors of my old classrooms back in Tanshelf. They'd accepted their fate in the same way. It didn't occur to them to scream or to flee. They all seemed to think, *So this is the way I die . . . that's fine by me.* And here they tumbled into the grass. Sometimes a sloppy shot would smash through a groin; then a guy would go down still alive, with blood squirting from between his legs. Even then they didn't seem overly perturbed that they'd just had their balls mashed by a dumdum bullet. One just rolled on his back, with one knee raised and the other leg flat to the ground; calmly, he stared at the clear blue sky as he bled to death.

"Those bundles," Madeline began. "They're moving."

I turned my attention to them. By now there were only eight of the creatures walking toward the wall. All of them raised bundles above their heads, like you or I would hold a sleeping bag above our heads if we were to wade through a river. Although they were in silhouette, making it impossible to identify them, I'm sure I saw one bundle change shape, as if it could move by it-self. One of the rifle rounds zipped above the Echoman's head to smash into the package or bag or whatever the guy held high in its two hands. Liquid streamed from it.

Dr. Saffrey gave an *uph* sound. "You see, they bring gifts, or what they believe are gifts. In my book that's powerful proof they have an intelligence that is alien to ours."

"What kind of gifts?" The package held above the Echoman's head still leaked. Now the figure was near enough to reveal that the liquid dripped into his hair. "Don't tell me this is a bring-a-bottle kind of party."

"They've brought all kinds of things in the past," Dr. Saffrey told me. "Food, drink, clothes. Once they even brought gifts of animals." Another hail of gunshots felled the last of the Echomen. A blond-haired woman took a dozen rounds to her torso that disintegrated the entire upper half of her body. As what was left of her dropped in bits to the ground the bundle fell, too. It lay squirming there.

I watched the screen as the doctor operated the zoom, expanding the image of the blob shape on the grass. My eyes widened and a cold, prickling sensation climbed my spine; it possessed all the revolting prom-ise of a gigantic spider creeping across my skin as the camera zoomed in toward the "gift" that the Echomen had gone to so much trouble to bring to us—and died trying.

"Ah . . ." Dr. Saffrey breathed. "Have you seen what they brought us this time?" She zoomed into a small face poking through the wrappings of cloth. "Babies. Tiny, little babies."

\*   \*   \*

Minutes after the final Echoman had been killed the soldiers moved into the strip of grassland that ran between the trees. Any of the creatures found to be still alive had their tenacity for life rewarded with a pistol shot to the head. Then the troops started zipping the bloody remains into body bags. I didn't see what they did to the babies wrapped in bundles of cloth. All this was revealed to us on-screen. A moment later Dr. Saffrey switched off the image.

"There you have it." She turned back to us. "What we do is unsanctioned by any elected president or prime minister. We're a coalition of security services from around the world—CIA, KGB, Mossad, and half a dozen others—many of them former adversaries."

"But now you're united against the Echomen."

"Absolutely."

Madeline frowned. "Why don't you inform the government?"

"First we must build up a dossier of documented proof. Our elected assemblies might decide we're deluded and simply close us down. Second, we still don't know how deeply Echomen have infiltrated national governments. So far the creatures are stupid. Once they are transformed from human to Echoman all they do is try to kill us. With the unique exception of Madeline here. Imagine, however, if they become more sophisticated and assume the form of senators, members of Parliament, senior civil servants and judges. We've no evidence of these developments yet, but we have to be sure before we trust anyone outside our inner circle."

She shook her head. "At the moment we're little more than janitors. We wait for one mess to occur, clean up the bodies, then wait for the Echomen to strike again, so we can be waiting with our metaphorical pail and broom. Before the Echo people came on the scene we had a similar protocol for terrorist activity. Failed terrorist attacks didn't even make it into the news because we kept the story bottled. Ten years ago a cargo ship called the *Oleander* arrived in a major Western port with a battlefield nuclear weapon in the hold. The timer failed, customs officers discovered the bomb, the army disarmed it, so the terrorists were disappointed not to see TV pictures of a mushroom cloud rising above a famous skyline. Due to a security error a report of the failed attack found its way onto the Internet. You had only to type '*Oleander*' into a search engine and you could read about a former Soviet nuclear bomb hidden beneath a cargo of roof slate. Certain security officers were given early retirement on health grounds for their snafu, and we swung into action and gave the World Wide Web a spring cleaning to brush out references to an incident that could have killed a hundred thousand innocents. Today we're still busy with our proverbial mop and pail, erasing any trace of damage when the Echomen attack."

"But today was different?" I nodded at the screen. "You laid bait and lured them in."

"Yes, indeed, the poor wretches. They simply strolled into our trap."

Madeline asked, "But why do they bring gifts?"

"You're better equipped to explain that; after all, technically you're one of those creatures."

Madeline shook her head.

Dr. Saffrey shrugged. "No? We don't know why either. They may believe we are stupid enough to be disarmed by their gifts if they bring food. If they bring babies perhaps they see those as human shields. One that will protect them from us."

"How wrong they were," I said with feeling.

"What happens to the babies?" Madeline asked.

"They're dealt with. That's all you need to know."

"Is there a technique to tell the difference between a normal human being and one that's turned Echo?"

"Absolutely nothing." Dr. Saffrey shrugged again. "Nothing is revealed by blood tests, at a cellular level, or in DNA. All we have so far is the physical change to resemble or, in your case, duplicate perfectly another human being. After that there is only the change in behavior. The instinctive drive to kill. Now . . ." She stood up. "It's time for you to enter your quarters."

"You mean quarantine?"

Madeline added, "Or jail?"

"You'll be very comfortable. Also, it won't be for long."

"But we have more questions," Madeline said, "don't we, Mason?"

Clearly she'd become as distrustful as I was. But then, she was a chip off the old biological block.

I agreed. "Around about another five hundred questions. After all, how come you're so confident you're not going to turn Echo? You've been close enough to me for the last hour or so. From what you've been saying I have only to e-mail some poor schmuck and they become my identical twin before you can say, 'Shazzam!' "

"I appreciate your concerns."

"Concerns? Believe me, I'm a raging inferno of concerns."

"All will become clear over the next few days."

"How come? You know precious little about the biology of these things."

"We are learning, Mason. Bit by bit."

"And I'm a bit you're going to learn from, aren't I?"

Anger surged through me. "You're going to watch everything I do."

The doctor nodded. "That and more. But I'm prepared to offer up my life for the preservation of our society. What will you offer?"

"If I go along with this, what happens to me?"

"Mason Konrad is already dead."

"Pardon?" Now that did take some digesting.

Dr. Saffrey continued briskly, "The media have reported that you killed your neighbors in Tanshelf when you lost your sanity. By the time the police arrived at your home you'd already turned the gun on yourself."

"Now, wait one minute . . ."

"There are eyewitnesses. Your body, or that of someone who resembled you exactly, was discovered in your home with lethal gunshot wounds. Remember, one of our roles is to act as that mop and broom. We'll tidy up the mess caused by the Echomen in Tanshelf. We'll manufacture a scenario of what happened the day of the slaughter and that will be the official history. There will be no further police investigation; no public inquiry. For the record: Mason Konrad is deceased."

"No way." My voice rose. "You're not taking my identity away from me."

"It's already gone. Don't fight it. Eve has surrendered hers, too. When this is all over you will be resettled under the good offices of the Witness Protection Program with new names. Even though the circumstances are different, the WPP is good at giving people new lives."

I began to speak, but the doctor held up her hand. "I know you could ask me questions for the next week, but I have things to do, and you'll need to settle into your new quarters. Tomorrow our people will start work. The experiments the Echomen conducted at the old school were clearly designed to expand their capabilities. What you can tell us will be invaluable. Your capacity, Mason, for transforming people into Echomen, even if it is involuntary, is so potent I can't risk your coming into contact with any of my staff. I'll show you to the Rose Garden myself."

"Wait a moment—why are you so sure whatever I carry won't affect you?"

A smile touched her lips. "I've been around Echomen for longer than you can imagine. If they haven't transformed me now, I figure I must be immune. Step this way, please."


# CHAPTER THIRTY-FIVE

The Rose Garden. Ah . . . the name suggests romance. But then, doesn't every new romance contain a hidden promise of nightmare? *I married the blowtorch murderer. . . . My girlfriend confessed to being a witch. . . . On my honeymoon I discovered my gal is really a guy. . . .* Hell's bells. This situation does that to you. Gets you paranoid. Makes you suspect your own shadow has homicidal intentions.

When Dr. Saffrey showed us through the door in the wall with the words, "This is the Rose Garden. Make yourself at home in the cottage," it was a warm, sunlit place, a pink sea of roses that released a delicate perfume into the evening air. What nicer place to walk hand in hand with the one you love? Only the girl I walked with was a female version of me. And I'd been through the Freudian hog-slosh before. I did not love Madeline. I was not sexually attracted to her. Okay? I felt a responsibility toward the woman. What was more, she'd helped save Eve's life back when the Echomen flooded what had been an empty swimming pool.

"Why weren't you here earlier?" A small guy with a shaved head furiously swept the path with a long-handled broom. He wore brown corduroy pants with brown lace-up shoes that were surprisingly glossy. On his top half he wore a blue jacket from a business suit that was way too big for him. It flapped like a sheet on a washing line as he attacked fallen leaves with the broom. "I'm hungry. I've had to wait for supper because you didn't come. And now the rose petals keep dropping off and I have to keep sweeping them up. 'Eddie, you won't get any supper if you don't keep the paths clean.' 'Eddie, sweep the steps.' 'Have you polished the brass yet?' 'Eddie, you swear too much.'" He'd changed his voice for the last part of his speech into something resembling the scolding tones of a schoolteacher.

Madeline said, "We're sorry. We didn't know you were waiting for us."

"I'm taking care of you." He chased pink petals against the wall, then instead of picking them up stamped them furiously into the soil. "I've got to take care of you, 'cause the others are scared of you two. I'm not scared of you. You don't know what I can do. I'm strong, me. I could scare you if I wanted."

I tried to put the angry little man at ease. "We'll be no trouble."

"Better not be." Grumpily he deadheaded a rose, then thrust the dead blossom into his jacket pocket.

"This is Madeline," I told him. "I'm Mason."

"All the chocolate in the drawer is mine—you're not to touch it."

"We won't get in your way; besides, we'll only be here a couple of days."

"That's what they said to me. I've been here for weeks. They make me do all the work. If it wasn't for me the place would fall to pieces. Do you know how many times I've swept up the rose petals today? Four times. Four! Can you believe it? You never see them lardy-dahs come out here and help." His bottom lip pushed out as a sulk took him. "It's just not fair. No supper, either. Not till you get here, they said. And you're late!"

"Sorry." Madeline smiled. "Can we do anything to help?"

"You can keep your thieving hands off that chocolate. It's mine."

"We will."

"Right. I've got to show you stuff." He thrust his hands into his jacket pockets, then stomped along the path between the rose beds. Any suggestion of seriousness on his part tended to be robbed by the fact that the jacket was so long he couldn't put both hands into his pockets at the same time. So, as he walked, he dropped one shoulder, then the other in an attempt to keep the hands lodged there. "Bloody roses," he grumbled. "Bloody damn crap roses. It's not fair."

The Rose Garden was perhaps as large as two tennis courts side by side. Surrounding it was a brick wall at least fifteen feet high. In the setting sun the brick had pink and orange tints that were as every bit warm as the roses. Like I said, in happier times, a lovely place for a romantic stroll. On the other side of the wall I could see the top floors of the safe house occupied by Eve, Dr. Saffrey, and the rest. As far as I could tell, the only entrance to the Rose Garden had been the formidable timber door we'd just passed through. At the far side of the garden was a row of four stables with pale green doors. Their red brickwork merged with that of the wall. And built into a corner of the garden was a small cottage with a single chimney protruding from its roof.

"You live there." The man pointed at the cottage. "You'll have the bedrooms. I sleep downstairs on the sofa. And that sofa's mine. Only I can use it."

"Thank you, Mr. . . . ?"

"Mister!" He made a high-pitched bark of a sound. "Mister? Nobody's ever called me mister. I'm Eddie."

I lagged behind on the path so I could whisper to Madeline as he marched off ahead with that odd see-saw gait as he tried, but failed, to keep both hands in his pockets at once.

"Madeline, didn't Dr. Saffrey tell us we'd be in quarantine?" I nodded at the angry figure stomping toward the stables. "Strange kind of quarantine if we're Eddie's houseguests."

Eddie turned to scowl from beneath eyebrows that were as bristly as his broom. "What's that you're saying about me?"

"We're not talking about you, Eddie," I said. "Dr. Saffrey told us we'd be alone in the Rose Garden."

"Alone? Ha! Yeah, right. Alone as I've been for the last week." He shook his head. "They keep bringing in more and more of you. At this rate I'm going to have to put up tents over these roses to keep you all in. Do you remember what I told you about the chocolate?"

"It's all yours."

"And don't you forget it. Hurry up. I'm ready for my

supper. It's not fair that they've made me wait. 'Eddie, make the guests welcome. Be sure they get enough to eat. Give them clean bedding.'" A crafty expression stole over his face. "'Eddie, be sure to tell . . . to inform them that it is *your* chocolate. They must not touch it.'"

Instead of leading us to the cottage, Eddie headed for the stables with the green doors. "I've been told to show you these," he told us. "Why it couldn't wait, I don't know. But it's either do this or no supper. And I'm starving. Do you know how many times I've cleaned up the crapping rose petals today? There's millions of them. It's not as though anyone comes to look at them. One bit of a wind and *whoosh*, them crapping petals drop off. And you know who cleans 'em all up? 'Eddie, sweep the paths.' 'Eddie, clean the windows.' 'Eddie, wash the clothes.'" That haughty schoolmistress voice again.

"You've got horses?" Madeline asked as we crossed the gravel to the doors.

"Horses? Why do we need horses?" He took his hands out of his jacket pockets so he could pull back the steel bolts. "Pets for them lardy-dahs indoors? More work for Eddie to do." He pushed out his bottom lip. "It's not fair. Watch your faces—these things swing back." After snapping back the bolts he violently yanked at the upper half of the door.

"This one's poorly," he said.

"Oh?"

"And it's all your fault." The moment Eddie crashed the upper half of the timber door back against the wall a figure sprang from the shadows. The face that shot toward me was easy enough to recognize.

Me. Some mutant copy of me, anyway. Madeline pushed herself between me and the man who howled in rage.

Eddie smiled for the first time. "Watch it. He's a biter."

The man caught Madeline by the hair; she screamed as he dragged her toward him; his mouth opened so he could sink his teeth into her face. Despite the gloomy interior of the stables I saw that steel bars caged the man. He had to wait until he brought the woman's face closer before he could start ripping flesh with his teeth. I slammed the heel of my hand through the gap of the bars into his forehead. With a hard shove I pushed his face back. At the same time I tugged Madeline away. She screamed as a clump of her dark hair ripped away.

A second later I'd hauled her back ten paces. Then I turned on Eddie. "Why didn't you warn us?"

He blinked in surprise. "He's a biter, I said. It's you two nitwits that got too close."

"Do you know who what he is?"

"That's Corporal Naylor. He doesn't like being in there."

"Didn't anyone tell you Echomen are dangerous?" Instead of waiting for a reply I checked Madeline as she pressed her palm to the side of her head. "It doesn't look bad," I reassured her. "But we'll get something for it. They must have a first-aid station here if it's a military base."

"If she wants first aid I'm getting some supper first. I've been waiting ages. If they don't, I'm eating that chocolate, rules or no rules; it's not fair that—"

"*Shut up.*" My tone stung him so much tears appeared in his eyes. "Why are they keeping an Echoman here?"

He took a step back as if afraid I might hit him.

"It's all right," Madeline said gently. "We won't hurt you."

"Don't bet on it." I shot him a look that he must have recognized as being downright evil, because his eyes widened in fear. "You're certain he's secure in there?"

"Bars," was the only word Eddie could manage with his eyes all huge and watery-looking.

I took a step forward, wary lest the guy charge the stall door again. In the gloomy interior of the stall that had been converted into a prison cell an Echoman stood hunched in the center; his eyes blazed at me with a kind of lusting hatred.

"Corporal Naylor?"

He flinched. "Look what you did to me! Bastard!" Saliva sprayed from his mouth.

I remembered what the doctor had told us. "You helped carry me into the house."

"And see the thanks I got." His words came in a series of barks. The man suffered, yet it wasn't pain.

Madeline stood beside me, resting her hand on my forearm so as to gain some reassurance from the touch. "He looks exactly like you. Transformation is faster than before."

"Yeah, yeah! You infected me." Naylor lurched forward to strike the cell bars. "And he's done the same to you, hasn't he, miss?"

The *miss* sounded at odds with his anger. I sensed he battled with what had been a crushing invasion of his personality.

"Corporal Naylor hasn't been defeated yet," I murmured. "He's fighting it."

"Yes, I'm fighting it. What the fuck do I want to become you for? I never asked for it. I don't want your face imposed on my skull." He raked his left cheek with his fingernails. Four bloody furrows streaked the flesh. "I'll rip this face off with my own hands if I have to. Because you know something? My face—my real face—is still under this mask. I believe that. Soon I'll prove it. Okay?"

Madeline trembled.

Naylor noticed her fear with some satisfaction. "I

know about Echomen. I've been killing them for six months. Echomen are ordinary people who catch a kind of bug that changes them into clones of carriers of the bug. You're a carrier, Mason. You infected me when I helped you into the house. And you must have infected the lady at some point, because though she's still a lady—a fucksome fine lady—she's got your face on her head, like I've got your face on my head, and like hundreds of other people have got *your* face on *their* heads. You with me so far?" He stepped into the light of the setting sun. Face-wise he was exactly the same as me. As for the body, he had the physique of a bodybuilder. This was a man who was an obsessive weight lifter. Knots of muscle the size of grapefruits bulged in his arms. The pair of hands that came up to grip the steel bars could snap Madeline's neck like a cracker.

"But you listen to this," he growled. "Echomen are changing. Your lady there isn't like the sort I blew to shit with my Uzi. Echomen change inside here as well as turning clone." He screwed his finger against his head. "They get a new instinct to kill anyone who isn't an Echoman. But your lady-clone isn't like that. She's not programmed to kill humans. Isn't that right, lover girl? You've been given another role to perform." The muscles bunched in his forearms as he squeezed the bars as if squeezing the woman's neck. "You know I'm telling the truth, Mason. Madeline's no human bitch; she's not like the other Echo bitches, either. She's got her own little fucking plan. A fucking plan that she'll spring on you, Mason, when she's good and ready. Ha!" He head-butted the bars. The clang made Madeline flinch against me. Blood dribbled down Naylor's forehead as he screamed with glee. "And when I get out of here I'm going to rip your faces off! There's only going to be one face like this." He slapped his jaw. "And it's going to be this one. D'ya hear me, Mason? I'm going to peel you like an orange. You fuck—"

The upper half of the stall door swung shut.

"Eddie, I—"

"Eddie? Don't you remember your little sister anymore, Mason?"

I blinked. After listening to Nalyor's bitter diatribe this was like emerging from a hypnotic trance.

"Eve?"

"Not too close, Madeline." Eve pushed Madeline away from me. "It still gives me the creeps when I see you touching my brother." She adjusted the strap of the submachine gun that dangled, muzzle down, beneath one arm. "Eddie, you were supposed to show my brother the rest. Open the next door." Eddie rushed to obey. Sis did look formidable with her death-dealing hardware hanging beside her slim waist. The military chic extended beyond the gun to camouflage pants in dappled greens. Ulric must have appreciated the tight green T-shirt she wore as well.

Her businesslike manner prompted me to ask, "Eve, what are you doing here?"

"Since you came back home, Mason, bringing trouble with you, I've discovered something about myself." She nodded as Eddie opened the stall door to the next cell. "I'm very good at torture." A grim smile tightened her mouth. "So in answer to your question, Mason, your little sister is here to inflict pain." Eve swung the machine gun into her two hands. "Okay, Eddie. Stand back."

# CHAPTER THIRTY-SIX

What remained of the sun that evening splashed a bloody light onto the brick wall that made a prisoner of the Rose Garden Madeline, Naylor, me, and probably Eddie, too. Eve I wasn't so sure about: someone had admitted her through the walls; they would let her out again, so why was she free to come and go?

What occupied me especially at that moment was wondering who was in the next stall, and what Eve would do with her machine gun. A figure already stood close up behind the steel bars when Eddie heaved back the upper half of the stall door.

I groaned. "Good God."

"See the bruising on the neck." Eve nodded at the female prisoner. "It's the same one we encountered before. Dr. Saffrey's people picked her up in Tanshelf."

"Come closer," Eve ordered the woman.

There she was, the biological Echo of my mother. Bruises still darkened her throat where Eve and Madeline had tried to strangle her, using the kettle cord as a ligature. A lack of expression smoothed Mom's—I mean the monster's face. My blood ran cold.

"Closer." Eve beckoned the creature with her free hand. When the clone almost touched the bars with her nose Eve stabbed the muzzle of her gun through the uprights. The violence of the jab rocked the creature back on her heels. When she recovered her balance I saw that the mouth of the barrel had left a black

O-shaped bruise in the skin above an eyebrow. The woman breathed a little heavier, yet she didn't so much as whimper.

"See?" Eve spoke with satisfaction. "They don't feel pain like we do."

"What are you going to do to her?" Madeline asked.

"The same as I'd like to do to you." Eve's grin had a savage quality. "But we need to study these monsters. One day soon, however . . ." She patted the gun.

The woman who wore my mother's face stepped into the bloodred light.

"Listen," she said, "the world is changing. What's happening to the human race can't be stopped. We're victims of it as much as you. But there's a way to make life better for all of us."

"You dying is a start," Eve told her.

Seeing Eve strike the facsimile of my mother was disorienting, to say the least; a sore-looking lump had formed above her eye from the blow. I nodded to the little guy in his oversized jacket. "Close the door, Eddie."

"No, wait." The woman extended her hand through the bars as if she wanted me to grasp it. Eve used the machine gun as a club; the blue-steel firearm cracked against bone. And you know something? This time the prisoner did grunt in pain. Even so, she didn't withdraw the arm back into the cell. Eve clubbed again.

Through clenched teeth the woman hissed. "I can take it as long as you want to deal it out. All I want is for you to listen— Ugh." A third smack of the gun across her wrist caused that grunt. "Want you to listen to what I say. Ah!" Blow number four. Grazed skin on her wrist produced speckles of blood. "Whatever's happened to us can't be stopped. Uhh . . . can't be reversed. No going back. But we can reach an understanding. I'll be your mother again. I promised before. It still holds. I'll be her for as long as you want me. We can be together. Ack . . ." That blow ripped away a fingernail. Red drops fell onto white gravel. Yet she still held her arm out as Eve struck with even more passion; tears rolled down my sister's cheeks. "I'll be your mother forever. We'll have Christmas like we used to. I'll drink my wine and you can tease me about the presents I've bought, when you tell me that you're too old to have them wrapped in cartoon paper. Reindeers, Santa— Ohh!" That savage swipe from Eve cracked against the woman's hand with a shocking *snap!*

"You're not my mother," Eve snarled. "Never, ever." Panting, she clubbed again.

"You're getting hurt for nothing," I told the woman. "We won't allow you to replace our mother. She's dead. You monsters killed her."

The woman found it hard to talk through her agony. "Monsters like her." Her eyes blazed at Madeline. "She's one of us. So how come you love her and not me?"

This time I lunged forward, ready to rip her arm from the socket. Madeline held me back. This earned a snarl from Eve.

"Don't touch my brother. If I have to tell you again . . ."

The woman drew her butchered arm back through the bars. It made me think of a wounded serpent sliding back into its lair. "Anytime," she whispered. "Anytime. I love you both. I'm ready to be your mother. Just give me a chance. . . ."

The door swung shut. "I'm hungry." Eddie scowled. "I want supper." However, instead of stomping off to the cottage, he drew the bolts back on the third stall door. "But I've got one more to show you."

In the third stall, a boy.

"Not any boy," I murmured to myself. "That boy. Camera boy."

Madeline watched the boy step into the light. With a pair of mucky fists he rubbed his eyes. She tilted her head as she studied his face. "You've met him before?"

"Look at him, Madeline. He's a ten-year-old version of me." I shot her a grim smile. "Just as you're a female version of me."

"I want to go home." The boy appeared dazed.

"You see," I began, "I found this *specimen* in my back-yard in Tanshelf. He'd been trying to photograph us, probably for the amusement of his Echo buddies. I chased him; he got away, but left the camera behind. The next time I saw him was when he fell down one of the old mine shafts near where I live. *Lived.* My facsimiles are hard to kill. The little monster must have somehow clawed his way out of the pit."

The boy stared in a daze. My words weren't sinking into his brain.

Eddie grunted. "The kid's camera's in the cottage. They told me to put it with your things. They took the film out, so don't think of photographing nothing."

The boy's plight struck a nerve in Madeline. "We shouldn't leave him locked in there. He's frightened."

"The kid stays," Eddie told her. "He's all right. He gets more to eat than I do. Little pig. It's not fair."

I tried to make out what lay inside the stall-cum-jail. A narrow bed against a wall. A jug of water on the floor. A chair beside a flimsy table on which stood a plate containing bread scraps. The walls were solid, so the child version of me had no opportunity of talking to or seeing his fellow prisoners in the adjoining cells.

I hated seeing him in there. "Eddie. Open the door. It's cruel to keep a child locked up."

"He's one of the Echo things."

"Nevertheless."

"Echomen are monsters. They don't feel pain."

"Open the door, Eddie."

The little man shook his head.

"Eddie?"

"Can't."

"Why?"

"They don't give me keys."

Seeing a younger copy of me imprisoned twisted something inside my heart. "Listen. What's your name?"

His brown eyes rolled. "Name?" He frowned. "I know it's Kirk."

"What you mean, you *know* it's Kirk?"

Madeline touched my arm. "Go easy on him, Mason. He's a child."

"You said your name's Kirk." I spoke more gently. "Does it seem as if the name isn't yours anymore?"

Kirk nodded, an expression of woe on his face.

I gave the bars an experimental tug. "Eddie, bring me a hammer. I should be able to break the padlock."

"Won't do any good."

Madeline chimed in. "Eddie, it's not fair to turn a child into a prisoner."

Eddie's sulk lip appeared. "I told you, it won't do any good. He won't come out of there."

"Why?

"Because he's scared."

"Of what?"

"He's frightened something will hurt him. The woman's scared of the same thing."

"But what scares them?"

"You better ask them things." Eddie turned away, his arms folded. *Stop asking me questions.* The body language couldn't have been any clearer.

*Damn Dr. Saffrey. Blast her dirty, rotten colleagues.* They'd set this up. No doubt this was part of their experiment. *Watch how I react to the prisoners! We're the ingredients! Mix us together to see what kind of confection you get! Damn them . . .* But then, if I didn't find out information for myself, who the hell was going to tell me anything?

"Kirk, listen to me. I'm not angry with you." When I saw the child's face behind the bars I saw myself as a schoolboy being pushed around by the bigger kids as they chanted, "Hey, hey, bastard Mason Konrad. Did you ever find out who your father was? Did he run off before paying your mother's fuck money?" After pushing me down they'd laugh while they chanted, "Who's your daddy, bastard boy? Who's your daddy?" The evil memory sneaked up and bit me. For years I'd forgotten all about the taunts, but looking into that face they became a riff of pure sorrow. It brought it all back to me. How the child me would stare at his reflection in the mirror and ask, "Why do they call me bastard boy? What do they mean about my dad not paying Mom? Why are they doing all this? I haven't done anything to them, have I?" The face in the mirror didn't have answers any more than the face behind the bars that was identical to mine—right down to the brown eyes that were so full of confusion and pain.

The boy drew a breath, as if he'd suddenly remembered something unpleasant.

"What's wrong?" Madeline asked.

"I know I'm called Kirk." His eyes cleared as if he'd emerged from a trance. "Only it doesn't seem like my real name anymore. You *feel* your name, don't you? I can't feel as if it belongs to me anymore." He spoke rapidly. "My name is Kirk. . . . Kirk Jones . . . Kirk Johnson?" He shrugged. "My first name is Kirk. I know that. I found the camera in the attic. It hadn't worked but I fixed it up myself; then I started photographing animals. I loved taking pictures of them. Snakes. Snakes are cool. They're hard to find, but I got really good at getting close-ups of adders and grass snakes. And . . . and I went to Tanshelf High to find grass snakes to photograph, because I'd show them to my mom and dad at home. They'd gone to the institute for the deaf, and then they'd married. It's hard for them to find work because some bosses are so stupid they think because people can't hear they've got no brains; that's not true. My mom and dad are intelligent, and they love to put my photographs on the walls." His eyes assumed a strange fixed appearance as he began to see more inside his own head than what lay outside. "So I went to the old school with my camera. I remember a lady there who said she'd lost her dog in the swimming pool building. When I got in there it wasn't like a pool anymore. Walls had been built inside it, and I thought that was funny. Someone had made it into pens, you know, like for animals? Only there was a man inside of it—and that man was you—Mason Konrad. The woman stopped talking about the lost dog. She made me stand close to the pool. I could see you sleeping on the floor. Then she made me"—his lips became dry—"stay there. I wanted to go home, but she wouldn't let me. When I ran a man brought me back. He kept me right above where you slept. I was standing on cage stuff. Then I started to feel funny. I began to think it was me lying on the floor of the swimming pool with my eyes closed. I didn't feel like me anymore. People say drugs make you crazy. I wondered if they'd given me stuff to make me crazy, but I don't remember any needles. I wanted to go home. But I knew I wouldn't be going home again." For a moment he swayed there behind the bars.

Madeline spoke gently. "Kirk? Why don't you sit down?"

Kirk shook his head.

Gently I asked, "Kirk? Why did you photograph me at my home?"

A painful dryness cracked his lips. He licked them, flinched at their soreness, then: "They told me to get a picture of you with the thing."

"What *thing*?"

The boy's eyes bulged. "You know what thing. You talk to it." He gulped. "We're all scared of it. We're terrified!"

I knew what he was talking about: Natsaf-Ty. But he was a product of my imagination, the old childhood pretend friend who'd remerged at this time of mental stress. And it was this nascent telepathic link that was festering in the minds of the Echomen. It allowed them a mystifying glimpse of the old mummy with its crust of red skin. But did I say *mystifying*? I should have used the word *terrifying*. The boy gulped and panted, and sweat ran down his face as if he were near to a panic attack.

Once more I realized that Natsaf-Ty must be my secret weapon. But how? I still didn't understand the mechanics of it entirely, just that it kept the Echomen off balance. So the last thing I'd do at that moment was identify the dusty gentleman of old Egypt who used to visit me when I was a boy and had recently returned.

Madeline spoke in softly reassuring tones, trying to ease Kirk's fear.

But I saw an advantage and drove over her kind words: "Listen to me, Kirk. I don't understand what your people have been doing. They send you to photograph the 'thing' that frightens you all, but why are you so hell-bent on killing me?"

"We aren't!" He all but screamed the words. "Not any longer!"

"What do you want from me, then?"

"You're the only one who can save us from that *thing*. It's a monster. It wants to hurt us!" With that the boy ran to the bed, flung himself down on it, covered his ears with his hands, then lay there, trembling.

"Suppertime," Eddie announced happily. He swung the stall door shut.

"Supper can wait," I said. A second later I yanked open the door to the female's cell—the Mom look-alike.

She blinked in what remained of the sunlight.

"Hey," I shouted, "what's your name?"

"Delph."

"No, Delph's my mother's name. What were you called before you changed?"

The woman nursed her bruised arm. (Eve had certainly held nothing back.) "I only know that name now. I can't remember anything from before. My life's purpose is to love you and your sister as a mother."

"Quit that fucking nonsense. Now tell me this: who is it that frightens you?"

"You know who, Mason." She winced as she moved her arm that bore the bruise stigmata of my sister's hate. "We've watched you talking to it."

"It?"

Her face paled. "Please make it go away, Mason. You don't know the effect it has on us. . . ." She pressed her lips together. She regretted telling me so much; maybe the pain had loosened her tongue. "Just get rid of it. I'll be Mom. I'll take care of you."

"Forget it. You know what my sister did to you, so I

wouldn't expect a long life." I gripped the timber door in order to close it.

"I'm sorry, Mason."

"Don't waste your breath."

"No, not for this. I'm sorry for the name-calling you suffered at school."

That made me freeze. "You can't know anything about that."

"I am your mother."

"My mother's dead."

"I am a copy of her. I remember what she experienced in life. I know the other children called you names for what I was forced to do."

*"Shut up."* A volcanic heat rose through my neck into my head. *Damn it.* I knew what she was going to say next. "Shut up!"

"You'd have been ten; Eve was little more than a baby. We were so broke, Mason. I couldn't afford to pay the bills—"

"Stop it. You don't know anything about us. You're a monster; you're not even human."

"I have your mother's memories in here." She touched her temple. "We were so poor. We had no money. I had men come to the house. They paid me for sex."

"You became a whore?"

"I tried so hard to keep it secret. I didn't want you to find out that I'd sold my body to keep a roof over our heads."

I stood there, listening. I couldn't move.

"Then one night I brought a man home, a real sleazeball. He said he had to go to the bathroom, but he let this gang into the house. They did things to me, really disgusting, painful things. I made so much noise that a neighbor called the police. After that, the truth came out."

"Mom, you didn't have to do that. You could have gone to my grandparents for money."

"Never that. I wouldn't go to them." Her voice grew hoarse. "Before I'd beg your father's parents for cash I'd rather suck off some stranger for a twenty."

I hurled myself at the steel bars. "Get out of my head! You're not my mother. You're lying. You're fucking lying!" The bars stopped me from killing her. I wanted to get my fingers under her eyelids and then rip off her face.

She sank away into the shadows. "I'm sorry, Mason. It's true. You know it's true. Remember what they told you at school."

"Bitch!"

Madeline wrestled me back, making soothing promises as she did so. "It's okay, Mason. It's okay. I'll take care of you."

Much to Eve's delight I pushed Madeline down onto the gravel path. She shot back with her arms and legs wide apart, scattering stones with her spreading feet. Eddie, meanwhile, slammed the door shut.

"Supper," he snapped. "It's time for supper."

# CHAPTER THIRTY-SEVEN

After supper I returned the camera to the boy. By this time darkness had gotten a grip on the place. The Rose Garden had become a pool of blackness. Beyond the wall lights blazed from the house. A faint beat of music reached me. For me the old mansion containing Eve, Ulric, Ruth, Paddy, Dianna, Dr. Saffrey, and her death squad could have been another world.

In the electric light of the stable cell the boy carefully examined the camera in case I'd hurt his much-loved instrument. "I never thought I'd see it again," he said. "Thanks, Mr. Konrad." I watched him go through his ritual of being reunited with the camera. He ran his fingers over the once-broken casing he'd glued together, then stroked a finger along the new strap as far as the heart-shaped buckle he'd used to replace the original.

"It's the only thing from my old life that means anything now," he told me. "Not even my name's important. But this?" He smiled. "I fixed this up. I saved up for the strap; that's the only new bit of it I could afford. Then I taught myself to use it because the instructions were missing."

"Then your camera's a lot like life."

"Pardon?"

"Life. We find it thrust upon us without asking for it. And the instruction manual doesn't come standard."

The kid grinned. "You mean we make it up as we go along?"

"Something like that." I tutted. "You'll have to watch out for that if you really are a younger version of me. Sometimes I find myself spouting wonky philosophy."

"Wonky philosophy? That sounds funny."

"Yeah, my philosophy about life is funnier than it is profound."

"No. I like what you said. We're born. We grow up without being told how to make our lives work properly."

"I like what you said, too, Mason." Madeline's voice came softly out of the shadows. "Thanks for giving the camera back to him." She stepped into the light falling through the open doorway.

Kirk beamed. "Can I take your photo? Both of you standing together?"

"No film in there. Sorry. They took it away."

Regretfully he rolled the wheel that would have advanced the film to the next frame. "Mr. Konrad, the thing you speak to frightens me. Sometimes it watches me through the wall. It's like I don't see it but I know it's there. If it comes tonight can I shout for you to come and check that I'm all right?"

After I'd closed the stall door on the boy I said to Madeline, "Anger blows all the garbage out of your head, doesn't it? When I got angry with the thing that looks like my mother I wanted to kill her. Two hours later I'm returning the camera to the boy; now I'm going to apologize for knocking you down."

"There's no need, Mason. I understand."

"That's the truth, isn't it? You're not shooting me a cheesy line. You do understand, because you're basically me now." I regarded her face in the gloom. It had become a pale disk. The only features I could make out were her eyes. "Madeline? Are there times when you see what I do?"

"Glimpses, but it's more like remembering something I've seen. Though I know I wasn't there at the time. You rode alongside a man in a truck. He tried to kill you."

"He started off as an Elvis look-alike; then . . . Well, I've no need to explain, have I?"

"He was trapped under the wheel. . . ." She paused. "You were warned that vehicles were approaching and you'd be caught."

"Do you know who warned me?"

As she tried to visualize what I'd seen a grunt escaped her lips. "No . . . I can't figure it out. When I get close to seeing who it was—and it was the same one who came to you when we were inside the cell—well, it's like I'm standing on the edge of a cliff that goes all the way down into . . . I don't know how far . . . forever and ever." An edginess made her voice quaver.

"Think harder."

"I am. Only the closer I get to seeing it the more I feel as if something's pulling me over the edge of the cliff. Mason . . ." At that moment she did topple as fear overwhelmed her. This time I felt a dizzying sense of vertigo as I held her firm, athletic body. Even the beat of her heart transmitted itself through her breast against my ribs. The scent of roses plunged through my nostrils into my stomach. It sickened me and sent a buzz of excitement through my veins all at the same time.

An explosive bang snapped through the air. It had to be a foot crashing against a door. From the first stall came an angry shout. "I know you're out there, Mason Konrad!" Naylor had been nurturing his fury behind closed doors. "You're not untouchable! I want my face back! And I'm going to take it back from you!" Another crash. "You just wait, Konrad. My name is Jacob Naylor. Army corporal. I know who I am. You're a fucking vampire, Konrad. I'm not letting you take away my ID. Do you hear me? You, too, bitch. I'm going to deal with you as well. I'm taking back what's mine—my name, my face. . . ." And so on as he pounded at the door to his cell.

I said, "He's not giving in without a fight. Maybe you only have to *want* to hold on to your identity hard enough; perhaps you can reverse the process. It has to be a question of willpower."

A female voice joined Naylor's grizzly-bear roar, "Mason! This is your mom. Let me out of here, please. My arm hurts. Please, Mason, sweetheart. Let me out of here. I'm frightened. . . ."

# CHAPTER THIRTY-EIGHT

In the sheltered garden the sun worked its searing magic. With the shadows gone it blasted emotional gloom away, too. The people from the big house left us alone. After an unusual European breakfast that could only have been ordered by Eddie of hot drinking chocolate and *pain au chocolat* (a kind of soft, sweet bread roll with a strip of dark chocolate piercing its core) we hit the garden. There we helped Eddie rake up the never-ending fall of rose petals that littered the paths. Maybe the scent of roses really is intoxicating, because I felt this incredible high. I'd enjoyed the chocolate-themed breakfast; I loved the sight of the Rose Garden enclosed by those brick walls that were blends of russet, orange, and tangerine. The blue sky didn't have a single cloud. For as long as I could remember I hadn't been this cheerful; I whistled as I raked the petals.

Madeline smiled as she followed me with a barrow to scoop up my mounds of petals, which she added to her own pink heap. We were relaxed with each other, and nothing momentous about Echomen or the deaths we'd witnessed needed to be uttered; in fact, we joked, or found minor things interesting, like a hairy caterpillar enjoying an undulating stroll along a branch, or pointed out squirrels jumping in trees on the other side of the wall.

The woman, the man, and the boy in their stable-cum-jail didn't make a noise, so I forgot they were there. Simple as that. At one of the CCTV cameras fixed to a wall Madeline stuck out her tongue. Then we undid all our labor by throwing handfuls of rose petals at the camera, treating anyone watching to the vision of a snowstorm in pink. Nice . . . too nice?

Madeline giggled. "How long do you think we'll stay?"

"Who knows?"

"I hope it's forever."

"Forever's a long time." I kept my face straight—but only for a split second. "Certainly more than a week."

"Idiot." Giggling, she hurled petals at me. Then, nearly breathless with laughter, she ran away into a tunnel made from a wooden frame on which more roses climbed. These were vinelike with tiny golden flowers. I found I laughed, too, as I chased her with a handful of petals.

"Madeline, I'm going to stuff these down your top."

She shrieked with laughter. Dr. Saffrey had arranged a change of clothes for her. Now she wore a pair of gym shorts that revealed her muscular thighs. Once again she reminded me of a female marathon runner. Her body boasted a lean firmness that glowed with health. The sleeveless top in lemon cotton revealed her broad, suntanned shoulders. When she moved her arms I could plainly see that they revealed what many an athlete would recognize as enviable muscle definition. At that moment I didn't even notice the Y-shaped scar on the back of her hand, the copy of mine that proved her nature as an uncanny clone. Instead of brooding, we cavorted, laughing like children. Even Eddie stopped his endless sweeping to watch in bemusement.

*Am I warming to Eddie? Am I ready to call him chum?*

"Watch out, Eddie, boy," I shouted as we tore past him so fast his overlarge jacket fluttered in the slipstream. At last even his sulky expression melted into a smile.

A day of miracles . . .

Eddie happy. Madeline and me chasing about the Rose Garden. Whatever next?

Yesterday seemed lost in a fog of misery. Listening to the female apparently recollecting my dead mother's memories of being a whore. Naylor's homicidal rant. Kirk's loneliness. All this on top of a bloody three weeks when I'd seen murder, committed murder myself, watched my mother drown. I'd lost my home in Tanshelf. Yesterday Dr. Saffrey had insisted that in the eyes of the authorities I was officially dead. That's right. Mason Konrad, age twenty-eight, no longer existed. What a twist of fate, especially ironic because somehow total strangers were becoming me. But even *I* wasn't *me* anymore. I would be forced to surrender my own identity. So who would Mason Konrad become? Go on, pick a name: Mattie Koenig? John Smith, John Doe, Levi Wrangler, Donald Starbuck, Fordster Kane, Melmoth P. Hellhole—good God, yes, there were thousands of names to pick from. From dark depression yesterday to sunshine and larks in the garden today. Yes, we're talking miracles.

Last night, after the yelling match with substitute Mom, Madeline coaxed me back into the cottage. Eddie served up cold beers from the fridge. The dark amber brew delivered a potent punch. By the time supper arrived from the big house I'd begun to unwind. From being tense and silent I began talking to Madeline as we sat at the kitchen table. There were roses on the drapes, as well as a rose pattern on the wallpaper—the interior designer had created an impression of the Rose Garden flowing in through the windows to occupy the cottage. The furniture appeared to be antique—old pine dressers, velvet-upholstered armchairs, blackened fire irons on the hearth.

Eddie ate his meal in a back room. Later he strolled into the kitchen, hoisted out a key that hung around his neck on bristly string that must have itched like hell against his skin, then unlocked a drawer in the cabinet.

Sliding open the door, he declared, "This is where I keep my chocolate."

Eddie didn't strike me as the fastidious kind. Granted, he had a fondness for the overlarge jacket he wore, but I didn't think he bothered much about being tidy. How wrong I was. Chocolate bars had been set out on an immaculate square of red satin. Each bar lay facing upward, each positioned a precise distance from its neighbor. They were formidable slabs of confectionery. We're talking Gideon Bible size, thick enough to crack a tooth if you took a reckless bite. To devour one of those beauties in one sitting would result in your either heading for the bathroom at full speed or confessing to Chocoholics Anonymous, "I admit it: I'm an addict. Back on the cocoa bean and on the road to ruin."

"I work hard for this." Eddie lovingly touched one of the chocolate bars. "Sweeping, washing, gardening—I do it all, you know."

For some reason he'd wrapped each slab of chocolate in a strip of gold cellophane, something like you'd find forming the band around a cigar. Whether he thought it looked sophisticated, or whether it possessed some pseudoreligious significance I can't even begin to know. Maybe that adornment really did, in his eyes, make the chocolate greater in stature than a sweet snack; it became a source of sacred nourishment. Here it is: Eddie's temple devoted to his milky holiness, the Chocolate God.

"My chocolate," Eddie breathed as he respectfully slid the door shut. "I had to do all kinds of things for that." He turned the key, then stood there for a while, perspiring, clearly moved by the act of showing us the objects he loved most in the world. After a respectful interval he pushed the key inside his shirt along with the bristly string that secured it around his neck.

By midnight Madeline had gone to bed. Eddie hung around, no doubt making sure I didn't jimmy my way into the chocolate temple. After a few attempts at conversation with him I called it a day, then headed to my own room. Madeline called a friendly good night as I closed my door.

More roses, I told myself. This time blue roses decorated the drapes across my bedroom window. Then I lay on the mattress for the best night's sleep in weeks.

Back to the present, the sunlight, the garden with its roses. I could still taste the sweetness of the breakfast chocolate on my tongue as Madeline flung petals at me while laughing breathlessly. The heat grew as the sun headed toward its zenith. Soon the temperature drove us into shade cast by the high wall. There we sat on a bench; on the far side of the garden Eddie still doggedly swept his paths; maybe he whispered prayers to the Chocolate God as he worked that broom.

For a moment we rested in the coolness; then Madeline said, "I feel nice."

"Me, too. I'm relaxed for the first time in days." A bee bothered Eddie. He crouched down with his hands over his head. "It's crazy to admit this," I said, "but I'm actually happy."

"Enjoy it while you can." She luxuriated in stretching her suntanned limbs. Twenty yards away the bee stopped bugging Eddie; he resumed sweeping.

For a spell I contented myself with sitting there in the shade. Even so, this wasn't holiday time. We were in quarantine. The thought worked its way deep enough under my skin to prevent me from dozing in the rose-scented air. "Let's recap." I closed my eyes so I could order my thoughts. "A matter of days ago I walked home. A stranger attacked me. He was identical to me. Paddy's gang rescued me. After that we were on the road, a squad of men and women who hunted down creatures that they called Echomen. Though I didn't know it at the time, they'd chosen me because I harbored some kind of special trait, and they were delivering me to Dr. Saffrey here, who's running a covert operation against the Echomen. It had spoiled Paddy's plan when I left them one night to return home. A mistake as big and as bad as you can get."

"You weren't to blame, Mason."

I opened my eyes. "Wasn't I? Anyhow, I learned about Echomen the hard way. At first, when I traveled with Paddy's gang, Echomen appeared to be ineffectual creatures. We trapped them easily; they didn't put up much of a fight when we killed them. What's more, it wasn't at all obvious that they resembled us. Ruth explained to me that the muscle structure under the face changed first. So they'd cut away the skin to find out who the Echoman resembled. To me, it was one of these 'eye of faith' situations. You had to *believe* you saw a resemblance, rather than there being an obvious similarity of features."

"That changed."

"Indeed. First time I noticed it . . . when the trucker who looked like Elvis gave me a lift. Within a couple of hours he'd developed this scar on the back of his hand." I touched the Y-shaped one on the back of mine. "Not long after that he talked like me, looked like me, must have been thinking like me, and I guess we started to pool ideas without realizing it at first. They say identical twins do likewise. They might be ten miles apart, but both decide to buy an iced coffee at the same time or simultaneously impulse-buy a . . . I don't know . . . a yellow shirt."

She nodded. *It's that thing she does, agreeing with everything I say, so I build up a momentum of ideas. Every idea I express she nods; the momentum continues.* So it happened then.

I watched a butterfly land on my knee. Its red wings made little trial flaps. "Now, that's a transformation," I said. "From caterpillar to pupa to winged insect. It makes our own metamorphosis look just a little bit crappy, doesn't it?"

"Maybe we should try harder." She smiled. "We might grow wings."

"Or have the magical power to make Egyptian mummies climb out of their coffins and come call on us."

Madeline tilted her head. "Why did you say that?"

"About Egyptian mummies? Nothing. Surely you know I have a bizarre sense of humor by now." The butterfly flew from my leg, up over the wall, to whatever lay in the outside world. "Now, back to the recap. After we met in the cell at my old school we learned that Echomen had become more resourceful."

"They also underwent the transformation faster. Look at me," she added.

"Absolutely. Remember what we found at the school later? All those copies of Eve and me. The other Echomen experimented on those poor wretches without mercy."

"And remember the one you've called Konrad? You hurt his face with the belt buckle."

"Now he seems to be the leader."

"He's probably still alive."

"Although we can't be certain. We know that there's something in my blood that makes strangers turn into clones of us faster than the others. Then they become hell-bent on killing ordinary human beings."

"Not all," Madeline said. "I'm not dangerous."

"No, you're the exception," I said in a light tone. "Do you know why?"

She shrugged. "There might not be a way of stopping people from turning into Echomen, but my case may be a cause for hope."

"You mean in the sense that when you underwent the transformation you weren't driven to kill me . . . or other human beings?"

"Yes."

"Then that is cause for hope."

"We discussed the possibility that this Echo syndrome might be a weapon created by beings from another planet."

"Who fear that other alien species might invade them."

She nodded. "Or contaminate them without malice on their part."

"I find the idea plausible. Eve didn't."

"Dr. Saffrey's people will find evidence of it."

"They will; I'm positive."

"No intelligent beings could risk the possibility that a

rival species will develop on a world where there is even the slightest chance of contact."

"Even radio contact," I added. "If humans received transmissions from an alien civilization it would remove the need for us to develop our own technologies."

"Knowing we weren't the only intelligent life-forms in the universe would be a huge psychological blow. We'd be robbed of our drive. It would destroy us."

"Destroy us completely."

"Mason," she said, "who or what is the figure you talked to in the cell in Tanshelf?"

Her eyes had a wide, friendly innocence about them, an open curiosity that didn't suggest she'd deliberately engineered a flow of questions and answers. A flow that would lead to my revealing the nature of Natsaf-Ty before I could stop my runaway tongue from spilling the beans by the vatload.

Across the garden Eddie deadheaded roses.

I licked my lips as thirst kicked in. "Isn't it amazing we're so cheerful today? In light of what's happened?"

"Its the relief of being safe."

"Something like that." I watched her face. She didn't appear put out that I hadn't answered her about the figure I spoke to in that swimming-pool cell. The same figure that terrified the Echomen, the very same figure that induced in her a catastrophic sense of vertigo. I bumbled along in a careless, chatty way, making a point of being relaxed; even so, my talk took a deliberately different route now. "You know, I figure being happy enough to mess about here in the garden with you is too good to be true. Okay, the sleep did me good, but I didn't feel in such high spirits when I got out of bed. It was after I'd eaten those chocolate pastries that I started getting"—I hunted for the appropriate word—"giddy."

"It's being safe again. No wonder we got a buzz."

"Some buzz," I told her. "There were times I became so exhilarated I could have . . . well, torn my clothes off, then yours, then done something not just wicked but that would have had sirens sounding in every psychiatrist's consulting room from Alaska to New Zealand." I glanced at the CCTV cameras mounted on the walls. "To speed up any experiment they'd planned for us, it would make sense to feed us drugs in the pastries to blow away our inhibitions."

"You think so?"

"Forget it, Madeline. I'm just being paranoid. Come on; let's find out if Eddie has some cold drinks stashed away."

I checked my wristwatch. Just minutes from noon. And just six hours until all hell would be let loose.

# CHAPTER THIRTY-NINE

Maybe Eddie warmed to us. We still weren't close to enjoying a taste of his chocolate; however, that night he brought a portable TV from his room. He told us he wanted to share his favorite show with us. It turned out to be a medical drama in Spanish with English subtitles. Eddie read the lines that appeared at the bottom of the screen aloud.

" 'Dr. Lupo, you are the first man I've wanted since my betrothed died. . . .' 'Nurse, remember your duty is to your patients. . . .' 'If you don't make love to me, Doctor, I will kill myself. . . .' "

I sat on the sofa; Madeline curled up in an armchair. Work in the garden had left us tingling pleasantly. We were relaxed enough to let the trashy drama wash over us. We each had a cold beer. The hot midnight air misted the green bottles, so little dribbles of condensation would peel away from the bottom to drop onto Madeline's bare skin above her top, then roll down the smooth gorge of her cleavage. The beer endowed my mind with that slippery quality when you're pleasantly drowsy. It skittered around recent memories, taking glimpses at random before darting to the next one. On-screen Dr. Lupo watched the raven-haired nurse slip out of her uniform to reveal legs encased in black stockings. On the screen inside my head I recalled Madeline when we were in the swimming-pool cell together. The first time I saw her she'd been naked. The heat pressed down on me with a weight that became nothing less than physical. Night formed a dark wall against the windows. No stars shone. Scarlett squirmed her way lasciviously into my head the same way she had squirmed her naked body against mine just a couple of nights ago. A vivid image surfaced of her red hair falling across her face as she straddled me; those physical feelings: warm, unctuous, tight, lubricious, a wonderful friction as she started that deeply erotic rhythm.

On TV the doctor freed the nurse's breasts from her bra. The camera loomed into close-up until a single nipple filled the screen. A soft female Spanish voice cooed lovingly from the speaker. Eddie's gaze constantly roved from the sex scene on TV to the drawer where he kept his chocolate. Erotic images triggered his cocoa craving. Another glistening bead of water dropped from Madeline's bottle onto her chest. I took a mouthful of ice-cold beer, swallowed; my nerve endings tingled.

The full-blooded thump lifted Madeline bodily out of

the armchair. Beer foamed from the bottle at the same time as a scream erupted from her lips. "Mason! There's someone at the window."

A white face slammed up against it; two fists pounded the pane. More striking than that were the two terrified eyes that stared out of the darkness at us.

Hands drummed as a voice called out, "Mason . . . Mason! Let me in!"

"Damn," I hissed. "It's the woman from the cell. She's managed to get out." I put the beer on the table as I got to my feet. "Eddie, what do you do when this happens?"

He blinked in shock. "It's never happened before."

"You must be able to talk to people in the house."

"Phone," he managed to say.

"Mason," called the thing with Mom's face. "Please let me in."

"Get away from here!"

"Mason, it's Naylor. He's out of the cell. He'll kill you."

From behind her a blur raced out of the darkness. A second later it slammed into the woman's back, and the momentum carried both of them through the window in a splash of crystal as glass panes shattered. The creature that begged to replace my mother had been thrust through the glass first. Shards bristled from her face. Blood spurted into the air. The dive through the glass left Naylor in better shape than the Mom-clone that he'd used as a protective shield. His powerful body bounded from the floor. I saw that copy of my face stretched tightly over his skull, distorting the features. Madeline threw herself forward to protect me from the powerful slash of thickly muscled arms. One pass of his hand effortlessly flung her across the sofa.

Eddie ran to the pine cabinet. "No, no, no . . ." His voice became a warbling screech as he fumbled around his neck for the string that held the key to the drawer.

"Eddie," I shouted, "phone the house. Tell them Naylor's out!"

"I warned you." Naylor advanced. "I'm not letting you take away my ID. This is Corporal Naylor!" He slapped his bare chest. "Give me back my face."

"I'm not responsible, Naylor. The change is spontaneous. Take it easy. Dr. Saffrey's team needs time to find out what's happening."

"Fuck you! I know what's happening."

Eddie whimpered as he struggled to get the key into the drawer, the treasure chest of his chocolate.

I bellowed at him, "For pity's sake, Eddie! Tell the house we need help!"

Meanwhile, Madeline moaned as she pulled herself upright by the arm of the sofa. At my feet the thing that pretended to be Mom bled on the rug. Naylor pushed his thumb into the side of his mouth as he glared at me. My trait when thinking hard—or when planning to act.

*Here it comes*, I told myself.

"Naylor. You've got to trust me."

"Trust you! You took my face away. See the scar?" He flicked the Y-shaped stigmata. "I never had that scar. It doesn't belong to me."

"Naylor—"

A huge fist buzzed the air. It connected with the side of my head, knocking me against the TV, crashing it to the floor. On-screen, the drama played on with the doctor sliding the nurse's stockings off her long legs.

I flung a punch back. It didn't bother Naylor much; hell, did he even feel it?

"Damn it, Eddie, call the house." The side of my head pulsed with agony. "Forget the drawer."

"I want my chocolate!"

"Leave it. . . ." Another punch from Naylor. The room rolled over. When my eyelids slid back I realized I lay on the floor beside the TV. The thing with my Mom's face, albeit sliced open by blades of glass, lay beside me.

"Eddie! Phone!"

Eddie wouldn't be phoning. Even though he desperately tried to rescue the chocolate bars, Naylor grabbed hold of him by the collar. The big man hauled the little man backward.

A cry burst from Eddie. "I've had enough! I want to go home! Let me go home. Please . . ."

Naylor didn't even break a sweat. Efficiently he pulled the string from beneath Eddie's shirt. Then he worked the string into a slipknot without taking it from the little guy's neck. That done he hoisted Eddie into the air, popped the loop over a nail in the ceiling beam, and left him to hang.

Even though the string pulled so tight into Eddie's neck the woven hemp vanished into his fleshy neck, he didn't let go of the chocolate bar he'd salvaged. It still gleamed there in its pristine silver foil with the cellophane band around it. Eddie spun around at the cord's end in the center of the room, his feet thirty inches from the floor. He didn't kick or spasm as he choked. Instead he drew his knees up until he formed a fetal position, knees tucked up into his chest. Mouth open, eyes closed, he brought the chocolate bar up toward his head. Then with the flesh of his neck turning purple as the crushing force of the noose ripped blood vessels under the skin, he lovingly pressed the flat upper side of the chocolate to his cheek. How cool it must have felt as his nerves blazed with the agony of hanging there, the narrow cord biting into his neck. It lasted a moment until his heart failed. The man's limbs suddenly flopped loose; slowly he twisted around, the chocolate bar slipping from dead fingers to the floor.

All this I saw in maybe five seconds, the time it took for Naylor to turn away from Eddie's dangling corpse and finish what he aimed to do: kill me. He bent down, that mirror-image face of mine contorted with hate; he bunched his fist to punch me as I lay there in a daze. Beside me on the floor the TV glared with garish images of the nurse lying naked on a bed. She teasingly caressed herself, running her fingers up bare thighs, a lascivious smile spread across her beautiful face.

A punch hit me with the force of a concrete slab toppling from out of the sky. The army had trained Naylor to kill people with his bare hands. I'd get the manual execution. He drew back his fist again, ready to smash my nose. A figure cannoned into him. The Mom-clone gripped his wrist. With her free hand she drew a glass sliver from where it had been embedded beside her mouth; then, with it gripped between fingers and thumb, she drove it into Corporal Naylor's eye.

Dear God, that hurt the bastard. He howled.

In a flurry of movement he shoved the woman aside and dragged the shard from his eyeball, bringing with it gouts of blood and jelly. The woman lumbered back across the room, knocking the body of Eddie in the process so he swung like a pendulum. Once more she launched herself onto Naylor.

With her hands around his head she dragged him away from me, shouting all the time, "Mason! Save yourself. I won't be able to hold him for long. Run!"

"Mom!" I helped wrestle Naylor down. "Don't let him hurt you." The emotion tore holes in me. I could barely speak. "Mom. I love you. I'm sorry. I should have stayed away."

"Don't worry," she breathed. "It's not your fault. I'll take care of this. You make sure you find somewhere safe."

Madeline crawled on all fours toward me. Above her the soles of Eddie's feet swished across her back as he swung. "Mason . . . she's not your mother. She only looks like her."

"Shut up!" My head spun. "Mom?"

All kinds of bloody crap oozed from Naylor's eye socket—not just blood (though there was a crimson abundance of that), but pink slivers of meat along with glistening pearls of jelly. All the time the woman with Mom's face did her best to hold him down against the floor.

Panting, she shouted, "Save yourself, son. Get out of here."

Okay, it must be the punches to my head, but it seemed as if my real, flesh-and-blood mother fought to protect me from Naylor. *This is the moment to redeem myself,* I thought. *I screwed up in the swimming pool. My mother drowned. If only I'd moved faster my real mother would still be alive.* Naylor lay flat on his back, his eye bloomed into a gory, crimson mess, but even though the woman sat on his chest so she could hold him down he got his fingers around her throat. Those thick, muscular fingers squeezed. A choking sound spurted from her lips; her eyes bulged.

The blows left me dazed. I wasn't rational, but as the Mom thing choked out the words that she loved me, that I should run for my life, and with Madeline trying to pull me in the direction of the cottage door, I tugged at Naylor's powerful arms. *I have to stop him from strangling her. This is my chance to make everything right again.* At that crazy, godforsaken, blood-soaked moment I really believed that I'd been given a second chance to save my mother. If I could only get the woman free of Naylor she really would be the woman who gave birth to me, who raised me and my sister, who sacrificed so much to give us a start in life. If only . . .

*If only* is the curse of humanity. If only the hijackers failed, if only nations signed peace deals, if only the firing mechanism in that bomb hadn't worked . . .

With a roar Naylor thrust himself up from the debris on the floor. One of his hands grabbed the woman by the hair. His free hand pushed me backward. My head cannoned into Eddie hanging by the neck. The blow dazed me and sent Eddie spinning a pirouette at the end of his line. Like the time in the swimming pool, even though I nearly burst my heart I tried to move so fast, it wasn't nearly quick enough. I saw it all so clearly. The TV still lay on the floor, presenting its show to chaos here in the room. The nurse with the long black hair lay on her back. In Spanish she begged for love.

Naylor knelt on the floor with the clone's hair gripped in his hand. A split second later he smashed her head down onto the case of the TV. Once, twice. The screen shattered; so did the Mom thing's skull. A river of blood discharged from the side of her head into the torn electrics of the TV. It sparked; smoke rolled in a black ball toward the ceiling.

Naylor rose to his feet. I ran to meet him head-on. He lifted his fists to finish me. The first weapon at hand was the remains of the TV that oozed blood and blue sparks from ripped wiring. I scooped up the smoking wreckage, then dashed it into his face. Live wires became grounded through the bloody wound in his eye. The electric shock smacked him off his feet.

To help her climb to her feet Madeline had used the

big antique cabinet that stood with its back to the wall. She still clung to it near the gaping drawer that contained Eddie's chocolate.

Roaring with fury, Naylor struggled to his knees. Black burn marks mottled his bloody face. "Mason! You're a dead man!"

"Madeline!" I gripped the dresser. "Push it over!"

Together we heaved the dresser forward. Naylor saw it coming. He held up his hands to stop it, but even his formidable muscular strength didn't cut it this time. The heavy furniture crashed down onto him, crushing him against the floor. Blood vented from the guy's mouth. Madeline and I blundered by Eddie's body dangling from the ceiling. For a moment I had a clear view of the little corpse's hand. A Y-shaped scar had begun to form in the skin, just in the same place as mine. Then we pushed by him out into the night air.

My plan now: to attract the attention of people in the house. But what I found out there in the Rose Garden killed that plan dead.

# CHAPTER FORTY

The time had rolled past midnight when we left the cottage in the corner of the walled garden. An early summer heat filled the inside of this enclosed space with a cloying rose-scented atmosphere that choked your lungs, a scent closer to sun-baked trash cans rather than flowers. Lights shone through the cell doors. Two were wide-open. Yet could they have been busted by Naylor, even though he had the muscles of a pro wrestler? What I saw lying on the ground didn't answer the mystery; it added to it.

"Paddy?" I approached the fallen figure. One look at the crooked neck told me Naylor had snapped the man's neck. Had Paddy opened the stall doors? But then, how could he do that? Surely the key wouldn't have been available to him. Come to that, why should he do it? Why release a pair of Echomen at midnight?

Madeline found the answer as she checked the body for life signs. "Mason? Look at his face. The shape of his nose is changing." Paddy's hand faced palm upward. Madeline turned it over to examine it in the spilled light from the doorway. "Oh, my God, take a look at this."

"I don't have to." I grunted. "Paddy had begun to transform. For some reason he freed Naylor and the woman. Naylor killed him."

"What if he's hurt Kirk?"

But right on cue a wail rose from the only cell still locked. Kirk screamed in absolute terror. "Mason. Help! It's back. Mason . . . Madeline . . . get it out of here." The scream rose in volume. "Please. Before it touches me!"

Opening the outer doors to Kirk's cell—the kid who looked like I did when I was ten years old—wasn't a problem. Shoot back the bolts, swing open the timber doors, a cinch. Only behind the outer doors a steel gate barred the way into the cell. Inside, the kid sat on his bunk with his back to the wall, a blanket pulled up to his face, which as a shield had to be as effective as fresh air. Of course, I knew what I'd find. The Echomen that were copies of me also got facets of my mind bundled with memories, thoughts, and the ability to sense the presence of Natsaf-Ty, if not to see him in his dusty red entirety, as I could. The Echo Mason Konrads appeared to glimpse "traces" of him that perplexed them, to say the least. Now it clearly terrified the creatures. Kirk's eyes bulged in terror as Natsaf-Ty stood in the center of the cell, arms limp by his sides, eyes closed, the tongue protruding slightly through the papery lips. Okay, the Egyptian mummy was my imaginary companion from childhood, so why did this figment of my imagination invoke explosions of horror in those clones of yours truly, Mason Konrad?

The kinder part of me almost told the kid, *Don't worry; he can't hurt you. You're seeing something I used to imagine when I was your age.* But still I recognized in Natsaf-Ty a secret weapon. The Echomen wanted me to fight Natsaf-Ty on their behalf. Yet in reality was there anything to fight? Okay, I could see Natsaf-Ty in Kirk's cell as the kid slobbered with fear. I could even describe him, because his appearance hadn't changed from when I was boy: *A gaunt figure with dark red skin. His eyelids are closed. There's no hair on his head; Egyptian priests shaved off all body hair. The scalp's a mess of cracks; there are gaping holes that expose a skull that's a dull brown. Few mummy wrappings remain. There are crisscrossed bandages over part of the chest, with more forming a loincloth around the waist.*

Kirk was terrified of the apparition, but what of Madeline? I turned to her. Eyes wide, staring, breath coming in shallow tugs; okay, so terror hadn't overwhelmed her, but the tawny phantom disturbed her. I remember how she described the tug of vertigo when she tried to picture Natsaf-Ty. Although something odd was happening . . . I knew the Mason Konrad clones couldn't see the mummy clearly like I could, so they failed to identify it. But when I studied Madeline's and Kirk's reactions I realized they didn't stare at the place the figure occupied; their eyes had a searching quality, as if they looked *around* it. As if they sensed it was far bigger than it really was, and they were trying to see something that had swollen to, I don't know, the size of an elephant? A house? A mountain?

"Wait here," I told Madeline; then I ran to the toolshed. There I found an ax that Eddie must have used to chop firewood in the winter. Seconds later I laid into the padlock on the cell gate. Each blow produced a gush of glittering sparks. Yet despite the firework display, plus the crash of ax head against padlock, neither Kirk nor Madeline could wrench their fascinated yet fearful gaze from the space around the dusty red guy with his pizza-crust flesh. After the fifth blow the hasp snapped.

I hoped Kirk would have readily sprinted for freedom. However, fear paralyzed him. In the end I picked him up, then carried him past the mummy.

"Good work," I murmured to my imaginary buddy. "I hope you've other hidden talents, because we're going to need them soon."

Of course the old gentleman didn't reply. After all, he'd not spoken to me since my teens. Imaginary friends are like that. Your conscious mind doesn't pull the puppet strings; it's the dark creatures in the abyss of the unconscious that have supreme control, just as they exert their power over your dreams and nightmares.

If the carnage tonight had flowed from Paddy's actions, then he'd done one thing right: he'd left the door in the wall unlocked. Madeline exited the Rose Garden first, with me following. Kirk appeared to weigh nothing in my arms; he didn't wriggle or utter a sound. *That must be the Natsaf-Ty effect,* I told myself. *The boy's mind and body have been shocked into shutdown.* That knowledge might come in handy later.

The next move would be to report what had happened, only the closer we got to the house it became obvious that not only the cottage in the Rose Garden had suffered an assault. A path led across the lawn to the mansion where we'd met Saffrey and where I anticipated that Eve, Ulric, and the others were billeted with the soldiers. From the house windows came a yellow glare that had nothing to do with electric light. Glass shattered from the heat of flames. Smoke gushed between the slates in the roof.

I nodded at a patio in front of the doors. "Naylor wasn't the only one to snap." Bodies lay in bizarrely twisted positions on the stone slabs. "They've been thrown from the upstairs windows. Here." I handed Madeline the comatose child. Her biceps bulged as she bore Kirk's weight.

"Mason, don't go in there. The whole lot's going up."

"I'll be right back." Even though it was night I could make out the area around the house as flames rolled through the windows. A cursory examination of the corpses revealed them to be military personnel who'd managed to hurriedly pull on their pants before tragedy overtook them. I checked the backs of their hands, half expecting to see the Y-shaped scar that marred my own flesh. This time the skin of these dead infantry men was unblemished, although they had wounds consistent with a twenty-foot-fall onto a stone surface and their skulls bore the signs of some fairly ruinous injuries. Half of them had ligatures around their necks, too. Therefore they'd died in relative silence, certainly quietly enough so we hadn't heard them from our cottage tucked away in the garden. A form brushed my shoulder. What appeared at first to be an attack turned out to be yet another corpse falling from above.

The guy in military fatigues smacked into the ground hard enough to shatter the stone patio slab beneath him. He'd had time to don a sidearm but not the opportunity to use it. I slid the automatic from his holster, then shoved it into the belt of my jeans. In the firelight I could see Madeline anxiously looking this way as she cradled the boy in her arms. Staying here much longer couldn't be wise, but I had to find my sister. First I tried the doors to one of the downstairs rooms, only chunks of burning debris were dropping from the ceiling. All that ancient timber that had been steadily drying for the last three centuries didn't just burn; it exploded into an inferno. The stench of smoke choked me. The heat now belching from the house seared my skin. That and the brightness of the flames had me scrunching my eyes shut so I could barely see.

"Mason." Madeline beckoned me. The heat had grown intense enough to force her away from the house. "Mason!" Then I saw she didn't beckon but drew my attention to a section of the building to my right. Through a door came a stream of figures. They were burning from head to foot. Yet they weren't screaming in agony. They moved purposefully toward me. That high pain threshold did nothing less than yell at me the word *Echoman*. They'd finished killing inside the house. Now they were going to mop up the humans on the grounds—me included. I drew the handgun from my belt. Three rapid shots burst the heads of the three monsters in the lead. Blood streaming from the bullet holes in their skulls extinguished their burning clothes in the region of their shoulders with a loud hissing sound. The three fell without a whimper. Behind them were twenty more, blazing zombie figures that didn't appear fazed by the fact that they were walking funeral pyres. I reckon I had maybe five rounds left in the gun. No need to waste them gifting the Echomen with an easy, pain-free death. I backed away. They kept advancing, but the burns had taken their toll. They lost sight of me as the heat destroyed their eyes. Another moment later one sagged to the floor. Their lungs must have melted as they'd inhaled superheated air inside the blazing building. The others were dying, too. One by one they sagged to the ground in a mess of burning flesh. A wave of roast-pork smell washed over me. Worse than the smell was the fact that another dozen Echomen had rounded the corner—don't ask me how I knew; I guess I'd developed an instinct for who was and who wasn't an Echo creature. These hadn't been touched by the flames. With there being too many to fight, I decided to retreat while we could.

When I reached Madeline I took the child off her with the command, "Run!" So with the blazing house at our backs we raced for the forest, where an unknown territory lay in wait for us.

# CHAPTER FORTY-ONE

Fortunately the boy—that ten-year-old facsimile of me as a child—appeared to weigh nothing in my arms. He still hadn't moved or spoken; come to that he hadn't given any indication of being awake. With Madeline keeping pace beside me we ran into the forest that rolled up to the mansion like a black ocean. At this time of night the world had become a compilation of faint grays, shadows, purples, and pools of utter blackness.

This journey was a voyage into the unknown. I didn't know the terrain. All I'd seen of it beyond the house was what appeared to be around a million trees with a narrow channel cut through them along which the Echomen had walked to their doom a couple of days ago. Far from the Echomen being idiot monsters, they must have somehow engineered an effective attack on Dr. Saffrey's headquarters. Now the building blazed like fury. A torrent of fire rose into the night sky.

So I didn't know where I was headed. Had the Echomen followed us? Was Eve dead? None of this I knew. All I had was the instinct to get away from the burning house. And that we did. Madeline accepted my plan, if you can call it a plan, without question. Unhesitatingly she placed her trust in me. The boy remained inert in my arms. Presently we adopted a steady, rhythmic pace. The massive columns of the tree trunks glided by. The warm night air possessed a hush that went beyond silence. It seemed to draw sound into itself, so I found myself half believing we glided through a black-and-white photograph of a forest at night. A still life where we were the only three creatures that floated through the darkness.

Above me, a canopy of branches hid the sky. Beneath me, soft dirt robbed my feet of any sound of their passing. And it was then, as we moved deeper into the forest, that I couldn't shake off the notion that we passed from this world into a separate reality. One that wouldn't obey the laws of physics—where up could be down, where yesterday might be in the past or still yet to come. This could be a place where life and death were simply masks that were switched back and forth on the face of a single, constant entity that was eternal.

My mind touched on memories as if they were promises of things to come rather than recollections of the past. An image came of my mother sipping white wine in front of the TV on a Saturday night as I combed my hair in front of the mirror. A ten-year-old Eve sighed, "I wish I was grown up. I want to go out at night." Then I lay in the bedroom of the house that Paddy's gang had occupied; the child's robot droned: "If you should die, do not lie screaming in your grave. . . ." The image of the Echo people who wore the faces of Eve and myself that were nailed to the classroom floor, and as they broke free to launch their attack on us.

"I'm lost," I told Madeline.

"We'll be all right," she replied.

"We could be going in circles. The bad guys might be lying in wait for us."

She gave me a sympathetic look.

"Aren't you afraid of being killed?" I asked.

"I'm with you. That's what's important to me."

We continued walking through the nighttime forest. Everything had become a uniform black—above, below, behind, in front. More than once I uttered, "I don't know where I'm going."

A faint glow appeared ahead. Instinctively I headed toward it. Moments later the glow resolved itself into a red figure.

"Natsaf-Ty," I murmured. "Keeper of the crocs." I glanced at Madeline. She didn't appear to notice our visitor. I spoke louder. "So, do you intend to be useful? Have you come to show us the way?"

A pale mist formed just above the ground. Even so I could still see the Egyptian mummy. I use the word *see* because even though the gaunt figure in bandages must have been a product of hallucination, it did appear real to me at that moment. I saw the thin arms, the closed eyes, the tongue protruding slightly between the lips. And complementing that image of the mummified priest was a characteristic aura of serenity. I'd grown up with Natsaf-Ty; he'd been my trusted mentor as I sat on the top stair at home and he seated himself on his habitual third riser from the bottom.

The years rolled back. In my arms an identical copy of me, age ten, slept. In the gloom I could see the shape of the face and pale bump of his nose. That was near the age when my world suffered the destructive attention of school thugs. Meanwhile, my mother's own life appeared to be on the verge of mental and economic collapse. Then the miracle. Natsaf-Ty stole into my life one night. He listened to my troubles, and in my childhood imagination, at least, he whispered answers to my problems. Was this coincidence? But at nearly the same time as Natsaf-Ty's arrival Mom landed a well-paid job in Tanshelf. Suddenly the world of the Konrad family became a happy one. Mom's spirits lifted; she sparkled with a healthy vitality I hadn't seen before. I wish I could report that the bullies suffered horrible injuries at the hands of a mysterious assailant (just picture the news story: "Police report traces of ancient bandage were found at the scene of the crime, while grains of sand found on the slain have been identified as Egyptian"), but life rarely delivers such a conveniently satisfying climax to episodes like this. Instead, the bully squad just faded out of the scene. Either they'd gotten bored with tormenting me, or they'd moved to other schools; I can't remember. All I am sure of is that school, if not exactly a shipload of laughs, became sort of okay. I made friends with Tony Allen; he had a knack for making everyone smile. From then on what I most remember about school were the jokes and the crazy adventures we enjoyed.

With these thoughts came a growing certainty that my life had followed a cycle. The dangerous times I'd known as a child, when there was a possibility our family would be torn apart, maybe with Mom needing psychiatric care, and me being remorselessly beaten down by classroom sadists—well, that kind of danger had returned. Only worse. I'd lost my mother, my career, my home, my identity; here I was lost in a forest in the middle of the night, in absolute darkness, with a distinct probability that in the next few hours I might lose my life. With me were monsters. Nothing less than that. Here was a girl who had been transformed into a female version of me. In my arms was a boy who had been rendered into a ten-year-old version of yours truly, Mason Konrad. When disaster threatened to fall on me when I was a child I'd visited the Tanshelf Museum. Along with the other kids I'd pressed my nose to the glass case that housed the mummy of Natsaf-Ty, keeper of the sacred crocodiles. We'd made silly comments about the shriveled body, or tried to peer through the gap in his loincloth while making willy jokes. Only everything changed for me. There I was on the brink of personal disaster. But when I woke at midnight to find that Natsaf-Ty had followed me home, seemingly with an interest in my welfare, that was when my life was saved.

So, whether this was the first sign of mental collapse in me I don't know, but I addressed the figure that glowed in the mist. "I've done everything I can to get through this. But I can't make it on my own. I need you again. Just like I did when I was a boy. Without your help I'm dead." The figure didn't move. When I spoke again it seemed as if I'd passed through a doorway of no return. "If you help me now, I'll give you whatever it is you need. Did you hear that? I owe you. I'll be in your debt." *You've just made a deal with the devil, Mason.*

*You've gone and sold your soul.* Those words came in a searing blast of revelation.

Madeline shot me a startled look. What was more, I could tell she was frightened, because she asked, "Mason, what is it you can see?"

"Don't you see anything?"

She shook her head, but something there in the wood troubled her so much that her eyes had that scared, searching quality, as if she knew a danger lurked just beyond her range of vision. Natsaf-Ty? Why did he panic the Echomen? What power did my old-time imaginary friend have to reach into their heads to hit all the fear buttons? Echomen couldn't see Natsaf-Ty. But they sensed him; that knowledge of his presence filled them with nothing less than supernatural dread.

I addressed the luminous shape in the mist: "Do we have a deal? Come on; we used to talk all the time when I was a kid. You can understand me. I'm promising to give you anything you want in return for getting us out of here. What's your answer?"

The ancient red face became suddenly clear through the vapor. That ruin of dried skin appeared to tighten. Lines appeared around the mouth. It lasted only a second; then the serene expression returned. But at that moment I told myself, *If I'm not mistaken, that was a smile.* A smile of friendship? Or a smile of triumph? Only time would tell.

I realized the red figure had begun to move. I hadn't seen him turn. This had to be nothing less than a re-assembly of his molecular structure. Where I'd been seeing the front of him, his face and chest, now I saw the back of his head with the cavernous hole in the skull.

"Come on," I murmured to Madeline. "If I'm not mistaken we're being shown a way out of here."

"Shown?" She didn't understand because she couldn't see Natsaf-Ty.

"Trust me. We're on our way to safety."

She did trust me in a way that had the power to be unnerving. If I asked her to douse herself in kerosene and light a match she'd do just that. Anyway, we followed the red sprite through the nighttime forest. For ten minutes we walked in silence. I kept my eye on the skull gliding through the darkness; sometimes, however, it looked less like a skull than a red planet drifting in the depths of space. One with an enormous black crater that scarred its surface. Then I realized a salient fact: the boy had become an inert weight in my arms.

"The child's dying," I said to the red globe as it drifted through darkness. "Can you do anything for him?"

A second later the boy woke with the words, "What are you carrying me for? I'm okay; I can walk."

I set him down. Without any difficulty on his part Kirk walked in between Madeline and me. We could have been some weird clone family out for a stroll in the dark. The other notion that struck me: *How helpful the old mummy has become tonight. For days he's been content to observe; now he's turned into the genie of the lamp, granting wishes like there's no tomorrow. Go on, ask him for a helicopter to fly us to safety. I dare you. And while you're at it, have him supply a sack full of diamonds so you'll be rich for life.* Flippant thoughts . . . they had their purpose, though: to mask an anxiety that sounded a faint yet persistent warning note inside my head.

We followed the red figure for at least an hour. The canopy of branches above our heads never broke once. Down at ground level the darkness possessed a quality that went beyond the mere absence of light. It felt as if I pressed my head into a thick fabric. Night filled my eyes; in an uncanny way it filled my ears and nostrils too.

*It's because you sold your soul to Natsaf-Ty,* came the voice in my head. *In return for saving your skin, Mason, he wants something from you. A big something. And big doesn't come cheap. This is one debt you'll wish you never owed. . . .*

Half a dozen shapes that I'd taken to be tree trunks suddenly came to life. The shapes hefted submachine guns; that much I could see. A light blasted into my face.

"Mason!"

One shape rammed into my chest with enough force to nearly topple me.

"Mason, how did you find us?"

"Eve?"

She pulled the dazzling beam from my eyes so she could light her own face. For the first time in days she was genuinely pleased to see me.

I asked, "Who else is with you?"

"There's Ulric. These five guys are from the commando squad. They were stationed at the house with us." She punched my arm. "But how on earth did you know we were here?"

Amid the trees a red object glowed. To avoid a complex—and undoubtedly problematic—explanation of the nature of Natsaf-Ty, I shrugged. "Put it down to instinct."

"Never mind," Ulric intoned. "You found us. That's what's important."

Eve used the flashlight to illuminate my traveling companions. "Uh, so you brought her with you?"

"I could hardly leave her, could I? The Echomen were killing everyone."

"And you picked up the other stray." My sister blasted the light into Kirk's face. "It's easy to see why. He's another copy of you."

"Eve, he'd be dead now if I hadn't—"

"I know, I know. But if you ask me, Mason, you've discovered a new dimension to narcissism. What you've got inside your head would keep a whole team of psychoanalysts busy for years." Then in an impulsive rush she kissed me on the cheek.

I smiled at Eve. "Does that mean, despite the murky depths of my subconscious, that you're actually happy to see your big brother?"

"Yeah, I'll give you a second chance. Even with your choice of menagerie."

One of the commandos grunted. "I don't want to spoil happy reunions . . . but we're exposed here, and to render it in civilian-speak, we don't know where the hell we are."

"Follow me," I said. "I met someone back there who showed me the way to the exit."

The soldier shot Eve a quizzical glance. "It's okay." She sighed. "My brother talks like this all the time. Now he must have tricked a guardian angel into looking out for him."

I gave a grim smile. "It's okay; my sister talks like *that* all the time."

Ulric added in precise Norwegian tones, "The pair of you must issue from an extraordinary bloodline. *Both* of you can be as perplexing as you are fascinating."

The commando stayed focused on the danger. "Around five hundred Echomen stormed the headquarters tonight. We exterminated plenty, but I figure there're probably at least three hundred in these woods searching for us."

"Point taken, Sergeant," Ulric said. "Mason, be so good as to lead the way, please."

Despite the carnage, Ulric's Scandinavian cool and good manners appeared in perfect condition. He stood aside to allow me to take the lead. Me and my odd little clone family.

The red beacon that only my eyes could see revealed the way. With Eve, Ulric, and the five surviving soldiers following, I walked into the darkness.

# CHAPTER FORTY-TWO

We reached the edge of the forest as the sun rose.

Eve gazed out over a valley where mists slid white fingers through the meadows. "Do you know what's missing?" she murmured. "The dawn chorus. There isn't one. Not a single bird wanting to sing." My sister slid the strap of the machine gun from her shoulder. "Nature's giving us a warning."

The boy blinked in the growing light. "I want to go home. I'm scared. . . ."

Ulric rested a hand on Kirk's shoulder. "What is there to be scared of? Do you see anything?"

Kirk shook his head; his eyes said it all, though: terror approached.

Then maybe old Natsaf-Ty exerted his unique aura on Kirk, who, after all, was an Echoman, albeit a junior one.

The commando sergeant's gray eyes scanned the grasslands. "If we continue this way, we leave the tree cover behind."

"You've got guns," Madeline said. She wasn't wrong.

These commandos carried a whole armory between them: submachine guns, sniper rifles, grenade launchers, a drab green cylinder that contained a wire-guided antitank missile. Add to that that Eve and Ulric toted submachine guns. There was formidable firepower here.

Even so Ulric shook his head. "We might have weapons, but the Echomen have got numerical power. Last night hundreds attacked the HQ. For all we know there might be hundreds of the creatures out there."

"Waiting for us," Eve added.

The sergeant who'd been staring at me with growing hostility slid back the bolt of his gun. "The real problem in the end wasn't the Echomen who stormed the building. Our force had already gone rotten. My men were changing." His eyes hardened. "They were turning into him."

Eve said, "It's not my brother's fault."

"He's a plague carrier. I saw my men with that same scar on the backs of their hands." He used the gun to point at the red scar on mine . . . the same one that blazed its Y-shaped stigmata on both the boy's and Madeline's flesh.

Another soldier added, "You can't trust anyone now. You start talking to your buddy, but by the time you finish he's gone and turned into that guy." He pointed an RPG at me. And at that moment I couldn't say for sure whether he pointed like it was an extension of his finger or he aimed the armor-piercing shell at my heart, ready to blow me all over the meadow in a sticky crimson paste. The other commandos gave a ripple of unease.

The hands of one tightened around the gun stock. "So what the fuck's happening with these two? How the fuck can this kid and the woman turn into versions of him? If they're Echomen why aren't they attacking us?"

"It's probably only a matter of time." The corporal clicked off the safety.

"And who's to say that this guy, Mason Konrad, isn't the leader of those things? The kid and the Echo bitch do what he tells them."

"Okay, okay." Ulric raised his hands. "Stay cool about this, huh?"

The sergeant growled, "But this guy might be infecting us. What if we turn Echo? We can't—"

"Listen to me. We brought Mason Konrad here for a reason. He is different from the rest of us. Yes, he can transmit the mechanism that causes the change, as do we all to a certain extent. We don't know how this occurs yet, but we're learning from Mason Konrad. Not all the people whom he 'infects,' as you put it, become hostile to human beings. That makes him unique."

Eve added, "It also means he could be humanity's greatest hope for survival."

"I'm also your greatest hope for survival right now," I told them. "I got you through the forest in one piece."

"We're not safe yet," grunted the corporal.

"Then trust me to go ahead and check whether it's clear."

"Yeah, so you're free to run back to your kind."

"I don't have a 'kind.'" I glared at the commando. "But if I scout ahead *alone* there's less chance of you looking in the mirror tonight and seeing this." I pointed at my own face. "Understand?"

"What about the boy and the woman?"

Eve answered this one. "Transformation relates to proximity. If they're far enough away you're safe from infection."

"She's right," Ulric said. "If they sit under the tree over there then there's no danger."

"You'd better be right." The corporal's eyes still flashed suspicion. "If one of these guys gets even so much as a rash on the back of his hand we're going start blasting."

For a second there was silence as we all digested the statement. By this time the sun had risen above the horizon; the mist in the valley turned the color of copper.

"Okay." I nodded. "We have an understanding. I'll check ahead. Once I know it's clear I'll come back." My eyes settled on the guns the commandos handled with a restless tension. "Only don't go pointing those things at me. Understand?"

The sergeant nodded. "But when you come back, keep your distance. Do *you* understand that?"

"You've got my word. Now keep out of sight until I give you the all-clear."

Before I left the huddle of people at the edge of the forest Eve handed me the machine gun with the words, "Remember, just point and squirt. Okay?"

With a nod rather than a heartfelt good-bye I headed down the grass slope into the valley. By this time Madeline had led Kirk by the hand to sit on the grass beneath a tree some fifty yards from the commandos. From the way her eyes followed me I knew she wanted to come, too. But what none of them could understand was that I didn't simply strike off on my own to see if the way ahead was clear; I still followed the red figure. A figure that none of them could see. How could I explain that I'd put my faith in something that I recognized as an imaginary friend from childhood? But just a few hours ago I had sensed that Natsaf-Ty had become more than that. If you wanted to get to the psychological guts of the matter I might, if pressed, suggest that the figure wrapped in scanty bandages and owning a dry crust

for a face was a component of my mind. A special part
that had become externalized in the familiar form of
that imaginary friend of yore. One and the same who
used to occupy the step at home in order to console
me and advise me after a trying day at school. But then
had it become more significant than that? People who
dowse using forked sticks will tell you that the ability to
find underground streams has nothing to do with the
hazel twig in their hands; it's a sixth sense that they're
born with that simply makes the muscles twitch so the
stick jerks over the hidden water source. As I walked
through the dew that was what passed through my
head. A growing sense of understanding, as if a hidden
picture slowly revealed itself to me until I was close to
the point of saying, *So that's what it is! I should have
known.* What I'm striving to express is this: Natsaf-Ty
wasn't an ancient Egyptian mummy who actually made
himself visible to me. If I walked up to him I couldn't
reach out to touch his dry face; I couldn't slip my finger
through the hole in his skull to wiggle bits of dry embalmer's rag in the brain cavity. Nor could I identify him
as simply a childhood imaginary friend. No. He was
more than that. Just what, I'd have to wait and see.

Therefore, make no bones about it, I talked myself
into placing my blind faith in the gaunt figure that
glided across the meadow in front of me. I even found
myself saying over and over, *I believe in you. You will
keep me safe. You're guiding me away from danger. You
have the power to protect us.*

*Dear God.* Natsaf-Ty had the power, all right. He had
the power to bring me face-to-face with the monster
that killed my mother.

# CHAPTER FORTY-THREE

"Mason?" The man smiled. "It's good to see you again."

I searched the meadow ahead for Natsaf-Ty. I'd followed him down through the early morning mist in a kind of trance. Now I woke up in the presence of the figure that sat on a wall beside the road. Of course he was every inch the replica of me, apart from one feature: the wound I'd made in his face with the belt buckle hadn't healed. In fact, it had degraded into a great open mouth of a wound. The lips of the crater in the side of his face formed a rim of wet flesh that had turned from red to black since I saw him last beside the road in Tanshelf. The bruising had become a veinlike pattern of dark lines, as if soon areas of the face would break away from one another before sliding from the front of the skull. At the center of the oozing crater were greenish cubes of hard material that could only be the remains of teeth embedded into a necrotic gum.

Bizarrely, that copy of me didn't appear perturbed by the hole in his face. He smiled warmly. The brown eyes were absurdly bright in that ruin of a head.

Cheerfully he tilted his head to one side. "I am really glad to see you, Mason."

"The sentiment's not mutual," I said. That sick clone of me didn't have a weapon that I could see, so I took my time unslinging the submachine gun. Already in my mind's eye I could see the satisfying sequence of pictures as rounds sped from the gun to burst the bag of pus that passed for a head. My God, I could even smell the rot from here.

As I stood there in the road I glanced back. By this time Eve and the others were a good half mile away back up the valley side. They weren't in view; neither was another single living soul. The decaying Konrad misinterpreted my action.

"Don't be concerned about traffic," he told me. "This is a private road on a military testing ground. Nobody will drive along here. See those houses across there?" He broke off a piece of grass to nibble on—those green lumps in his mouth *were* teeth. Casually he waited until I'd taken in the view of white houses on the hillside. "They're fake," he said. "The army uses them for training soldiers in house-to-house fighting. Weird, huh?"

"Not as weird as you." With a click the bolt slid back. *Point and squirt . . .* The monster would experience the full force of my generosity: he could have every single round in the thirty-capacity magazine. There'd be nothing left of his festering head after that. Perhaps a smear in the field behind. Nothing more.

"You know, Mason," he said, "I'm responsible for saving you. I knew you were being kept prisoner in the house up there in the forest where they were experimenting on you like a lab rat, so I had our people free you. Then I only had to *think* you here, and you came. With powers like that, doesn't it prove that we are the superior species?"

I firmed my grip on the submachine gun. "What's this about 'our people' and 'we are the superior species'?"

Smiling, he chewed his grass stalk.

I got to the point. "You're a monster. You aren't even human."

"I'm a copy of you. A perfect copy."

"Didn't I shit your face up?"

"We're closer than twins. All this is so new, so unexpected, there's bound to be some conflict at first. Look at Madeline; she loves you. Yet she's still to learn that our kind have risen above love and hate. We're forming into a single organism, physically separate units, agreed, but joined by telepathy into a seamless entity of unimaginable power. Remember what I just told you? I willed you to come here to me; that's exactly what you did."

"You sure it wasn't something else?" Natsaf-Ty guided me here. He wasn't showing me a route to escape; he'd brought me here to confront my tormentor, not hide from him. But if only he could have warned me. Damn his crusty hide.

"All I have to do is plant the idea in Madeline's head to join us and she'll soon come trotting down the lane. After all, she is close by, isn't she?"

Despite the growing urge to blast his stinking head I wanted to see the expression of shock on his pus-filled face when I told him what Madeline and I had worked out in his swimming-pool jail. "We know exactly what you are. You're the equivalent of a hand grenade thrown into a café, or a bomb left on a crowded commuter train. Your purpose is to cause chaos."

He smiled broadly enough to squeeze a yellowish gel from the crater in his cheek. "I must have left you both in the cell too long. You talked each other into swallowing peculiar theories."

"No more peculiar than yours. You're deluded if you believe we're part of some new super race."

"We are the super race, Mason. The master race. You

should be proud. Nature has decided you are the perfect model."

"And so Nature transforms the entire human race into copies of me?" I lifted the gun so it pointed at the thing that wore a corrupt edition of my face. "Hardly."

"You're our god, Mason. I know, I know, a short while ago we wanted you to leave us alone. Now, however, we realize we were wrong. Your biology has special qualities. Mason Konrad is a miracle. You're the source. All of us flowed from you. The miraculous spring that gives us our new life. You even have the power to transform other Echomen into versions of yourself. That's unheard-of. And that's the reason Dr. Saffrey wanted you so badly at her HQ—so her experts could study you."

"I'm your god? Then you'll do as I tell you."

Mason threw the grass stalk aside. "When people worship gods they try to manipulate their deities' actions through prayer. Those devoted believers don't for one minute want to have to obey their gods' or goddesses' orders. Now, that would be chaos. Free will out the window." He stood up as I trained the weapon on him. "Gods are revered from a distance, and then only on certain days of the week. And they should never actually intervene in humanity's schemes."

A hand shot into my field of vision—a hand with a Y-shaped scar. It gripped the muzzle, then pushed it harmlessly up into the air. More hands followed to wrestle the gun from my hands. Another hand snatched the automatic from my belt, leaving me unharmed, yet strangely triumphant.

"See," I told him as a dozen copies of yours truly—young, old, male, female—formed a ring around me. "Some god you chose. I didn't even know your rabble were creeping up on me." With that I punched out at the one nearest to me, a silver-haired Mason Konrad; then I ran.

The sun burned away the mist. Its heat brought out the cloying smell of hemlock growing at the side of the road. At that moment all I could do was drive myself to run as hard as I could. Yet as I raced downhill, fury took hold. Natsaf-Ty had delivered me into a trap.

"Why did you let me down . . . after all this time . . . ? Why did you do it?" The red figure remained out of sight. "I put my faith in you. Why stab me in the back?"

The road plunged downhill. Ahead of me more Echomen stood in the roadway, so I cut across a field that led down toward a clump of trees, where a stone church steeple poked at the sky. At that moment running like a crazy man had to be preferable to being the creatures' god. Their god? Me? A mad, barking laugh escaped my lips. *This proves their insanity. What poor, flawed monsters they are.*

A hundred yards from the church I reached a low wall that separated the field from the road. Just in time I stopped myself from jumping it because I saw that the other side plunged ten feet down to road level. If I broke my leg now the Echomen could carry me to their damned Mason Konrad temple for worship or other divine activities—no doubt as anomalous as they would be perverted.

Instead of leaping the wall I climbed onto it, then ran along its top in the direction of the church. Even though the building occupied a military site, it looked like the real deal: stained-glass windows, a cemetery, headstones, the works, all enclosed by a five-foot-high wall in yellow brick. Glancing back up the hill revealed a mass of Echomen walking along the road in my direction. If this was a pilgrimage to me they were mistaken. I'd take off, leave the monsters to their fate. Ahead of me a flatbed truck stood in the center of the road with a gap of around five feet at each side before the blacktop reached the high wall. I continued running along my side of the wall. My shadow followed against the other curtain of brick, flung there by the rising sun. A plan formed in my head as I saw the truck there. If the keys were in the ignition I could simply roar out of here in my own steel chariot. The notion filled me with a surge of exultation. I'd escape this place. Then I'd return with the military to reduce these creatures to piles of bloody flesh. In my imagination I could see flamethrowers at work already. The screams, the burning smells, the dance of death. Laughter gurgled in my throat. The surge of adrenaline the chase had pumped through me had knocked common sense out of kilter. What seemed like a cogent plan—leaping nimbly onto the back of the truck from the wall, then driving away—turned to crud. The leap I accomplished with ease. The landing I did not. I threw my upper body forward too enthusiastically; it left my feet trailing behind in the air. So when I landed on the back of the truck I slammed chest-first into the boards from a height of five feet. My head whipped forward to crunch against solid matter. The excruciating pain, coupled with a nauseating sense of slippage inside my skull, suggested that the collision of man and machine had resulted in my brain tipping out through my forehead. I groaned. Wet stuff (brain matter; it had to be cerebral stuff) slid through my fringe of hair into my eyes. Ribs aching like hell, choking back the pain, I rolled onto my side. Touching my forehead revealed that I hadn't spilled my fool brain, but my fool blood painted my fingertips red. *Damn* . . .

I managed to sit upright on the truck's boards. There, flowing down the road toward me between the five-foot-high walls, were Echomen. Hundreds of them. All me ... I shook my head. ... *No—these are monster-clones of me, not really me.* They were culled from both sexes and all ages. I saw a withered old man with my face—a grotesquely young face on an old head. He approached the truck with shuffling steps, his pants sagging from a narrow waist. Too dazed by the fall to do more than hoist myself into a sitting position, all I could do was watch. The river of human beings grew closer—human beings? No, these were like the clone monsters from the school. They'd been ravaged by experiments conducted by their own kind to discover how much punishment they could absorb before they ceased to function. Yet more of their species suffered an assortment of hideous wounds from fighting their human foe.

I saw men and women with arms missing, with gashes in their bellies that had released red fronds of intestine; others were burned offerings to their god, Mason Konrad. Eyes peered bleakly from charred faces. Acid burns had stripped scalps from heads. Bullet strikes had robbed some of hands, jaws, eyes—they'd die soon, but not soon enough for me. They all moved toward me. A single purpose drove them; their eyes blazed with a kind of hunger that made my blood run cold. As they got nearer—twenty yards, fifteen yards—I shuffled back along the truck's boards. I saw in my mind's eye how they would drag me off the vehicle, then enter into whatever passed for a sacred—and very physical—communion with their creator, their godhead.

In the early morning sun they approached, hauling their torn bodies closer and closer, their eyes shining with such a fervor that they surely couldn't have felt the hurt from their hundreds of wounds. A boy held his face to a head that had been torn half away by shrapnel. The flesh of the face had long since died. A green moss formed on the skin, but still a trace of Mason Konrad remained in its features, while behind the mask of skin the boy's flayed skull oozed blood that now resembled black treacle.

With an effort I tried to stand, but a concussion had exploded my sense of balance. After a second attempt to rise I sank back to accept my fate at the hands of the look-alikes.

*Ten yards, five yards, four, three, two, one—they're here.* I closed my eyes, breathed as deeply as my sore ribs would allow, then held my breath as I waited for the hands, all those hundreds of hands with Y-shaped scars marking them out as my spawn. I waited for them to seize me.

And yet I felt nothing. I raised an eyelid. They were flowing by. All looked me in the eye as they passed, all those hundreds of faces, some with the most appalling wounds imaginable, but they kept surging by as I sat on the truck. At last I did climb to my feet. I had to see where they were headed. Soon it became only too apparent. They marched on the church. But why?

Again a wait of a few seconds revealed the reason. Behind the church wall I saw the appearance of heads. Even though it was fifty yards away I recognized Dianna and Ruth. With them were around a dozen soldiers, more survivors from the big house. Just beyond the church I saw burned-out cars that had been stopped at a barricade of trees that had been felled across the road.

Ah, how clear . . . how transparently, awfully clear . . . Ruth and the other survivors must have fled through here in their cars, only to be stopped by felled trees blocking the way. They'd taken refuge in the church. Now the Echomen closed in. Gunshots rang out. The creatures at the front toppled. The old man with the young face clutched his forehead as a rifle slug ripped his skull.

Despite the vicious hail of bullets the humans soon fell back to the church as their magazines ran dry. Still, the inexorable tide of transformed men and women flowed by me, engulfing me in a river of *me*. When they reached the graveyard they spilled through the gates to turn the cemetery into a sea of living bodies—one that flowed above those bodies buried in graves six feet down beneath the sod. At the church the Echomen piled against the walls. Their bodies formed a growing ramp against the stonework. Within moments the stained-glass windows sagged as unnatural flesh pressed against the panes. Then nothing could stop them. The creatures engulfed the church. Of course there were gunshots. I knew that many must have been killed by Ruth and her comrades in arms. But there were not enough bullets in this entire valley to stop the invasion. Soon the guns were dead.

A voice came from behind me. "Mason. Are you all right?"

"I'll live. For now," I replied as the copy of me with the pit in his face climbed onto the back of the truck. A fatalism infected me now. Where could I run? What could I do? My survival—or lack of it—depended on the whim of fate now.

A moment later he crouched down to examine the head wound with an expression of genuine concern. "We'll get someone to take care of that for you. That's a nasty cut." He rubbed his hands together. "But first we have a surprise for you."

# CHAPTER FORTY-FOUR

I sat there on the back of the truck, some seven feet above the road, as the Echomen flowed past: nothing less than a river of monsters converging on the church. Their heads were at the height of my waist, so I looked down into the faces. Male, female, old, young, injured, uninjured—a mixture of racial backgrounds, yet it appeared as if some evil magic had copied my face, then pasted it onto a thousand or more strangers. Still dazed from my concussive landing on the truck's boards, I watched the flood wash by. The guy with the gaping hole in his face that I'd inflicted just days ago at my old school had promised me a surprise. That should have sounded warning alarms, yet all I managed to accomplish at that moment was to stare in a dull way at the tightly packed flow of heads.

Crouching, he handed me a handkerchief that was surprisingly clean. "Here. Press this to your head; it should stop the bleeding. Although you might need a stitch."

The pain caused by the misguided leap onto the truck returned with a vengeance. An invisible drummer must have mistaken my skull for a hi-hat, the way it throbbed. The off-the-wall thought produced a grunt of laugher in my throat.

My clone tilted his head as he checked my face. "Pale, very pale . . . is your vision blurred, Mason?"

"You mean, do I see more than one of you?" I managed a groggy wave of the hand. "There are dozens of you. Hundreds . . . probably thousands . . ."

"You know, Mason"—he pushed his thumb into the corner of his mouth—"I've been thinking about what you said. That the mechanism that creates duplicates of other men and woman is a kind of time bomb planted in the DNA of our ancestors millions of years ago."

"Ah, the engine of the transformation." Still holding the handkerchief to my forehead, I nodded. Concussion now made me feel as if I'd gulped down half a pint of vodka. "Hidden in our DNA, it bided its time until we developed intelligence . . . technologies; it waited until we came close to traveling to other worlds and thereby ran the risk of contaminating other civilizations. Scientists say that when two cultures encounter each other, the least advanced will suffer."

"So millions of years ago alien beings sprinkled their secret weapon into the DNA of life-forms on earth. Then, whenever a creature becomes too intelligent, the mechanism activates, and that mechanism has the power to transform a person into an exact copy of another."

I managed the woozy nod again. "I thought we just said that."

"Sorry, I'm just trying to get in clear in my head, Mason."

"Did anyone tell you you've got a rotten head? There's a hole in your face."

"I have noticed it, thank you."

"I did that."

"I know."

"Angry?"

"No."

"Should be."

"Mason, you've explained the history of how our

kind came into being, but I still don't understand the purpose."

"Let me tell you what I think is going on here. No, rip out the word 'think.' This is what I KNOW is happening. Scientists might not be able to prove it for fifty years, but my gut instinct tells me this is the truth: An alien civilization created a weapon. It infects all life on Earth like a virus. Once a life-form on Earth develops intelligence—in this case human beings won the IQ prize—the 'virus' activates some mechanism, some mysterious mechanism that causes the transformation. And that purpose is simply to cause chaos. There is no noble agenda, other than for you clone people to become an aberration; you're nothing more than a mixed up mess of human and alien DNA. Because once the change takes place all you evil little clones become hostile to genuine human beings. You try to destroy us . . . so we'll never ever pose a threat to the extraterrestrial cowards who created you. A threat that might not even be real. For all we know the creatures that seeded our planet's life with this disgusting little bug might be extinct themselves now. Think of the irony . . ." I groaned. "I'm going to lie down now. My head's really . . ." A grunt came from my lips.

"You're going to wait for your surprise, aren't you?"

"If you insist, my dear twin. Ouch. Must've banged my noodle harder than I . . . uhm . . ."

"Stay awake, Mason. Your surprise is coming."

"Keep it till Christmas." The moment I closed my eyes he shook me awake.

"We haven't finished discussing why all these people became a copy of you."

"You're nothing more than a minefield. No alien race

can risk being damaged or destroyed through contact
with another culture. Your purpose is chaos. To mess
civilization up so much that we're too busy repairing
the damage to even think about allotting resources to
building big, sexy spaceships."

"I've heard you talk about this before. It's bad manners, I know, but back at the school, when you and
Madeline were in the cell, I eavesdropped. As an explanation of our nature it was distinctly shabby."

"Shabby? Ouch. You know, I can't even say the word
without it hurting my head."

"I'm sorry."

"But don't we have a telepathic link? You should be
saying, 'I feel your pain,' and meaning it."

The man with the hole in his face smiled, pus welling
from the crater. By now flies buzzed in, drawn by the
odor. "Do you feel the wound in my face?"

"Now that you mention it, an itch." I grimaced at the
ache in my skull. "Ah . . . you said my explanation of
your nature is shabby. But then up there on another
world, cowardly aliens have played a shabby trick on
all of us. Maybe it's the cosmic equivalent of spitting
bubble gum on a bus seat to spoil the clothes of whoever sits there later. Some low-down skunks on Planet
X, Mars, or wherever it is, intend to spoil the progress of
a life-form that they don't even know exists. Imagine if
the Echo process results in the substitution of world
leaders who start wars, or ordinary men and women
being replaced by copies of themselves who commit
terrorist atrocities. If they detonate a bomb in your
town every day, how long would it be before you
stopped visiting the supermarket there or going to
work? Ancient Rome didn't collapse solely because of
an invasion from outside; it went rotten on the in-

side . . . people stopped going to the office . . . 'No more office for me,' they said. 'I'm going fishing. . . .' " My head sagged as pain overwhelmed me. "Got any morphine . . . anything to take the pointy corners off this?"

The thing with the holed face continued with an obsessive fire in his eyes. "If this 'spoiler theory' is true, then is it such a bad thing? It stops humanity from spreading its virus of violence into the universe. So aren't we doing God's work? Who wants the human race knocking on their planetary door when we're addicted to war and terrorism, and suffer such irrational behavior that we have an inability to agree on international boundaries, food standards, religion, or even what constitutes physical beauty? Let's face it: the human race is a problem child. It can't be let out of the cage we call Earth yet. Agreed?"

"We are quarrelsome to the point of being self-destructive. But it'll pass. One day nations will live in harmony. So there's no need for Echomen to wreck society and our capacity to progress. Therefore, we will destroy you monsters."

"But what if we aren't this time bomb that you and Madeline have dreamed up between yourselves?" His ruined face loomed toward mine. "What if we are the next stage in evolution?"

I didn't answer. My head hurt too much.

"Hmm?" Flies swarmed in the wet mess in the side of his face. "At this moment in time, which side is winning? Human beings or us?"

For a moment I didn't reply; then my head cleared as an idea formed there. "When I was in the cell with Madeline someone else arrived. You didn't put him in there. He just strolled in to visit me. Remember that?"

His eyes hardened.

My turn to smile. "Yes, you do remember, don't you? And I've heard that you and your people were none too happy with it. In fact, the stranger who can walk through walls to visit me scared the daylights out of you. Isn't that correct?"

Instead of answering he abruptly stood up. "I promised you a surprise, Mason. Here it is."

The pain in my head suddenly wasn't important anymore. What I saw being brought toward me had the effect of a stinging slap in the face. Enough to dispel the vertigo and bring me to my feet in a second.

"Let them go," I said.

"But this is your surprise." The ruined face grinned hard enough to squeeze gobs of yellow from the wound.

The flow of Echomen had reversed itself. They now walked uphill, away from the church. Only that flow carried with it Dianna and Ruth. Sooty marks around the women's noses revealed the intensity of the gun battle. They must have fired hundreds of rounds into the monsters as they crawled through the shattered church windows. Now the Echomen brought their captives to me as a gift.

Ruth blinked in the sunlight. "Mason?"

"Don't worry," I called to her. "They've decided I'm responsible for their creation. I'll order them not to harm you." I flung the bloody handkerchief that I'd been clamping against my forehead to one side. "Listen to me," I shouted to the things that I'd unwittingly spawned. "These two women are my friends. You must not hurt them."

Diana shrugged herself free of the hands that held her. "Mason. They attacked the house last night. There were hundreds of them."

"I know. And some of us are safe." I couldn't afford to

be any more explicit than that. "And don't worry; it won't be long before help arrives."

Meanwhile, the sea of faces gazed up at me—a sea of *my* faces. That brought the vertigo back. All those Mason Konrads watching me. "Don't lay a finger on these two women," I told that sea of staring eyes. "I order you not to hurt them." Then I turned to the two women who stood on the road just twenty yards from me. "Ruth. Dianna. Don't run; don't make any sudden movements. Just walk to the cab of the truck and get in. I'll join you in a moment."

They moved at an easy pace toward the truck. A germ of an idea formed inside my head. *Join them in the truck. Drive out of here to safety.*

"Mason, you don't understand." The man beside me sighed. "We offer these two women as a sacrifice."

He nodded at the crowd. They swamped the two women in a second. And what could I do? Well, I'll tell you. All that monster maker Mason Konrad could do was stand there and watch as Dianna and Ruth were torn apart by dozens of bare hands. Torn apart? Think of old T-shirts torn apart to polish the car. Newspapers torn apart to light a fire. Lettuce leaves torn apart to feed a pet rabbit.

But a human being torn apart?

The forces necessary are immense. Let me tell you those forces were present that day. Driven by sheer bloodlust, my clones ripped the hair from the heads of the two women. They heaved at fingers until sinews gave way. Arms are tougher. A mass of eager hands had to participate to separate a human arm from a shoulder. Ruth's and Dianna's screams were so full of pain that I found myself hating the sun for still daring to illuminate the scene. And all I could do was stand absolutely still, watch, listen, smell, experience their deaths. And deaths that had to be the bloodiest I've ever witnessed.

# CHAPTER FORTY-FIVE

They swarmed up onto the truck. The first carried the heads of my two dead friends; the twenty that followed celebrated with lumps of raw meat. One boy held aloft a fistful of crimson human offal as if it were a floral bouquet.

I thought, *They're smiling. These things really do believe I'm pleased by what they've done.*

"You see"—the man with the crater in his face was satisfied—"they'll die for you . . . and they'll kill for you."

"You bastards . . . you filthy, murdering bastards." I punched one grinning youth with a handful of bloody hair. He toppled back onto the brutes who crowded in tight around the vehicle. Their heads were just about level with my feet as I stood on the back of the truck. Something that, in my enraged state, was temptation beyond my power to resist. I delivered full-blooded kicks to those faces—my copied face—noses shattered; eyelids ripped open in bursts of blood.

The man approved. "People don't want a kind god; they need angry, vengeful gods. They'll love you even more for what you're doing to them."

My shoe cracked against a gray head. "Shut your mouth. I'm not their god."

"Oh, but you are. As I said, they'll kill for you, die for you, but they won't obey you." Smiling so much his face wound oozed pus, he approached me. "This is the plan. We'll take you somewhere safe. Then in a day or two, when you're rested, we'll bring ordinary men and women to you. You'll put your hands on their heads as if you're blessing them. They will, of course, turn into copies of you in a matter of hours. That way you—and us, your disciples—will inherit the earth."

From my vantage point high on the back of the truck I noticed what the man and his vermin hoard hadn't. Eve and the others must have been so concerned about my nonreturn that they'd followed me into the valley. Now they were uphill in the center of the road. They'd seen the Echomen clustered tight around the truck. What had to be a big downside for me was that they couldn't differentiate between the real, bona fide Mason Konrad and the swarm of copies. To them I was just another member of the mob. A hundred yards away the commandos deployed the bipod legs of the green tube that contained the antitank missile. Whether they intended it for defense or for attack I didn't wait to find out.

I shoulder-charged a woman who carried Ruth's blood-soaked head. She fell back onto the crowd below; they were so tightly packed that she slammed onto crammed shoulders and heads without falling through to the pavement. I jumped, landing with both my feet on her soft belly; then, with the Echomen's upturned faces gazing adoringly at me, I ran across them. The soles of my shoes slapped down onto noses, foreheads, mouths, leaving a bruised mess behind me. Using the tightly packed heads as stepping-stones, I bounded toward the wall, hopped onto it, then raced back the way I came.

Not ten seconds too soon, either. From a hundred yards away the tube spat the rocket. A ball of fire crackled through the air, dragging the wire behind it that allowed the soldier to control its flight. With neat precision the missile slammed into the truck's cab. The explosion sent a blast of hot air into my back. But I kept running. I glanced back only when I knew my balance was sure. Behind me, the truck had become a fireball. Hemmed in by the confines of the high walls a hundred or more of the creatures must have died, consumed by burning fuel from the truck as much as killed by the detonation of the antitank warhead.

"They want a vengeful god, they want a vengeful god. . . ." This I panted as I raced back to Eve, Madeline, and the rest. By now the surviving Echomen had surged back up the hill to wreak their revenge on their attackers. The firepower of even just that small group had a formidable effect. Submachine guns rained a flurry of red tracer at the men and women as they ran along the channel formed by the walls. Bullets struck them with sufficient force to kill the ones in the lead, then pass through their bodies to take the lives of those who followed.

When I felt the slipstream of bullets tugging at my hair I realized that running along the top of the wall was about as sensible as my headlong dive onto the back of the truck earlier. I leaped down to the meadow side of the wall; then I sprinted at a tangent away from the road as the guns flung hot metal faster than the speed of sound into the faces of the monsters.

A bullet snapped by my ear. Fifty yards away Eve drew back the bolt of the rifle, then snapped off another round at me. It gouged the earth near my feet.

"Eve!"

The next time she took a shot I anticipated that her

aim would be dead on the nail. I flung myself into the long grass as she fired. The bullet seared the air where my chest had been a second before.

"Eve." I raised myself on one arm to wave with the other. "Eve, don't shoot; it's me."

*Of course it's me*, I all but shouted at myself. *But then, all the hundreds streaming up the hill toward Eve and her squad are versions of me also. She can't tell the difference between flesh-and-blood brother and bogus look-alike.*

A bullet cracked through grass stalks just above my head, showering me with gobs of green pulp. I rolled to one side, then knelt up.

"Eve, don't shoot."

My sister aimed, squeezed the trigger. At that moment Madeline ran in front of her, shouting. She'd realized that the genuine me occupied Eve's gun sights. Eve fired. Madeline clutched her side, her knees sagging. But she still pointed toward me, and I knew she was shouting at them not to fire at me. That here was Mason Konrad. The real deal. Not fake, not a copy. Eve gripped her rifle in one hand, its muzzle pointing upward; with her free hand she beckoned furiously.

"Mason," she yelled. "Hurry! Before they get here!"

A second later I bounded to my feet, then raced up through the meadow toward where they stood on the roadway. Meanwhile, the commandos and Ulric still poured a stream of gunfire down at the advancing Echomen. One man fired a grenade that felled ten of the monsters. Sometimes the death toll was so great at the front of the mob it formed an obstacle in the roadway; they had to clamber over the bullet-ravaged corpses so they could continue.

By the time I reached the group Eve had begun to help Madeline to her feet. Madeline winced with pain. Her face had become bloodlessly pale. She pressed her hand against her hip where Eve's bullet had caught her.

"Don't worry," Eve said. "It's just nicked the flesh; you'll be all right."

The compassion in Eve's voice caught me by surprise. I had to look at my sister a second time.

Eve gave a grim smile. "You heard right. I do care about your friend. Madeline really is on our side."

Ulric warned. "Fall back. We can only slow them down. We need to regain the cover of the forest."

I shook my head. "Not this time. I'm going to call for reinforcements."

They looked at me with open mouths as if I'd gone crazy.

"If it doesn't work, save yourselves . . . or at least try. Eve? Will you take care of Madeline and the child?"

Eve didn't know what I planned, but the look in her eye told me she trusted me. Whatever I did next would be fine by her. "Okay." I held up my hand. "Stop firing. I'm going to meet this bunch halfway."

With that I walked back down the hill toward them. Here it was. My last card. I knew that with the same kind of clarity as the sun shining down into the valley. If it worked, that is. If it didn't, I doubted that I'd have time to reflect on what a funny little life we have. A few years of events, ambitions, planning, some setbacks, some successes . . . and then what? Like I said, no time to dwell on it, nor the quality of our lifetime. Ahead of me, the man strode up the road with that shining crater in his face. Behind him came his army. They wanted blood. This time it might even be mine.

# CHAPTER FORTY-SIX

The sun had risen high enough in the sky to deliver a beefy slug. Its heat struck me in the back of the neck as I walked down the road to meet the masses of me. A thousand Mason Konrad copies advanced along the road. Behind me Eve, Madeline, Ulric, Kirk, and the commandos watched in silence. In a moment that might be symbolic of nothing or everything, a black cat ran across the stretch of road that separated me from the guy with the crater face and his murdering hoard.

When we were twenty yards apart the man stopped. Those following stopped abruptly, too. I saw that most had been wounded either in this or earlier conflicts, or had been subject to the sadistic experiments. Shrapnel wounds studded their faces. From other parts of their bodies sharp pieces of metal jutted that reflected the sunlight. There were survivors from the school building back in Tanshelf. Six-inch nails protruded from faces and limbs. For some reason this mutant faction of the human race had been driven to test themselves to destruction. Now their ranks needed replenishing. Clearly they expected me to "infect" regular human beings so they turned Echo, too.

I might not have started this epidemic of random cloning deliberately, but at that moment I knew that if I had a single remaining purpose in life it was to stop them. Stop them dead. Stop them forever.

And what did I have left in my arsenal? Yes, indeed. My secret weapon.

The man with the ruined face that oozed pus fixed his gaze on me. "If you come with us now," he said, "I promise that your friends won't come to any harm."

I shook my head. "No deal." A ripple spread through the mob; they were ready to charge. "Wait." I held up my hand.

"They won't obey you," the man warned.

"I think they'll be interested in what I'm going to do next." The mass of eyes locked on me with a searing intensity. "Someone visited me in that cell you kept me in. Remember? You sent the boy to photograph the individual at my home. But it wasn't curiosity that ate you up; it was fear. Because I've got a friend who terrifies you. Only you don't know why."

"Mason, that doesn't matter anymore. We've got what we need—you."

I smiled at the monsters. "Too late. I've called him. He's already on his way. Can't you feel it in the air? You can sense his presence growing here, can't you? Put out your tongues." I laughed. "You can taste it, can't you?"

*What now? I asked myself. Do I put on a show of summoning my childhood imaginary friend? How would it sound if I called out. "Come now, Natsaf-Ty, keeper of the sacred crocodiles"? Wouldn't that be too much like a conjuror's stage act? Or do I force myself to picture him standing there on the road between us? But what can an imaginary friend do if he's only a sort of dream that exists inside my head? For some reason this thought process that creates Natsaf-Ty disturbs the Echomen. But can it have any real destructive force? Once they've recovered from their initial shock they might simply carry me off to be the equivalent of their queen bee to duplicate more of their kind. In that case Eve and the rest will soon be dead.*

"What are you waiting for, Natsaf-Ty?" I called the

words into the air. "Aren't you going to show yourself to us? Just like you used to when I was ten years old?"

The sun blazed down; the intensity of it felt like hot metal pressed against my skin. Insects buzzed among wildflowers at the side of the road. Crows circled overhead, black cross-shaped things floating through a blue sky.

"Come on. What are you waiting for?" My throat had become as dry as the dusty road. "Show yourself, Natsaf-Ty. . . ." I planned to smile, to demonstrate my coolness, that I was in control of the situation, but the realization forcing itself on me was, *Here I am, one man facing a hoard of killers, with no plan B, and plan A falling apart by the second.*

The Echomen began to move forward. Mere seconds from now they'd rip apart Eve and the rest just as they'd butchered Ruth and Dianna. My voice rose louder. "When I was a child . . . when my life was in ruins, you came and got me through it. You weren't even real, but I loved you." I closed my eyes. What more could I do? Natsaf-Ty was where he always had been in reality: back in the glass display case in the Tanshelf Museum. An empty shell of a corpse in a bandage loincloth to be joked over by schoolkids. He'd only ever lived in the imagination of an unhappy child, one Mason Konrad, who was being bullied into the ground by other kids at school, and whose family had begun to disintegrate, as his mother couldn't afford the upkeep of their home.

*"Please!"* Memories rolled back of Mason Konrad, the child, sitting at the top of the stairs. The other kids had ripped my books, then punched me to the ground. My mother had sobbed herself to sleep with a pile of unpaid bills on the bedside table. Eve had been three years old. She'd been too young to understand what

had happened, but trauma is contagious. Painful sores had broken out on her eyelids. She'd stopped eating; Mom and I watched the flesh fall away.

Now, here in the sunlit valley, the man with the hole in his face had walked to within ten feet of me. "Come with us," he murmured. "Promise me you won't look back at your old friends. After all, you've got us now."

I glanced over my shoulder. Eve stood with her eyes on me. She helped support Madeline. Ulric and the others watched, too.

"I tried." My voice came as a whisper. "Believe me, I tried."

I turned back to the creatures who'd stolen my face. A mask they could hide behind as they slaughtered innocent men, women, and children.

Then a change came into the world. For a moment I didn't know what had happened. I listened. Where had the noise of the insects gone? The heat of the sun simply vanished. A cold breath touched the back of my neck. Shivers ran down my spine. The mob noticed something, too. They stopped advancing. The man with the gaping wound in his cheek looked around him as if expecting to see some threat.

At last I felt a smile steal across my face. "He's here. Are you ready for him?"

The sun threw shadows across the road, yet one of the shadows appeared red rather than black. I willed myself to see it as the ancient mummy, the same dry figure with cracks in its face, closed eyelids, tip of the tongue protruding through the lips, only . . .

. . . only it wasn't quite like that this time. The red figure appeared as an indistinct pillar between the mob and myself. Once more they moved, but it came as a ripple of heads, as if they tried to advance on me but couldn't move their feet. They had the same reaction as the boy back at the house when he'd panicked in the presence of Natsaf-Ty. They didn't look directly at the figure. Instead their eyes had a searching quality: they scanned the air above the figure and then to each side, as if they were dimly aware of some huge, but only partly visible object in front of them. I heard the quickening breath as fear crept through their nervous systems. Above me the sun dulled until it resembled a disk of brown foil pasted onto the sky. And what had been a flawless blue sky degenerated into a smeary purple dome that rested on the hills. As this change took place the temperature cooled until my breath misted the air. And as a mist rolled from the meadows into the road the sun became a yet gloomier ghost of its former self. However, the red figure in front of me grew correspondingly brighter. Within seconds it appeared to be lit from within, but it still hadn't formed the lines of the familiar figure that had manifested on the stairs at home. As the world darkened around me, and the Echomen became indistinct shadows that were paralyzed by terror, I found the telepathic link that I'd experienced before working itself into my mind. A throb started in my forehead. When I blinked it seemed as if I looked at the lone figure of Mason Konrad standing on the road. I saw through the eyes of the Echomen. That throbbing inside my skull was the throbbing of their emotions and the pain of their wounds fused into a pulse of feeling that had no trace of rational thought. I sensed their brute nature—they were driven by the instinct to conquer. Pain or despair or grief at losing one of their own kind would be alien to them. All that mattered was their lust to overwhelm the human race.

I moved closer to the luminous red figure in front of me. It had become the brightest object in sight.

Then I did something I've never done in my life before. I reached out my hand and touched the figure that I'd always known as Natsaf-Ty. Only at that moment did I understand I'd been wrong all this time. My juvenile imagination had willed myself to see this pillar of red light as the Egyptian mummy from the museum. Maybe that had been the only way I could form a relationship with what I was beginning to see clearly for the very first time.

The moment my fingertip made contact with the body of red light was the moment we moved outside the world I'd always known.

# CHAPTER FORTY-SEVEN

Vertigo. That sensation engulfed me as I stood there in the road. Vertigo . . . falling . . . a drop into an abyss that had no bottom to stop me from plunging down and down and down . . .

The vertigo wrenched my mind inside out, making me want to grab for anything to halt the plummet into a dark void, yet there was nothing to catch hold of. For me, the vertigo scrambled my thoughts into that panic-stricken sense of suddenly falling from a high place. But the impressions feeding into my head from the Echomen were of a terror amplified by the vertigo they experienced. They felt the descent multiplied a thousand times as much as I did. So this was what horrified them when they were in the presence of Natsaf-Ty. An overwhelming impression that the earth had split open beneath their feet to swallow them into a bottomless pit. An elevator descent of surreal intensity. A hundred white-knuckle theme-park rides mated with the downward swoop of a plane dropping like a stone when it hit an air pocket.

Only here there were no seat belts to fasten, no bars on the carnival death-ride car to grip. This was the scream-your-lungs-bloody plummet into the Grand Canyon of the universe.

But still I didn't tumble out of control. When my eyes focused I saw that I stood alongside Natsaf-Ty. Just for a second that column of red light became my imaginary friend of yore: a rust-colored Egyptian mummy with closed eyes and tongue protruding slightly through the lips. He turned his head so he could "look" at me in that uncanny way of his—as if he'd read every thought that had roamed through my mind ever since I'd been born.

What I'd taken to be air blasting past me now seemed more like some force streaming *through* me. A hurricane blast of particles that roared through my blood, flesh, and bones.

"Mason! What have you done?"

I blinked. We were still standing there in a group, as before: me, then the red figure in the middle, then the Echoman with the rotten crater in his face, then the hundreds of clone creatures tightly packed together, clinging to one another. Only now they were locked in a paralysis of terror; their faces, which were copies of mine, were the epitome of panic, eyes frozen wide-open. The man with the ruined face was the only one who appeared able to speak. Speak? What exploded from his mouth was a panic-driven yell.

"What is it?" he screamed. *"What have you brought into the world!"*

"What have *I* brought into the world?" Cascades of ice poured down my spine. The red figure in front of me oscillated between good old friendly Natsaf-Ty, clad in fluttering bandages, to something that I can think of only in terms of *other*. An *other* life-form not connected with the Earth, nor connected with the time and space of our universe.

The guy with the face rot, my archenemy, had opened my eyes. I sensed the other-place nature of the red figure. No longer was he the dusty gentleman of ancient Egypt. My childhood imagination had shaped the red smear of light that visited me nightly into the mummy, which had become my imaginary friend. In truth, Natsaf-Ty, the museum exhibit, had been exotic, yet familiar enough to form an acceptable shape to represent the thing that fell through darkness with us. All the conversations I'd had with him as a boy must have been one-sided. To me they'd seemed real, of course— as real as to the child who talks to a toy and fantasizes that the toy replies. And yet, those conversations had helped me through dark times. The luminous visitor on the stairs had allowed me to discuss my worries, and then, more beautifully and profoundly than Natsaf-Ty answering my questions, it was me, Mason Konrad, who'd found the answers inside myself. Without knowing it, I'd cultivated wisdom and maturity, together with the mental and emotional apparatus to manage my life. In turn I guided myself along the sometimes dangerous road from being a child to becoming an adult. And, before these catastrophic events, a happy, well-balanced adult, at that.

Meanwhile, this fall through darkness. A fall in the company of a pillar of red light that grew taller, that penetrated the void beneath our feet. The red pillar was becoming a glowing filament that ran through the body of the universe. We, the Echomen and I, rode along it, a pulse of thought along a bloodred nerve.

The one with the ruined face screamed, "How did you do this to us?"

Vertigo's grip on me began to ease. When I spoke it was calmly. "Imagine a child who has been deserted. He's alone. He sits on a wall beside a busy highway. Cars stream by, thousands of cars, millions of them, all speeding by in a blur. Eventually a driver might notice the abandoned child and stop. At that moment the child doesn't know whether the driver's intentions are good or evil. Now, imagine a child who is broken-hearted, who knows his family is disintegrating, that his mother is close to suicide. Visualize the child sitting on the top step of a flight of stairs at midnight. Now picture this: in our universe, radioactive particles are falling through our bodies all the time, things like gamma rays and electrons. Imagine that riding this stream of radiation, like cars use a road, are beings with minds. In all their millions riding through our world, isn't it possible that one might notice an unhappy boy or girl and stop?"

"But is that to help or cause harm?" His face was a picture of horror. "Have you let something into this world that will destroy us?"

"Us?" I shook my head. "You mean your kind. The Echomen."

"No. All of us. I'm talking about the death of life on Earth! Mason! Haven't you seen what it is yet?"

The figure had elongated to a red line that threaded itself through the blackness of the abyss into which we descended at incredible speed. Above us the luminous ribbon of light appeared to have no end, and when I looked down beneath us it curved away into the darkness, growing more and more slender until I could see it no more. The group of men and women who wore my face sped along the crimson strand that I'd once thought of as Natsaf-Ty, my humble imaginary friend who would listen with such rapt attention as he sat on his customary third step from the bottom. Back then I'd tell him how I stood up in class to read from *Catcher in the Rye* as my best friend pulled faces until I couldn't speak for laughing. Or I'd solemnly ask the dusty old gentleman's advice about girls, or confess that I was afraid about going on the school's camping expedition.

No, I hadn't understood the true nature of my not-so imaginary friend. I looked into the scared eyes that were a replica of mine in the ruined face. "I haven't seen what he is yet," I told him. "But I know this: soon we'll find out."

"What have you done, Mason? *What have you done?*"

The huddle of Echomen appeared to ripple as terror crackled through them like a wave of energy. They ducked their heads. Eyes stared wide into the burning pillar of light that grew steadily brighter as we fell . . . not through the universe but through the spaces in between . . . between the atoms. . . . My mind whirled as vertigo took hold again, sending pulses of sensation through me that made me so dizzy I could barely see.

Then out.

Out across the face of an alien world whose landscape of spiked rock thrust from the ground like the spines of a sea urchin. Purple clouds swirled around the needlelike columns of stone. Above us twin suns revolved around each other.

Being so near the red twine that was flung across the abyss saved me. It created a nexus of protection that spared me from the vacuum, the heat of the sun, the withering ordnance of radiation that must have seared these worlds. However, the creatures that we called Echomen began to die. The withering heat took them; I watched as they opened their mouths and screamed not sound, but atomized droplets of blood from ruptured lungs. From dozens of mouths gusted clouds of scarlet vapor. Then, as suddenly, a killing cold replaced the heat. Blood particles jetting from their mouths became vermilion snowflakes. The zone of destruction crept closer to where I stood beside the red cord. Dozens more were obliterated by temperatures that were cold enough to liquefy the air in their throats. A tongue in one of the creatures' heads turned into a hard, black mass. Expressions of pain and terror became fixed on their faces. Hands darkened, then shattered. Gradually faces caved in on themselves—a slow-motion implosion as soft, moist tissues inside the heads contracted as body temperatures plunged to absolute zero.

Meanwhile, the journey continued through a sea of golden lights that might have been fireballs or even entire galaxies. I had no sense of dimension. The red line along which we flashed like thought along a nerve might have been as thick as a girl's waist or might have exceeded the circumference of our sun. So what may have been a mist of photons could equally have been silver dust motes or another field of stars, each with planets that contained life. More worlds rolled beneath us, one awash with a yellowish ocean in which strangely human faces floated. They looked up with eyes the size of islands as we flowed by, high above the surface. In those eyes beneath smooth foreheads that were as broad as prairies I saw the light of intelligence; call it intuition, but I sensed they knew something of my life and my world.

Then they were gone. By the light of a blue star I saw that the group of surviving Echomen numbered about a hundred. These were the ones closest to the red column, that nexus of protection from the hostile elements that ached to rob us of our lives. Even so, those copies of me were all damaged, either by heat or by cold. Bare skin had blistered; lips were blackened by frostbite; they panted as their lungs suffered from exposure to toxic gases; radiation burst blood vessels under their skin to form strange random tattoos. Hair fell from heads like trees shedding dead leaves in the fall.

A woman stumbled to her knees. She held out her arms toward me so I could help her rise again. The moment I took hold of her two hands in mine the skin slid off them like a pair of gloves; a second later she died. Whatever protected me from the lethal forces also ejected the detritus. Instantly she was flung into such heat her body turned into a smear of vapor.

The man with the ruined copy of my face spoke. "There's nothing you can do to save us now. Or, for that matter, your own kind. Don't you realize you created a bridge to our planet from this? Eighteen years ago you invited this . . . *death* into our world."

By now, heat and cold had taken its toll on the man. His lips turned blue; he had difficulty breathing, as if the intense heat surge had scorched his lung tissue. When he raised his hand to touch his injured face I saw that his fingertips had turned black; what was more, his nails had begun to flake off from the flesh. Frost formed in the deep crater in his cheek. Ice crystals twinkled there in the light of the blue star. At last the panic left his eyes; that went for the others, too. Instead, they'd become passive; they calmly accepted that their destruction wasn't far away.

He moved his head to indicate something in the distance toward which we hurtled. "Not far now. Can you feel it?" A ghost of a smile reached his mouth. "You've nearly reached your destination . . . or should that be destiny?"

The red line along which we glided now had an ending. This sinuous filament entered a globe that glowed with the same luminous red. For a while it grew only gradually in size; then suddenly it expanded into a vast body that filled my field of vision. Once inside we seemed to fall by other entire worlds. A globe lined with valleys passed beneath us. The valleys were filled with mist, and through the vapor dark shapes swam. And often we didn't so much as bypass worlds as fall through their centers. Cold, poison gas, heat, they all stripped more Echomen away from the edge of the group. Disintegrating bodies tumbled away, dwindling our group to little more than twenty.

In this red world we moved more and more slowly until we stopped, suspended in a ruby light.

The man with the ruined face had grown weaker; his shoulders sagged under their own weight. By willpower alone he managed to remain standing as he regarded me. "Tell me now, Mason, what is it you're thinking? When you look out there, do you see what I see?"

"They say that before the universe existed there were only two states of reality: here and now. Space didn't exist, so there wasn't an 'over there,' or a 'behind you,' or an 'up above.' Time didn't exist. So there was only now. You couldn't have a past, so there was no history. Back then everything that occurred happened all at once and in the same place." I blinked. "When I was a boy I pictured the . . . what do you call it? Entity? A figure? That doesn't seem an adequate description anymore, does it?" I took a deep breath. "Anyway, my mind construed this red appearance as an Egyptian mummy by the name of Natsaf-Ty. It seems almost homely now. A three-thousand-year-old priest popping into my home at midnight for a chat; me sitting at the top of the stairs, him on his customary third from the bottom. And what a good listener he was." I gazed at what the man had indicated, and I saw that from the shadows a shape had begun to resolve itself into something that made my heart beat faster. I found myself grow breathless with anticipation. "Now I can reinterpret what I saw. I believe that there are intelligent beings who ride through the universe like radiation. Normally you don't see them, can't detect them, but they're flowing through worlds and everything on them as if that solid matter isn't there. Then one took notice of me and stopped."

"And baited a trap, Mason. You let them in. You've killed us all."

"How can you know that?" I shrugged. "What I saw on the stair wasn't the whole organism. It was a tiny part of it. Maybe only a single atom of its body. But in our universe it manifested itself as something the size of a man. Call me naive, but at this moment I believe we've been invited into the very being of my old visitor."

"Your visitor is Death."

I looked into the darkness, where a figure came into view. "Would Death show us that?"

Vertical planes of a hard paleness contained a fog of shadow. Into it stepped a shape. Of course I recognized it. Up there at the top of the stairs a ten-year-old Mason Konrad saw the figure for the very first time. The boy who was me stared down, apparently into my eyes. On his face an expression of awe replaced the one of fear.

"Why are you here?" the boy whispered. "What do

you want?" The eyes widened. "Hey. I saw you today. You were in the glass case at the museum." The child that was me smiled in delight. "I remember what they called you. You're Natsaf-Ty . . . you're the keeper of the sacred crocodiles. Whatever they are." He laughed as he sat down on the step. The brown eyes twinkled as the smile on his face dispelled the sense of gloom that had surrounded him after a day at school when the bullies had pushed him around. A day when he'd heard his mother cry herself to sleep in her bedroom over money worries.

What I saw at the moment, as I looked out through the strangely—surreally—closed eyelids of Natsaf-Ty was a boy already on his first steps to maturity.

"You'll never guess what happened to me today." He made himself comfortable on the top step. "These kids shoved me around, called me names. I was so frightened I wanted to kill myself. But tonight I'm talking to you. Imagine talking to you, an Egyptian mummy that's been lying in the desert for thousands of years. But if I'm not scared of you, why on earth should I be scared of some stupid kids who call me names? That wouldn't make sense, would it? If I'm not frightened of ghosts then a couple of idiots at school shouldn't bother me." The boy clapped his hands together as he realized a fact. "But do you want to know something?" He leaned forward with a friendly smile. "You're not frightening, are you? And you know something else? You've got a . . . a . . . what do they call it . . . a good . . . no, you've got a *wise* face. That's it: wise! You're here to help me, aren't you?"

I looked up at the boy whose face shone with renewed hope.

A shiver rippled through me. "That's the moment when I realized I'd won the first battle."

The man beside me shook his head. "No. That was the moment that I and my kind lost the war." He closed his eyes; tremors shuddered through his chest.

If scientists and priests do agree on one thing, it is that there is a unity in all things, or a singularity in the universe. This had to be the example presented to me now. In a single moment of time I looked up the stairs to where a ten-year-old Mason Konrad happily talked to his visitor. Already he sensed that his life would soon change for the better.

In that same moment I saw a plain that I wouldn't describe as vast or tiny, for the simple fact was that it didn't possess dimensions I could understand. It's sufficient for me to say I saw an openness on which stood red figures. Just as the openness had neither beginning nor end, the red figures extended down and up into infinity (if those words could be accurate in this context). A little while ago I would have imagined they all looked like Natsaf-Ty, keeper of the sacred crocodiles.

Now I knew better.

Didn't I?

I blinked. The sun pressed against my neck, a body of heat that made my skin tingle. Insects buzzed among wildflowers at the side of the road. In front of me a much-reduced group of Echomen formed a ragged cluster on the road. Most were sinking to their knees; some were already dead. Extreme switches between heat and cold had damaged their bodies so much that their deaths were not only inevitable but just moments away. It didn't seem long ago that the Echomen had become a formidable force that were destined to sweep Homo sapiens away and replace them with a race of copied Mason Konrads.

Now they are fragile things, defeated by a power that had brushed them away as you or I might bat away a mayfly. When I was fifteen I witnessed a neighbor's dog killing a rat that had crept from its nest under a shed. At the time I'd been thrilled to see how the dog pounced. With a shake of the head the terrier had snapped the rodent's neck. I'd cheered the dog as a heroic defender of the neighborhood against the verminous attacker. Only later did I pity the rat. It had only been doing what its nature directed it to do. I remember it had dark, inquisitive eyes; its brown pelt was sleek, nothing that could be described as repulsive. The animal had probably been foraging for its babies; when the parent didn't return they'd have died of hunger. Damn it, the rat didn't seem so much a villain at the end of the day.

Now the Echomen died. They'd only obeyed their nature. Maybe they couldn't even have been described as evil.

Most of the Echomen lay on the ground now, breathing their last. The one with the cratered face managed to remain on his feet. The wound released a pulsing stream of blood down over his jaw. The hole dilated to the extent that it took his left eye, causing it to deflate into a wrinkled pouch. Around his right eye the skin had turned black. Meanwhile his breathing had deteriorated so much that his chest rose and fell as he tried to claw oxygen from the air.

"Don't look so pleased with yourself, Mason." He gasped. "You believe you saved the world from us. But are you sure you haven't built a bridge between this planet and the *thing* that enjoys your company?"

"I haven't. What we saw is beyond good and evil. But it helped us get rid of you once and for all."

"But at what price, Mason . . . what price?" The color left his face. "What does *it* want in return?"

Blood gushed from the man's mouth. With a sigh he collapsed to the ground to lie there dead with the rest of his kind.

Have you ever answered questions in such a way that your statements are the complete opposite of what you know is the truth? You say yes; you mean no. But you're not being mean or dishonest; you are endeavoring to protect the person asking the questions.

Example: a child asks, "But, Mommy, does Santa Claus really exist?" Parent replies, "Of course he does, dear."

The boy waiting for the bus that will take him back to camp takes hold of the girl's hand. "You do still love me, don't you?" When she hugs him she secretly glances at her wristwatch, not wanting to be late for her new flame. "Of course I still love you."

Patient to doctor: "The operation was a success then? You got it all?" "Don't worry, Mr. Johansson; you'll be back playing golf in no time at all."

Widow to priest: "There really is a heaven, isn't there, Father?" "Oh, assuredly so, Mrs. Johansson. Your husband is in paradise."

I don't want to hammer the point too remorselessly, but you get my drift? Sometimes a white lie hurts less than the truth.

So when I returned to the knot of people standing on the road—Eve, Madeline, Ulric, Kirk, and the commandos—the first three questions asked of me I answered truthfully.

"Are all the Echomen dead?"

"Yes."

"What will happen to Kirk and Madeline?"

"Whatever infected them is leaving their bodies. Look at the backs of their hands. The scar's gone." I showed them my own Y-shaped scar that wouldn't leave me so easily. "They're reverting back to who they were."

"Has the change stopped now?"

"Yes, I'm sure of it. The epidemic is over. There is, for want of a better word, an agency that has intervened. It won't allow any more people to be transformed."

Madeline frowned. "What is this agency? Are you saying something like an angel?"

"Life-forms have immune systems to protect them. The universe has, too. Otherwise so many bad things would happen, chaos would run out of control and destroy everything."

Ulric regarded the mound of corpses just a hundred yards from us. "What happened to them? Why did they all die so suddenly?"

One of the commandos added, "You stood talking to the guy with the bite hole in his face and they all just flopped down."

So, my friends hadn't seen the sun darken, or me and the Echomen vanish from the face of the earth for what seemed to be a significant period of time. Then Natsaf-Ty, or the thing he symbolizes, has many talents. "The Echomen simply weren't viable. The transformation process they used, whatever it is, was too random. Some people turned into copies of me, some didn't. Some of us are immune to being duplicated, some aren't. Their fundamental nature is chaotic. Ultimately, their own biology couldn't sustain them."

Ulric gave one of his rare grins. "Then this is a happy ending?"

"Oh, yes." I nodded. "This is a very, very happy ending."

Remember what I told you a page ago? When I stated

that the first three questions asked of me were the ones I'd answered truthfully? Even as we walked away from that little valley of death the cluster of neurons inside my head that had a propensity for showing me Natsaf-Ty revealed a figure standing beside the road. It seemed for a moment that I saw the phantom of the man with the hole in his face. He fixed me with accusing eyes as his voice reached me like a breeze sighing through leaves on a tree: *Why are you so sure you haven't built a bridge between worlds? Listen to me, Mason Konrad, you invited Death onto the earth. He will want something in return; you are in his debt, remember?* Then the shadow that wore my face evaporated before the brilliance of the sun.

"It's over," I told them. Madeline smiled at me as we walked by banks of wildflowers. "We're going to be all right."

My breath caught in my chest as I waited for a lightning bolt to crash from the blue sky and turn me to ashes. I watched the meadows in case the thing I called Natsaf-Ty arrived with millions of his kind to lurk redly amongst the grass until they decided to make their move against humankind.

But no killing lightning struck. No invasion of ruddy figures. So maybe the Echoman's spiteful prophecy of me, Mason Konrad, being the cause of a global catastrophe was merely the last bullet in his arsenal. One last vindictive shot before he ceased to be.

Hey, I survived. My name is Mason Konrad. This is me. The real deal. The genuine article. Today is the start of my new life. So, until that dusty red gentleman tells me otherwise, this isn't really the end. I go on to face my future, whatever that will be, under the same skies and stars as you.

# THE DELUGE

# MARK MORRIS

It came from nowhere. The only warning was the endless rumbling of a growing earthquake. Then the water came—crashing, rushing water, covering everything. Destroying everything. When it stopped, all that was left was the gentle lapping of waves against the few remaining buildings rising above the surface of the sea.

Will the isolated survivors be able to rebuild their lives, their civilization, when nearly all they knew has been wiped out? It seems hopeless. But what lurks beneath the swirling water, waiting to emerge, is far worse. When the floodwaters finally recede, the true horror will be revealed.

ISBN 13: 978-0-8439-5893-5

# DEMON EYES

## L. H. MAYNARD
## &
## M. P. N. SIMS

Emma had just started her new job as personal assistant to Alex Keltner, the charismatic and powerful head of Keltner Industries. So when he asked her to attend a party he was throwing that weekend at his secluded estate, she knew better than to refuse. It would be her first party amid the extremely wealthy and powerful elite....

It will be a party she'll never forget...if she survives. At first it will be simply odd. Mysterious warnings. Strange, seductive guests. An atmosphere of lust and sexuality. Video cameras in the rooms. But as the weekend progresses, Emma will slowly learn the true nature of the guests and her mysterious host—and the real, grotesque purpose of the party.

ISBN 13: 978-0-8439-5972-7